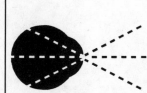

MIRIAM AND THE STRANGER

MIRIAM AND THE STRANGER

JERRY S. EICHER

THORNDIKE PRESS
A part of Gale, Cengage Learning

GALE
CENGAGE Learning·

Farmington Hills, Mich • San Francisco • New York • Waterville, Maine
Meriden, Conn • Mason, Ohio • Chicago

GALE
CENGAGE Learning®

LIBRARY OF CONGRESS CATALOGING-IN-PUBLICATION DATA

Names: Eicher, Jerry S.
Title: Miriam and the stranger / by Jerry S. Eicher.
Description: Large print edition. | Waterville, Maine : Thorndike Press, 2016. | ©2015 | Series: Thorndike Press large print Christian romance | Series: Land of promise ; #3
Identifiers: LCCN 2015037227| ISBN 9781410485755 (hardcover) | ISBN 1410485757 (hardcover)
Subjects: LCSH: Amish—Fiction. | Mate selection—Fiction. | Large type books. | GSAFD: Love stories. | Christian fiction.
Classification: LCC PS3605.I34 M56 2016 | DDC 813/.6—dc23
LC record available at http://lccn.loc.gov/2015037227

Published in 2016 by arrangement with Harvest House Publishers

Printed in Mexico
1 2 3 4 5 6 7 20 19 18 17 16

MIRIAM AND THE STRANGER

CHAPTER ONE

Miriam Yoder opened the schoolhouse door and looked across the ball diamond where only a couple of hours ago the children had played softball at recess. The sunbathed, open Oklahoma landscape stretched off into the horizon. Miriam paused with her hand on the doorknob. This little one-room schoolhouse had been hers for the past two years. She was the teacher, and the Clarita Amish community had become home to her. Here she had found a land of promise in which to heal and to grow after the tragedy of her beloved Wayne's death — even if that now meant she might have to walk alone as a single woman for the rest of her life.

A smile filled Miriam's face when Star's whinny from the small weather shelter broke into her thoughts.

"Yah," Miriam hollered. "I know I'm late, but you don't have to be in such a hurry."

Star tossed his head as if he understood, and Miriam closed the schoolhouse door behind her. Aunt Fannie would have supper on the table by now. She shouldn't have worked so late, but at least she had managed to finish correcting the last of the arithmetic tests. Tomorrow the scholars would be happy with their grades. Her entire third-grade class of four students had received scores above ninety, which was an accomplishment after last year when all four had struggled so hard. She had spent time this term with the students whenever there had been a spare moment. The other grades also needed a fair share of her attention, but the extra effort with the third-graders had paid off. Their faces would glow with happiness when she told them the news, and further joy would fill her own heart. Her fourth teaching term had begun this fall, and what grace the Lord had granted her that she could play even a small part in the development of these precious children's lives. The Lord had surely been with her since Wayne's passing during that awful tornado.

Star lifted his head as Miriam approached, and she rubbed his nose. The white mark on his forehead was highlighted in the soft afternoon sunlight. Miriam traced the outline of the imprint while Star held his head perfectly still, fully enjoying the attention.

"The Lord has guided me well these past years," Miriam whispered to him. "And this is one of my signs that the way was opened by His hand. You are my Star." Miriam brushed the silky hair on his neck.

Star whinnied again.

Miriam laughed. "*Yah,* you are a dear. But now we'd best be heading home before it gets much later."

Miriam hurried to hitch Star to the buggy and drove quickly out of the schoolyard. Star lifted his feet high and pranced down the road. Miriam laughed and allowed contentment to fill her again.

She was happy even if the prospect of marriage had not been granted her these past years. *Yah,* she would always mourn Wayne, but in her heart healing had come. That the two could occur together seemed impossible, yet both were true. Uncle William and Aunt Fannie had experienced the grace of the Lord along with her. The tornadoes that had swept through the community and brought so much sorrow were a distant memory now. And back home in Possum Valley, the latest news was that her sister Shirley had fallen in love and would marry Glen Weaver next month. She would travel to Ohio for the November wedding. The Lord truly had blessed again. And now *Mamm*'s last letter had hinted of a new happiness soon to enter Miriam's life. *Mamm* hadn't given details, saying only that she was to trust in the Lord and in *Daett*'s guidance, which sounded like *gut* advice whatever this new thing should be.

Miriam pulled back on the reins to slow Star for the stop sign. With a quick look each way she turned west. She should be very thankful, Miriam reminded herself. A heart could be broken into a thousand pieces, and yet the Lord knew how to put them all together again. She still struggled at times with submission to the Lord's will for her future. Was there to be a man in her life or not? No unmarried man in the community had paid her more than a passing glance these past two years. And surely the news *Mamm* wrote about couldn't be about a man.

Miriam sighed. Not often did she dare entertain these thoughts. Daydreams weren't wise, and even if another unmarried Amish man with an interest in marriage looked her way, could she open her heart again? At almost twenty-four years of age, she was an old maid in the Amish world.

All the unmarried men from the community were younger than she was. Maybe she should travel more and put herself out there before she was a hopeless case? Miriam frowned and pulled back again on Star's reins for the stop on Highway 48. She turned south after a quick check each way.

The road was the main thoroughfare through the community, but traffic was usu-ally light — unlike Possum Valley near Berlin, Ohio. There the place usually buzzed with people and automobiles. She couldn't imagine Clarita, Oklahoma, jammed with cars like Berlin was on Friday nights. Clarita, with its empty streets, was an island of sanity on any day of the week. Its peace and quiet comforted the soul. The small Amish community followed course with its laid-back attitudes and slower pace of life. Not too many unusual things happened here. Even the violent fall storms had been quiet the past two years, as if their fury had been expended for a time.

Miriam hung on to Star's reins and shiv-ered at the memory of the evening she had spent in Uncle William and Aunt Fannie's basement. Outside the winds had lashed from the tornadoes. Many of the *Englisha* people in Clarita had perished that night, and the Lord would not exempt the Amish

11

from the tragedy. She did not blame anyone for Wayne's and his sister Lois's deaths — most certainly not the Lord. His thoughts and purposes were high above what anyone on this earth could comprehend.

Miriam slowed down as her Uncle William's greenhouse with its rows of plants and bushes came into view. She turned into the driveway and pulled to a stop near the barn. A car was parked at the greenhouse door, which was unusual at this hour, but perhaps Uncle William had a late customer. Miriam climbed out of the buggy and unhitched Star. With another quick glance at the car, she led Star into the barn and left him in his stall with his nose deep in a bucket of oats.

Miriam slipped out of the barn and crossed the lawn. The car was still parked in front of the greenhouse, so perhaps a salesman was having a late conversation with Uncle William. She shrugged and entered the front door of the house and called, "*Gut* evening. Anybody home?"

"In here." Aunt Fannie's voice came from the kitchen.

Miriam peeked through the doorway with a big smile on her face.

"My, are we cheerful tonight?" Aunt

Fannie asked, looking up from the kitchen stove.

"Students all got good grades on their arithmetic tests," Miriam answered. She held out her hands to chubby baby Jonathon — who wasn't a baby anymore but a toddler. He didn't hesitate but ran out from behind the stove to greet her.

Miriam snatched him up to kiss both of his cheeks. "You sweet little thing! I hope you behaved yourself today."

Aunt Fannie chuckled. "He's been a *gut* little boy. William says he's easy to train, but that we must not allow our heads to swell with only one child. The Lord will surely humble us once He's given another little one." Aunt Fannie glanced down at her middle with a wry look.

"You'll be great parents to a dozen children," Miriam reassured her aunt as she gave Jonathon another peck on his cheek.

Aunt Fannie smiled at the two of them. "Now don't you be worrying, Miriam. I can hear it in your voice. There'll be someone along for you. You'll be a *frau* and a *mamm* someday."

Miriam made a face. "I don't think so. I'm an old maid now."

"That's not true," Aunt Fannie protested.

Miriam smiled and changed the subject.

"So what can I do to help with supper?"

Aunt Fannie waved her hand around. "I'm a little late as you can see, but the food's ready. You can set the table. They'll be one extra plate. Set that near William's place."

"We have company tonight?" Miriam paused to set Jonathon on the floor. "Surely you're not inviting someone here to meet me?"

Aunt Fannie chuckled. "I only wish. *Nee,* it's an *Englisha* man who stopped by today. William took a fancy to his project — whatever that is, something about the Amish — and invited him for supper. They want to continue the conversation. William says the man has an interest in tasting the full flavor of an Amish home." Aunt Fannie's hand fluttered about. "It's supper that he wants, I'm sure. A man and *gut* food. The two always go together, which is why I've been tense all afternoon and late with supper."

"I'm sure you did just fine," Miriam assured her. She walked over to one of the pots and lifted the lid off the green beans to take a deep breath. "Perfect!"

Aunt Fannie laughed. "Thanks for trying to comfort me. I don't know why the man has me so confused. It's not like I haven't made food for *Englisha* people before."

There you go," Miriam said, setting the

first plate on the table. "This man will be so impressed he'll want to come back every night."

"One night will be plenty, thank you." Aunt Fannie fanned herself with one hand. "Although I'm grateful for a husband who is so hospitable to strangers."

"So what's this man like?"

"Oh, he's just another *Englisha* man. I saw him for only a few seconds." Aunt Fannie looked the table over with satisfaction and said, "Now, Miriam, please remember to talk with the man. Help make a *gut* impression on him. We can't have him thinking that Amish women are backward or stuck-up."

Miriam laughed. "So that's what you're worried about. Well, don't be. I worked for an older *Englisha* man for more than three years — Mr. Bland? Remember? I was with him almost every day, and they are just like everyone else, so relax. You'll be more than comfortable around this *Englisha* man."

Aunt Fannie took a deep breath but looked skeptical. "Everything is fine here. Now you run upstairs and put on a fresh dress. Take Jonathon with you."

Miriam scooped the boy up and tickled him as they went up the stairs to Miriam's room.

CHAPTER TWO

Thirty minutes later Miriam was holding Jonathon on her lap with one hand and clutching the edge of the kitchen table with the other as low voices murmured in the living room. Jonathon looked in that direction and chirped loudly, "That's *Daett*."

"*Yah*," Miriam whispered and silenced him. "*Shhh* . . . you have to be quiet now."

Jonathon appeared puzzled, as if he couldn't understand why quiet was required around his *daett*. This had never happened before in his little world. But how did one explain to a three-year-old that a strange *Englisha* man was in the house. In spite of her earlier words to Aunt Fannie, she was tense herself. A glimpse of the *Englisha* man's face had unnerved her. She set Jonathon on the floor and nudged him toward the kitchen doorway. "Go meet your *daett*. It's okay."

Jonathon toddled off, pausing at the living

room doorway to glance over his shoulder, and Miriam motioned him on. She listened as happy laughter filled the living room. Now she was alone in the kitchen. Aunt Fannie had rushed off without a word the moment they caught sight of the two men coming across the lawn from the greenhouse. Uncle William's lengthy beard and homemade clothing had made quite a contrast to the young *Englisha* man's clean-shaven chin and his fancy clothing.

Miriam jumped as Uncle William appeared in the kitchen doorway with Jonathon in his arms. "And here's our charming schoolteacher who's staying with us," Uncle William called over his shoulder. He motioned with his hand. "Miriam, meet Tyler Johnson. Tyler, this is Miriam Yoder."

Miriam felt herself flush. Surely her face was the color of red beets. Mr. Johnson stuck his head in the kitchen doorway as if he was perfectly at home. "Hi," he said. "Glad to meet you, Miriam Yoder."

"And you . . . too," Miriam managed, which was a perfectly stupid thing to say to a fancy *Englisha* man. What was wrong with her? Thankfully she'd never see the man again after tonight. She'd pray that her face forever be a fog in his memory.

"An Amish schoolteacher!" Tyler studied

Miriam with an appraising look.

"Yep, and the best!" Uncle William declared. "A real jewel."

Please don't say that, Miriam wanted to say.

"What is your alma mater?" Tyler asked.

The room swam in front of Miriam's eyes. She had no idea what the man meant. Mercifully Uncle William covered for her. "We choose our schoolteachers for their excellent character and reputation. Miriam has plenty of that, I can assure you."

So Uncle William didn't know what an alma mater was either, Miriam thought with a smile . . . but at least he had his wits about him sufficiently to formulate a sensible response. Why was she always such a dunderhead? No wonder she didn't have a husband yet.

"Well, I suppose that makes good sense. After all, this is an Amish community," Tyler allowed.

"*Yah,* it is," Aunt Fannie spoke up, appearing out of nowhere. "And supper is ready. Please come have a seat, Mr. Johnson, right here beside William. We'll have the food served in no time."

They all sat down, and Tyler focused on Aunt Fannie's potatoes and gravy steaming on the table beside the freshly cut bread. A smile spread across his face. "Looks delicious, ma'am."

Aunt Fannie's faced colored, but she said nothing.

Uncle William broke in. "Let's pray. We shouldn't waste any more time before the food gets cold."

"I agree," Aunt Fannie seconded as the two bowed their heads.

Tyler hesitated only a moment before he followed their example. Miriam knew she shouldn't follow the man's every move, so she too closed her eyes and focused on the words as Uncle William concluded, "And now our most gracious Father in heaven, we give into Your hands this evening and the night that lies ahead. Be with us and give us Your forgiveness and blessing as we also extend to others the grace that You have bestowed upon us. Amen."

A ghost of a smile played on Tyler's face when Miriam looked up. He had probably never heard a prayer like that before, but Aunt Fannie had said he wanted to experience Amish life, so he shouldn't be surprised. Heartfelt prayers were an everyday occurrence at Uncle William's house.

Miriam returned her gaze to the table for a few more moments before she looked up again. Aunt Fannie's hands were a whirlwind of motion as she passed the food. Tyler still had his smile as he took small portions from each bowl.

Uncle William noticed Tyler's selections and teased, "Come on, now. Heap it up high. This is Amish country, and you have to experience the fare like the locals do."

"There will be seconds," Aunt Fannie said at once, "so don't pay any attention to William."

Tyler grinned. "Everything looks very good, ma'am. I'm sure I'll have seconds and eat nothing tomorrow to make up for it."

"Now, that's city talk," Uncle William said with a chuckle.

"Yes, but we don't all work like the Amish do, you know."

Miriam tried to smile, but couldn't. What was wrong with her? She had never been affected by an *Englisha* man like this. She must remind herself that after tonight she would never see Mr. Johnson again. Maybe then she could at least eat.

"So what do you do for a job?" Aunt Fannie asked Tyler as she filled her own plate.

"I'm a freelance journalist," Tyler replied. "I usually only pursue stories that interest me, but I take some work on assignment, like the story I'm on now."

"A writer!" Aunt Fannie glowed. "A real one."

Uncle William laughed. "*Yah,* I think he's real all right."

Tyler appeared amused at the third-person address but said nothing as Aunt Fannie continued. "Oh, that is so *wunderbah*! What are you writing about?"

Tyler set his fork down before he answered. "My current assignment is an article about the severe tornadoes that came through here two years ago. The focus is to be the Amish, as I believe quite a few of your farms were damaged. We've been told that Amish have quite a record of community involvement in the cleanup and reconstruction afterward. My editor thinks your loss and response could be of wide interest to the public."

"This is true," Aunt Fannie allowed, "but there were lots of people in Clarita who had losses — not just us."

"I agree," Tyler said, "and that's not being ignored. But you're the only Amish community affected by the tornadoes. In addition, readers are interested in the community's life. They want to know how you're doing now two years later . . . how this has affected your outlook on life, and especially how you all managed to rebuild without insurance. On top of that, my research shows that the Amish community made quite a large contribution to the Clarita Community Relief Fund. That's of great interest to the public. How did the Amish rebuild without insurance and still have a large amount of money left to give to others? Apparently there is much to learn from your lifestyle. Much we English could learn from it."

Tyler smiled disarmingly, but Miriam saw in her aunt's and uncle's faces there was no need. Neither one had objections to his article, though normally there would be hesitancy about any outside scrutiny of the Amish community. Uncle William must feel an obligation to be open about the matter. But *how* open? Miriam paled at the question. Certainly Uncle William's lips would be sealed about the two million dollars she had given Deacon Phillips, the monies Mr. Bland had left her in his will. No one in the community had spoken of the matter since the tornadoes that had caused such havoc and had taken Wayne's and his sister Lois's lives.

"We can all learn from each other," Uncle William said with a sober look. Thankfully no one looked her way at the moment to see her pale face.

"Yes, indeed. I'm sure we can learn from our different cultures," Tyler said with a smile. "And that's why I'm here." Tyler turned toward Miriam. "But I won't attempt any teaching on my part. I'll leave that to our esteemed schoolteacher."

They all laughed, and Miriam tried to join in. When the laughter quieted down, Uncle William spoke up. "Like I told you earlier, Tyler, you're welcome to tour the greenhouse again tomorrow. And I can give you the addresses of some of the community's storm-damaged properties. Most of the buildings were rebuilt right after the storm, and some of the houses were added on to. I imagine you want pictures, but you'll have to sneak those when no people are in the scene. Beyond that I can't speak for anyone. You'd best speak with Deacon Phillips about money questions. He was the one who handled contributions to the relief fund."

"I will do that," Tyler agreed as he finished the last of the food on his plate. Aunt Fannie grabbed the mashed potato bowl and passed it around again. With a boyish smile, Tyler took a large spoonful and ladled on some gravy. He reached for a piece of bread and added thick slabs of butter followed by jam. "This is amazing food, ma'am," he said. "I'd be a fattened hog in no time if I stayed around here very long."

"We'd just have to work you all the harder," Uncle William said with a grin.

Tyler turned to Miriam again, and she caught her breath. "So what does an Amish schoolteacher of impeccable character teach in her classroom?"

Miriam's mind whirled, but she finally managed to form her thoughts. "Lots of things, I guess. We had arithmetic tests today. All the grades did pretty well, but the third grade especially."

"All the grades?" Tyler appeared puzzled.

"She teaches all eight grades," offered Uncle William, who regarded Tyler with a steady gaze. "That's how we do things."

"All *eight* grades?" Tyler repeated. "I thought there were twelve grades before college."

Uncle William shook his head. "Not for us, there aren't. This system of eight grades used to work for everyone, but the public schools stopped teaching the basics years ago."

Tyler's surprise was evident. "I see." He turned back to Miriam. "Eight grades and one teacher. That's quite an accomplishment."

"Thanks." Miriam tried to smile. Nothing

seemed to work right in her brain right now. If Tyler weren't so handsome and charming, maybe she could think straighter.

"So your children only go to the eighth grade?" Tyler seemed to be processing the information further. "That's . . . unusual."

Aunt Fannie gave Tyler a quick glance and bounced to her feet. "Okay, enough of that for now. Is everyone ready for pie and homemade ice cream?"

Tyler grinned. "Sounds great to me."

So this was why Aunt Fannie had been late with supper. She must have left the ice cream in the basement so it wouldn't melt but had failed to inform her. This was her chance to move away from Tyler for a few minutes and catch her breath.

"I'll get the ice cream," Miriam said as she got up and headed for the basement. As much as she hated to admit it, the truth was she found herself starstruck at Tyler's presence. Surely it would pass by tomorrow morning. After all, everyone had weak points, and this was hers. This would be a much-needed lesson in humility. Heat crept into Miriam's face at the thought. She rubbed her cheeks with both hands before she found the crankcase of ice cream near the stairs and carefully opened the lid to dip the creamy contents into a large bowl.

When the bowl was full, Miriam paused for several deep breaths before she attempted the return trip. She had to sober up and act like the decent Amish girl she was.

With her face set, Miriam climbed the stairs to enter the kitchen again. She even managed a decent smile when Tyler looked up. This was much better, Miriam told herself, but the man still exuded charm that made her weak all the way down to her toes.

CHAPTER THREE

The following Sunday at the morning service, Miriam shifted on the long church bench for a better view of the visiting minister. He had stood to his feet a few minutes ago to begin the main sermon. His face was serious and thin, his shoulders narrow. He wasn't tall, but his pinched features made him appear so. His gaze pierced the room as silence fell over the gathered congregation. Clearly this was a man of God who took his calling seriously, Miriam thought, as she sat up straighter.

Without warning, the memory of Tyler Johnson, the *Englisha* man, as he laughed last week at Aunt Fannie's kitchen table floated in front of Miriam's eyes. She pushed the image away at once. Tyler Johnson was a most inappropriate thought to have in the middle of a Sunday morning service. But ever since that evening, visions of Tyler Johnson appeared at unpredictable moments. If this kept up she would have to confess her weakness to someone, preferably only Aunt Fannie but perhaps also Uncle William. What an embarrassment that would be. Both of her relatives thought so highly of her while the truth of the matter was that their schoolteacher couldn't keep thoughts of an *Englisha* man out of her mind. Miriam dropped her head for a moment. Why did she continue to see Tyler's handsome face in her mind? The question sent chills all the way through her.

Miriam looked up again and the piercing gaze of the visiting minister seemed to settle on her. But that wasn't possible, Miriam told herself. The man didn't know her — unless her guilt had drawn his attention. Could he see straight into her heart?

Thankfully, the minister's gaze moved on, and he continued to speak in a low voice. "Dearly beloved brothers and sisters in the Lord," he said. "We are gathered again on this morning of the Lord's day to prepare our hearts once more for a life of obedience and service. This determination must continue while we breathe and walk on this earth. Let us pray that mercy and grace would be given us, and that we might live humble and broken lives before the almighty God in heaven."

Those words were exactly what she needed to hear, Miriam told herself. Maybe she'd find true repentance in her heart from her fascination with Tyler Johnson. Where this minister had come from, she had no idea. She had seen him before the service as he climbed down from Deacon Phillips's buggy. She had noticed no wife, so the man must be single. No Amish man traveled any distance without his *frau* unless there was a disaster in another community and the menfolk had gone to help with the work. But this community had experienced no crisis recently.

Miriam focused on the sermon again. She studied the minister's face as he spoke earnestly, "Can light and darkness dwell together? Can good and evil take up residence in the same heart? I warn us, dear brothers and sisters, that these things cannot be. Either we serve God or we serve the world and all its evils. Let us look well this morning on where our feet are leading us and beg for grace to change our lives if we have gone astray."

Miriam shivered and breathed a quick prayer. "Help me, dear Lord, and please guide my feet. I'm sorry about my feelings toward that *Englisha* man, Tyler. I know I shouldn't have felt what I did, and worse . . .

what I still feel."

There! She had confessed it to the Lord. Was that not the first step in the right direction? Maybe now thoughts of Tyler Johnson and his charm would no longer haunt her.

Miriam froze as the minister's gaze settled on her again. He still spoke, but his eyes didn't move on after a few seconds. She waited, unable to look away. Had the Lord given his servant a glimpse into her soul? This couldn't be, Miriam told herself as a tender look crossed the minister's face. Did the man know her? That also wasn't possible. Thankfully, the minister's gaze had moved on again, and she could breathe. She really needed to do something about her feelings for Tyler Johnson. Her guilt made her imagine way too many things. More prayer was needed to cleanse her heart . . . and soon!

The sermon continued, and Miriam kept her head down for the next thirty minutes. It was best that way, and she could still hear the sermon. The words of exhortations to holy living were what she needed.

As the message concluded, Miriam took a long breath of relief. Thankfully her thoughts had calmed down, and she hoped Tyler Johnson was banished from her mind completely. Miriam stood up after the last prayer to volunteer her help with lunch and was assigned to the married men's table. With her hands full of jelly and peanut butter jars, Miriam approached the rows of bearded men. They politely moved sideways on the benches to give her room to work, and her hands were soon empty.

On the second trip, Miriam caught Aunt Fannie's bright smile of encouragement from the married women's table. Thoughts of Tyler Johnson seemed far away and unreal at the moment. How could she even think of an *Englisha* man in such a way? This was where her joy was filled to its fullest. She was the community's schoolteacher and loved for her dedicated service. If anyone knew her thoughts . . . Miriam paled and almost stumbled on the hardwood floor. *Nee,* she must not allow Tyler Johnson to disrupt all that. Certainly the Lord would protect and guide her through this weakness. Aunt Fannie would love her even if she found out Miriam had experienced a starstruck moment over a handsome *Englisha* man. Hadn't Aunt Fannie experienced moments of weakness in her *rumspringa* time when she had dated an *Englisha* man? Yet Aunt Fannie had survived and made the right choices. That was a comfort she must hang on to.

As Miriam approached the other end of the married men's table, Deacon Phillips looked up to say, "Well, if it isn't Miriam Yoder, our schoolteacher, serving the tables today. What a blessing you are."

"Don't say that so loudly," Miriam whispered back. Heat crept up her neck. The visiting minister was sitting right beside Deacon Phillips.

Deacon Phillips chuckled, and the minister turned around to look up at Miriam. The tender look from earlier in the day filled the man's face. "So this is Miriam. I thought she might be the woman I was told about."

"*Yah,* our very own Miriam," Deacon Phillips said with a grin. "And Miriam, this is Mose Stoll, from near your area in Possum Valley. He's visiting us for a while."

"Hello." Miriam choked on the word. What was she supposed to say?

"*Gut* to meet you," Mose said, the tender look still on his face.

Deacon Phillips continued as if Miriam wasn't present. "She's as faithful a member of the community as one could wish for, Mose, and a *gut* schoolteacher on top of that. I don't know what we'd do without her."

The bowl of peanut butter slipped from

Miriam's fingers and dropped to the table with a loud bang. Her face must be blazing. What on earth was Deacon Phillips up to? Why was he singing her praises to this strange man?

Mose regarded Miriam with a steady gaze. "The Lord guards the hearts of men and maidens alike," he said. "It's *gut* to know His work produces such comely results."

Deacon Phillips chuckled again. "*Yah,* like my own *frau,* Katie, Miriam is a jewel. Any man who can capture her heart has done well."

"I can see that," Mose said with a nod. "This Miriam has been blessed by the Lord indeed."

Miriam fumbled with the last peanut butter bowl and nearly dumped the contents into Mose's lap. What had gotten into Deacon Phillips? In a quick motion, Miriam pushed the bowl away from the two men. It slid across the table and stopped with a clink against the red beet dish. Splashes of red juice went airborne and then landed on the tablecloth and spread out in a slow stain. Several bearded men looked up with surprised expressions on their faces. They had been involved in their own conversations and hadn't heard the flattery about her. Well, they would have to think her a clumsy klutz. She was not about to explain. With quick steps Miriam fled back to the kitchen and slipped into a corner to calm her nerves.

This wasn't like Deacon Phillips at all. Nor was it like a visiting minister to pay so much attention to an unmarried woman — unless the man was here on a search for a *frau*. Miriam's hands tingled. Could this be true? Was the minister on a search for a *frau* to replace one who had passed away? He was too old to have never been married. And he didn't appear nervous around women. That could mean only one thing. He had been married before to a godly *frau* who had honored and obeyed him.

Miriam tried to breathe deeply. The married men's table still needed attention, and she was in no condition to help. But surely she was wrong about the visiting minister. No Amish man of such high regard would simply appear in a community and pick her out of the crowd.

"Get a grip," Miriam whispered out loud. Thankfully none of the other women heard her in the loud bustle of the kitchen, but she would have to go back. Miriam filled her hands with bowls again and headed for the married men's table — at the other end this time.

"We could use some more bread," a man's soft voice spoke. Miriam jumped.

She gave John Kuntz, the father of one of her students, a nervous smile. "*Yah,* of course. I'll be right back." After a quick dash to the kitchen, Miriam handed the plate of thick homemade bread to John.

"How's Carrie doing in school?" John asked.

Miriam tried to relax. "Carrie's doing *gut.* She tries hard and thinks she has to get one hundreds on her papers all the time. That's not necessary, of course."

John's laugh was soft. "Her *mamm* and I have told Carrie that, but the girl is driven to succeed. I think she takes you as her example."

"Now, don't say that," Miriam scolded. What was this? Compliment the school-teacher day?

"It's true, nonetheless," John said. "We're blessed to have you in the community, Miriam."

"Thanks," Miriam managed as she turned to flee once more to the kitchen. How could the men of the community say such *wunderbah* things about her? They certainly didn't know about her starstruck moments with an *Englisha* man. Thankfully the married men's table now had all the food it needed. Miriam stayed in the corner of the kitchen until Bishop Mullet announced the closing prayer of thanks. Silence fell among the women, and Miriam bowed her head as the bishop's clear voice led out in the benediction.

When Miriam opened her eyes, Aunt Fannie approached her with a tense look on her face and clutched Miriam's elbow. "Katie just spoke with me. That visiting minister wants to stop by our place this afternoon."

Miriam froze. "Who? Mose Stoll?"

Aunt Fannie stared at Miriam. "You know his name?"

"Well, *yah,* it's no secret. Deacon Phillips just introduced us. But why is he coming to our place?" Miriam managed.

"I'm not exactly sure why. All I know is, he's coming," Aunt Fannie said, and moved on.

Miriam took several deep breaths and pinched herself. She would soon wake up from this dream and find herself the community's schoolteacher with no visiting minister showing her interest and, most especially, no thoughts of a handsome *Englisha* man!

CHAPTER FOUR

Later that afternoon Miriam stood at the stove churning the popcorn popper with one hand while holding on to the handle with the other. Heat from the stove rose around her and flushed her face. Behind her, the low murmur of the men's voices rose and fell in the living room as Deacon Phillips and the visiting minister, Mose Stoll, spoke with Uncle William. Aunt Fannie was squeezing oranges at the kitchen table while Katie, Deacon Phillips's wife, stirred the mixture into a large pitcher.

Miriam could feel the frequent glances both women sent her way. Her suspicions at the Sunday service must have been correct. The visiting minister was interested in her attentions, and Aunt Fannie must have approved. But that wasn't a great surprise. Aunt Fannie would accept any Amish man as her husband, even if he wasn't a minister. The question was how Mose Stoll had learned so much about her that he would travel all this way in search of a *frau.* Or had Mose noticed her for the first time this morning? That seemed unlikely, but obviously Mose Stoll was interested in her now. Perhaps this was the blessing *Mamm* had referred to in her letter. But how had *Mamm* known?

She had tried to stay out of sight when Mose arrived an hour ago with Deacon Phillips and Katie by slipping out of the washroom door with Jonathon and playing with the neighbor children in the yard. That had lasted until Aunt Fannie had called her in on the pretense that they needed someone to make popcorn.

Now Katie's whisper grew louder. "Don't you think we had best tell Miriam?"

Miriam didn't turn around. She wouldn't act as if she knew a thing until Katie volunteered the information.

"I think we should," Aunt Fannie answered in the same tone.

Clearly she would have to respond now, Miriam told herself. Above the sound of the popping popcorn, she asked, "What is it you think I should know?" Her arm slowed, and the white kernels pushed against the lid, spilling some out of the popper. Miriam quickly dumped the contents into the large bowl Aunt Fannie had placed on the counter.

Katie stood to her feet before she answered. "I don't want this to come too suddenly, Miriam, as I know you are perfectly happy in the work the Lord has given you as the community's schoolteacher."

Miriam pasted on a bright smile. "*Yah*, I am." Perhaps the less said, the better.

Neither Katie nor Aunt Fannie had a hint of a smile. Katie clasped and unclasped her hands as she stepped closer. "This is *gut* news, Miriam, of the very best kind, but of course it may come as a shock. I know I still haven't gotten over my own surprise once I heard why Mose was here."

"Why *is* he here?" Miriam tried to keep her pasted smile in place.

Katie's face appeared tense. "Mose Stoll has taken a serious interest in you, Miriam, though I know you don't know the man at all."

Aunt Fannie spoke up. "I know what you're probably thinking. *What in the world?* Or *how is this possible?* But you shouldn't say no at once. It's perfectly explainable . . . and so exciting!"

"Maybe you should start explaining then." Miriam leaned against the counter, her smile gone now.

Aunt Fannie's face brightened. "She's considering it, Katie. I knew she would."

"I don't know about that," Katie said as she sat down again and took a deep breath. "But let's see. How did this all happen? First of all, Mose arrived at our place last week with a letter of recommendation from your bishop in Possum Valley — Bishop Wagler, I believe?" Katie paused and Miriam nodded. "Anyway," Katie continued, "Bishop Wagler said all the usual things about how Minister Stoll is an upstanding member in his own district in Wayne County and has impeccable personal standards. All that stuff . . ." Katie's voice trailed off for a moment. "We wondered at once why an Amish minister would be traveling by himself all the way out here. That he was looking for a *frau* was our guess. So we made him feel welcome but dropped hints that there weren't that many unmarried women in the community his age. Mose didn't respond until later the next morning when he enlightened us that his *frau*, Rachel, had passed this spring and that he had someone very specific in mind — *you*, Miriam. He proceeded to ask us all kinds of questions about you, which we answered in the most glowing manner possible. I mean, what else

could we say with your *wunderbah* character?"

"But . . . I . . . shouldn't someone have
told me? Why should I be the last one to
know about all this?" Miriam sputtered. She
covered her face with both hands.

Katie reached toward Miriam to stroke
her arm. "The truth is that Mose already
knew quite a lot, and in fact he has spoken
to your *daett* about a relationship with you."

"Isn't this just so exciting!" Aunt Fannie
interrupted. "I'd say this is almost straight
out of heaven. Just when we had all given
up hope!"

"Who says I had given up hope?" Miriam
protested.

Aunt Fannie ignored the question and
continued, "Isn't this just something? In
your heart, Miriam, you must know this is
right."

Miriam opened her mouth to object, but
Katie was already speaking. "I'm very sorry
about the suddenness of this, but sometimes
these miracles do happen out of the blue."

Miriam's thoughts spun. Surely this wasn't
already decided! Katie and Aunt Fannie
knew she had a say in the matter. And yet
did she? If she severely disliked the man,
that would change things, but so far it
hadn't. And there was her preoccupation

41

with Tyler Johnson that no one knew about. Maybe the Lord had sent her help in a way she hadn't expected. An Amish husband would solve her fascination with Mr. Johnson.

"It's such a miracle," Aunt Fannie continued. "It's one of those moments we pray and long for, and then the Lord moves in such clear ways. Think of it, Miriam. Mose had already spoken with your *daett* before he made the trip out here."

More than likely that was so Mose wouldn't waste his time, Miriam thought, but this was not a moment for snide observations, and Mose was a godly man. She could do much worse.

"Mose would like to speak with you this afternoon," Katie added. "In fact, he's probably been waiting impatiently this past hour."

"Then we should let him get on with it," Aunt Fannie declared. "Miriam will gladly speak with the man."

"Is that okay with you?" Katie asked with a tender glance toward Miriam. "We don't want to rush you into anything."

Heat rushed into Miriam's face, and she lowered her head.

"That's all the answer we need," Aunt Fannie said with a broad smile. "The girl's in love with the man already!"

Katie nodded and appeared satisfied. "I'll go tell Mose you'll speak with him then."

"You can go right out on the porch and talk with Mose there," Aunt Fannie said, even before Katie was out of the kitchen. "I'll personally keep the children away so you can enjoy some peace and quiet. Oh, Miriam, how *wunderbah* this is, and you'll have lots to speak of in the short time he'll be here. Surely Mose will bring you home from the hymn singing tonight. Tell him to stay for supper. Then he can drive you there with our buggy and bring you home. I'll make a temporary bed for him in the basement, and he can make his way back to Deacon Phillips's place tomorrow. Oh, Miriam this is so exciting!"

Aunt Fannie would have the wedding planned by this evening, Miriam told herself, and a wry smile crept over her face. She sobered moments later when Katie returned to say, "It's all settled now."

Aunt Fannie bubbled over with joy. "They can go out on the front porch with their popcorn bowls."

"That's perfect," Katie agreed. She reached over to touch Miriam's arm. "This is still a little sudden. Are you sure it's okay?"

"She's fine," Aunt Fannie answered. "Remember that Miriam is a mature and sensible girl. And after what she's suffered, she deserves this."

Miriam attempted a smile. "It's okay. I'll speak with him, and we'll go from there."

Katie nodded her approval. Moments later Miriam found herself out on the front porch with Mose Stoll seated beside her. The transition was a blur that didn't quite register. She remembered Mose's pleased face in the living room, followed by Uncle William's encouraging smile as he held open the front door. Aunt Fannie deposited the popcorn bowls in their laps and made a hasty retreat. Now Mose seemed at a loss for words as they both gazed across the open prairie beyond Uncle William's greenhouse.

"So you're from Wayne County?" Miriam asked, gathering her wits.

Mose's smile was a little tense. "*Yah.* I'm from the district of your soon-to-be brother-in-law, Glen Weaver."

"Oh!" Miriam couldn't keep the delight out of her voice. "Shirley's promised man."

"*Yah.*" Mose seemed to relax and regain the confidence he'd displayed earlier in the day. "They are a sweet couple for sure, and Glen's a *gut* friend of mine. It's through his

44

suggestion that I'm here. Glen spoke right highly of you when he learned that I felt the time had come to move on with life. Because I guess you know that my *frau* passed this spring."

"*Yah,* I know." Miriam let her gaze linger on the distant horizon. "I'm sorry to hear that."

"Glen told me you've had your own similar loss," Mose said. "You must have suffered greatly. I at least had some warning when the cancer came. But you have done well, Glen said."

"Thank you," Miriam managed.

Mose was silent for a moment before he continued, "Anyway, for the rest of my story . . . I finally traveled down to your district a few Sundays ago and preached for them." A smile played on Mose's face. "But my real reason was to speak with your *daett,* which I did after the service."

"And *Daett* said what?" Miriam asked.

"He spoke very highly of you," Mose answered. "As has everyone I've asked about you. And I clearly see it is all true. You have impressed me greatly so far, Miriam."

Miriam looked away as the man's gaze pierced into her soul. If *Daett* had approved of the man, that counted for something.

Had not *Daett* spoken that *wunderbah* blessing to her over two years ago? She could still hear the words: *"You are a woman among a thousand, Miriam, full of the grace and the glory of the Lord. Blessed may your days be on this earth, and may a thousand people see the light of heaven in your life. May you live fully and walk the fruitful path that has been chosen for you. And remember that your mamm and I will always love you."*

"Did I say something wrong?" Mose asked, his concerned eyes peering at Miriam.

"Oh, no." Miriam collected her thoughts. "I was just thinking of something *Daett* once told me."

"I'm sure they were *gut* words," Mose said as he settled back into his seat with a smile. Clearly *Daett* had made an equally decent impression upon Mose.

"*Daett* and I are close," Miriam managed.

Mose looked up with a pleased expression. "You don't have to explain yourself to me. A *daett*'s approval speaks well of any woman. I'm honored to have been told about you and to meet you, Miriam. Thanks for consenting to spend this time with me."

"I am glad you came," Miriam whispered.

Mose's face had its tender look again. "I hope you'll consent to seeing a little more of me — perhaps a lot more in the next few weeks. I can't stay in the community very long, but I'd like to spend some time with you — whatever is decent, of course. I know this is all sudden, but I'm a cautious man, and I've proceeded the best I knew how. I didn't feel comfortable writing a letter when you'd never heard of me, even though your *mamm* offered me the address."

Miriam stole a quick glance at him before she said, "*Yah, Mamm* wrote there was a surprise coming my way, but I didn't know it was you." Mose was nothing like either her childhood sweetheart Ivan, or Wayne, the man she had planned to marry, but maybe she should allow the Lord to choose her husband this time. Didn't his request have all the markings of the Lord's direction? There was *Daett*'s and *Mamm*'s approval, and that of Uncle William and Aunt Fannie, and Deacon Phillips and Katie.

"It's okay," Miriam said softly.

Mose's pleased expression returned. "How do you spend your Sunday evening around here when you're dating? I'm afraid I was married long enough to have forgotten."

"I think Aunt Fannie already has the evening planned," Miriam said with a smile.

Mose's happy look remained on his face as he took his first bite of popcorn. They had forgotten to eat, Miriam noticed. She quickly picked up a few kernels herself.

CHAPTER FIVE

Tyler Johnson closed his laptop and slipped it into his carry-on bag. He couldn't use the device for his meeting with the Amish Deacon Phillips Tuesday morning, but his technology would go with him on the trip regardless. How the Amish lived without such necessities of modern life was beyond him. He assumed there were side benefits. Maybe a connection could be made between a slower pace of life and the Amish's fabled record of honesty and hardwork. That and the rosy-cheeked maiden named Miriam who had blushed at his presence the other evening.

Tyler grinned at the memory of his meal with the Bylers. The community's school-teacher was no dashing beauty, but she exuded a wholesomeness and depth of character he liked. The world could use more of those qualities. All the Amish he had met on this trip were good examples of what society should be. His article would have no criticism of the Amish, despite their old-fashioned refusal to adapt to modern American life.

His editor would be happy at that. The man had made it clear he wanted an article complimentary of the Amish, and especially of their unselfish efforts in that horrible tornado season a couple of years back. The two million-dollar donation to the Clarita Relief Fund had been impressive. But he wondered, where did these people find that kind of money to donate? And that wasn't the only question that niggled at him. Had the funds been collected in small donations from here and there? That was difficult to imagine. The community only had so many members. Still they seemed prosperous enough, and friendly. William Byler and his wife, Fannie, had welcomed him into their home on the slightest of introductions. He could have been a mobster on the FBI's most-wanted list for all Mr. Byler knew, but his story had been accepted without question.

Tyler shook his head as he left his motel room and allowed the door to slam behind him. His cell rang on the walk to his rental car. Tyler checked the number before he answered. Ah. Hilda.

"Good morning, dear," Tyler said, tossing his carry-on on the backseat.

"Where are you, Ty?" Hilda cooed.

"Amish country," Tyler chirped.

Hilda was nice enough, Tyler reminded himself, but he had no illusions about their relationship. He was a rich trust-fund kid, which did have an upside in addition to getting dates. For one thing he took on writing projects only when he wanted to — projects he liked.

"Amish country?" Hilda questioned. "What is Amish country?"

"You should educate yourself," he teased. "The Amish are nice people."

"I didn't say they weren't, but why are you with them?" Hilda probed with tension in her voice.

"Because I'm on an assignment, and they are the subject."

"Oh, yes!" Comprehension dawned, and Hilda said, "I think I did hear about them once. They are a Stone Age people, aren't they?"

Tyler laughed. "Something like that. So what can I do for you, dear?"

"Just wanted to hear your voice and ask when I'll see you again."

"Maybe when I'm back in town," he hedged. "Don't know when that will be, though. This might take a while."

"What is there to know about Stone Age people?" she pouted. "They can't be that interesting. Not like me."

"No, that's certainly true," Tyler chuckled. "But assignments are assignments."

"Okay." She didn't sound convinced. "But don't forget to call."

"How can I forget, dear?"

They both knew he wouldn't have the chance. Hilda was the one who called him, and she would be the one to do so again.

"Goodbye," Hilda twittered, and disconnected before he did.

Tyler slipped his cell phone back into the clip and climbed into the car, the face of the young Amish schoolteacher drifting through his mind. He couldn't help but compare her simple grace and unadorned face with that of Hilda. Tyler grinned. Now there was a comparison. Hilda was a fully modern, dashing woman. She didn't step out of the house without her beauty aids. Nor did a week pass without her appointment with the hairstylist. Not that he cared; he did admire the results.

Tyler shook his head at the comparison between the two women and drove out of the parking lot. In a very real sense, to people like Hilda the Amish *were* a Stone

Age people. Even to him, the Amish world was a foreign world. But he had tasted a sample of their life the other evening at the Bylers's home, and foreign or not, he had liked it. It was in some strange way . . . well . . . appealing. He had seen a genuineness in Miriam Yoder that he liked. Were the Amish all as kind and peaceful as the ones he had met? Were there no closets with skeletons in them? Perhaps this morning's interview with Deacon Phillips would be revealing. Maybe a flaw would pop up. He didn't like the prospect, but the Amish lived with the same human nature as everyone else, even if they tried to hide out in communities. The truth was he hoped the Amish would survive the scrutiny. He didn't need an additional ring of cynicism around his heart.

Tyler checked both ways before he drove into Coalgate's main street. The midmorning traffic wasn't heavy. He had eaten earlier at the Iron Cafe while what passed for the morning rush hour was on. Compared to Oklahoma City, it wasn't worth a mention.

Tyler turned on the radio as he drove out of town. He flipped through the stations but shut off the volume when only country stations came up. Country music wasn't his first choice, and besides, he needed to think and prepare himself. Deacon Phillips had given no indication what his answers would be in response to questions about the relief fund. Tyler knew he would have to dig, but with the Amish's reputation for honesty, he thought he would receive straight answers if he asked the right questions. He also had another meeting this afternoon with the chairman of the Clarita Relief Fund, Mr. Westree. From Mr. Westree he had sensed all the usual signs of a man who could obfuscate and dodge with the skill worthy of a smooth politician.

Mr. Westree had reminded him, "We value and respect the wishes of our list of donors and recipients, Mr. Johnson. Remember that."

"You know there are state and federal laws governing the disclosure of information," Tyler had shot back.

"I will gladly tell you what I can about the generosity of the Clarita community following the tornadoes," Mr. Westree had responded somewhat coolly.

He would have to dig here too, Tyler told himself, but unless there was corruption hidden somewhere, he doubted he would find anything of interest. And how was corruption possible? Surely in such a sleepy community, things must run aboveboard.

Crimes and misdemeanors seemed unlikely, but he would still ask. Perhaps he would be stonewalled, but there were ways around such things. If he could land a scoop out of his digging, so much the better. So far in his freelance writing career, all the really juicy scoops had eluded him. Likely the same would happen here. The Amish were too honest to have some sordid scandal associated with the relief fund. Still, how did they manage to donate so much money?

Tyler pulled to a stop at Highway 48. This was the main drag running north and south near Clarita and through the Amish community. He'd gathered from his conversations the other evening with Mr. Byler that Amish farms lay on either side of the highway. Tyler slowed as the greenhouse came into view, but he didn't stop. Too much of an invasion of anyone's privacy wasn't decent. Maybe he should stop by the schoolhouse and say hello to the schoolteacher. How would that go? Miriam might no longer be the flustered woman he had seen the other evening — but in a way, that would be a disappointment. It was refreshing to find a woman who could act so bashful and be so unaware of his trust-fund money. Nor would Miriam be impressed if she did know. Likely the girl had never possessed more than a thousand dollars in her bank account at any given time. If she even had a bank account.

Tyler sobered at the thought. He should squelch his fantasies of Amish schoolteachers with sterling character qualities. He'd only corrupt their virtues with close contact. Still, he had to admit, he did find Miriam irresistible in some strange way. He would speak with her again, somehow, somewhere. Tyler slowed for another turn and moments later pulled into Deacon Phillips's driveway. Two buggies were parked beside the barn, and Tyler pulled in beside them. He climbed out to survey his rental car — the best SUV the agency owned. The car gleamed in the morning sunlight. The contrast with the two dark-clothed buggies couldn't have been starker. *Which about sums up the situation,* Tyler told himself.

Deacon Phillips's voice called from the barn door behind Tyler and pulled him out of his reverie. "Howdy there, Mr. Johnson. *Gut* to see you again."

"And you too." Tyler turned around to smile. The open friendliness of these people still surprised him. "Hope I'm not taking up too much of your time this morning."

"*Ach,* no!" Deacon Phillips exclaimed. "The Lord has given us the whole day, has

He not?"

Tyler chuckled as Deacon Phillips continued. "We can speak in the barn unless you want comfortable seating on the couch in the living room."

Tyler grinned. "The barn is fine. I'll try not to keep you long."

Deacon Phillips opened the door wide. "Then come on in, and I'll finish putting down the straw for the horse stalls. You can ask all the questions you want while I work."

"Maybe I can help," Tyler offered.

Deacon Phillips laughed. "We wouldn't want an *Englisha* man's fancy clothing messed up, now, would we?"

"I guess not," Tyler agreed. He looked down at his jeans, practically new and of the latest style and cut. No, he would not like to have them damaged by farm work.

The deacon seemed oblivious to Tyler's introspection as he spread straw with both hands. "So what were these questions you have about the relief fund?"

Tyler cleared his throat. He might as well get right to the point. "It's become public record that more than two million dollars was donated by the Amish community. Could you give me details on where those funds came from? That seems like a huge amount coming from such a small and . . .

well . . . unwealthy group of people."

Deacon Phillips didn't answer for a moment. "Well, first of all, I regret that such records were kept by the relief fund people, much less made public, but of course we cannot control such things. I had hoped the Lord would reward those who gave in secret. As you likely know, we shun the knowledge of man when it comes to our generosity."

Tyler cleared his throat again. "I suppose that's a nice sentiment to have, but it's a little unrealistic, don't you think?"

Deacon Phillips shrugged. "In this world perhaps, but we seek to live by the Lord's laws."

Tyler glanced at the barn floor for a second. He might as well ask the question. "This amount of two million dollars. Did that sum come from the community locally, or were there donors from out of state?"

Deacon Phillips reached for another bale of straw. "You know, I'd rather not answer the question."

"But surely you can tell me that much." Tyler held his breath for a moment.

"Well, *yah,*" Deacon Phillips finally allowed. "Some of the funds came from Possum Valley. A vanload of men came out during that time to help rebuild."

"In what amount?" Tyler pressed on. "The community here doesn't seem that prosperous. Or am I missing something?"

"The Lord provided." Deacon Phillips gave Tyler a sharp glance.

Clearly he had been pushed far enough, but Tyler couldn't resist. "Would you give me the names of the major donors?"

Deacon Phillips shook out the straw bale vigorously before he said, "That person wishes to remain hidden, and I ask you to respect her privacy."

Tyler tried to hide his delight. "So there was one person, and a woman at that? Perhaps an elderly widow who left her property for the storm relief?"

Deacon Phillips's face reddened. "I'm sorry, Mr. Johnson. I shouldn't have told you that information. I'm not used to talking about these things. Forgive me for saying this much."

"That's okay," Tyler told him. Further questions appeared useless. The deacon had clammed up, his lips set in a firm line. "Thank you for your time, then," Tyler offered with a smile. "I really shouldn't be keeping you."

"You will remember the Lord's ways," Deacon Phillips told him. The look on the deacon's face showed more hope than expectation.

Tyler pushed his surge of guilt aside. "I thank you again, Deacon Phillips. May the Lord bless you."

"And you too." But Deacon Phillips didn't appear too happy.

I am a hypocrite, Tyler thought, as he beat a hasty retreat. But a story was a story, and this could prove a good one if he could find further details. His editor would love the tale of a widowed Amish woman who left her life savings to storm relief instead of to her children or grandchildren . . . if such was the case. And surely it was something like that. What else could it have been?

Outside of the barn Tyler's phone beeped with an incoming text message. He checked to find a note from the chairman of the relief fund, Mr. Westree. "Emergency has occurred. Meeting canceled this afternoon. Apologies."

There was no emergency, Tyler told himself. Mr. Westree had made no offer to reschedule.

"Well, happy hunting," Tyler said aloud with a glance toward the sky. "And may the Lord bless me. Looks like I could use it."

CHAPTER SIX

About the same time Tyler Johnson was leaving Deacon Phillips's place, Mose Stoll jiggled the reins of the deacon's horse, Ralph, to get him moving. Mose had borrowed the animal for a tour of the community and was just arriving at Bishop Mullet's house. He still wasn't used to the horse's quirks, such as his penchant for quick starts at stop signs. A deacon shouldn't drive an unsteady horse, Mose told himself. He hoped it wouldn't reflect on the deacon's character.

The last few days had crept past slowly. Mose wasn't used to all this idle time, but he supposed the downtime was necessary if he wished to marry the schoolteacher, Miriam Yoder. He should relax, Mose told himself. His farm back in Wayne County was in the capable hands of his brother, and so far his time here in this small community had borne fruit. No one had given him a negative answer when he asked questions. Still, at times he wondered why he had traveled all the way out here to find a wife. There were single girls and widows available at home within easier reach. It had been Glen Weaver's glowing testimony of Miriam's character that had brought him here. Of course, his conversation with Miriam's *daett* had drawn him in deeper. The family seemed endowed with an outstanding head of the family. And so he had to check out the matter with a trip to meet Miriam at least. How could he go wrong with that choice? From the reports, Miriam seemed incapable of wrongdoing. Miriam was no raving beauty, but she wasn't bad looking either. Far from it. Outward beauty had been made by the Lord, Mose reminded himself as he pushed the thought away. But the Scriptures said such things faded with time, and beauty of the heart was the desired virtue. That was why he had traveled so many miles and thankfully hadn't been disappointed. He would ask more questions of the bishop today. The man might know a fault of Miriam's that had escaped the notice of everyone else. Hopefully the matter wouldn't be a deal breaker. What a shame to have traveled all these miles and have his hopes raised only to return to Wayne County empty-handed. Perhaps a few chuckles would circulate in his home community over his travails, but he could live with that. The important thing was to choose a *frau* who walked in the fear of the Lord.

"Whoa there," Mose called to Ralph as he pulled into Bishop Mullet's driveway. With a shake of his head, the horse stopped beside the barn. Mose climbed down to tie him to the hitching post. The knot secure, Mose approached the barn door. Faint noises were coming from inside, and Mose stepped inside to holler, "Anybody home?"

The bishop's voice came from the back of the barn. "Over here, working on some stalls."

Mose found his way past the cow stanchions and greeted the bishop with a smile. "Hard at work, eh?"

"As always." The bishop chuckled. "I see you arrived just in time for lunch."

Mose laughed. "Guilty. I've been out touring the community and surely enjoyed it. Worked up an appetite, though."

Bishop Mullet picked up another board to size it up. "So what are your conclusions?"

"About what?" Mose hedged. "The church or . . ." He couldn't say Miriam's name out loud. Not in the bishop's presence. Not yet, at least.

Bishop Mullet grinned. "I'm thinking the two are tied up in your mind."

"I suppose so," Mose allowed. "But that's how it should be, don't you think?"

"Of course," Bishop Mullet said at once. "Although Miriam really has nothing to do with our Amish church life out here on the prairie."

"But I'm going partly by your approval of her," Mose shot back.

"True enough," Bishop Mullet agreed. "Now we're back to my original question. What do you think of us?"

Mose shrugged. "It's hard to tell in so short a time."

Bishop Mullet gave him a sharp glance. "Don't beat around the bush with me, Mose. You have eyes in the back of your head, unless I miss my guess."

Mose allowed the feeling of pleasure to sink in for a moment before he answered. "I take that as a compliment, and *yah,* I do have some questions about your practice of tractor farming and about your small number of young people. Where have they all gone? Have you been losing many of them to the world?"

Bishop Mullet's face shadowed. "I wish I could say we're perfect in keeping our youth, but we did lose two more young men last fall, the Mark Yoder boys. They left about the same time, for the usual reasons, I suppose — lusting for the world and its allure. But beyond that, we've managed by the Lord's grace to keep our young people in the community."

Mose shrugged. "Not perfect, as you say, but not a cause for great concern. We lose ten to twenty percent in any given year. Each loss tears at our hearts, but a man must make his own choice."

"Very true," Bishop Mullet agreed. "And we sorrow here also. Now on the tractor farming subject, *yah,* we do farm with tractors. That change in the *Ordnung* was pushed on us by the soil conditions, which are out of our control. We felt like . . ."

Mose held up his hand. "I know. Deacon Phillips already filled me in. I don't agree, but it's a local matter and shouldn't affect my interest in Miriam."

"You're a deep thinker." Bishop Mullet paused to nail on a board. "So what do you think of Miriam so far?"

Mose looked away. "She seems to be what she's reported to be. But I should ask you. You know her better than I do."

"I know her quite well," Bishop Mullet agreed. "Miriam's a real asset to the community, and everyone loves her."

"She's almost too perfect," Mose said. "But I take comfort that at least she has experienced sorrow in her past with the death of her fiancé. And I hear that her childhood sweetheart from Possum Valley jilted Miriam before she moved out here."

Bishop Mullet nodded. "This is all true, and I have nothing to add. I assume Deacon Phillips told you about the money an *Englisha* man left her in his will."

Mose pulled himself up with a start. "Money? Left in a will! What does this mean?"

Bishop Mullet waved his hammer about. "Miriam doesn't have the money any longer, so don't worry. She gave it all away."

"Oh." Mose let out a long breath. "You had me there for a moment."

Bishop Mullet chuckled. "Couldn't let it look as if you're marrying for money?"

Mose remained sober faced. "Not just that, but an abundance of money calls one's character into question — at least in my book. I'm surprised Miriam's *daett* didn't tell me this if it's to her credit."

Bishop Mullet grinned. "Sounds like you're having a difficult time believing the reports already. Maybe Miriam's *daett*

thought she should tell you this about herself."

"Then you shouldn't have told me either,"
Mose said, raising his eyebrows.

Bishop Mullet didn't back down. "I think
Miriam will be glad I told you. She doesn't
like to speak of the matter — not to anyone,
and I am the bishop."

Mose nodded. "So tell me more about this
money. Are we talking about a few thousand
dollars?"

Bishop Mullet sobered. "No, try two million."

"Two million!" Mose paled.

Bishop Mullet had a shy look on his face.
"Are you wishing perhaps that Miriam
hadn't given the money away?"

Mose sputtered. "Of course not, but . . .
oh, my, that's a ton of cash. Did she really
give it all away? That would take a character
fashioned of the Lord's hands indeed."

Bishop Mullet hesitated. "It's not like I
saw the money, but Deacon Phillips assured
me she handed him a two-million-dollar
check made out to the Clarita Relief Fund.
If she spent a few dollars before that, what
does it matter?"

Before Mose could think of a response,
the barn door rattled behind them, and the
bishop's *frau,* Ellen, called out. "Lunchtime,

you two. Or do you plan to talk about church matters all day?"

"Coming," Bishop Mullet called back. "We were talking about . . ." The protest died on his lips when the barn door closed.

"Does your *frau* think well of Miriam?" Mose asked.

Bishop Mullet snorted. "You are an impossible man, Mose. After what I told you, you still have questions?"

Mose looked away. "I know. I guess I'll never stop asking questions. That's just me." He followed Bishop Mullet out of the barn toward the house.

Bishop Mullet turned with an amused look and said, "Soon Miriam will be asking questions about you if you don't make up your mind."

Mose laughed. "Oh, I've made up my mind. It's just that the questions keep coming."

The two chuckled as they entered the house and sat down at the kitchen table. Ellen joined them, and they bowed their heads in thanks for the food laid out on the table.

With the amen said, Ellen pointed to the bowl in the middle of the table. "Dish it out. It's potato soup, and I have pecan pie for dessert. Not much, but we'll have more if you stay for supper."

"You should, you know." Bishop Mullet glanced at Mose. "Ellen sets a nice spread for supper."

Mose filled his bowl with steaming potato soup before he answered. "Thanks, but I have to see Miriam tonight. I'm sure Ellen's a fine cook, but I'll have to find out more some other time."

"Oh, she's the best," Bishop Mullet assured him. "Why don't you ask Ellen how Miriam can cook? That's one question I haven't heard you ask, and it's one I can't answer."

Mose grinned. "Don't you think I've asked enough questions for one day? I'm sure the woman can cook."

Ellen smiled but still answered, "I don't know that much about any of our young community girls's cooking, but Fannie is among the best, and I can't see where she'd have failed to teach Miriam — if Miriam hadn't already learned at home. Possum Valley is known for its tasty dishes, is it not?"

"That it is," Mose agreed as he took another spoonful of soup. "This is excellent, by the way. And thanks for the hospitality."

"Mose was afraid he'd starve," Bishop Mullet teased, "if Miriam agreed to wed him."

Ellen eyed Mose for a moment. "Miriam is dear to our hearts, you know. She's had a rough row to hoe when it comes to men."

"That's what I've heard," Mose managed. "You don't think I'd . . ."

"I'm just expressing my concern," Ellen said. "Miriam doesn't need her heart broken again."

"I wouldn't, of course . . ." Mose searched for words. He hadn't expected this line of questions. "Surely you don't think I'd give the woman hope only to jilt her?"

Ellen gave him a sharp look. "I just wanted to get in my two cents. If you walk away now, Miriam won't get hurt, but don't decide in a few months to leave her after you've made wedding plans."

"I will treat the woman properly, as the Lord directs," Mose protested.

"I think my *frau* means this well," Bishop Mullet replied, taking charge again. "This just shows you, Mose, how well-regarded Miriam is in the community."

. "I do see this," Mose allowed. "And I assure you that I'll be careful with Miriam's heart."

"That's all we can ask," Bishop Mullet said.

Silence settled in the kitchen as they finished their soup. Ellen got up to bring over the pecan pie from the counter.

"This is *gut* cooking, that's for sure," Mose offered as he took a large bite.

Ellen smiled. "So how are you finding the rest of the community?"

"Friendly and open," Mose said. "I have no complaints."

"I'm glad you're enjoying yourself." Ellen pushed the pie pan toward him. "Another piece perhaps?"

Mose shook his head and finished moments later. They bowed their heads, and Bishop Mullet led out in a final prayer of thanks.

Mose pushed back his chair and stood to his feet. "I'm so glad you had me in to lunch, and everything was delicious. I'm sorry I can't come back for supper."

"Maybe next week," Ellen said with a smile.

"We'll have to see, I guess," Mose said as he took his leave. He untied Ralph to drive north toward the schoolhouse. He pulled his pocket watch out to check the time. At two o'clock school would still be in session. Maybe he could catch the last recess if he hurried. Afterward he'd stay and watch how the classes were run. He was sure Miriam would have things in order, but he wished to see for himself.

Mose jiggled the reins and pushed Ralph to a fast trot. He soon saw the playground ahead filled with schoolchildren, and he slowed down. The children stopped in their play to watch him drive in, but no one paid him any further attention once he parked his buggy. After Mose tied up at the hitching post, he approached the schoolhouse doorway. Miriam met him there with her eyes downcast.

"You have come to visit?" she whispered.

"*Yah,* if I may." Mose regarded her with a steady gaze.

Miriam seemed flustered but welcomed him inside with a small hand motion. "I'll ring the bell in a few moments, but you're welcome to look around."

"I'll do that," Mose said.

She led him up the steps, and Mose glanced around. Everything appeared neat and in order, even for the end of a long school day. This spoke well of Miriam. If she could manage a schoolhouse, she could keep their house in order and raise any *kinner* the Lord gave them with decency and decorum.

"You can have a seat over there," Miriam said, motioning with her hand again as she reached for the bell, "if you want to stay longer."

72

Mose smiled and nodded. "I believe I will, if you don't mind."

"Things can get a little hectic the last period." Miriam glanced down again. "But I have nothing to hide."

"It's okay," he assured her. "Everything looks as it should."

She appeared relieved and moved to ring the bell. Mose settled on the bench and observed the students as they entered. No one ran or stared at him after their first brief glances in his direction. By the time Miriam called the next grade to come up for their time with her, the students seemed to have forgotten him.

This was how a decent school was run, Mose told himself. Miriam was clearly a fine teacher. A fine woman. Truly the Lord had led him all the way here to find a virtuous woman the likes of which he hadn't dared imagine. With a smile on his face, Mose slipped out the back door and untied Ralph. He'd see Miriam again tonight, and his approval of her would only increase. Of this he was certain.

CHAPTER SEVEN

An hour later Miriam watched from the schoolhouse window as the last of her students' buggies disappeared in the distance. Her head still hurt from the tension of knowing Mose had been sitting on the bench near the window scrutinizing everything with an intense gaze while she had tried to keep a normal flow to the schoolhouse routine.

Thankfully, he'd left before she dismissed school, but her headache hadn't. None of the students had asked embarrassing questions about her relationship with Mose before they left. Likely plenty of little minds would have queries for their *mamm* and *daett* at home, but that was to be expected. Most of the community knew about Mose Stoll and why he was here, and knew that Bishop Mullet and Deacon Phillips both approved of his mission. The whole world seemed to approve.

So why wasn't her heart drawn in? Or had events simply happened too quickly? She hardly knew the man other than her experience with his sharp and inquisitive glances. She hadn't seen much more of the tenderness of his first looks. She understood that Mose wished to cover all the angles in his investigation of her. As a minister, Mose wouldn't want a *frau* who would cause trouble for him once they had said the marriage vows.

Miriam sighed as memories of Wayne flooded her thoughts. Mose certainly didn't court her like Wayne Yutzy had. She couldn't imagine sweet nothings slipping out of Mose's mouth or even an "I love you so much, Miriam."

"But the Lord has taken Wayne away from me," Miriam whispered to herself. "I shouldn't complain over His choices."

And *Daett* could be trusted in his judgment of Mose, Miriam reminded herself. Hadn't *Daett* been right about the two million dollars? She had experienced nothing but trouble when she had kept the gift a secret. *Daett* hadn't complained about her deception, but his heart had been much troubled once he found out about the two million dollars. And *Daett* had been right.

She would trust *Daett* with Mose, Miriam

told herself. There was no other way to live. Hadn't her heart proven itself deeply unworthy with its recent attraction to the *Englisha* man, Tyler Johnson?

Miriam steadied herself on her teacher's desk with one hand. With the resolution a measure of peace settled on her, and her breathing became easier. Mose would see her again tonight, and perhaps things would go better when they spoke on Aunt Fannie's couch. They could talk and relax in a more homey setting. That was what she needed.

Miriam turned away from the window but paused as a car appeared in the distance. Not too many *Englisha* vehicles came up the school road at this time of the day. Miriam studied the car and pulled in a sharp breath as it came closer. Her head tensed again until it throbbed. It was the *Englisha* man's car. Surely Tyler Johnson wouldn't stop in at the schoolhouse. He had no business with her, and yet this was surely his car pulling in and halting right where Mose Stoll had parked his buggy not an hour ago.

Miriam clasped and unclasped her hands. Should she hide in the closet? But the schoolhouse door was unlocked, and Tyler would know someone was around. And if she didn't see him today, he'd only come back tomorrow. Weren't reporters like that?

Persistent? Tyler certainly seemed to fit the bill. Miriam gathered herself together. She would control her emotions in front of him, and he would soon leave. Then she would never see him again.

Miriam set her face in a tight smile and went to open the door. Tyler was standing there, ready to knock. He paused with his hand upraised and said, "Howdy there, Miss Yoder. Remember me?"

He appeared much too pleased with himself. Of course she remembered him. Her face burned from the memory, but he didn't seem bothered by her tongue-tied condition.

He spoke again, "If this isn't a good time, I can come back later."

Miriam found her voice. "No, this is okay. The students left a while ago, and I haven't started grading papers, and Mose . . ." Miriam cut off the words. Tyler had no right to all this information, and neither should he see her turn into a blubbering mess.

Tyler continued in his pleasant manner, "Then perhaps you have a few moments for some questions. And a tour of the schoolhouse afterward? This would go along well with the article I'm writing on the Amish." He flashed a grin.

"Well, maybe . . . *yah,* come on in." Miriam stepped aside. "I do have a few minutes."

That sounded too eager. She should order the man to leave, but that would have been unwomanly and unkind to boot. Even pushy strangers must be treated with respect. If only they weren't so handsome and didn't take her breath away.

Tyler followed her inside and looked around. His glances weren't piercing like Mose's had been. He appeared genuinely interested. "So this is where it all happens."

"I suppose so," Miriam allowed. "I know you don't have a very high opinion of our one-room schools, but I do try."

"I'm sure you do a fine job," Tyler assured her. "And one-room schools are great for what your community needs." He appeared concerned and stepped closer with one hand out. "Are you okay? You look a little pale. I'm not startling you, am I?"

"I don't faint easily, Mr. Johnson." Miriam met his gaze but looked away at once. His eyes were so blue, so clear — his chin with the slight stubble was . . . Miriam tried to breathe evenly. Maybe she *was* going to faint.

"It's Tyler," he said. His hand came down gently on her arm. "Maybe you'd better sit down. Over here perhaps."

Miriam allowed him to guide her, and sank down at a student's desk. Tyler peered at Miriam before he settled into a seat beside her.

"I'm okay," she assured him. At least her face didn't burn like a gas lantern right now. There didn't seem to be much blood left in her body. It had all drained to her feet.

"Are you sure?" he persisted. "I could call 911." He reached for his phone.

Miriam gasped. "No, not that! Don't call." She grabbed his hand, and he lowered the phone. Horror gripped Miriam. How could this be explained if the community found out she had been alone at the schoolhouse with Tyler, and worse if an ambulance was called.

"Okay. If you say so," Tyler finally said, but his gaze didn't leave Miriam's face.

Miriam struggled to collect herself. "You had some questions," she whispered.

Tyler hesitated. "If you're sure you're okay."

"I'm fine," Miriam insisted, but she knew her smile was crooked and lame. And her face still had no blood in it.

"Tell me how a one-room schoolhouse works, then." Tyler settled back into his desk. "The last time the general public used one of these was an awful long time ago."

"We're not backward." Miriam sat up straighter in her desk. "We use the latest curriculum. If you plan to write a bad story about our school, you'd better leave now."

Tyler chuckled. "Heaven forbid I do such a thing. I like the Amish, and my editor wouldn't publish a negative story anyway."

"Oh." Miriam relaxed. She should still ask him to leave, but she didn't have the strength. And his presence soothed her ruffled spirit. Perhaps this came from the years she had taken care of the ailing Mr. Bland in Possum Valley. That would explain why she was somewhat comfortable around *Englisha* men. Miriam's face began to burn as she stole a glance at Tyler's face.

Tyler noticed and smiled. "Feeling better, I see. Apparently I must ask charming questions."

Miriam tried to glare at him, but her face wouldn't cooperate. The effort must have appeared as a horrible grimace because Tyler laughed. "You *are* feeling better."

Miriam set her face into an emotionless expression. She took a deep breath and rattled off the words. "Well, this is how it goes. The schoolchildren arrive and put their horses in the shelter if their parents don't drop them off. They play in the yard until I ring the bell at nine. When they come in and have caught their breath, we open each morning with a short reading of Scripture and a prayer, after which . . ."

He leaned forward in his desk and interrupted her. "You lead out in reading the Bible and with prayer?"

"Why, of course."

Tyler smiled. "Just asking. It just seems your community has some very patriarchal ideas, and I would have expected a man to arrive each morning to read the sacred pages."

Miriam stared at him. "Do you think a woman shouldn't teach or read the Scriptures to her students?"

"No." His face darkened. "Not me. Them! The men of the community. I would have expected them to object."

Comprehension dawned. "It's not like that at all," Miriam hastened to say. "Our men lead in the home, but here I'm the teacher."

"Okay." Tyler looked like he was ready to say more but didn't.

If Tyler knew about Mose Stoll and how their relationship had begun and proceeded, he would think quite ill of everyone, Miriam thought. Which was exactly why Tyler wouldn't find out. Such things were not for an *Englisha* ear. Especially not handsome men who wouldn't understand how love really worked among the Amish.

Miriam gathered herself again and continued. "After prayer we go straight to classes with a schedule I've drawn up and worked the bugs out of over the years. The students know when the class time for their grade is scheduled, and I call them up and go over the next lesson and answer any questions they have. It's all very effective, really."

"I can imagine." Tyler smiled again. "Can I look around?"

"Sure!" Miriam followed Tyler to his feet.

"I'm impressed," Tyler said after he had poked around the desks. "Can I look at the workbooks?"

"Of course." Miriam didn't hesitate. "Their grades aren't too bad. They're good students."

Tyler grinned. "With a teacher like you, I'm not surprised."

Miriam felt herself color again. "You don't have to say that."

"I don't just say it," Tyler protested. "I mean it. I think I would have learned a lot more in a school like this and with a teacher like . . ." Tyler sent Miriam a meaningful look.

Miriam lowered her head and didn't respond. The words seemed stuck in her throat at the moment. She had to remember that this was an *Englisha* man, and he often used flowery words that had no meaning. But if Mose Stoll would use more of them like Wayne Yutzy used to, she . . . Miriam clutched her hands together. What terrible thoughts she was having about a minister, and one who sought her hand in marriage. She shouldn't complain about what the Lord had sent her way.

"You could have taught me quite a few things, I think." Tyler still looked at her, and Miriam's heart pounded. She needed to break her fascination with this man. But how?

"I'm sure you have a college education and could have taught me much more than I could ever have taught you," Miriam finally managed.

He laughed. "Always humble. Are all your people like that?"

"We try to place others above ourselves," Miriam said at once. "It's the godly way."

"But not the human one," he teased. "Aren't you still human?"

If he could hear her heart beat, he'd know the answer to that question. With her face ablaze, Miriam turned away from him. "And over here is the blackboard where we work out problems with the students. They learn better with a hands-on approach than

83

with hearing only lectures."

"That's true enough," Tyler allowed.

He acted as if he didn't notice her discomfort, but the man didn't miss much. Well, now he knew she was human. Thankfully she'd never have to see him after today. She would confess her weakness to the Lord tonight and beg for forgiveness. Maybe she should confess to Mose, but that would send him on a straight beeline back to Wayne County . . . which she didn't want. There might not be another Amish husband sent her way anytime soon, or one who came with such high recommendations.

"You wouldn't know who gave more than two million dollars to the Clarita Relief Fund, would you?" Tyler cut through Miriam's thoughts. "I understand it was a woman."

Miriam choked for a moment. "Did Deacon Phillips tell you this?"

Tyler shrugged. "Not really, but he said enough that I got the gist of the idea. This is correct then?"

Miriam pressed her lips together. The suddenness of the question left her cold. Nothing she could say could make things better. And what if the secret slipped out of her mouth? That must never happen.

Tyler looked at Miriam closely. "I take it

you know who this person is?"

Miriam managed to show no expression. "That's not a proper question to ask among the community people."

"I'm sorry," Tyler said quickly. "I'm not trying to offend anyone, but this would be considered a great honor among my people."

"You'd publish such a thing in your paper?" Horror tinged Miriam's voice.

Tyler seemed to ponder the point. "I guess we do have a different perspective on the matter."

Miriam remained silent.

Tyler tried another tack. "Would you tell me if I didn't publish the name of this woman in my article?"

"No!" The word sprang from Miriam's lips. "I would never tell you. And now it's time for you to leave."

Surprise was written on his face as Miriam ushered Tyler toward the door with one hand on his arm.

"I'm sorry about this," he tried again. "I didn't mean to offend you in any way."

"Just go." Miriam opened the door and pushed on his shoulder. Tyler left with a quick backward glance, as if he couldn't figure out her sudden change in attitude.

As the sound of Tyler's car died away in

the distance, Miriam collapsed at a student's desk and held her head. Now she still had all her grading of papers ahead of her, and Mose would be at Aunt Fannie's for supper tonight. She couldn't be late. Oh, how had this happened? She had entertained an *Englisha* man in her schoolhouse for more than an hour. There was no other way to look at this. Neither Mose or anyone else must ever find out about this. Never! Or how far her heart had strayed from the straight and narrow. How could she have such feelings for an *Englisha* man? Only Tyler's sudden question about the two million dollars had brought her out of the stupor she had been in.

CHAPTER EIGHT

Later that evening Miriam was filling the water glasses on Aunt Fannie's kitchen table in preparation for the meal. Moments earlier, Mose Stoll had arrived, and Miriam had shaken hands with him. The blush on her face had clearly been interpreted by Mose to mean she had feelings for him. Miriam could see the delight spread across his face.

Aunt Fannie came up beside Miriam and whispered, "He's so handsome, isn't he? I saw you turn all sorts of colors when he arrived. Oh, aren't the Lord's ways just *wunderbah*?"

The comment shouldn't be allowed to pass unchallenged, Miriam decided. She whispered back, "I might have had other reasons, you know."

Aunt Fannie still glowed with happiness. "Don't try to dodge the point, Miriam. You already love the man."

Miriam forced a smile. Aunt Fannie would have to think what she wished. Now if she could forget Tyler Johnson for the evening . . . but the memory of the stubble on his chin wouldn't go away. Miriam turned her back to hide her face from Aunt Fannie.

"Call the men for supper," Aunt Fannie said more loudly.

Miriam peeked around the edge of the kitchen doorway before she stepped out to announce, "Supper is ready if you are."

"Sounds great to me," Mose said. He stood slowly to his feet with a broad smile on his face as Miriam beat a hasty retreat.

Uncle William had a grin on his face when he carried Jonathon into the kitchen. He set the boy on the back bench and declared, "There you go, little man. All settled in for supper time."

Aunt Fannie waved Mose to his place, and he sat down as if he owned the place. Miriam forced a smile as she took a seat across from Mose. At least Aunt Fannie hadn't seated them side by side. Aunt Fannie must know she needed a little breathing room with the speed at which this courtship was proceeding.

Aunt Fannie took her own seat and smiled. "I think we're all ready."

"Then let us pray," Uncle William announced.

They bowed their heads as Uncle William led out with the first words of the Lord's Prayer, "Our Father, which art in heaven, hallowed be Thy name. We come tonight to give You thanks for this food prepared for us. You have blessed us with so much, we can never give You thanks enough. Be with us now. We give You praise and glory that . . ."

Miriam snuck a look at Mose across from her. His beard nearly touched the table below his bowed head. His face was solemn, filled with holy thoughts of thanks, Miriam was sure. Why couldn't she give thanks for this great blessing the Lord had sent her way? Here was no doubt a *wunderbah* husband who had landed right in her lap. She didn't even have to look for him. He was surely prosperous — in a reasonable way. She wouldn't have to worry about financial difficulties if a dozen *kinner* were given to them by the Lord. Mose was a minister, and she would hold a position of honor in the community in Wayne County. This would all be achieved overnight without effort on her part. All she must do is go along with things. But instead of feeling thankful, all she could feel were the clear, blue eyes of Tyler Johnson as they pierced into hers.

"Please help me, Lord." Miriam whispered her own prayer as Uncle William pronounced the amen. The words caught in her throat, and Miriam coughed into her apron.

Aunt Fannie glanced at Miriam with concern on her face. "Is everything okay?"

Mose half rose from his seat.

Miriam managed a painful smile. "Something caught . . ." Miriam rubbed her neck. This had to stop. But how? Maybe if she'd think more about Mose, the memory of Tyler would fade into the distant past?

Mose had settled back into this chair. "You had me worried there," he teased. "I thought my presence had unsettled the dinner table."

Miriam forced a laugh. "No, I'll be okay. I'm glad you're here."

Uncle William gave Miriam a strange look. No doubt that was a little forward of her to say, but she had to get Tyler Johnson out of her mind.

Mose appeared pleased, though, responding, "I'm also glad to be here. And oh, if I didn't say it plainly enough this afternoon, your school was very well run. The children appear well taught and well behaved."

Comprehension seemed to dawn on Uncle William's face. "So that's what the nervous attack was about. I'd be weak bodied myself if someone had inspected my schoolteaching."

Mose waved aside the comment. "You don't have to worry. Miriam passed with flying colors, as I'm sure you all knew she would."

"We expected nothing but the best," Uncle William said, his tone sober. They all laughed, and even Miriam managed to join in.

When the laugher died down, Mose said, "By the way, Bishop Mullett told me this afternoon about the two million dollars Miriam inherited and gave away. Why didn't anyone tell me this before?"

Miriam coughed again and kept her head down. This was not her place to speak.

Thankfully, Uncle William answered for her. "I take it as a compliment to Miriam that she hasn't told you, and we didn't think that was our place either."

"I suppose not," Mose allowed. He appeared quite pleased. "That was a very courageous and righteous act, Miriam. I commend you for it."

"Thank you," Miriam whispered. Now she had turned all sorts of colors, and not because of Tyler Johnson.

Aunt Fannie reached over to touch Miriam's arm. "Miriam has been through her trials. But the Lord has seen her through them all and has never stopped the blessings."

Mose smiled. "When one does the will of God, it always ends well. We should remember that even in our darkest hours."

Everyone nodded. After that *gut* word, the Lord would surely remove Tyler Johnson from her memory, Miriam told herself.

For the next several minutes, the chatter was light, and Miriam relaxed and even laughed at some of the banter. Finally, Aunt Fannie bounced up to announce, "And now for dessert."

Miriam motioned with her hand for her aunt to seat herself again. "I'll get the pies."

She noticed out of the corner of her eye that Mose was impressed. She hadn't intended to make a statement, but Mose's further approval might help remove her obsession with Tyler Johnson.

Miriam brought the pies from the counter, and Aunt Fannie began to cut large pieces. Mose lodged a protest, "Just a small piece for me, please." He patted his stomach. "I've been sitting around for days now with no work, and the pounds are staring me in the face."

Uncle William chuckled. "I can put you to

work tomorrow in the greenhouse. Or you can pull weeds in Fannie's garden."

Aunt Fannie glared at Uncle William. "I'll get to those weeds tomorrow. I was making supper today."

Mose laughed. "Far be it from me to introduce disharmony into a family's life. The garden looked fine to me."

"Thank you," Aunt Fannie replied. "See there." She gave Uncle William another glare. "The man's on the poor woman's side."

"My deepest apologies for my error," Uncle William said with mock gravity. "I see I could not have been more wrong."

"Men!" Aunt Fannie grumped, but a smile played on her face as she settled into her seat and took a slice of pie.

A comfortable silence settled over the kitchen.

Uncle William finished his last bite with a sigh. "Nothing like cherry pie to settle the mind and body at the end of the day."

"You can say that again," Mose seconded. "Even a small piece has that effect."

Laugher filled the kitchen again, and moments later they bowed their heads for a prayer of thanks. Miriam was on her feet seconds after the amen.

Aunt Fannie waved her out of the kitchen

at once. "You've been enough of a help, so go, Miriam."

Go meant go off to the front porch with Mose. Miriam opened her mouth to protest, but Mose was already halfway to the kitchen doorway. She could do nothing but follow. They walked through the living room and found seats outside on the far end of the porch. Dusk had begun to fall, and the occasional lights from a passing *Englisha* automobile flickered from the road.

"Nice evening out here on the prairie," Mose said. His gaze swept the horizon. "Have you become fairly attached to the place?"

"I like it," Miriam said, "but I'm not fastened to the prairie like some people are." Mose still probed, but he didn't have to worry. She had learned that the Lord's grace reached wherever one lived.

"That's *gut* to hear." Mose's voice was low. "I really meant what I said about your school and the fact that you gave away those two million dollars. I must say nothing I've heard about you was exaggerated in the least."

"You shouldn't say such things." Miriam hid her face. "I'm just an ordinary woman."

"But with extraordinary grace given to you." Mose studied Miriam. "I feel very

94

blessed to have met you, Miriam." Silence settled for a moment before Mose continued, "But what about you? Do you have any questions for me? Here I'm asking all the questions while you must also have some. I drop in out of nowhere, and . . ." Mose let the words hang.

She really had no questions, but Mose would expect some. Well, she was interested in his former *frau.* She could ask about her.

Miriam framed the words with care. "Your *frau,* Rachel — can you speak of her? What she was like?"

"Sure." Mose didn't seem uneasy. "We dated for several years before we were married. Happily, I might add. The only sorrow we had was that the Lord failed to add *kinner* to our union, but that was His choice, which we didn't wish to question. We had several happy years together, but cancer came soon after that, quickly and without warning. Breast cancer." Mose's voice faded for a moment. "Rachel was a dear woman, too *wunderbah* for me. I never could see what she saw in me, but we had been sweet on each other since our *rumspringa* days. I suppose she didn't think it worth the effort to look for someone else." Mose let out a deprecating laugh. "I was deeply attracted to Rachel, and a piece of my heart passed with her. Only lately have I found the strength to look again for a woman to walk with me . . . mostly for my ministry's sake, I guess. A minister needs a *frau* by his side. But if I may be so bold, Miriam, I must say that you have moved my heart deeply. I didn't expect to find another woman like Rachel, whom I could both respect and love."

Miriam didn't meet his gaze as she whispered, "I don't know what to say about that. You praise me too highly, I'm afraid. But I'm glad to hear that things had gone well between Rachel and you."

Mose nodded solemnly. "That is a *gut* observation, and one I would expect from you. A bad first marriage would likely lead to a bad second marriage. I hope and pray this time that I can spend many long, happy years with my second *frau.*"

Miriam held her breath for a moment. Mose hadn't proposed outright, but he had come close. She would have said *yah* if he had asked, but thankfully the moment hadn't arrived. She needed a little more time to prepare her heart.

"Is there something else?" Mose's voice was gentle.

"You have a farm, I assume?" The words slipped out. Now she sounded like a financial concern was the second most important thing on her mind.

Mose chuckled. "Women would think of such things. Can I afford a family, in other words?"

Miriam began to protest, but Mose silenced her with a motion of his hand. "Your character has already been established when it comes to money, so don't worry. You have a right to ask. Any woman would. So here goes. My farmhouse sits on more than one hundred acres. Not all of the mortgage is paid off, but enough that I'm comfortable with the payment. And Wayne County's farmland is known for its abundant production of crops. So unless the Lord has other plans, I should be able to raise a family with my next *frau* and not face starvation."

Will the Lord give you kinner this time? Miriam almost asked. Mose seemed so certain, but she had never borne children for a man. What if she failed him in this area?

"You don't object to *kinner,* do you?" Mose glanced at Miriam.

"No, no, of course not," Miriam sputtered.

"Then you fear how many the Lord would give you?" Mose's gaze pierced again.

Miriam hid her face with both hands. "No, Mose," she whispered. "I'm satisfied with what the Lord gives. But please, let's speak of something else."

"That is well said." Mose settled back into his chair. "You respond with shame like a virtuous woman should, and I am grateful."

Miriam clung to the sides of the chair and wished for dusk to fall completely. Yet Mose seemed to understand. He allowed long moments to pass before he spoke again, "Perhaps we should go inside and spend some time with your Uncle William and Aunt Fannie."

"As you wish," Miriam heard her voice tremble.

Mose smiled. "I hope I can see you again this week. Maybe on Thursday evening for supper?"

"If Aunt Fannie will fix a meal." Miriam tried to smile. "I can come home early from school to help, but . . ."

"Your Aunt Fannie has already invited me, so the matter is settled," Mose interrupted. He regarded her for a long moment. "I have enjoyed my time with you tonight, Miriam, and I hope you have also."

Mose didn't wait for an answer as he led the way back inside the house.

CHAPTER NINE

Two days later Miriam hitched up Star and headed the buggy out of the driveway toward the schoolhouse. The brisk morning air stirred around her. The sun had risen only moments before and was now flooding the prairie with golden light. Long shadows stretched across the road in front of the buggy.

Miriam had risen early as usual, even though classes didn't begin until nine o'clock. She was accustomed to arriving at the schoolhouse early and spending quiet moments alone preparing for the day's work and having some time of communion with the Lord. This morning she especially needed that time of prayer. Her next date with Mose Stoll was tonight. He would be at Aunt Fannie's for supper. Mose might even propose a wedding date, since he had announced his plan to leave after the coming weekend. Mose was both cautious and practical. That much she had figured out. And since she had passed every test he had placed in her path with flying colors, why should he not return home with his mission accomplished?

Miriam winced at the thought. She didn't usually make such prideful observations, with a touch of bitterness also included. The man was so full of himself. Had some of that spirit rubbed off on her? But Mose did live a righteous life, Miriam reminded herself. She shouldn't think evil of the man. The problem was her own heart. She enjoyed knowing she had passed Mose's rigorous inspection. She had pleased him. More than she had imagined possible. Streaks of heat warmed Miriam's face in the cool morning air at such plain thoughts.

"Whoa there," she called out to Star as she turned into the schoolhouse driveway. Moments later she parked and climbed out of the buggy to unhitch Star from the shafts. All she wanted was love from a decent Amish man. She hadn't exactly envisioned that man as Mose, but still . . . why object? Miriam tied Star inside the stall of the small shelter and patted his nose.

"There now, be happy for the day," she said as she dropped half a bale of hay in his stanchion. Star lowered his head to munch away as if he didn't have a care in the world.

The crunch of tires on the schoolhouse's gravel lane brought both of their heads up with a start. Star stared along with Miriam through the shelter door as the car approached. Miriam felt a weakness creep through her entire body. She knew this vehicle, and it shouldn't be here. Why had Tyler Johnson come back again when she had made herself so abundantly clear? She wanted nothing to do with the man. But here he was so early in the morning. There went her quiet time with the Lord, to say nothing of her preparations for the day's lessons. She could never settle down after this even if she could get rid of Tyler at once. Why did the man have this effect on her? What if Mose found out about this visit? Neither Uncle William nor Aunt Fannie had said a word in Mose's presence about a strange *Englisha* reporter who was asking questions of those in the community.

"Good morning," Tyler called out to Miriam as he closed the car door with a loud thump.

Miriam turned her face away and didn't answer. This was horribly ill-mannered for a Christian girl, but she couldn't help herself. Here she had thought so well of herself only moments ago.

"Am I disturbing your morning?" Tyler seemed genuinely concerned. "I can make an appointment for later. I would have, but of course you don't have e-mail or a cell phone . . . and I didn't really want to stop in at your aunt and uncle's."

And they both knew why, Miriam told herself. This was a most inappropriate call, and Tyler knew it. Yet here he stood. Had she somehow given him a reason to take this liberty the last time they spoke? Perhaps as an *Englisha* man her flaming face in his presence had been all the permission Tyler needed.

Tyler stepped closer. "I really need to speak with you, Miss Yoder. It's important."

"But why?" she croaked.

A smile played on his face. "Well, we could go inside to talk about this — if you have the time right now."

"I think it would be better if you just left," she said, her voice not even trembling.

Tyler regarded her with a tilt of his head. "I'm sorry this is uncomfortable for you. I just want to ask a couple of questions for my story, and then I'll leave . . . if you really want me to."

He had read her correctly, Miriam told herself. Oh, why couldn't she have feelings for Mose like the ones that were racing through her heart right now? This was an *Englisha* man, and he was completely out of her league. Miriam forced out the words, "I don't think I have any answers that would interest you."

"You might be surprised." Tyler was his confident self again. "Can we go inside now? I'll take only a few minutes. And your classes don't begin for a while, do they?"

Miriam couldn't speak, so as an answer she led the way to the schoolhouse and held open the door for him.

"Thank you," Tyler said, sporting that same grin that made her stomach flutter.

Miriam led Tyler up the aisle and took her usual place behind her teacher's desk. That left Tyler to sit where the students sat on the benches. She needed to establish some control over the situation even if she couldn't restrain her own emotions. Perhaps the one would affect the other now that she could sit down.

She stole a quick glance at him. He smiled at her from his lowered position. The man had enough charm to . . . Miriam pushed the thought away to ask, "So why are you here?"

"To get some answers," Tyler replied, still smiling.

Miriam looked away. They'd go around

this point all morning, and yet she felt totally helpless. Was this the Lord's way to humble her? If it was, the job was well done. She didn't have a smidgen of self-respect left.

Tyler regarded Miriam for a long moment. "I now know who gave the two million dollars to the Clarita Relief Fund."

Miriam's head spun. How could Tyler know? Had Deacon Phillips told him? But that wasn't possible.

Tyler seemed to read Miriam's question. "I asked one of your students yesterday on his way home from school. Doesn't your Bible say, 'out of the mouth of babes'?"

Miriam clasped her hands together until they hurt. The man was brilliant. Even she wouldn't have thought to ask the schoolchildren, but of course they would know and think the matter of small concern. Such things couldn't be kept a secret in the small community.

"Who would have thought?" Tyler had open admiration on his face. "It was you who gave the money. Will you confirm this?"

I could lie, Miriam told herself, but that wasn't possible even at this horrible moment. She was who she was. And Tyler might expect her to deny it, and this would only motivate him to dig deeper. What if

Tyler went to Deacon Phillips or Uncle William for confirmation? Mose might even hear of the inquiry.

"*Yah,* I did give the money," Miriam said, finding her voice.

His eyebrows went up. "So you really did?"

"I see that was the wrong thing to say," Miriam snapped.

"Well, I didn't think you would lie." Tyler was sober-faced now. "So let's backtrack a little. That means you once had two million dollars. Can I ask how you came into the possession of such a sum? Have you been married before?"

That's none of your business, Miriam almost said. But the words would sound bitter.

"Of course, you don't have to tell me," he said. "I won't use this for my story. I respect you, and I respect your privacy."

He was a reporter, Miriam told herself, but Tyler appeared sincere, so the words spilled out. "I once worked for an older man for three years, a Mr. Bland in Possum Valley. He could take care of himself during the night but needed someone with him during the day, for meals, and making sure he took his medicines. I also kept the house clean and that sort of thing." Miriam's voice died off.

Tyler remained silent while she searched for words.

"I had grown to love Mr. Bland. He was generous to me with wages, and we needed the money at home badly. *Daett* isn't that *gut* handling money." Miriam bit her lip. She shouldn't have said that, but Tyler didn't know *Daett* and never would. Miriam hurried on. "One morning I arrived at his house as usual and helped him get out of bed and buttoned his shirt for him. Mr. Bland said he had dreamed of his *frau,* Thelma, that night. He said it was a lovely dream. As I helped him to his front porch rocker while I fixed his breakfast, his face just shone with the memory of his dream. When I came back with his breakfast, he was gone . . . to join Thelma." Miriam felt a tear well up at the memory.

"And he left you the money," Tyler finished.

Miriam could only nod.

"He must have loved you a lot," Tyler said.

Miriam glanced at him in alarm, but Tyler only smiled back. He understood, Miriam thought, and more tears welled up.

"You must have been close." Tyler stood to take a Kleenex from the desk and hand it to Miriam. She took it and wiped her eyes.

"*Yah,* we were," Miriam allowed. She finally collected herself. What if one of the students walked in early and found her in tears with the *Englisha* man? What had come over her? Words to dismiss him from the schoolhouse rose to her lips, but his gaze made them die before she could speak.

"How did you decide to give the money away?" Tyler's voice was gentle.

Miriam looked away. She couldn't share those intimate details with an *Englisha* reporter. But at the moment Tyler didn't look like a reporter. He didn't even look *Englisha.* His face was clean-shaven this morning as an unmarried Amish man's would be, and she could almost imagine him with an Amish haircut.

So the words tumbled out. "My *daett* has very strong opinions about money, so I kept the inheritance a secret from him and *Mamm.* Which was wrong, of course, but it seemed like the wisest course at the time. Anyway, I had some trouble with a sort of ex-boyfriend. Everything got all tangled up. I came out here to get away for a while and ended up falling in love with a local Amish man and became engaged to him. We had planned to marry when . . ." Miriam couldn't go on.

Tyler nodded. "Your deacon told me that

part of the story. He died in the tornadoes. He and his sister. I'm sorry for you, Miriam. I really am." Tyler handed her another Kleenex.

Miriam wiped her eyes. "*Yah,* that's what happened." She tried to smile. "But the Lord has been with me all these years."

"I suppose so." Tyler stared at her.

Miriam stood to her feet. "Now, I think you'd better go. The children will be arriving soon and I have some work to do."

Tyler stood with her and moved a step away, but he paused to turn around. "I'd like to speak to you again, Miriam. Some time when it's convenient."

"You can't do that." Miriam twisted the Kleenex into her hand. "You really can't."

"Why not?" His blue eyes pierced hers.

"The community . . . I mean it's not proper . . . because . . ." Miriam shut her mouth. Now she had only made the situation worse.

"I'll see you in a few days then." A slight smile played on his face.

Before Miriam could speak, Tyler had gone out of the schoolhouse door. Miriam glanced down at the floor where little pieces of Kleenexes lay scattered about. She ignored them to rush over to the window and watch Tyler's car leave. Once the vehicle was out of sight, Miriam brought herself out of her trance with a sharp pinch on the arm. She must get out of this dreamworld somehow. Slowly the Kleenex particles beside her desk came into focus again. Miriam hurried back to the closet and grabbed the broom to sweep them up. With a quick dump of the dustpan she emptied the pieces into the wastebasket.

There, at least the evidence of her behavior during Tyler's visit was gone. But what about the unseen evidence in her emotions? Her heart had betrayed her again. And where should she go from here? This was only getting worse. Perhaps she should confess to Mose tonight. He'd understand, wouldn't he? But she knew he wouldn't. If he knew what had happened at the schoolhouse this morning, Mose would leave tomorrow on the first Greyhound bus out of Coalgate.

CHAPTER TEN

After supper that evening Miriam and Mose sat quietly on the front porch of Aunt Fannie's home. Miriam turned her face so the cool evening breeze could blow across her cheeks. The last of the sun's glow was fading in the western sky, and the kerosene lamp on the porch flickered on Mose Stoll's face. He had insisted they bring a light so they wouldn't sit in the dark. What a holy man Mose was. He wanted only impeccable standards applied to their relationship. A flush of shame filled Miriam's face. She should confess and tell Mose about Tyler Johnson right now, but the words stuck in her mouth. And Mose seemed happy with the silence on the porch as behind them the low murmur of Aunt Fannie's and Uncle William's voices came from the living room.

There was an excuse for her weakness, Miriam assured herself. In the years she had taken care of Mr. Bland, she must have become comfortable around *Englisha* men. Perhaps *too* comfortable. Was that the explanation for why she had such an unusual reaction to Tyler Johnson? No wonder *Mamm* had entertained misgivings about her job with Mr. Bland. Still, the Lord would see her through this difficult situation. In the meantime she wouldn't spill her thoughts to Mose. It wasn't necessary. They might even marry this wedding season, and as a minister's *frau* her past would lie forever behind her.

"You seem comfortable enough with me tonight." Mose's voice interrupted Miriam's thoughts. He turned to face her with a pleased expression on his face.

"Just thinking, that's all." Miriam forced a smile. "About us and the future."

Mose nodded. "That's *gut.* I'm glad you're taking this seriously. I'm planning on leaving after the weekend, and I'm thinking we should see each other only once more before then. Perhaps on Sunday evening?" He smiled. "I can bring you home like a proper dating couple."

Miriam lowered her head. "Whatever you think is best is okay with me."

Mose seemed pleased again. "Can I look forward to a letter writing time between us once I return to Wayne County?"

Miriam's head spun. Would there be no marriage proposal? Was a time of letter writing all that Mose offered after this week of intense scrutiny? Did Mose pick up the discord in her heart over Tyler Johnson?

Mose leaned forward to ask, "Or do you need more time to think about this?"

"Oh, no!" Miriam let out a little gasp. "*Yah,* I can write letters."

"So it's settled then." Mose had a big smile on his face. "We must take this slowly . . . even though I could use a *frau* at home in Wayne County next week."

What was she to say to that? So she said nothing.

Mose continued. "I know that my house is empty, and I'm lonely, but I can't think of taking you away from your schoolteaching job before the term is over. And more time would also give each of us a chance to think about whether marriage is what the Lord wants for us. I hope you understand that I meant no harm by my sudden appearance in the community or by my suggestion that we correspond by letter for a while. I understand that a woman's heart turns slowly, and I have been grateful that you've been as open to me as you have been."

Miriam cast her gaze to the porch floor.

There was only one proper response, and she must say it. With a steady voice Miriam spoke. "I will pray about this, and I'm not offended by your attentions. I can understand your position, and I trust *Daett* and *Mamm*'s judgment on the matter. They haven't led me wrong before."

Admiration filled Mose's face. "You truly are a woman blessed by the Lord, Miriam. I continue to be amazed."

"Oh, I do have my faults," Miriam managed to whisper. "For which I ask forgiveness each day."

"Ah, but we all do," Mose said. "Faults are nothing to be ashamed of. They keep us humble and walking in the Lord's strength."

She could breathe again, Miriam told herself. Slowly the throb of her conscience drifted into the background.

Mose cleared his throat beside her. "But there is something I wish to tell you before I leave."

"Yah?" Miriam glanced up at his face. Surely the man wouldn't confess detailed faults of his own. Mose would expect her to follow his example after that.

"I understand that you'll be coming to Possum Valley for your sister's wedding soon."

"Yah."

Mose smiled. "I'll be seeing you of course when you do."

"Sure," Miriam said at once. "That's better than reading and writing letters."

Now why had she said that? She sounded overeager again.

Mose spoke as if he hadn't noticed. "I should tell you another thing. There might be a change, a serious change, in my ministry before long." Mose let out a nervous chuckle and seemed to gather his courage. "Far be it from me to know the mind of the Lord or to even think of my own worthiness for such a high and holy calling, but it would be remiss of me if I didn't mention the possibility. You would think for sure I was trying to hide something from you."

Miriam waited with her gaze fixed on his face. She whispered a silent prayer, *"Please, no secrets."*

But Mose appeared pleased with her attention and began to speak again. "Our district is ordaining a bishop this fall at communion time. We've been without a bishop for a year now, and I guess it's time. What I'm saying is that there is a chance the lot might fall on me. If it does, I beg the Lord for mercy and strength for the task. But this would be one more thing you should consider in a marriage relationship

114

with me."

Miriam stared at him. "You might be made bishop?"

"Yah." Now Mose studied her. "Is that a problem for you?"

"No, of course not." Miriam folded her hands on her lap. "You know this would be a great honor."

"And one I am unworthy of," Mose added at once.

"And so would I be unworthy." Miriam's fingers dug into her palm. She might be a bishop's wife? The thought took her breath away. So this was where the Lord's plan was leading her? No wonder the road had been so rough and difficult. One didn't become a bishop's *frau* without preparation. A great light seem to shine right out of heaven into her heart. This explained so much of her past sadnesses and even her temptations with Tyler Johnson. The Lord had clearly been testing her. She had been too blind to see before this. And yet, she had somehow been able to trust the Lord and prevail.

"You have nothing to say to this?" Mose had turned in his chair to face Miriam.

"It's . . . it's just so much to fathom, I guess," Miriam managed. "I'm just a school-teacher."

Mose smiled at this description. "You're

also quite humble, and before the Lord's eyes that's of great value. We will submit this to the Lord and await His decision, but I'm glad I told you and that you're still willing to continue the relationship."

Had Mose really thought she wouldn't? Or had he wanted to see her reaction? Either way she had apparently passed the test. Mose studied the darkened horizon beyond Uncle William's greenhouse. "Your sister Shirley is getting a *gut* man, you know."

The bishop subject must be over, Miriam told herself. She responded, "*Yah,* I know. Glen is *gut* for her."

She could play along with Mose's light conversation, but she would have appreciated a few more moments to ponder this turn of events. Becoming a bishop's *frau* was not a light matter. She still hadn't absorbed the full implications. *Mamm* would be so impressed, and *Daett* would glow with joy from ear to ear. That was if Mose was chosen in the lot, but somehow she knew he would be. Likely Mose would get most of the votes, but it only took three votes from the members to make any of the ministers a candidate. Surely the Lord would pick Mose, Miriam told herself. Too many things pointed in that direction.

"Maybe we should go inside." Mose stood to his feet, not waiting for an answer before he headed for the front door.

Miriam followed him. Once inside, the smiling faces of Uncle William and Aunt Fannie greeted them. There was no sign of Jonathon, who had already been sent to bed.

"Time that I should be on my way," Mose announced. "Thank you so much for the supper, Fannie, and for the way both of you have taken me into your home this week. I am most grateful."

"It was a great pleasure," Aunt Fannie gushed. "Do you want another piece of pie before you leave?"

Mose laughed. "And swell my stomach to indecent proportions? I think not. But thanks anyway."

Miriam winced. She should have thought to offer Mose food before he left, but her mind wasn't working very well.

"I'll see you on Sunday then." Mose smiled in Miriam's direction and then opened the front door and was gone into the night.

"Abrupt sort of man," Uncle William muttered. "But a solid man too."

"He certainly needs a *frau*," Aunt Fannie added. "He's way too skinny, whatever he says. Only a *frau* can fatten up that kind of man."

Uncle William grinned but didn't say anything. Miriam moved into the kitchen to hide her red face. This conversation disturbed her, as did the rest of the evening.

Footsteps followed her into the kitchen, and she heard Aunt Fannie's gentle voice. "I'm sorry if I offended you, Miriam. I didn't mean my comments about Mose to sound the way they did."

Miriam forced a smile. "That's okay. I'm troubled about something else."

Aunt Fannie took a seat at the kitchen table. She looked up with a smile on her face. "Did Mose propose tonight, and did you accept? Is that it? I can see where that would be a big adjustment."

Miriam shook her head. "He didn't propose. Mose wants to write letters for a while. He doesn't want to take me away from my schoolteaching job until the end of the term."

Aunt Fannie's face lit up. "Then that's a proposal of sorts. It's obvious your heart has fallen for the man, and I can see why you would. Mose is such a solid man and so decent, and a minister."

"Make that a bishop," Miriam said. "They're having an ordination this fall."

Aunt Fannie appeared startled. "But Mose wouldn't know this, or has he somehow gotten all the votes? The man's an amazement, but even that's going a little far."

Miriam pressed her lips together. "No, but the lot will be in his book. Too many things point in that direction."

Aunt Fannie shrugged. "You should leave this in the Lord's hands, Miriam, but I can see why you would be troubled. Being a bishop's *frau* is a high honor indeed and a great responsibility."

Miriam forced herself to speak. "And there's something else, Aunt Fannie. That reporter Tyler Johnson stopped by the schoolhouse again to ask questions. He now knows that I gave the money to the relief fund." There, the words were out of her mouth.

Aunt Fannie regarded Miriam strangely. "And you told him this?"

"No, he asked one of the schoolchildren."

Alarm now showed on Aunt Fannie's face. "Will he write a story about your gift?"

Miriam fiddled with the edge of the chair. "He says he won't."

Comprehension dawned on Aunt Fannie's face. "So Tyler must greatly admire what you did. Oh, Miriam! Take this as another sign of the Lord's blessing on your life. And forget about the fact you gave the money or who knows. That's part of your past and is behind you now."

Miriam remained silent. What was there to say? She couldn't tell anyone about how the Lord had tested her heart and how much fault had been found there.

Aunt Fannie soon stood to give Miriam a hug and a quick kiss on the cheek. "I think we'd better all get to bed now. This is still the middle of the workweek, and all this excitement has exhausted everyone."

"Yah," Miriam agreed.

At least she had opened up partially about Tyler Johnson, and Aunt Fannie didn't seem worried. The Lord would take care of her heart, Miriam assured herself. She would trust, and she could sleep in peace now.

Miriam took the stairs slowly and entered her room to prepare for bed. She had so much she could be thankful for. She might someday be a bishop's *frau.* She would think about Mose and not Tyler Johnson. How many unmarried Amish women would turn down the offer Mose had brought from Ohio?

CHAPTER ELEVEN

At close to noon the next Monday, Tyler Johnson eyed the man seated across the table. The restaurant fan hummed above their heads, but the sound didn't drown out the conversation or that of several other patrons at tables near them.

When they had come in, Tyler had tried to steer Mr. Westree, the chairman of the relief fund, toward the far corner for some privacy, but to no effect. Mr. Westree had made sure they took a table in the center of the room. The man's motives were transparent and obvious, but Tyler could do little about it. They served only to sound further alarms bells about the man's character beyond the questions he already had.

"Excellent cod you serve here," Mr. Westree told the waitress as she dropped off the plates they had ordered. "And you're pretty as a belle today, my dear."

The girl blushed and beat a quick retreat.

Mr. Westree knew the place well, Tyler thought. He should have insisted on a meeting place of his choosing, but Mr. Westree wouldn't have agreed. This arrangement had been difficult enough to finagle.

"Have you found the area's entertainment pleasing?" Mr. Westree asked. His gaze lingered on the door the waitress had disappeared through.

Tyler didn't respond.

A grin spread across Mr. Westree's face. "You've been hanging around our fair town long enough to have made some nice connections. I thought something serious might be afoot, which I couldn't blame you for. They come lovely on the prairie."

Tyler gave the man a sharp glance. "Let's get serious for a moment, Mr. Westree. I think I may have found a problem with the relief fund. That's what I want to ask you about."

"Then fire away," Mr. Westree said, pasting on a cheesy smile. "We have nothing to hide here."

"Okay," Tyler began, "a large portion of the distribution of funds goes to Wymore Building Supply here in Coalgate." Mr. Westree's smile didn't fade. "Of which you are part owner, I believe."

Mr. Westree gave a short laugh. "Are you

expecting to find some fraud and corruption to spice up your story? If so, I'm afraid there's nothing for you there. I kept myself out of any individual decisions on distributions of the money that was donated. Those decisions were made by the board. But if you're suspicious about my character or the character of any of the other members of the board, let me tell you what you should already know. The other two lumber companies in the area, Howard Truss and Western Lumber, received monies on a carefully calculated formula based on their total market share. That should satisfy anyone's suspicions."

"And are you willing to make those calculations public?" Tyler probed.

Mr. Westree laughed. "Not a chance. That's private information, which you should also be aware of. Besides, you don't see either Howard Truss or Western Lumber complaining, do you? If they're content, so should you be. I'd advise you to write your little article on the Amish involvement as you're supposed to and forget about any attempts to uncover a scandal you imagine might have transpired."

Tyler forced a laugh. "Now, how do you know what my assignment was?"

Mr. Westree took a large bite of his fish

lunch and pointed to Tyler's plate. "Your fish is getting cold. I strongly suggest you enjoy your lunch and forget about that Pulitzer prize you're dreaming about."

The man was clamming up. Tyler nibbled at his meal, all the while trying to come up with a question that would unseal Mr. Westree's lips.

Tyler finally decided it was no use. He took a bite of his cod and said, "I suppose since you have nothing else to tell me, my next step will be visiting each of your competitors to see what they have to say."

Mr. Westree had just finished his plate and leaned forward. "That's a fine idea, son. Do you know what I think you'll find? I think you'll find a lot of decent and upbuilding stories of how the recovery effort brought relief to suffering and hurting people. And how the Amish people contributed a large sum, as you know. That's the story here. That's the story I'm interested in reading."

Tyler tried another angle, "Speaking of that, do you know where the Amish came up with two million dollars?"

Mr. Westree laughed. "No. I don't practice looking a gift horse in the mouth. Surely you're not imagining fraud and corruption, or the fleecing of poor community members for donations? That kind of notion is dead in the water with the Amish. They're good folk, as are all of us in these parts."

Tyler didn't respond, so Mr. Westree went on. "Son, you should get out of the city more. It'll put your suspicious mind to rest when you get to know some decent small-town people."

The waitress appeared and asked, "Dessert anyone?"

"Not for me." Tyler pushed back his plate.

Mr. Westree thought for a moment but shook his head.

"I'll get you a box," the girl offered with a glance toward Tyler's half-eaten meal.

"That would be great," Tyler said with a smile. He could eat the rest tonight in his motel room, if nothing else.

"Thank you, sweetheart." Mr. Westree glowed in the girl's direction. She left the check on the table and vanished again through the door to the kitchen.

Tyler picked up the list of donors Mr. Westree had set on the table. He caught Mr. Westree's glance out of the corner of his eye. Fear was showing on his face. Tyler paused and followed the look at several names displayed above where his fingers touched the paper. Small donation amounts were listed to the side. He hadn't paid them any attention earlier. Fraud was perpetuated best where large sums of cash flowed, not small amounts.

Mr. Westree was on his feet now, but Tyler sat down again. "One last question, please," he said.

Mr. Westree tried his best to smile. "I think we're through here today, son." He turned his back but didn't move away from the table.

"Olga Corporation. Westby Tabled. Eastern Indian Market," Tyler read out loud. Mr. Westree still hadn't turned around. "What did these suppliers contribute to the relief effort?"

"You'll have to ask them," Mr. Westree said.

"I will," Tyler allowed, rising to his feet as Mr. Westree walked on ahead.

Tyler took the check and the box of uneaten cod with his gaze on Mr. Westree's retreating back. The man went out the door, climbed into his car in the parking lot, and drove away without a backward glance. A nerve had been touched, Tyler told himself, and purely by accident. It could be that he was imagining things, but his instincts were usually correct.

Tyler looked up as the waitress reappeared at the register and accepted his credit card. While waiting, he thought a moment and then asked, "Do you know Mr. Westree well?"

The girl didn't answer right away. "He comes in here sometimes," she finally said.

"Seems like a jolly fellow," Tyler probed.

"A pillar in the community, as they say." The girl's look betrayed her praise.

Tyler didn't push. "It was an excellent meal. Thank you for the box."

The girl smiled. "You're welcome. And come back soon. We have a nice prime rib special on Friday nights."

"I'll keep that in mind." As Tyler climbed into his car, he wondered, *Now what? Should he continue what might well be a wild-goose chase? What were the chances he'd find anything? Not good.* All he had were looks and insinuations. These were country folks. They wouldn't embezzle relief funds. The accusation was ludicrous.

Tyler rubbed his eyes as he drove out of Coalgate. He would look into the donation matter later. Right now he needed a distraction. The real reason he was lingering in town was because of a blushing Amish schoolteacher. He hated to admit such a base motive, but the girl gripped his imagination. Her story was absolutely fascinating, but he hadn't mentioned anything about her in the first article in the planned series he'd e-mailed to his editor last night. Surely the next article would have to have more substance to it, or the editor would be disappointed.

He knew he wanted to show Miriam the story he had written, and he wanted to see her again. Yes, she was from another world — one he could barely imagine, let alone understand. That first night when he ate supper with the Bylers, he had felt the effects of their lifestyle. The stillness and peace of the house had undergirded their quiet conversation. He'd at first attributed Miriam's red face to the heat from the stove in the kitchen, but it had been more than that. He was obviously as strange to Miriam as she was to him, but she was perhaps not immune to his charms. That stroked his vanity more than he wished it did. Perhaps that was what drove him to ignore Hilda's recent texts.

Oddly, his exposure to the Amish was pricking his conscience about his cavalier attitude toward Hilda and the several girlfriends who had preceded her. He couldn't imagine Miriam taking up a relationship with the same kind of detachment he showed toward Hilda, a detachment he had always justified to himself. But with Miriam things were different. Although he had no business disrupting Miriam's life, he somehow couldn't resist. And his excuse was flimsy. If this kept up he might actually feel some guilt about the way he treated the women who liked him.

But in the meantime he would stop again at the schoolhouse after he checked on the loose ends Mr. Westree had left him. Miriam would have finished with her schoolday by then, and she'd be alone. He liked that picture. There was something primitive and personal about Miriam's presence. Her persona was so open and aboveboard, unlike Mr. Westree's or Hilda's. What would it be like to date such a girl? He liked that idea too — more than he wished to admit.

Tyler glanced at the donor list. Westby Tabled's address was south of Clarita, but he had the time, so he headed in that direction with his thoughts still on Miriam. The whole thing about the two-million-dollar gift still seemed impossible. Was someone not telling the truth? Surely Miriam had been truthful. Her employer for three years had been a Mr. Bland. He could check on that, just to be sure. That would be easy enough. Newspapers published obituaries. Tyler glanced at his watch before he pulled over into a cattle lane. He turned off the engine and pulled up the Internet feed on his iPad. He searched and found the website for the largest newspaper in Sugarcreek, Ohio. With a broad search of five years and the last name Bland, two obituaries came up. One of them was for a thirty-five-year-old man. The other matched Miriam's description, and the only surviving relative was a sister, Rose.

Well, what did you expect, Tyler asked himself, *that Miriam would lie?*

Clearly Miriam was as honest as she appeared. He wanted her to be wrong about something. Underhanded or devious was too much, but a little flaw in Miriam would make him feel better for some odd, unexplainable reason. Then perhaps his fascination with the woman would end. But since nothing like that appeared likely, could he possibly ask her out? On a dinner date? Did the Amish even do that? No, he was sure they didn't. Even if she said yes, it would likely get her into some kind of trouble with the community. He had learned enough about the Amish to know that much anyway.

Miriam would rebuff his advance, Tyler was certain. And there would go what little access he had to her. The thought troubled him more than he wished. No, he would be the perfect gentleman. He would see her again only after he had visited the offices of

Westby Tabled, though in his present frame of mind he probably couldn't focus enough to ask coherent questions, let alone sniff out corruption.

Tyler rubbed the stubble on his chin and drove his rental car back onto the road.

Chapter Twelve

About that same hour in Coalgate, Mose Stoll paused in the door of the Greyhound bus to wave goodbye. Miriam and her Aunt Fannie were standing on the sidewalk nearby to see him off on his return trip. Miriam had found a substitute teacher for the school day, even though Mose had insisted this wasn't necessary. He had shaken hands with both of them moments before and had hoped they would return to the car. Their driver, Mr. Whitehorse, had driven them all into town to catch the bus, but Miriam wouldn't leave until the bus pulled away. It just seemed to her the right thing to do.

Mose gave one last wave and climbed up the bus steps. The bus driver gave him a grin. "Did you have a good visit?"

"*Yah,* I did," Mose answered as he looked back through the bus for a seat, finally settling into a seat across from two middle-aged women and laying his head back on the seat. Out of the corner of his eye, Miriam's face appeared again on the sidewalk. She waved again. Mose lifted his hand in a feeble response. Miriam likely didn't see him through the tinted bus windows anyway. She smiled though, and wisps of her hair were blowing out from under her *kapp* and across her face.

Mose looked away. Miriam was a decent and holy woman, but he hadn't seen a woman's long hair unbound for many months now. Miriam's hair would be beautiful flowing across her shoulders, Mose told himself. He wished now he had asked her last night to wed him. Perhaps his conscience would be more open to these thoughts of Miriam if she was his promised one. But last night he had been too cautious to make such a fast move, much as he wanted to wed Miriam this fall. Mose chided himself. He should have given in to his first impulse, but he couldn't overcome his scruples. He would have to wait now. Miriam would be his *frau* in a year or so. He felt confident of that, and he'd feel better if she went ahead and completed her promised year of teaching. Then she'd be free to marry him without inconveniencing anyone. That was how he liked things done. Duty first, followed by pleasure.

The bus pulled out of Coalgate, and Mose watched the landscape pass by the window. He liked this part of the country, but he wouldn't want to live here. Thankfully Miriam had voiced her willingness to return to Wayne County with him. He had gotten that far with his proposal of marriage. More could be said in the letters they would exchange, though probably not the proposal itself. A woman wouldn't want a proposal on paper. When she came for her sister's wedding, perhaps he could ask her then.

The Lord was blessing him greatly, Mose told himself. Women of excellent character sometimes lacked in outer beauty, but Miriam did not fit that description. Neither had his former *frau,* Rachel, who had been both lovely to look on and possessed of a most gracious character. He had been ready to accept Miriam if she lacked outward blessings of the Lord, but in this he had been pleasantly surprised. *Yah,* he had been more than pleasantly surprised. He still couldn't fully grasp how the Lord had chosen to bless him twice with beautiful women who would honor, obey, and love him like the Scriptures instructed.

He hoped the Lord would give Miriam and him *kinner.* They were both young, and he wanted children with the *frau* he married this time. But that would depend on the Lord's will, he supposed. One could not dictate such things, but it would be a shame if the bishop's lot landed on him and he could never have *kinner* of his own. The community would try to understand, but they would wonder why their bishop wasn't blessed of the Lord — even with his second *frau*.

Mose stared out of the bus window, but he saw only Miriam's face in front of his eyes. *Yah,* he would have to trust the Lord. He could be cautious and careful, but sometimes a man couldn't control everything, and *kinner* was one of those things. Miriam had passed all the scrutiny he had placed on her, and she seemed to still respect him. That wasn't an easy accomplishment, even if a woman was blessed with a submissive spirit. Mose felt love stir in his heart for Miriam. He had meant to keep this strictly on an evaluation basis, but more had happened in the past week than he had planned. There had come a moment last night when he had leaned over to touch her hand, and Miriam had looked up at him. He had almost taken her in his arms and kissed her right then and there. Miriam would have returned the affection, he was sure. She seemed so willing to accept this

135

sudden change in her life. Maybe he had made a mistake to wait until the next wedding season to say the wedding vows with Miriam. But impatience had never been in him, and here he was, impatient. That was an unexpected outcome of this trip.

The bus slowed for the next town, but Mose was lost in his thoughts and didn't notice. New voices filled the bus, and a few people departed. Mose saw only vague forms out of his side vision as his mind whirled with thoughts of Miriam.

"Is this seat taken?" A cheerful woman's voice interrupted his thoughts.

"No, it's open." Mose didn't look up but scooted further to his side of the bus.

"Are you Amish?"

Mose finally looked up. The young woman was well dressed. A faint whiff of perfume hung in the air. Her beauty was obvious to him. *"Yah,"* Mose managed.

"I thought so," the woman chirped. "You look quite Amish. My name is Cindy."

When he was silent, she continued, "Are you sure you don't mind. I mean . . . I can sit somewhere else."

"No, that's okay." Mose forced a smile. "The seat is empty. My name is Mose."

The woman stood to toss her large handbag into the overhead compartment. The smell of her perfume became stronger as the bus lurched forward again and Mose hung on.

"So what brings you to Oklahoma? Or is Oklahoma your home and are you visiting another community?" Cindy was obviously in a talkative mood.

Mose thought for a moment before he answered. "I was visiting a community in Clarita."

"Is your wife along, or are you single?" Cindy glanced over her shoulder to take in the rest of the bus.

Mose shook his head. "My wife died a while ago."

"Oh, I'm so sorry," Cindy cooed. She reached over to squeeze Mose's arm. "Was it sudden?"

"We had some warning," Mose muttered. "Cancer. Breast cancer."

"Oh, that must have been hard." Cindy's hand was still on his arm. "You haven't married again?"

This was none of the woman's business, Mose thought, but a man of God must not be rude. And he didn't want to offend her, but he pulled his arm out from under her fingers before he answered, "I'm waiting on the Lord to provide . . . in His time."

"Oh, that's so dear." Cindy didn't seem

offended by him removing his arm. "So how will you know when the Lord has provided? Does the woman make the first move? Is this how second marriages happen among the Amish?"

Mose almost laughed but managed to keep a straight face. "No, the man still seeks out a suitable mate, which the Lord provides."

"And you're looking then?" Lights seemed to go on in Cindy's face. "How fascinating. How's the search going?"

Mose looked away. This conversation had gone into deep waters, but he didn't know how to extricate himself. "Well . . . I'm . . ." He tried, but nothing presented itself that he wished to say out loud.

"That's okay." Cindy patted him on the arm. "You don't have to tell me, although that would be a most fascinating story — an Amish man's hunt for a mate."

That was a most gruesome way to describe things, Mose told himself. But the *Englisha* had different ways about them.

"Are you some kind of newspaper reporter?" he asked.

Cindy laughed. "Oh, no. Just curious."

Mose wasn't convinced. *Englisha* reporters were trained to deny who they were. What if this made its way into a local news-

138

paper? No one from his community would read the story since it was published out here on the prairie, but this Cindy knew his name now, and such things could get spread far and wide on the Internet. Cindy might even snap his picture secretly on her phone and print that with the story.

"You don't believe me?" Cindy watched Mose with her eyebrows raised.

Mose managed to mumble, "One can't be too careful these days, you know."

"A skeptical Amish man." Cindy appeared deflated. "I expected better things of such a holy people."

Mose swallowed twice. "Okay, I'll tell you this much. I was looking for a *frau* this past week, and I think I have found one by the Lord's grace." There, he had said the words. He certainly couldn't leave an outsider with the impression that the Amish faith produced hypocrites. That was the worst kind of implication.

Cindy's face lit up. "That's wonderful. How did it all come about?"

He had said enough, Mose told himself. Marriage and courtship led to wedding vows, and that was sacred territory. On the subject, he would not speak words lightly even to his own people. Few in his Wayne County community would learn the details of his week in Oklahoma. Surely Cindy should be able to understand that.

"We treat marriage with great respect," Mose said. Now he felt more comfortable with the subject, so he continued. "Perhaps we had best not speak too much about the things which the Lord's hand has so clearly led me into."

"You *are* a holy people," Cindy allowed. "I can respect your private feelings on such matters. Well, the best to the two of you. Was she willing? At least tell me that."

"I didn't ask yet." Mose held a smile back.

"But she will say yes?"

"We leave such things in the Lord's hands." Mose smiled this time.

Cindy chuckled. "Of course."

Mose sent a silent prayer heavenward. *Thank You, dear Lord, for sealing my lips.* He wished Cindy nothing but the Lord's blessings, but she obviously lived in a world he wanted no part of.

"So where are you from?" Cindy asked when Mose remained silent.

"Ohio."

"All that way to travel for a bride!" Cindy exclaimed. "And on a Greyhound bus."

Mose shrugged. "It's the best way for us."

"I know you don't have personal transportation," Cindy said. "Oh, except for your

140

buggies. You've never owned a car, have you?"

Mose looked away. How was he supposed to answer the questions of this woman? Cindy's face had lit up again. "Likely you owned one in your *rumspringa* time. Isn't that what you Amish call sowing your wild oats?"

Mose finally met her gaze. "The Lord has mercy and forgiveness for our mistakes, and, *yah,* even for those days when I did things I shouldn't have."

Cindy had a gleam in her eye. "Did you ever date a girl like me in your *rumspringa?*"

Mose felt the heat flame up his neck. The truth was he had, but the words stuck in his throat. This was why he took such care in his choice of a *frau.* He wanted nothing the world had to offer. He could never imagine Miriam asking questions like these. No decent Amish woman would.

Cindy chuckled beside him. "Must have seen something you didn't like? Am I that bad?"

"The Lord bestows His grace on all of us."

"I see."

"We all have our faults," Mose said, and wished he hadn't. A hurt look filled Cindy's face, but he didn't know how to comfort her without further damage. He couldn't touch her arm like she had touched his. That was what she likely wanted. He would have to wait until this awkward moment passed. "I'm sorry if I hurt your feelings," he finally said.

Cindy remained silent, and Mose didn't try again.

What would the community back home say if they learned of this conversation? He couldn't be fully blamed, but he had somehow allowed himself to speak familiar words with a very worldly woman. And she had felt at home enough to sit beside him on the bus. Those things were not easily explained. He would ask the same hard questions of any man who allowed himself to fall into such a trap. If this incident made its way back to the ears of his district in Wayne County, it would remove all his votes for bishop this fall, and he wouldn't blame anyone but himself.

Thankfully he was far from home, and no one would ever find out. That was poor reasoning, but it was all he had. In the meantime he would think again of Miriam and what a holy woman she was. He would have Miriam soon to help him and stand beside him while they walked through the life the Lord had planned for them.

Cindy took a long breath beside him and

exclaimed, "Apology accepted. I guess I'm a little touchy."

"I'm not always what I should be myself," Mose acknowledged, and a comfortable silence settled between them. Cindy debarked from the bus at the next town with a wave of her hand and a smile.

Mose smiled back, but he didn't wave.

CHAPTER THIRTEEN

Miriam hopped out of Mr. Whitehorse's car when they arrived back from Coalgate and ran up the driveway to the mailbox.

"What's the rush?" Aunt Fannie called after her with a laugh. "There'll be no letters from Mose yet!"

Before Miriam could answer, Jonathon raced out of the greenhouse to welcome his *mamm* home, and Aunt Fannie bent down to wrap her arms around the little figure.

Miriam opened the mailbox to find the usual pile of magazines and bills. Most of them were addressed to Mr. William Byler. Miriam held them in one hand and searched deeper with the other. She shrieked in delight at the sight of *Mamm*'s handwriting on a white envelope. With the mail in both hands, Miriam hurried back toward Aunt Fannie.

Aunt Fannie had paid Mr. Whitehorse by the time Miriam arrived back at the car.

Jonathon jumped up and down as she approached and leaped into her arms for a quick hug.

"I'm working for *Daett* today," he announced and wiggled out of her arms to race back toward the greenhouse.

Mr. Whitehorse smiled and slowly backed his car out of the driveway.

Miriam held the envelope high in the air to show Aunt Fannie. "A letter from *Mamm*!"

"Gut!" Aunt Fannie declared. "That will cheer you up over Mose's leaving. Now tell me what your *mamm* wrote."

"I'm afraid I'll have to read it later," Miriam said. "I want to check in with Betsy at the schoolhouse and see how today went."

"Oh, I'm sure she did just fine," Aunt Fannie assured her. "Relax a little. You've worked hard enough today, I say."

Miriam blushed at the implied compliment. She *had* worked hard on pleasing Mose, but wasn't that what a *gut* prospective *frau* should do?

"I need to go," Miriam said hurriedly. "Betsy probably knows what she'd be doing, but I'll feel better if I check in with her."

"Always thinking of your duty," Aunt Fannie said, clucking her tongue. "Let me

145

at least help you get Star hitched. You'll have to hurry to make it in time."

Miriam tucked *Mamm*'s letter in the dress pocket and handed the rest of the mail to Aunt Fannie. She hurried toward the barn to throw the harness quickly on Star's back. When Miriam led Star outside, Aunt Fannie held the shafts of the buggy high in the air, and Star was ready to go in no time. Miriam hopped in, and Aunt Fannie threw her the lines. With a quick wave, Miriam was on her way.

Star seemed to understand the need for haste, or perhaps he was feeling frisky since he hadn't been driven all weekend. She had ridden with Uncle William and Aunt Fannie on Sunday morning, and Mose had picked her up with his borrowed buggy for the hymn singing on Sunday evening.

She had wanted last night to be a special time for her and Mose. But to her surprise, memories of her weekends with Wayne had intruded. She had seen Wayne's face again and heard his laugh even while Mose was in the buggy with her. She had pushed the thoughts away at once. She had no right to compare Mose with Wayne. Mose was older and more mature, as was she now. She should no longer need warm flashes to her face and poundings of the heart to thrill her. Nor did she need kisses. She had told herself this several times last night. Yet how would it have been to kiss Mose? He had acted like he wanted to kiss when they were seated on the couch. She would have let him, though her face would have turned beet red. *Yah,* Mose was a man, and she had kissed a man before. She almost wished Mose would have followed on his impulse. But he was too proper to indulge in the usual affections of dating couples, but surely he would eventually. Wasn't that part of marriage?

Miriam held the reins tight as Star took the next turn at a rapid clip. Mose probably figured they should wait until their marriage vows had been said before they kissed, or at least until he proposed. Mose thought she was decent, but he didn't know everything. Somehow Mose had missed the fact that she had kept the two million dollars a secret for so long. That was her weakness. She could pretend well. In all that time *Daett* and *Mamm* had never suspected that she had such a large sum in the bank. They only found out because she had finally confessed.

Miriam's fingers dug into the rough leather of the reins as she thought of another of her faults. Tyler Johnson. But she wasn't about to confess her feelings for him. Those would go away soon anyway. That secret need never be told. If Mose had missed one of her faults, she wasn't to blame. With all the scrutiny he had given her, it served him right that he had missed one. That meant Mose wasn't perfect either. Miriam smiled and relaxed her fingers. That she found pleasure in the thought was downright sinful, but she couldn't help it.

"Everyone should be human," Miriam muttered out loud.

She certainly wanted a husband who was human. Mose likely thought he was too perfect, but she was sure the man had flaws of which he wasn't aware. She hadn't dug for them because Mose would have taken that as a serious flaw in her own character.

Miriam drove the buggy into the schoolhouse lane as the children were bursting out of the classroom door and scattering around the schoolyard. Two of the older girls threw a softball back and forth, while their brothers brought the horse out of the small shelter. Miriam smiled at the sight and brought Star to a stop by the fencerow. She would wait a few minutes until the students were gone before she drove on in. The single gravel lane could only handle so much traffic.

Several students passed Miriam with

happy smiles on their faces. They waved but didn't stop to speak. Betsy must have done a good job if the students had such a *gut* cheer about them. But on the other hand, perhaps Betsy had allowed them to goof off all day. That would make children happy, but it wasn't *gut* for them. Betsy wouldn't allow that, Miriam assured herself at once. All the young women of the community were taught that duty came first, which was exactly why she wouldn't allow herself to return to the playful days when she was in love with Wayne. How young she had been and so dreamy. Not unlike a schoolchild who saw only marvels in a day that contained no work. Now as an adult she knew of the test that lay ahead of her . . . as did the Lord. The truth was that Mose was better for her than Wayne would have been. At least now she must believe that and not doubt.

Miriam pulled herself out of her thoughts as more of the students worked their way past her. They all smiled and waved. A few hollered out, "Hi, teacher. See you tomorrow."

"See you too." Miriam smiled and waved back.

She loved these little ones with all her heart, as the Lord must love her with all

His heart and wanted only the best for her life.

Miriam was still encouraging herself when moments later she drove Star forward to stop by the hitching rack. She would only tie up, Miriam decided. Star could stand outside in this nice weather. With a quick jump she made her way down the buggy steps and snapped the tie rope on Star's bridle. Up the walk she went and met Betsy at the schoolhouse door with a worried look on her face.

"Oh, I'm so glad to see you," Betsy gushed. "I'm all nerves and twitters. What if I ruined someone's life today?"

Miriam laughed. "They all appeared healthy to me."

Betsy clasped and unclasped her hands. "That's so *gut* to hear you say. I was so worried."

"You don't have to be." Miriam took Betsy by the hand and led the younger girl inside. "So tell me how English class went. I know some of the grades were having trouble last week."

Betsy took a deep breath. "I don't know. I tried to explain things, but half the time my voice squeaked so much I knew everyone had to be laughing."

"I'm sure you did just fine," Miriam assured her. "Thank you so much for filling in for me."

"Did you see Mose off on the bus okay?" Betsy's eyes grew large.

"Yah." Miriam felt a blush burn on her cheeks. Betsy's open admiration of the relationship caught her by surprise.

"He's so handsome and manly." Betsy caught herself and clasped a hand over her mouth. "I'm sorry. I shouldn't say such things. He's not my boyfriend. But see what I mean. I haven't been able to say anything right all day."

Miriam forced a smile. "I understand. Mose can be a little intimidating, but he's a man like everyone else."

Betsy didn't appear persuaded, but she nodded her head in agreement.

"Well, I'm here now," Miriam said with a happy sigh. "Can I help you get anything ready to leave?"

"I just have my carry bag in here." Betsy gave a nervous laugh. "The horse *Daett* had me drive, Ronny, is a little skittish. Maybe you could help me get on the road."

"Of course." Miriam led the way outside again and waited until Betsy brought out the driving horse. True to predictions, Ronny tossed his head repeatedly while they hitched him to the buggy.

151

"He'll be okay once I'm on the road," Betsy said with another nervous laugh.

Miriam hung on to the bridle until Betsy had climbed in before she let go. Then Betsy waved as the buggy went by, and Miriam waited until Ronny had cleared the driveway before she breathed evenly. But Betsy had been right. Ronny calmed down and settled into a steady trot. Miriam turned toward the schoolhouse and as she walked, she reached into her pocket to find *Mamm*'s letter. She pulled the envelope out to unfold the pages. *Mamm* had written three pages in all, so there must be plenty of news from Possum Valley.

Miriam read the first words . . .

Dearest daughter Miriam.

Greetings in the name of our Lord and Savior Jesus Christ. I have waited to write until I felt sure that Mose Stoll had left the community. If I've misjudged the timing, that's okay. I just didn't want to disturb you while he was still there. I'm sure you enjoyed your time with him, and maybe you're a promised woman again by now. My heart leaps with joy at the thought. I had so hoped that eventually the Lord would supply your need for a husband —

152

because you do need one, Miriam, even though you thought that life had settled down to a blessed state without a husband. There was still a need, and *Daett* and I have such high hopes for Mose and you, which is why I waited on the letter. I know that you should arrive at these decisions on your own without undue pressure from your parents. But that being said, we are thrilled to the bottom of our hearts with the gracious way Mose has spoken with *Daett* about the matter, and with the concern the man has for a godly *frau*. I know you fill the requirement perfectly, Miriam, but he had to learn that for himself, I guess. Which I'm sure happened in the past few days.

Besides all that, we are in the middle of Shirley's wedding preparations. That is also such a great blessing in our lives. Shirley is getting such a decent Amish man, and to think how things could have turned out — my heart shudders to even write these words, so I will think only of what did happen. That being said, below is the list of all the table waiters and the witnesses.

Miriam paused again to take in the long

list. This explained the extra pages. *Mamm* continued to write:

Now don't you feel one bit guilty about not being here to help out. I know you're taking off the week of Shirley's wedding, and that's more than can be expected from a busy schoolteacher in Oklahoma. Shirley wanted to tell you that Mose will be a witness with you. *Daett* will speak with him once he returns from Oklahoma, and I'm sure Mose won't object. Neither should you, now that you are likely his promised one. And even if you aren't, I'm sure Mose will make his intentions of marriage clear very soon.

Mamm had drawn a huge smiley face, and Miriam felt her face grow red. She lowered the page to push open the schoolhouse door and walk back inside. *Mamm*'s letter was one more sign that she was on the right path with Mose. She would love the man someday just as she had loved Wayne, and if not — then marriage was still the Lord's will. He would supply the grace needed.

CHAPTER FOURTEEN

An hour later, Miriam closed the notebook where she had written out Tuesday's lesson plan, and stood to her feet. Darkness on the prairie was still a few hours away, but Aunt Fannie would have supper on the table soon and she should get home. Since Betsy had driven out of the schoolyard, Miriam had been absorbed in *Mamm*'s letter and her school work, but that was finished now.

Miriam's thoughts drifted to Mose. He would still be settled in on the Greyhound bus, the long night ahead of him. Thankfully the memory of Mose from the weekend now seemed distant, as though she had known the man only in a dream. But that was how things should be, wasn't it? Life should move on. She had met Mose only a little over a week ago, but time would change all that. She would see him again at Shirley's wedding, and things might go better in Possum Hollow than they had in

Oklahoma. Mose might not be as suspicious on his home turf.

Miriam pulled herself out of her reverie and hurried through the front door of the schoolhouse. With her hand still on the doorknob, Miriam came to a sudden stop. She had not heard anyone drive in, but a familiar car was parked beside her buggy. Miriam tried to still the quick intake of her breath. Tyler Johnson had come back.

Miriam's hand twitched. She was tempted to dash back inside and hide, but Tyler had already seen her. He had climbed out of the car with a big grin on his face. He waved toward her. Miriam forced herself to breathe. The man had more nerve than two foxes in a henhouse.

She would get rid of him quickly and that would be that. Miriam set her chin and walked toward the car. Tyler didn't wait by his car but met her halfway.

He greeted her with a solemn, "Good afternoon, Miss Yoder."

"It's practically evening." She tried to speak calmly. "And I have to get home."

He smiled. "Don't you have a few moments for a friend?"

You're not my friend, she wanted to tell him. But that wouldn't have been right. Tyler was a human being and deserved the respect she should give him.

"I'll take that as a yes . . . or should I say a *yah*?" Tyler grinned again and pulled a paper out of his pocket. He held it toward Miriam. "Here's the article I wrote. I thought you might wish to see how harmless I turned out to be."

You're not harmless to me, Miriam wanted to say but pressed her lips together.

Tyler didn't seem to mind her continued silence. "When you get a chance to read it, you'll see that your name isn't even mentioned, or your secret. That lies between us and will go no further."

"You do take your liberties though, don't you?" she finally said.

A slight smile played on his face. "I have been accused of that, but I've been gracious enough by the standards of journalism."

Miriam stared at the ground. She wasn't used to the *Englisha*'s ways, so Tyler might be right. But by the standards of the community, Tyler was on dangerous ground with her, or rather she was with him. That he was even here was . . .

"Sorry if I've offended you." Tyler interrupted Miriam's thoughts. "I guess I forgot how different things are in your world, but I mean no harm."

Miriam still said nothing but kept her eyes

157

on the ground.

"I really am sorry." Tyler retreated a step. "Please accept my apologies. Now if you will excuse me . . ."

"Please." Miriam spoke quickly. "I didn't mean to criticize you. I guess I'm touchy right now. Will you . . ." Miriam's thoughts whirled. She couldn't ask him into the schoolhouse. She wanted to, but she simply couldn't.

Tyler waited in silence, his hand half raised as if he meant to speak but had decided not to.

"You'll come to supper at the house perhaps?" Miriam asked instead. "Aunt Fannie will have the meal ready by the time we get there."

Now Tyler stared at her. "Are you serious?"

"I think you would be welcome." Miriam tried to smile. "That is, by Uncle William and Aunt Fannie, but I'd also . . ." She stopped, red-faced.

He smiled. "I'd be honored to accept."

Miriam tried to focus, and the words tumbled out. "You'll come then? You know where we live?"

His smile grew wider. "Yes, but I can follow your buggy."

Miriam flinched. "Perhaps you shouldn't.

That will look like . . ."

His smile didn't waver. "I understand. I'll be there soon then."

Miriam stared after Tyler as he walked back to the car and climbed in. Where had that come from? Well, at least it was on the up and up and not a secret meeting in the schoolhouse. Anything but that. With Uncle William and Aunt Fannie present, nothing untoward could be said . . . or suspected.

Still, as she untied Star, she prayed, "Help me, dear Lord! I don't want to be blushing all evening around an *Englisha* man. Take this wrong thing out of my heart. I don't want to live with secrets again."

Miriam untied Star and drove out of the school driveway. Tyler's car was already a faint blip in the distance. Thankfully, he turned toward Clarita at the stop sign and soon vanished from sight. Miriam would have urged Star to take up a faster pace, but he seemed to have wings for feet all on his own. They made the trip in the shortest time Miriam could remember.

No one was in sight when Miriam pulled up to Uncle William's barn. She climbed out of the buggy to unhitch Star and take him inside. After the horse was in his stall, Miriam hurried out the barn door and arrived in the house out of breath.

159

Aunt Fannie came out of the kitchen wiping her hands on an apron. "You're in an awful big rush. Calm down, Miriam."

Miriam tried to speak but no words would come.

Aunt Fannie beamed. "What is it? Did the memory of Mose have this effect on you?"

Miriam shook her head and exclaimed, "The other man! He's coming tonight! Tyler! I invited him."

"Tyler?" Aunt Fannie's mouth dropped open. "The *Englisha* man?"

"*Yah,* I'm sorry, but I had to invite him. He had a paper he showed me, and I . . ." Miriam held out the article as if that explained everything.

"It's okay," Aunt Fannie said as she collected herself. But she didn't look twice at the paper. "I guess we are supposed to invite strangers home when we have a chance, and the man has been here before, so why shouldn't you do so again?" Aunt Fannie appeared puzzled but soon turned to rush back into the kitchen.

Miriam joined her. A quick glance around showed the table half set and pots of steaming food on the stove.

"Just soup," Aunt Fannie said when she caught the look. "I hope that's okay."

"Of course!" Miriam exclaimed again.

Aunt Fannie appeared relieved and continued, "You can set the table if you want to."

Miriam moved quickly, but she wasn't finished by the time car tires sounded in the driveway.

"William will take care of Tyler," Aunt Fannie decreed.

Miriam wasn't sure about that. How would Tyler explain the invitation? He might not know enough about Amish ways to say the right things and could easily get her into trouble. "Lord, help us," Miriam whispered as she finished setting the table.

"Straighten the tablecloth quickly," Aunt Fannie ordered.

Miriam responded, and Aunt Fannie set the pot of soup in the middle of the table.

"At least I have pie for dessert," Aunt Fannie moaned. "I should have meat and potatoes and gravy for such fancy visitors as Mr. Johnson."

"He's not that fancy," Miriam protested, and she wished she hadn't said the words. It implied an intimacy with the man she shouldn't have.

Aunt Fannie didn't seem to notice. "If you'll call Jonathon, we'll be ready. He's down in the basement playing."

Miriam opened the basement door and

called down the stairs, "Jonathon, time for supper."

Miriam waited, and Jonathon soon pattered slowly up the stairs. Miriam gave him a quick hug when he arrived and helped him take his seat on the bench. He sat there with hands folded as if he knew company had arrived. But then, this was the way Jonathon had been trained to sit at the table until a prayer of thanks had been given. Tonight tears pressed against Miriam's eyelids at the sight. If she were ever given *kinner* by the Lord, this was how she wished to raise them — obedient and in the fear of God. For that to happen she must banish all thoughts of Tyler from her mind. But oh, how had she sunk so low.

Miriam pulled in a long breath when Aunt Fannie reappeared with Uncle William and Tyler in tow. Tyler nodded toward Miriam with a slight smile. Miriam dropped her gaze at once, but not before she caught the look on Uncle William's face. He didn't appear displeased, so Tyler must have used the proper approach when he explained the supper invitation.

Miriam kept her gaze on the tablecloth as the men settled in.

"Let's give thanks," Uncle William said. "Our visitor is back with *gut* news. I read the article he filed with his editor, and I'm well pleased, so I'm glad Miriam invited him to supper."

Miriam stole a look at Tyler before they all bowed their heads. The man must have a slick tongue, but then she already knew that. Somehow he had gotten a supper invitation out of her. How had that happened? Miriam ran the conversation outside the schoolhouse through her mind as Uncle William led the prayer. Every statement in her memory sounded perfectly innocent, so maybe Tyler hadn't manipulated the situation.

As Uncle William said amen, she raised her head and was able to match Tyler's small smile. As uncomfortable as this supper would be, it sure beat talking to Tyler in the privacy of the schoolhouse. That had the appearance of impropriety, and if that was ever noticed . . . Miriam shuddered.

Tyler turned to Uncle William. "I appreciate the confidence you've just expressed in my article. Do you think you could help me with another matter?"

Aunt Fannie interrupted them with a wave of her hand. "No planning until the food is eaten."

"That's perfectly fine," Tyler assured her. "I shouldn't have barged in here like this,

163

but I did want to speak with Mr. Byler, and after she saw the article, Miriam was kind enough to invite me."

"That's all right with me," Aunt Fannie said. "I only wish I had known sooner. I would have had a meal fit for visitors."

"Oh, this is excellent, I'm sure," Tyler said with a warm smile. "It definitely beats restaurant food."

"The soup, please," Uncle William interrupted. "I'm hungrier than I knew."

"I can say the same," Tyler agreed, as he filled his bowl.

Aunt Fannie handed him the cracker plate. Tyler took several, but he waited until Uncle William had broken his into the soup before he did the same.

Tyler was out of his element here, Miriam thought to herself. Yet he acted so normal and found a way to blend in. Deep admiration was all she could feel for the man. He was very intelligent and yet humble.

Right now Tyler's laugh filled the room as Uncle William lowered his voice and said something she couldn't hear.

"No secrets at the table," Aunt Fannie ordered.

"Mr. Byler just asked whether I planned to join the community," Tyler explained. "I guess my article must have been sympathetic enough."

"Well, why not? You're still hanging around," Uncle William said. "I believe you've been here as long as Mose Stoll, and he was courting Miriam."

Tyler jerked his head toward Miriam but recovered quickly. A soft smile spread over his face. "So I missed the real story, I see. Right under my nose. So who is this Mose?"

Uncle William laughed this time. "You want me to spill the beans, I see. How will *that* article look?"

"Better than the first one." Tyler didn't miss a beat.

Uncle William laughed, but Aunt Fannie spoke first. "I think Miriam should tell the story. That is, if she's comfortable telling it. But it's such a blessed tale of the Lord's grace."

"I would love to hear the story," Tyler said.

His face was kind when she dared a glance in his direction.

"Well," Miriam began. "*Mamm* had written that there was a surprise coming my way, but I had no idea a man would arrive who wished to court me."

"Oh, it's such a *wunderbah* story," Aunt Fannie gushed.

Miriam waited a few seconds before she continued. "I had accepted my lot in life as that of a single woman. At least I thought I had." She gave Tyler a quick look. She wanted him to hear this. "But when Mose arrived and stated his intentions, I saw at once the Lord's hand in the matter, and now my heart is open again to what life might hold for me, even a husband, *kinner,* and . . ." Miriam's voice caught. She couldn't say the word "love." Not in front of Tyler.

"Oh, I'm almost moved to tears," Aunt Fannie whispered.

Miriam noticed Tyler's face had lost its smile.

"And who is this old fogy who is hiding behind the will of God?" Tyler couldn't keep the sharpness out of his voice.

Uncle William looked up in mild surprise. "Well, he's maybe a few years older than Miriam, and a widower, and a minister. Quite impressive, if I must say."

And almost a bishop, Miriam came close to saying. She looked at the tabletop instead. Tyler wouldn't be impressed with that.

"That's a little better," Tyler allowed. "But still . . . well, it's none of my business. Now what I wanted to ask you about, Mr. By-ler . . ."

Miriam got up to bring the pies over to the table. Tyler's abrupt change of the

166

subject stung, and her ears rang. Why did an *Englisha* man's opinion mean anything to her?

CHAPTER FIFTEEN

That Thursday evening Miriam turned Star into Deacon Phillips's driveway. A long line of buggies already lined the barnyard, and a volleyball court had been set up behind the barn. Miriam caught a glimpse of the game in progress as she approached. She was late, but she had had to grade tests again after school. That wasn't the real reason, though. She could have finished the papers in the morning before classes began. In reality she hadn't wanted to face the sly looks and glances from the other young people now that Mose was gone. Everyone would assume she was engaged to the man.

And she couldn't blame them. She was a part of the community. They had a right to know the basics of what had transpired. But what was she supposed to say? *I'm being dated by an Amish minister?* They already knew that. Maybe, *We're writing?* But Mose's decision to write sounded a little weak, coming from a widower who no doubt wanted a *frau* as soon as possible. Everyone would assume she already had wedding plans. Still, Mose deserved to court her in his own way, and she shouldn't spill his secrets.

At least Tyler was no longer a secret. Her spur-of-the-moment invitation on Monday had been an inspiration. Everything was aboveboard now, and Tyler hadn't shown his face at the schoolhouse again.

Miriam climbed down to unhitch Star from the buggy. She didn't want to think about Tyler, so maybe an evening spent with the community's young people would clear her mind. In hindsight she shouldn't have worked late at the schoolhouse. She needed the company of people her own age.

Miriam left Star in the barn and walked along the line of buggies. She stopped short at the sight of a familiar rental car parked behind the buggies. Her head began to throb at the sight. Tyler was *here*? Why? She hadn't invited him. Maybe Deacon Phillips had. But why would Deacon Phillips invite Tyler? Now her haven for the evening was the most dangerous spot in the community. She should go home, but she couldn't. She'd have to do too much explaining if she harnessed Star to the buggy again and drove out of the lane.

Miriam forced her feet forward. She would live through this somehow. She'd have to remember that none of this was her fault. She had invited Tyler to supper at Aunt Fannie's, but not this.

"Howdy there," Deacon Phillips's oldest daughter, Ruth, called out as she stepped away from the game to run toward Miriam.

"Hi," Miriam greeted her, trying to keep her wits about her.

Ruth reached out for Miriam's hand as she exclaimed, "You must be late from working at the schoolhouse! We're glad you made it."

"Well, I'm here," Miriam managed. She glanced down the line of buggies. "Why is the *Englisha* car here?"

"Oh, that." Ruth's face lit up. "*Daett* invited Tyler Johnson to attend a youth function. He's very interested in the Amish community, *Daett* said. But come." Ruth pulled on Miriam's hand. "We have a spot still open for you right beside me." Ruth's voice dropped to a whisper. "And the *Englisha* man is playing on the other side of me. Isn't that exciting?"

Miriam nodded and followed Ruth across the field. She couldn't blame Ruth for her excitement. The community didn't believe in *rumspringa,* so Ruth rarely spoke with handsome *Englisha* men. And look how her own feelings responded to Tyler's attentions. She was the one who should be ashamed, not Ruth.

"Hi, Miriam." A chorus of voices greeted her as the two approached the group.

"Hi, everyone," Miriam managed.

"Right over here." Ruth pulled on Miriam's hand again.

Miriam kept her gaze averted, but she had to look up when Tyler called out, "Look who's here. The pretty Amish schoolteacher herself."

Smiles spread on the faces around them. No one seemed to wonder how Tyler knew her sufficiently for such an intimate greeting. Shame gripped Miriam. These people trusted her, while her heart wasn't pure.

"Hi, Tyler." Miriam got the words out, wishing at once she had called him Mr. Johnson instead of Tyler. She looked away at once and placed Ruth between them.

"Did you have to spank one of the children? Is that why you look so disturbed?" Tyler leaned around Ruth to tease.

Several of the youth chuckled as the ball was served. Miriam concentrated on its flight and didn't answer.

But Ruth had no compunctions about a

talk with Tyler. "Miriam is such a *gut* teacher, she's never had to spank any of the children in the three years she's taught here."

"I see," Tyler mused. "Has she over-whelmed the evil with her holy presence?"

Ruth seemed puzzled by the statement. "I suppose so," Ruth allowed.

Tyler hid his grin, Miriam noticed. Amish young people obviously had a different sense of humor from what he was used to. That she had understood was to her own discredit. The ability must have come from the years she had taken care of the elderly Mr. Bland. What would Mose say when he took her as his *frau* and found out she had picked up *Englisha* ways?

"Did you ever spank a scholar?" Tyler interrupted Miriam's thoughts to ask. Ruth had stepped forward to set the volleyball up for the front row, and their view of each other was unobstructed.

Miriam answered without looking at him. "Maybe I'm shirking my duty."

Tyler laughed. "I doubt that. I'll stick with my theory. And thanks for the supper invitation the other night."

"Shhhhh," Miriam said, and wished at once she hadn't. Ruth had returned from the successful play with her face flushed but

172

with her ears obviously wide open. "That was very *gut,*" Miriam encouraged. She hoped that would distract the girl.

"Thanks," Ruth responded. She glanced between the two of them. "You invited Tyler to supper, Miriam?"

"At Aunt Fannie's, *yah,* he . . ." Miriam stopped. Excuses wouldn't help. Ruth might be young, but she wouldn't be fooled.

"Tyler was at our place for supper too, but *Daett* invited him," Ruth said.

Miriam tried again to make her innocence known. "Uncle William invited him the first time, and he had an article I wanted to show Aunt Fannie, so . . ." It was no use, Miriam decided. Ruth would have to think what she wanted to.

"It was a very good supper," Tyler offered. "I had a long conversation with Mr. Byler afterward. He's going to get some information I need."

Thank you, Miriam almost said aloud. Ruth appeared satisfied, but how had Tyler known he should help her out?

Tyler had a big grin on his face when she glanced at him. The man knew way too much, that was for sure. And it was no use protesting. Her face had betrayed her.

"Are you going back again for supper?" Ruth asked Tyler.

173

Tyler kept the grin on his face. "I haven't received an invitation from Mr. Byler, but maybe you could give me one. Your mother served excellent cherry pie . . . or was that your handiwork?"

Ruth appeared puzzled for a moment. "Oh, you mean, did I make the pie?" Ruth laughed. "I'm afraid not. But I'm going to learn soon. Piecrust in an art all to itself, *Mamm* says."

"I'm sure it is." Tyler gave Ruth a smile. "You'll have to let me know when you've learned."

Ruth turned bright red but nodded with vigor. "I will if you're still around. Are you staying long in the community?"

"I don't know." Tyler focused on the ball that was flying in a high arch above his head. A moment later he stepped forward to whack the ball back to the other side of the net.

"You should have set it up," Ruth reprimanded him, her earlier question apparently forgotten.

Tyler chuckled. "I suppose I should have. You'll have to teach me how. I didn't play much volleyball in school."

"Oh, it's nothing," Ruth said. "We just learn what little we know in the youth group. And I think you already know how."

Tyler reached over to squeeze Ruth's arm. "Thanks for the confidence."

Ruth smiled but said nothing more as the game continued.

Surely she wasn't jealous of Ruth, was she? Miriam thought. This had become completely ridiculous. What was wrong with her? Beside her Ruth kept up a friendly chatter with Tyler. From the sounds of things, the two had spoken freely with each other when Tyler had been in Deacon Phillips's home. Their conversation was innocent, though, unlike her thoughts. Several of the other girls joined in with Ruth's easy banter. Miriam tried to stay a step back whenever the ball came her way. Ruth seemed more than happy to take the play. That was fine with Miriam. It helped keep the focus off her.

Darkness soon crept across the horizon, and gas lanterns were lit. Ruth's *mamm,* Katie, appeared around the corner of the barn near the end of the third game. She called, "The ice cream is out. Come before it all melts."

This brought the game to an end and produced a stampede from the boys toward the house. The girls followed at a more dignified pace. Miriam hung even further back but quickened her steps when she noticed that Tyler wasn't in front with the other young men.

Before Miriam got too far, Tyler's voice called out from behind her. "Growing older, are we?"

"Speak for yourself," Miriam snapped. "I don't see you in the front of the pack."

"That's because I want to speak with you."

Miriam rolled her eyes. He apparently didn't understand her predicament as well as she hoped he had.

"You heard right," Tyler said. "I can't stay quiet about this. Surely you're not marrying that man from out of town — the minister. How can a lovely girl like you do something like that? Tell me I didn't hear something right the other night."

Miriam didn't know what to say. What if the others heard her conversation? Oh, this was so wrong!

"Is he handsome perhaps?" Tyler probed. "Or does he come with tons of money? Is that what's driving this?"

"This is none of your business," Miriam squeaked. "And shhhh!"

"Let's say I'm making it my business," Tyler shot back. "Maybe I can do one good thing for you before I leave. Because this isn't right, you know."

"Tyler . . . *Mister* Johnson . . . this is really

176

none of your business!" No further words would come out, and Miriam focused on breathing.

Tyler regarded her for a moment before he continued. "I asked your uncle some questions and also Deacon Phillips, all in the guise of my admiration for how the community does things, and I don't like what I'm hearing. This man arrives and spends all week investigating you. Does the man even *love* you, Miriam? Or you him for that matter?"

Miriam's face blazed red. Was it embarrassment or anger? Probably both, she thought as she turned to face Tyler. "How we do our marriages is none of your business. I think I made that clear already."

Tyler's hand waved in the air as he exclaimed, "But this is so medieval! So feudal! So archaic! And hello . . . so very *wrong.* You must know this is true, Miriam. You're a teacher. You can't be completely uneducated."

"We live as the Lord decrees," Miriam barely whispered. "I wouldn't expect you to understand."

"Answer my question, then," Tyler demanded. "Do you love the man?"

When Miriam remained silent, he continued. "That's what I thought. You'll just marry him in cold blood. How can you do something so chilling when you have such a warm personality?"

Miriam gathered herself together and took a deep breath. "What I am is also none of your business, Tyler. Now can we stop this conversation before someone hears us?"

A look of triumph filled his face. "See what I mean. You are a captive. That's why you can't talk with me."

"I just did talk to you," Miriam said. "I have been more than free with you. But this has gone far enough."

He studied her face for a second. "Well, I don't like any of this. You can't marry a man you don't love . . . and who doesn't love you."

"Would you *please* go away and leave all of us alone?" Miriam pleaded.

Tyler sobered but shook his head. "I've heard that line before, and it doesn't work on me."

"But I beg of you." Miriam reached out to grasp Tyler's arm. "My future is my own to choose. Isn't that what you *Englisha* say? Why won't you let me choose mine?"

"But marriage to an old fogy? Do you really want this, Miriam?"

"Mose is not old," Miriam's voice trembled.

"But do you want this? Really *want* this?" Tyler stepped closer. "Tell me the truth, and I'll leave you alone."

Miriam met his blue eyes as they pierced hers. She tried to speak but failed.

"Aha! That's what I thought," Tyler mumbled. "God help us all."

Miriam struggled to get a protest out, but Ruth cut off her efforts as she raced around the corner of the barn. "Oh, there you two are. Are you coming?"

"Right away." Tyler smiled in Ruth's direction.

Miriam fell in step behind him. Thankfully, Tyler didn't take her arm. That was what he wanted to do, she was sure. Still, Ruth looked suspiciously at them.

Miriam forced a laugh instead. "Tyler and I were just having a disagreement about a matter. I think he should conclude his investigation of the community pretty soon and move on. Don't you think so?"

Ruth wrinkled up her face. "I don't know," she said. "I think it's nice to have him around."

"Thatta girl!" Tyler reached over to squeeze Ruth's arm, and the two walked on ahead of Miriam. She hung back as the thought struck her. Once more she had a secret, and the shame burned deep inside of her.

CHAPTER SIXTEEN

It was Sunday afternoon, and Miriam laid Mose's letter on her upstairs bedroom dresser. She had read the letter twice. With a trembling hand, she walked over to the window and fingered the dark drapes. Outside she could see the slanting sunlight flooding the plants set near the greenhouse with a soft glow. Autumn was nearly over, but winter didn't arrive as quickly on the prairie as it did in Possum Valley. Sometime before Christmas Uncle William would move everything inside. The only plants that could stay outside as the cold set in were Christmas trees, and Uncle William didn't sell those. Once in a while an *Englisha* customer asked for Christmas trees, and Uncle William would smile and say, "We don't handle those."

The message would be transmitted in a gentle way that the Amish didn't celebrate the birth of Christ like their *Englisha* neighbors did. Eventually the questions would stop when everyone in the area had learned the young community's ways.

Now if Tyler Johnson would only interest himself in questions about Christmas trees, how much better her situation would be. Miriam sighed and turned away from the window. She hoped Tyler's continued conversations this past week with Uncle William were about other matters. Surely Tyler wouldn't ask more questions about Mose and herself. But what else was Tyler interested in? She couldn't imagine. Whatever the subject was, Tyler might have invented it so he could continue to hang around. Yet what would he gain by such actions? Did Tyler really think she was a prisoner in the community? He seemed to, but how could he think that? She was no princess in an *Englisha* fairy tale. She was an old maid, while Tyler was handsome enough to qualify as a prince. Miriam groaned out loud. This attraction between them must come to an end. She could not fall for an *Englisha* man's charms, nor he for his need to rescue a princess.

Surely Tyler would soon leave the area, or perhaps she could leave early for Shirley's wedding. That would place an extra burden on Betsy, her substitute. Betsy had already been a bundle of nerves when they spoke today after the services about the upcoming week of substitute teaching. But somehow Betsy would manage the schoolhouse just fine. The children were good students and wouldn't make her job harder.

Miriam seated herself on the bed and focused on the letter from Mose. She would be his *frau* soon, and from then on there would be no further questions of where her loyalties lay.

Miriam reached over to retrieve Mose's letter from the dresser. She opened the pages and read the greeting again, "Dear Miriam . . ."

Miriam looked away from the page. How was she even worthy to date this man? Mose was a minister, and perhaps soon would be a bishop, and all while she had awful things hidden in her heart. Perhaps Mose would soon suspect something. Wouldn't a holy man see right through her? That hadn't happened when Mose was here. But it might when she saw him again at Shirley's wedding.

Miriam continued to read,

Greetings in the name of the Lord. I trust you have kept yourself in the fear of God since we have seen each other.

There is much in this world that tempts us and draws us away from all that is pure and holy. I comfort my heart that you are a woman who seeks only what is right, and rejects evil in all its ways.

Miriam laid the page down to stare out of the window. Mose was correct on one point; she did try to live right, even if she wasn't doing very well right at the moment. Of course, she hadn't exactly done anything wrong yet, Miriam comforted herself. Perhaps Mose would find a little mercy in his heart if he knew the full story. She had not gone looking for this temptation called Tyler Johnson.

Miriam looked down to read again,

I looked into your face often while I visited in Oklahoma, and I told myself you are both beautiful and holy. It's not often that a man is given such a gift, Miriam. I don't wish to speak too boldly, but you have been greatly blessed of the Lord. I find my heart lifted in gratitude to God that I have been allowed to live to see this day. I never would have wanted Rachel to leave me and this earth, but the Lord decides such things. His grace also supplies our needs, and in this area great grace has been given me in that I have met you.

Calmness crept over Miriam's heart. Mose's words were what she needed. He spoke both rebuke and comfort. Miriam got to her feet. She would not think about Tyler anymore. Mose and she would stand together against the world and all that threatened them. That was the end of the matter.

Miriam approached the dresser again and took out a tablet. She should have written Mose earlier, but she hadn't. She would write now. She would thank him for his kind thoughts toward her, and for words that both rebuked and comforted.

Miriam began to write,

Dear Mose,
    Greetings in the name of Jesus. I received your letter on Friday, and I have read it through several times now.

Miriam paused to study the words. Were those too plainspoken? Mose might think her forward. Still, it was best that Mose see her heart and know that she did long for him. What woman wouldn't want to long for her future husband?

Miriam continued to write,

I should have written sooner, but I did want to wait until I received your first letter. I'm hoping you had a decent trip back home on the Greyhound. I couldn't see you through the window when you left Coalgate, but I was waving. I've thought of you often since then and pray that the Lord will keep watch over you. Thank you so much for your kind words and also for the words of rebuke and warning. I know that I am a creature subject to failure, and often ask the Lord to keep me on the straight and narrow. Your concern is much appreciated.

I spoke with my substitute teacher again today about my visit to Possum Valley for Shirley's wedding. A longing has come over me to travel there sooner, but I don't know if I should indulge myself or not. It doesn't seem quite right to impose a greater burden on Betsy than she already carries . . .

Miriam wrote for twenty minutes before she folded the pages and slipped them into an envelope.

There, she had written her first love letter. Ivan, when he was after her money, had once written to her and she had responded, but those hadn't been love letters. Not in this way. Mose would be her husband next year unless something terrible happened again.

Miriam laid the letter on the dresser and slipped out into the hall and down the stairs. Aunt Fannie looked up from her rocker with a smile. From the other rocker Uncle William's gentle snore filled the living room. Miriam tiptoed across the floor.

Aunt Fannie's smile broadened. "Don't worry. He's slept long enough for a Sunday afternoon."

"I heard that," Uncle William muttered, straightening up in his rocker. "Is the popcorn ready?"

"So like a man," Aunt Fannie scolded. "What about *my* nap?"

"I'll get the popcorn," Miriam said with a laugh. Their lighthearted teasing warmed her heart.

Aunt Fannie rose from her rocker to follow Miriam into the kitchen. "Are you missing Mose?" she teased. "Tomorrow it will be a week he's been gone."

Miriam kept her voice steady. "I was reading his letter again, and I wrote him back."

"That's so dear," Aunt Fannie cooed. "I never had a chance to write William letters because we both still lived in Possum Valley. But that would have been so romantic."

Miriam bit her tongue and didn't say anything. Aunt Fannie would take her silence as embarrassment, which was sort of true. She was embarrassed over her lack of proper feelings for the man she was to marry. What she had written in the letter moments earlier sounded almost too personal. She didn't have a right to say the words.

"I think we're going to the hymn singing tonight," Aunt Fannie announced. "You've inspired me, and I feel young again. I hadn't expected to have a dating girl in the house so soon."

Miriam managed a smile. After a moment of silence, she changed the subject.

"I'm thinking about leaving early for Possum Valley. Do you think that would be overly selfish?"

"Oh, that would be perfectly fine," Aunt Fannie gushed. "You're in love, and I'm sure the schoolboard will support this decision, unless . . ." Aunt Fannie's face fell. "Does this mean Mose will steal you away from us before the term is over? Maybe you shouldn't tempt him."

Miriam felt the heat rush up her neck. "I'm not a temptation, Aunt Fannie."

"Oh, but you are." Aunt Fannie clucked her tongue. "I'm comforted that a man has finally arrived with the sense to see it. You're being courted now by a minister, and perhaps even a bishop in a few weeks." Aunt Fannie stopped short. "When is the ordination, by the way?"

"I don't know."

Aunt Fannie paused a moment. "It's the week before the wedding, I think. That's when most of the churches around Possum Valley have their communion time. Don't tell me you didn't think of that. You should be there, in attendance. What better way to show support for Mose?"

"But how will that look if I walk in and . . . I'm not even promised to him yet?"

Aunt Fannie was on her feet in an instant. "I'll slip a little note in with your letter," Aunt Fannie declared, "and it will be taken care of, and oh, Miriam, this is such a dream."

"Is my popcorn about ready?" Uncle William roared from the living room. "All I hear is women's voices chattering like magpies."

"The nerve of the man," Aunt Fannie muttered, but she hollered back, "Yes, dear. Coming up."

"Maybe you should go calm him down," Miriam teased.

Aunt Fannie chuckled. "That's the spirit. I'm thinking Mose is already doing you a lot of *gut*. The two of you will raise a household of *kinner* for the Lord and bless the whole community in Wayne County. Isn't that so *wunderbah*?"

Miriam didn't answer as she turned the gas burner on the stove to high and poured in the popcorn. With the handle twirling in her hand, Miriam asked, "Is Tyler . . . Mr. Johnson . . . still talking to Uncle William?"

"Ach, *yah*." Aunt Fannie sounded exasperated. "The two jaw together worse than women. In fact, Tyler asked if he could stop by this afternoon, so we'd better make extra popcorn, now that I think of it."

Miriam stopped in midspin. "He's coming? This afternoon?"

"Yep," Aunt Fannie replied cheerfully. "You know, sometimes I think the man wants to join the community. Wouldn't *that* be something if William and I had a hand in another of the Lord's *gut* works? And you've played your part too, I think."

"That would be *wunderbah*," Miriam managed, "but I haven't done much." Miriam whirled the popcorn popper even faster.

"Oh, you have," Aunt Fannie insisted. "I think Tyler sees in you the perfect picture of what's so lacking out in his world. Not many women are like you, Miriam. Tyler finds it easy to speak with you, and that's also *wunderbah.*"

If Aunt Fannie only knew, Miriam thought. The loud popping of kernels filled the kitchen, and Miriam emptied the popcorn into a large bowl. Aunt Fannie stepped closer to pour a stream of golden butter over the white kernels, followed by salt from the shaker.

"William will love that," Aunt Fannie said as stray sunbeams played on the popcorn.

Outside an automobile drove into the lane, and Miriam breathed a quick prayer. "Help me, dear Lord, and protect me from temptation today."

CHAPTER SEVENTEEN

That evening after the hymn singing had let out, Tyler took the reins of Star with a firm grip. The faint sounds of the young people's voices could be heard behind them as the buggy wheels lurched forward. Ahead of them, Miriam's uncle and aunt's buggy was leading the way home.

He should have let Miriam drive home, but he wanted a try at this — if he didn't end up in a wreck.

"Are you sure you don't want me to drive?" Miriam asked. "It's not like you're used to this."

"No, I want to try it." With that, he took a firmer grip on the reins. "There are only so many things that can go wrong."

"And what if you do all of them?" Miriam asked. "I think you're just trying to show off for Uncle William."

"Don't worry," Tyler teased. "I'll save the princess tonight, even if I can't keep her from the evil ogre."

Miriam's tone turned tense. "This is not a teasing matter, Tyler. You shouldn't even be with me tonight, and you wouldn't be if you hadn't charmed my aunt and uncle and come up with that excuse about . . . well, I'm not even sure what it was now."

"Learning to better know the community." Tyler snuck a quick glance at her before he fixed his gaze back on the road. "You're not really upset, are you? And everyone found my presence tonight perfectly explainable. I didn't understand everything your uncle said, but they all know that I'm innocent and pure as the wind-driven snow."

Miriam snorted. "That's because you've never given them your freeing-the-princess speech."

"That's for your ears only," he said. "You understand. They don't."

"I don't understand any of this," Miriam said. "I don't understand your coming this afternoon, your staying around, your charming my uncle and aunt, or your finagling a ride with me in my buggy from an Amish hymn singing. What exactly do you think this will accomplish?"

"I have my hopes." Tyler gave Miriam a wicked grin. "I want the best for you."

He really did, Tyler reminded himself. His

conscience still pricked him a little, but this was all for the best. He couldn't see this woman married off into who knew what without an effort on his part to stop her. And he had his own reasons for his actions tonight.

"You seem to think this is funny, but it's not," Miriam said. "None of this is funny. You think it's easy — our life, the way we live, the years I've put into building my reputation. If you wanted the best for me, you wouldn't put me in a situation where I have to explain this to . . ." Miriam stopped and let the words hang.

"The ogre, perhaps?" Tyler teased.

"He's not an ogre, Tyler. Whatever that means. He's a man who wants me as his *frau.*" Her tone turned wistful. "Why do you fault me for wanting the love of home and family, and a . . ." Her voice caught. ". . . a man in my house?"

Tyler didn't respond at once. Miriam's sincerity was obvious, and he was touched, so he proceeded with caution. "That's admirable, Miriam. I'm not saying it isn't, but surely you don't have to settle for the kind of situation that has been described to me. This is an older man, and a little harsh, I think. He takes you for granted. He shows up suddenly and expects that all the questions are his to ask. If I measure him correctly, he never seriously thought you'd turn him down. Am I right?"

Miriam's silence was answer enough.

"So tell me why I shouldn't object to such a one-sided arrangement?"

Her answer was soft. "Because love doesn't always come like you think it does, Tyler. You come from the world where people take up and throw away each other on a weekly basis. That's not how we are. When we pledge our hearts to each other, the Lord gives us feelings . . . in His time. It's better to have feelings that come slowly than ones that last only a week."

Tyler took a deep breath. Miriam's words stung. There was no question about that. His love affairs lasted for more than a week — usually. His with Hilda had. She'd still be there when he arrived back in Oklahoma City — if he wanted to resume the relationship. But it wasn't for the sake of any feelings that he had for Hilda. Not in the way Miriam meant the term. He was certain of that.

"Isn't this true?" Miriam probed gently.

"I won't argue the point," Tyler allowed. "But this still isn't right."

Miriam hurried on. "So I'm thinking that after tonight we won't be seeing you again.

You'll leave me alone?"

Tyler took a deep breath and countered the question with one of his own. "What if both you and I have these feelings?" Tyler clutched the reins again. Driving a horse wasn't easy. He focused on the road. Miriam half turned to face him, her mouth open. He had her attention at least.

"What if you and I have feelings for each other before you get them for this . . . what shall we call him? You don't like ogre. How about the mystery man? Or the shadow perhaps?" Tyler tried to chuckle, but Miriam's expression stopped him.

"Tyler, you mustn't say such things. You and me? Tyler, you're not of us. Such feelings are forbidden."

"But they're there, forbidden or not. This is true . . . isn't it?"

He pulled back on the reins for a stop sign as the lights from Miriam's uncle and aunt's buggy pulled away. The soft glow of their headlamps illuminated a cattle lane by the side of the road. Tyler waited at the sign for a moment, and Miriam didn't protest. When Tyler let out the reins, he turned into the lane and bounced to a stop.

"My uncle and aunt will wonder why we stopped," Miriam whispered.

Guilt gripped Tyler. Why did he insist on

disturbing her world? He could wreck her life, he knew. And yet . . .

"I'll tell your uncle I wanted to enjoy the moonlight from a buggy." Tyler stuck to a lighthearted tone.

"There is no moonlight."

Tyler didn't answer but took her hand in his. Miriam trembled under his touch.

"You don't have to be afraid of me," he said.

"Please, Tyler," she whispered. "We shouldn't do this."

Tyler looked toward Miriam's face. The soft lamplight revealed only the faintest of outlines. She was beautiful, he told himself. Not beautiful like Hilda or the other girls he had known. Somehow this beauty was deeper, yet it shone through in her face. It was no trick of the shadows.

"We need to go." Miriam's voice was insistent. "This can't be, Tyler. Our hearts are not to be trusted. You cannot be what I am, and I cannot be what you are."

"Are you sure? I haven't even tried yet."

"This is beyond ridiculous, Tyler, and you know it." Miriam pulled her hand out of his.

"Stranger things have happened," he said, seeking her hand again. This time Miriam didn't pull away. "Maybe this is from the

Lord, as your folks in the community might say. Did you ever consider that possibility?"

"No. Such things don't happen in our world."

Miriam pulled her hand away again, and Tyler sighed. "Maybe you're right. I do have a history with girls, and not a good history, I have to admit."

Miriam didn't move or show a shocked expression. At least not that he could tell. Tyler began again. "You could make a decent man out of me."

Miriam turned away. "You speak as the world and not as those who follow what is right. A woman is supposed to obey her husband, not change him. We must go, Tyler. This cannot go on."

Tyler waited as thoughts raced through his mind. She was a brick wall, and one not torn down easily. Somehow he must win this girl's heart. But how?

"Tyler, please?" Miriam begged.

He let out the reins, and the horse seemed to find his own way back to the road. Silence settled over them, broken only by the whirl of the buggy wheels and the steady beat of the horse's hooves on the pavement. This was Miriam's life, and he was privileged to be on the inside even for a moment, Tyler told himself. A feeling of sadness crept over him, and Miriam felt the same, he was sure. So why must they fast approach the moment when they would part tonight? His senses screamed a protest, but words would fail to persuade her. He was sure of that.

Miriam's fingers brushed his arm in the darkness. "Thank you, Tyler, for stopping such talk."

He managed a laugh. "I'm not an ogre; that's why."

"And neither is Mose." She seemed to smile up at him. "You just don't understand him."

The touch of her hand was gone. Tyler could make out the Bylers's homestead in front of them and pulled back on the reins to turn into the lane. A light was on in the house, but the barn was dark. The buggy they had followed earlier sat empty in the barnyard. Miriam pulled in a sharp breath, and Tyler hurried to reassure her. "I'll come in and explain. Okay?"

They climbed out and unhitched in the light of the headlamps. Tyler fumbled with the tugs and tried to follow Miriam's lead. When the horse blocked the view, he simply guessed. Miriam stuck her head around the horse's bridle and nodded her approval.

"Hold the buggy shafts," Miriam told him,

as she led the horse forward.

Miriam disappeared into the barn, and he waited. A small beam bounced against the barn window, so, he figured her uncle must keep flashlights hung on the inside wall. His guess proved correct when Miriam reappeared and paused to leave an object behind her.

After Miriam returned, Tyler led the way toward the house. He reached for her hand, and Miriam didn't resist, but her fingers slipped from his as they approached the front door. Tyler stepped back to allow Miriam in first. He noticed that she tried to hide her flushed face behind her hand.

William's voice greeted them from his rocker. "There they are. I was ready to come looking for the two of you."

"We're back," Miriam said, but she kept her head down.

"I was driving," Tyler offered. "And I had to stop and enjoy the moment. It's not every evening that I get to ride home with a beautiful Amish woman."

Miriam fled toward the kitchen as Uncle William chuckled. "I thought I saw you pull over. I hope you were properly impressed. There's nothing quite like a buggy ride after dark."

"That's what I found out," Tyler replied

as he took a seat on the couch.

"I asked around some more tonight," William said, glacing toward the kitchen doorway and lowering his voice. "No one so far received any funds from the companies you mentioned. But I'll have to ask some more. And your presence does make the questions easier — people think you're sympathetic to the community."

Tyler allowed a smile to fill his face. "That's what I had hoped, so I might hang around a little longer if you don't mind. And I do like the community. It's quite different from what I'm used to."

"I suppose you're looking for some kind of fraud with your questions?" William gave Tyler a sharp glance. "I'll warn you, though, not to involve the Amish in any way. I hope that's understood. I'm only doing this as a favor to you. You did write a decent article about the community, so I'm trusting you to do only what's right and proper."

"Understood," Tyler agreed as Aunt Fannie appeared in the doorway with plates of cookies and lemon bars. Miriam followed close behind with glasses of milk.

Fannie beamed at him. "Hungry, are we?"

Tyler didn't hesitate. "I'm always hungry. But I wasn't expecting this."

"Amish tradition after the hymn singing,"

Fannie pronounced.

"Or at least for dating couples," William laughed. "I guess there's nothing wrong with memories of the past."

"To Amish traditions then." Tyler took a piece of lemon bar with a broad grin on his face. "This looks awfully good, Mrs. Byler. Thank you so much."

Fannie waved away the praise. "It's what we do. I'm glad you enjoyed the evening and the hymn singing."

"Oh, very much," Tyler assured her.

Miriam set down her items and fled back to the kitchen. She would have to come out soon. Too much time away would draw attention.

Tyler sat back and waited as the memory of her fingers in his hand as they walked toward the house lingered. She had not objected, Tyler reminded himself. He would not forget that moment or the rest of this evening anytime soon.

CHAPTER EIGHTEEN

The following Sunday morning, Mose Stoll took his seat in the circle of chairs set up in Deacon Yoder's upstairs bedroom. Below them the congregation's voices rose and fell as they sang the familiar hymns. Mose moved his chair a few inches and cleared his throat, but he didn't speak. A visiting bishop, Bishop Miller, was in charge this morning. They had asked him to lead the local bishop's ordination in two weeks, and with his responsibilities heavy on his shoulders, Bishop Miller would expect a full account of Mose's recent trip to Oklahoma. As a contender for the new bishop's position, his quest for a *frau* would be subjected to questions, but he was ready. Miriam had passed every test he had put her through. She also had a quiet, natural beauty, but he wouldn't mention this to his fellow ministers. Beauty of the heart was the only matter they would inquire after.

Mose cleared his throat again and waited. Why he was nervous, he couldn't imagine. Bishop Miller was an older man and wouldn't subject him to a harsh interrogation. Minister Kemp and Deacon Yoder were another matter. They would, but they had a right to. If he became the bishop they would have to submit to his authority. This would go the hardest for Minister Kemp because he was the oldest of the three. But in spiritual matters the bishop always led out, regardless of his age.

Across the room Bishop Miller finally looked up and ventured a smile. "The Lord be praised again this morning."

"Amen," they responded in unison.

"My old body grows weary," Bishop Miller continued, "but the spirit is ever quickened again in the work of the Lord."

"*Yah,* it is," they all murmured.

"I hope we still have unity about this matter of the ordination." Bishop Miller launched right in. "I can't say I approve fully of how you're doing this, but I give way. After all, I'm getting old and can't keep up with the newfangled ways you young people have." Bishop Miller coughed, followed by a strangled laugh.

Each of them glanced at the other, and as the oldest, Minister Kemp spoke first.

"Forgive us, Bishop, if we have taken up newfangled ways, but we all thought this had been done before — choosing a bishop from the three of us and ordaining another minister when things have settled down after a year or so. It seemed to us more disruptive to ordain another minister first and wait another year before we have our own bishop. I mean, we've already imposed on you enough."

"True," Bishop Miller grinned. "I can see the point. I know it has been done before. I was only teasing."

They all chuckled and Mose relaxed. Bishop Miller was in a *gut* mood this morning, so the questions for him would be light. And the other two had better be careful how difficult they made things for him. It wasn't too late to change his mind and object to this plan. In that case they would ordain a minister in two weeks instead of a bishop. This would cut Deacon Yoder from consideration a year later when a bishop was ordained. As part of this compromise, they had agreed to include the deacon as a candidate. The inclusion was quite an honor for Deacon Yoder. If they waited a year, Minister Kemp and he would make sure the deacon wouldn't be eligible for the lot. That was the normal practice among the Amish communities. In the meantime the odds of the draw wouldn't increase or decrease for himself.

Bishop Miller coughed into his handkerchief. "Let us proceed then. But first, has anything new come up that needs our attention? Perhaps some *Ordnung* breaker has been plowing in the fields with his *Englisha* neighbor's tractor?" Bishop Miller laughed at his own joke but soon sobered. "I hear Mose is fixing to get himself a new *frau.* Perhaps we had best hear about that matter . . ."

The other two nodded, but they didn't look at Mose. Mose began at once. Maybe if he spoke quickly this would go away. "I had a *gut* trip out to Oklahoma," he said, "and I spoke at length with Bishop Mullet about his member, Miriam Yoder."

Mose felt his neck burn a little. There was no need for embarrassment, but Miriam's name spoken right out in the open like this affected him. Miriam's presence in the buggy beside him had the same effect, but that had been in private. He couldn't imagine how it would feel to hold Miriam's hand when they said the wedding vows or to have her cook meals for him in his house where Rachel used to stand. But he must not think such thoughts now. If he appeared embarrassed, the others would think he had something to hide.

"I see." Bishop Miller smiled. "I'm an old man, but I still can rejoice to see the younger ones find themselves a *frau* and marry. But did you have to travel that far? Don't we have some *gut*-looking single women in this area?"

They all chuckled and Mose joined in. "I suppose so," Mose allowed, "but Miriam came highly recommended, and I had to investigate at the very least."

"I see," Bishop Miller said, still smiling. "I don't know the woman, so we will have to take your word for it or that of the ones who recommended this Miriam to you. Has she been married before?"

"No, but that makes no difference to me," Mose hastened to say. He hadn't expected this line of questioning.

"The ones who have been married before are safer sometimes." Bishop Miller nodded wisely. "They've been tested and have demonstrated their walk well before the Lord and the community. In your case, perhaps that would have been a wiser option, considering the bishop ordination coming up. I suppose it makes no difference in votes either way, but if . . ." There was a long pause from the bishop. "Shall we say, if the lot is drawn by your hand, a proven *frau* would be the best choice."

"I suppose so," Mose allowed. "But I . . ."

Bishop Miller silenced him with a lift of his hand. "We don't have to argue. No doubt this Miriam is a *gut*-looking woman, and you've fallen hard for her."

Mose didn't join in the laughter this time. Bishop Miller had now made Minister Kemp's questions easier, and this he also hadn't expected. Had the bishop suffered a sleepless night after all?

Minister Kemp rubbed his hands together when the bishop motioned that it was his turn to speak. "Perhaps Mose can tell us what details he found out concerning Miriam Yoder's character. From the few questions I've asked, I understand she once was left a great sum of money by an *Englisha* man. I believe she used to work for the old fellow. Does she still have this sum of money? And if not, I'd like to know how she got rid of it. And beyond that, why was the woman given the money in the first place? That simply doesn't happen to an Amish woman — at least it hasn't in my lifetime. What do you say to these things, Mose?"

Mose took a deep breath. Here the questions came, and he still wasn't ready. But these were questions he would have asked if the tables were turned. Had he not asked them in Oklahoma? The answers were solid enough to him, but how could he explain Miriam's character in a way that didn't make matters worse? The reports given by Glen, and Miriam's *daett,* and Bishop Mullet, and Deacon Phillips, and William and Fannie Yoder — the list was quite lengthy — they might be his best answer. He hadn't been able to speak of how he felt while he rode beside Miriam in the buggy, or sat across the table from her at William and Fannie's home, or noticed her gentle grace, or watched that soft rush of color that filled her face when he stared too long at her.

"Is Mose tongue-tied about this?" Minister Kemp asked. "Surely he would not rush into something like this without the proper questions being asked?"

"I did ask them!" Mose's words came out in a rush. "From all the people involved! They all said not one word that cast a shadow upon Miriam's character. I was told that Miriam spent hardly a dime of the money and gave the rest to a relief fund when the tornadoes hit the area some years ago. You remember that, don't you?" Mose cast a quick appeal around the circle.

Bishop Miller helped him out, "I think I

do remember. And does Miriam say the same thing?"

"*Yah,* she does," Mose assured him, "and so does their Deacon Phillips. The man handled the check himself, he told me. Not a shadow could be cast on Miriam's character over the matter."

"You could perhaps expect that," Minister Kemp replied. "But why was she given the money in the first place?"

Mose steadied himself and put on his sternest look. "Miriam worked for the *Englisha* man for more than three years under the strictest standards of conduct. He highly appreciated Miriam's care. Glen Weaver told me this — the man who is to marry Miriam's sister Shirley sometime this wedding season."

Minister Kemp snorted. "Nothing like family for getting a *gut* name."

Mose gave Minster Kemp a glare. "The *Englisha* man was an old man, and Miriam never stayed for overnight. That her family saw to. Miriam is reported by everyone who knows her to be an upstanding, decent, and honorable woman. Nor does Ivan Mast, whom she used to date, speak ill of her. We all know a woman's character cannot be turned on and off like a spigot. So why was the money given? I don't know, other than the *Englisha* man liked Miriam's work. Is that a sin?"

Bishop Miller gave a low grunt. "Let's not be taking offense, Mose. The question was a fair one, and you would have asked the same thing, I'm thinking, if the shoe were on the other foot."

Minister Kemp appeared relieved and continued, "I have to remind you, Mose, that my sister Bethany is available. Her two small children need a *daett*, and that would be the more responsible choice, I think. And we wouldn't be having this conversation about her character either."

"Thanks for the offer," Mose said, pasting on a smile. "But I think I'll pass."

So that was Minister Kemp's motivation, Mose thought. But it wouldn't be proper to disparage Minister Kemp's sister. They all knew Mose had the freedom to choose the *frau* he wanted.

Bishop Miller grunted again and turned to Deacon Yoder. "So what about you, Deacon? Any questions?"

Deacon Yoder waited a second before he said, "There is something. When do we all get to see this *wunderbah* woman?"

Laughter filled the room, and Mose joined in. Thankfully, Deacon Yoder had defused the conversation.

"I am glad you are getting a decent *frau*," Bishop Miller added, once things had quieted down. "I'm sure you miss Rachel a lot. I know I would my *frau*, Millie, if she were to pass."

"Thank you," Mose mumbled.

He had passed the test, and nothing more would be said about the matter. The conversation continued around him as Mose's thoughts centered on Miriam. In truth, Minister Kemp's questions bothered him more than he wished to admit. Thinking of Miriam in tender conversation with an *Englisha* man, even an elderly one, bothered him. And those conversations would have occurred in the three years Miriam took care of the man. What if he had missed something? From a distance Miriam's character seemed almost too perfect. Yet the whole Amish community in Oklahoma loved their teacher. Was that what blinded him? Or was he in love already? That he hadn't planned on. With his second marriage, he had planned to fall in love after he said the vows with the woman. It seemed safer that way. But he hadn't reckoned with Miriam Yoder.

"I think it's time we get back to the congregation." Bishop Miller's voice rang in Mose's ear.

He looked up and from the expressions of the others, the bishop must have spoken twice already.

"Are you at least in unity with our plans, Mose?" Bishop Miller asked with a twinkle in his eye.

He had no idea what those plans were, but there was only one correct answer. "*Yah, I agree,*" Mose said.

"I thought so." Bishop Miller got to his feet with a big grin on his face and the others followed.

He would soon be the laughingstock of the community, Mose thought. One could always depend on a woman to reduce a man to such a state. That was exactly what wasn't supposed to have happened to him.

CHAPTER NINETEEN

Early on Tuesday evening Miriam drove her buggy into Deacon Phillips's driveway. The schoolboard had suggested the visit to gain the deacon's final approval on Miriam's early departure date for Possum Valley. She had plenty of reasons for the request, Miriam reminded herself. Shirley and *Mamm* could use her help with the wedding preparations, and there was the bishop ordination in Mose's district. That would probably bear more weight with Deacon Phillips than the wedding preparations, which was why she hadn't asked for this extra time off before.

Betsy had been all in a tizzy when Miriam had spoken with her again after the Sunday service. But Betsy's eyes had also contained a gleam of excitement. "I might get to teach for two whole weeks!" Betsy had exclaimed.

Miriam knew Betsy would do well once she got into the flow of things.

Miriam slowed down to park in front of

the hitching rack and climbed out to secure Star. Tyler's continued presence in the community was the third reason she wanted to leave the area early, but she couldn't say that in anyone's presence. She hadn't even told Aunt Fannie, who seemed oblivious to the attentions Tyler was paying her. But someone was sure to notice soon if they hadn't already. Her deliberate absence for two weeks would speak well to her own opinion of the matter. How things had come to this state, Miriam couldn't fathom. How had she even allowed an *Englisha* man to speak words to her the way Tyler had the other Sunday evening? And to have driven her home in her buggy? That the buggy ride was at her uncle and aunt's insistence made little difference. She should have made a big fuss. At least she had survived the incident without a scandal, and since then Tyler had behaved himself. He was a constant presence in the community, though. The man even drove a different car now, which must mean he had dropped off the rental and purchased a vehicle of his own. Obviously Tyler didn't plan to leave soon. No one else in the community had commented on the switch of automobiles, and Miriam wished she hadn't noticed, but everything about Tyler made an impression on her.

Miriam arrived at Deacon Phillips's front door and knocked. She was greeted at once by Katie's cheerful voice. "Come on in. You know our schoolteacher is always welcome."

"*Gut* evening." Miriam returned the greeting and stepped inside. "I hope I'm not interrupting supper."

"Already finished," Katie assured Miriam. "The girls are washing dishes in the kitchen."

"*Gut* to see you," Deacon Phillips greeted, looking up from his *Budget* with a smile. "I hope you haven't come to report trouble with that Mose of yours?"

"Now, Phillip," Katie scolded. "Miriam just got here."

Miriam blushed and dropped her gaze to the floor. Thankfully, Ruth stuck her head out of the kitchen doorway at that moment and chirped, "Hi, Miriam. We're washing dishes in here."

"I should help," Miriam said at once.

"You will do no such thing," Katie ordered. "You didn't come to wash dishes."

"*Yah,*" Miriam allowed as she reached for a chair beside the stove and sat down.

Deacon Phillips looked up again to regard her soberly this time. "Surely there's nothing wrong at school," he said.

"No." Miriam tried to laugh. "I need to ask your opinion on something. I cleared it with the schoolboard last night, but they thought I should also speak with you. Would it be okay if I took an extra week off from school for Shirley's wedding so I can also take in the bishop ordination in Wayne County?"

"Oh!" Deacon Phillips's face lit up with interest. "That's true. There is an ordination soon in Wayne County. Mose must have told you."

"Of course he did," Katie interrupted. "Mose plans to wed Miriam."

Miriam quickly hung her head and looked away.

Deacon Phillips chuckled. "I'd say that's a great idea, Miriam, even if Mose doesn't draw the lot. You'd spend some time with him and show the proper concern a future *frau* would have for her husband."

"Thank you." Miriam still kept her head down.

Deacon Phillips cleared his throat. "I know this is none of our business, so don't tell me too much, but it does concern the school, so we should ask."

"Yah?" Miriam clutched the side of her chair and waited.

Deacon Phillips proceeded with caution. "There wouldn't be a chance Mose plans to take you away from us before the school term is over this year?"

Miriam allowed a smile to creep across her face. "No, I don't think so. He . . ."

Katie reached over to touch Miriam's arm. "You don't have to say more. We shouldn't have asked this much, but we were worried. Mostly because we have no idea where we'd get another schoolteacher to replace you this year." Katie laughed. "Or next year for that matter. At least we now have time to think about this and plan. And we all knew you wouldn't last forever — that some man would soon be along to snatch you up."

"I don't know about that," Miriam responded. Katie's praise was nice, but they both knew she had been well on her way to spinsterhood and could be thankful for any offer of marriage from an Amish man.

Deacon Phillips chuckled. "Then it's settled, and my mind is relieved."

Miriam jumped to her feet and declared, "And now I'm helping Ruth and the girls. I insist!"

"As you wish," Katie said with a laugh, and Miriam made her way into the kitchen. Ruth had soapsuds up to her elbows and a big grin on her face. Two of her younger sisters scurried around as they gathered up the last of the supper dishes and scraped them clean. The bucket of slop sat on a kitchen chair within reach of their small arms.

"How about if I dry dishes for you?" Miriam asked.

Ruth shooed both of her sisters out of the kitchen at once. At the last minute she handed the slop bucket to one of them and ordered, "Dump this over the fence, and then you're done for the evening."

Miriam watched both small girls run out with big smiles on their faces and then turned back to Ruth. Clearly, Ruth wanted to speak about something private if she got rid of her sisters so quickly.

True to Miriam's suspicions, Ruth whispered, "He's coming here tonight," her arms in the soapsuds again.

"Who?" Miriam whispered back, but her heart felt like it had sunk already.

"Tyler Johnson. The *Englisha* man." Ruth's face glowed. "Oh, my heart pounds at the very thought of him."

Miriam picked up the dish towel but didn't say anything. Did Ruth want a rebuke or an encouragement? Perhaps neither. Ruth must simply want a sympathetic ear to spill her secrets to. Ruth's *mamm,* Katie, obviously wouldn't tolerate such talk. Guilt crept through Miriam. Her own actions at the volleyball game must make Ruth think she could tell her these things.

Right away, Ruth began to chatter. "I don't exactly know what he wants, but it's something to do with *Daett,* I think. They are talking all the time, and *Mamm* mentioned Tyler should be invited for supper, but *Daett* said no. Oh, Miriam, do you think the man plans to join the community?"

Miriam finally found her voice. "We really shouldn't be speaking of the man, Ruth. He's not from the community, and . . ."

Ruth looked at Miriam in surprise. "But you were speaking so freely with him the other evening."

"I know." Miriam frowned at the memory. "Maybe I don't always do what's right, either."

"But there was nothing wrong with what you did," Ruth insisted. "I know because *Daett* was pleased you made Tyler feel so comfortable around our young people."

Mose wouldn't be happy about that. The words almost slipped out, but instead Miriam said, "I still don't think you should get your hopes up about Tyler joining the community. I imagine he's got other things on his mind."

"Don't you even think there's a small chance?" Ruth's face had hope written all over it.

Miriam sighed. Ruth was so innocent and pure in her heart. If Ruth knew Miriam's own feelings at the sight of Tyler's handsome face, all of Ruth's respect for the community's schoolteacher would be shattered.

"Not really," Miriam said.

"Well, I think there is at least some hope," Ruth insisted.

Miriam tried to keep her words gentle. "Sometimes a young heart gets ideas that don't pan out later, Ruth. I think you should be very careful with what your heart is feeling. Tyler is much older than you are, and he hasn't even mentioned joining the community, which I don't think he ever plans to do."

Ruth's face had fallen. "Has Tyler told you this?"

"No, but I can guess." Miriam forced a smile. Shame threatened to send a rush of color into her face at the memory of what Tyler had said in her buggy. Those had been very intimate words they had shared. Ruth was still very ignorant of the ways of the fallen heart.

"You were once promised to Wayne,

weren't you?" Ruth asked, studying Miriam's face intently. "You lost him. Is that why you're so skeptical?"

"I hope not," Miriam managed. "I just think you should be very careful about Tyler Johnson."

"I'll try to be patient," Ruth sighed as she finished the last dish. "But it does so hurt inside. I feel like I could cry sometimes."

Miriam reached over to hug the young girl. "That's the way the Lord has made our hearts, Ruth. We are to love a man someday, and bear his *kinner* and raise them in the fear of the Lord. Surely a *gut*-looking girl like you will have no problem getting a husband."

Ruth tried to suppress a smile. "I hope so . . . but you know I'm not that *gut* looking."

Miriam wiped the last of the dishes with a quick whisk of her towel before she answered. Pride was an awful thing, and she didn't want to swell Ruth's head, but right now the girl did need encouragement, so Miriam said, "You're quite a beauty, Ruth. You're much better-looking than I am, so you don't have anything to worry about."

Ruth's face sobered. "*Mamm* says the character of the heart is much more important than the beauty of the face."

"And that is true," Miriam agreed. "But every once in a while you can comfort yourself with the thought that the Lord has given you a beauty on the outside that will someday fulfill a man's dream. Someone you love will look at your face, and you will make him very happy."

"Oh, Miriam." Ruth leaned against her. "You speak such *wunderbah* things. I will ponder them well in my heart. And I'm sure *Mamm* would agree. I've heard *Daett* tell her how *gut*-looking she is, and *Mamm* turns all red." Ruth leaned closer to whisper. "I even saw them kiss once in the hallway. Oh, Miriam, will that happen to me someday?"

Miriam looked away. "If the Lord wills it, *yah.* But you must wait for His time."

"Have you been kissed by a man?"

Miriam swallowed hard, but no words came out. Wayne had kissed her often enough after they had been engaged, and the memory of those precious moments down by the creek blazed through her mind. All these years later she still hadn't forgotten, even if she was almost promised to another man.

Ruth's eyes had grown large. "So you did, and you were not married."

"A man can kiss you before you're married," Miriam managed.

"Has Mose kissed you?"

Miriam strangled a laugh. "No, but please, Ruth, we must not speak of this anymore."

"Do you love the man then? You must if you . . ." Ruth let the question hang.

Miriam laid the towel on the counter. "I really must be going. It's been nice chatting with you, and I hoped that I helped. But give up the idea of the *Englisha* man, Tyler. Okay?"

"I suppose I should," Ruth allowed.

Miriam waved a quick goodbye to Deacon Phillips and Katie as she dashed out the front door. "Got to get home before dark," she said as she passed.

"Thanks for helping with the kitchen," Katie called after her.

Hopefully Katie would appreciate the advice she had given her young daughter, Miriam told herself on the rush out to her buggy. Ruth likely was too shy to speak with her *mamm* yet about such matters, but that day would come, as it had for her. In the meantime, strangers were sometimes easier to speak to than one's own parents.

Miriam untied Star and climbed into the buggy. There was no sign of Tyler as she raced out of the lane. Tyler must have run late, and thank the Lord for that. The last thing she needed was to see him tonight. Maybe she should have a long talk with *Mamm* about all this once she arrived back in Possum Valley. Her parents had been the last to learn of her two-million-dollar gift from Mr. Bland. Maybe they should be the first to know about her heart's wanderings after a young, handsome *Englisha* man.

A car appeared in the distance, and Miriam kept her head down until it passed. She still caught a glimpse of Tyler's smile. He had seen her, she was sure, and knew she had avoided him. This would only make things worse in the long run, Miriam was certain.

CHAPTER TWENTY

A little more than a week later, Miriam peered out of Mrs. Faulkner's car window. The fall foliage crept past as they made their way through the town of Sugarcreek. Miriam was coming home to Possum Valley during a beautiful season of the year. Even more, she had left Tyler Johnson far behind for two weeks at least. Maybe by the time she returned her heart would have found some peace and settled down. Her mixed-up feelings for the *Englisha* man were a complete disgrace.

"You came at a perfect time of the year." *Mamm* echoed her thoughts from the front passenger seat.

Mrs. Faulkner turned around to say, "I suppose you haven't forgotten how crowded it can get with the tourists around here. You hardly have that in Oklahoma."

"No, we don't," Miriam allowed. "But I don't think I mind the tourists right now.

I'm just happy to be home."

Miriam watched as more familiar sights came into view. She had forgotten how much she missed Possum Valley. Once she married Mose, they wouldn't live that far from here, and she could visit often.

Miriam sobered as she thought of Mose. She had tried not to think of when she would see him again. His last letter had arrived in Oklahoma and now lay unread in the bottom of her suitcase. She had intended to open the envelope and read the pages on the long bus ride, but she had postponed the moment. Maybe she'd feel able to read the letter now that the joy of home filled her again.

Mrs. Faulkner slowed for the turn off of Highway 39. *Mamm* and Mrs. Faulkner continued the conversation they'd been having.

"*Yah,* Shirley's been through a lot," *Mamm* was saying, "but she's ready to settle down now. Really, she's been ready for some time, I think."

"I've been praying for your family," Mrs. Faulkner said. "Charles and I never had any children, so living next door to your family I watched everyone grow up and always hoped that things would turn out well for them all."

"By the Lord's grace we've made it through some difficult times." *Mamm*'s smile was grateful. "Thank you so much for your concern."

"You're welcome," Mrs. Faulkner responded. "And thanks for accepting the use of our pole barn for the wedding reception. It's a great honor for us. Charles and I feel almost like family."

Mamm's smile brightened. "We're the ones who need to thank you. I don't know what we would have done otherwise. Perhaps we'll even have to bother you again soon."

Mrs. Faulkner glanced over her shoulder and teased. "Oh. Are there any more weddings coming up?"

Mamm laughed. "We hope so."

Mrs. Faulkner chuckled. "Come on now, Miriam. Your secrets are still secrets with me. You know that."

"Well," *Mamm* said, "maybe Miriam should tell the story. She's more up-to-date than I am. But I do know she came home early for a very important date next Sunday."

"Oh my . . ." Mrs. Faulkner cooed. "That's sounds romantic. Who's the lucky man?"

"I think I'm the woman who should be

228

happy she has a chance at a husband," Miriam said.

No joy leaped up in her heart, though. Not like she had felt moments ago on her arrival. Why did Mose do this to her? Only it wasn't Mose but her own heart that was to blame. Tyler knew how she felt about him. He had enough confidence to show up near the Greyhound bus station to see her off. Aunt Fannie hadn't noticed him, as Tyler had stayed out of sight a block away and waved as the bus passed. That was the real reason Mose's letter had remained unread in the bottom of her suitcase on the long trip home.

"Miriam's just being modest," *Mamm* said. "Mose Stoll is a real catch, if I must say so myself. My mother's heart is gladdened. I had begun to think our oldest daughter would be an old maid."

"I am an old maid," Miriam said, and *Mamm* and Mrs. Faulkner laughed.

She didn't join in. If she messed up this relationship with Mose, she would be an old maid forevermore. No Amish man would come close to her with a marriage proposal again. So perhaps it was time she bared her soul to *Mamm* tonight and received some *gut* advice. *Mamm* would know what should be done.

Mrs. Faulkner made another turn, and the old homestead where Miriam had grown up came into sight. Miriam sat up straight and began to wave at Shirley and Naomi, who were standing in the yard waiting for her. Their smiles became even wider as Mrs. Faulkner came to a stop and Miriam dashed out to embrace both of them at once.

"Welcome, Miriam!" the two said together.

"You both look so *gut,*" Miriam gushed. She let go of Naomi to hold Shirley at arm's length. "Glen must kiss you every time you come into his sight."

Shirley reddened a little. "He has been more than kind to me. That's why I'm marrying him."

"What about me?" Naomi teased. "Don't I look kissable to a man?"

"Stop it, girls," *Mamm* ordered. "Here I was bragging about how all of you turned out so well."

"Kissing is perfectly normal and healthy," Mrs. Faulkner chuckled. "I can't say I don't still like a few from Charles."

Naomi gave a little shriek. "I can't wait!"

"This is totally inappropriate, girls," *Mamm* told them, but a smile played on her face.

"With my wedding just next week," Shirley

reminded her, "talk of kissing is allowed until Glen and I have said the vows. Then life can go back to normal."

They all laughed, and the girls walked toward the house hand in hand. *Mamm* stayed behind to pay Mrs. Faulkner. Once inside the house, Miriam pulled out a chair at the kitchen table and sat down.

Shirley paced the floor, chattering away, "Two serving couples — Emil and Lois, and Ronny and Laura — have canceled. They have a conflict with a cousin's wedding. The cousin contacted them later than I did but lives closer. I can understand that. Travel is expensive, which, by the way, Miriam, thanks for coming early — for coming at all. I know how far away Oklahoma is, but I so wish Aunt Fannie and Uncle William could also have come."

"They're both thinking of you," Miriam assured Shirley. "Of course, I also came early so I can see Mose next Sunday." Miriam attempted a smile. Maybe if she acted as though she were deeply in love with Mose, the proper feelings would follow.

Shirley read the look on her sister's face and said, "I sure hope Glen hasn't gotten you into something you don't want. Mose is Glen's friend and all, but to be honest, Mose always appears so stern. I can't imagine being wrapped up in his arms for a kiss. He'd probably bite if . . ." Shirley stopped as Naomi giggled. "Sorry, I forgot you were over there."

Miriam felt her face color as Naomi's giggles continued. "Mose has a kind heart!" Miriam declared.

"Have you . . ." Naomi struggled to get her giggles under control.

Miriam didn't answer, which was all the answer Naomi needed. "See, Shirley might be right. You should kiss him *before* the vows, just to make sure."

"You're pretty young to be dishing out advice," Miriam retorted. Naomi meant no harm, but the remark still irritated her.

"That's okay." Shirley patted Miriam on the arm. "I was just afraid Glen had gotten ahead of himself. But I see you have made up your own mind."

"Mose might draw the lot for bishop on Sunday." Miriam lifted her chin a few inches higher. This was so unlike her, but she needed a boost to her ego.

Both of her sisters' eyes widened. "Wow," Naomi said. "You'll get to kiss a bishop after the wedding."

"Enough about kissing," *Mamm* said, appearing in the kitchen doorway. "Don't you girls have anything better to talk about?"

"I'll get right back to work." Naomi put on a repentant look and dashed off.

"Phew!" *Mamm* exclaimed as she took a seat at the kitchen table. "Here, you're home at last, Miriam. I can't say I believe it myself. It's been more than two years now since you've visited Possum Valley, hasn't it?"

"*Yah,* at least that long." Miriam reached over to give her *mamm* a quick hug. "It's so *gut* to be here."

Shirley cleared her throat and changed the subject. "What did Mrs. Faulkner want? You were talking with her for some time."

"She just wanted to talk about the wedding." *Mamm* smiled. "She'd like to help in some way beyond the use of her pole barn. Do you think we could find something for her to do that wouldn't offend anyone from the community?"

"She's our neighbor," Shirley mused. "People would understand. But we have our own ways, and we can't stand around explaining things all day, especially if Mrs. Faulkner would like to serve as a cook. That's about all an older woman can do at an Amish wedding."

Mamm sighed. "That's what I told her. But I promised Mrs. Faulkner she would be welcome to attend both the morning and

233

the evening services. I said we would be greatly honored with her presence."

"I agree," Shirley said. "So whatever you think is fine. Now I have work to do upstairs. Talk to you later, Miriam."

Miriam felt a sense of relief. It was good to see Shirley again, but her being upstairs would give Miriam some time to herself with *Mamm.*

With the kitchen now empty, Miriam took her chance. "*Mamm,* I need your advice."

Mamm turned to face Miriam. "Are you and Mose having problems already?"

"Not that I know of," Miriam managed. "I don't have any real feelings for him, but I do appreciate his character and how dedicated he is to our way of life."

"There you go." *Mamm* appeared satisfied. "And the lack of feelings is a common concern of older girls. They've often had a relationship earlier full of emotion and youthful vigor, and now the man is older, and they're older — it's almost like a second marriage, really. But you shouldn't be worried about this. If everything else is right, your feelings will come for the man once you've said the vows." *Mamm* paused to glance at Miriam. "Since you girls have been talking about it, I'll ask. He hasn't kissed you. Is that the problem?"

Miriam's gaze was fixed on the kitchen wall.

Mamm clucked her tongue and scolded again. "Mose is the limit, but men who have been married before are often that way. Not that I would know from personal experience, but I've heard the talk at the sewing. They're afraid their emotions will get the best of them, so they come across a little cold. All that goes away after the wedding, Miriam. You just have to believe that."

Miriam took a deep breath. "But there's more, *Mamm.* A young *Englisha* man hangs around the community and pays me attention. I wonder sometimes . . ." Miriam fell silent, and her face flamed.

Mamm's gaze became alert. "Does Fannie know about this?"

"About the *Englisha* man, *yah.* But she doesn't seem to notice the attention he gives me."

"Then it's nothing." *Mamm* relaxed. "This young man probably stirs up memories of Wayne and your experiences with him. Perhaps he brings up thoughts that have been long dead and buried. But how like life! When the Lord's will is revealed, something else is always offered. No, Miriam, you have nothing to worry about unless you've returned his affections, but then you wouldn't. Not to an *Englisha* man."

Miriam swallowed and wet her lips. "I have told him my heart is settled on Mose."

Alarm filled *Mamm*'s face. "Then you have spoken this plainly with the man?"

Miriam kept her head down. "He has spoken with me. He is not shy about saying such things."

"But you have told him this cannot be?" *Mamm*'s hand reached for Miriam's.

"Yah," Miriam assured *Mamm* as their fingers clung to each other. "I have told him."

Mamm searched Miriam's eyes. "My oldest daughter, I trust you with all my heart, so don't worry about this. You have been strong through your troubles with Ivan and your engagement with Wayne. You helped us when Shirley strayed from the truth. The Lord will give you strength for the trial that's been placed upon you. But remember that no great honor comes without an equally great temptation. I have withheld my tongue so far, but I will say it now. You have lightened my old age, Miriam, with the thought that my daughter should be a bishop's *frau.* This is more than we should even speak of, but there, I have said it."

"Thank you." Miriam squeezed her *mamm*'s hand. "I knew you would tell me what I needed to hear."

"So relax now and stop worrying," *Mamm* said. "Mose will be by this evening to see you. I don't know where you can go to court the man properly, but maybe he'll take you for a short drive."

Miriam stood to her feet. "If Mose is coming, then I have something I have to do."

She hurried into the living room before *Mamm* could speak and retrieved her suitcase. Moments later she was upstairs and had Mose's letter in her hand. Miriam took a deep breath. With that load of guilt off her shoulders, she could at last read Mose's words with an open heart.

CHAPTER TWENTY-ONE

Later that evening at the Yoders' supper table, Naomi leaned over to whisper to Miriam, "He's here."

Miriam had heard buggy wheels come in the driveway moments before but hadn't wanted to act overeager. Not that she felt eager, but wouldn't a woman in her shoes be expected to be eager to see her suitor? Miriam forced herself to rise quickly to her feet.

Daett looked up from his plate of potatoes and gravy with a smile. "Mose is a little late for supper, I'd say."

"He wasn't planning to come for the meal," *Mamm* said. "Mose said he didn't want to disturb Miriam's family time the first night she was home."

"I'd say he's disturbing Miriam's whole evening," *Daett* teased. "But run along, Miriam. You'd better let him in."

Miriam stood and gripped the back of her

chair as she tried to gather herself together. Already *Mamm* had forgotten their earlier conversation about Tyler Johnson. *Mamm* thought the problem had been resolved, and it had been, Miriam reminded herself. She simply had to believe that things would now be different when she returned to Oklahoma. All her past memories of Wayne and the *wunderbah* times she used to have with him were what caused her present reaction. She wasn't to blame for the feelings that surfaced when Tyler paid her attention. And she must not compare Mose with either Wayne or Tyler. Mose was a world of his own — a much better world. She was privileged that he had even come to call on her.

"Go on — Mose is waiting." *Daett*'s voice interrupted Miriam's thoughts. He sounded a little impatient, and Miriam hurried out the kitchen doorway.

"The girl's all *fahuddled,*" *Mamm* said to *Daett* as Miriam left. "But you can't much blame her. Mose appeared a little suddenly in her life."

"He'll be *gut* for her," *Daett* responded.

Miriam trembled as she forced herself to open the front door. The chill of the evening struck her. Miriam paused for a second on the porch. Should she return for her shawl?

Nay. Mose stood beside his buggy with an expectant look on his face. He appeared a little irritated that she had made him wait this long. What would Mose think if she dashed back inside again? She was *fa-huddled,* like *Mamm* had said. There was no doubt about that, and flighty and forgetful tonight on top of everything. Neither description sounded like Miriam Yoder, the esteemed schoolteacher from Oklahoma. She had to gain control of herself. Early impressions here at home were important. Mose would soon wonder if she was a different girl in Possum Valley than the one he had met in Oklahoma. *Nay,* she would not go back inside. There was a buggy blanket behind the seat, and Mose surely wouldn't object to its use.

Miriam took measured steps off the porch and approached Mose with a smile. "*Gut* evening. Did you want to come inside?"

"Maybe later." He took her appearance in with a quick glance and appeared pleased.

Miriam climbed into the buggy, and Mose followed. He handed Miriam the buggy blanket.

"Thank you." Miriam draped the blanket over her lap and let the ends fall down toward the floor.

Mose grinned at her and asked, "Have you

enjoyed your time at home this afternoon?"

"*Yah. Mamm* and I had a good talk." Miriam forced a smile. "I had been looking forward to that."

Mose nodded. "*Yah,* that is a *gut* thing. A *mamm* and her daughter need to talk." Mose glanced at her again. "I thought we might drive down to an auction that's going on tonight. That would give us a chance to do something productive with our evening. I need some farm parts they'll be offering. Is that okay with you?"

"Of course — whatever you wish." The words rushed out. "*Mamm* just said you'd be by, and anything you have planned is okay with me."

Mose nodded and clucked to his horse. "So how was the bus trip?"

"Okay." Miriam forced a laugh. "As *gut* as Greyhounds can be, I guess."

Mose snorted. "I don't like bus travel myself, but a little sacrifice in the Lord's service is *gut.* We wouldn't want to become like so many and long for the ease and pleasure of private transportation. Even hiring a van goes a little too far for me, but I guess it's necessary sometimes. Especially if it's for a funeral or a wedding when people need to get there and back on a tight schedule. Work on the farm's important too."

"Oh, before I forget," Miriam whispered, "thanks for your last letter."

"And for yours," Mose returned, concentrating on the road. "I'm not much of a letter writer, but I try. And I'd have made better plans for this evening if I'd known you were coming earlier than you'd planned."

"That's okay. I guess it was all sort of on the spur of the moment."

Mose appeared concerned. "Did something come up here at home? Your *mamm* didn't say anything when I spoke with her."

"Everything's fine," Miriam said. "It'll be nice to help out with the wedding a week before, and the schoolboard was very understanding. And now I'll get to . . ." Miriam stopped. Did Mose not approve of her being in attendance when all the ministers drew lots for bishop?

Mose didn't seem to pick up on her discomfort. "You were saying . . ." He sounded impatient again.

Miriam tried to look properly submissive before she asked, "Is it okay if I attend the communion service and the ordination on Sunday?"

Mose regarded Miriam with a stern look. "Is that why you came early? You plan to be there when we draw lots? You do know that I might not be the one chosen."

"Of course, but I wanted to be there as your . . ." Miriam choked on the word. What exactly was she to Mose? He hadn't really defined their relationship, other than implying things.

"You're not my *frau* yet," Mose said sharply. "And if I do draw the lot, you mustn't make a scene."

"I hadn't planned to." The words continued in a rush. "I don't have to come, Mose. I just thought with how things were going . . . and you did speak of this in Oklahoma. Don't you want me there?"

Mose regarded Miriam for a long moment and softened his gaze. "I suppose it would be appropriate. And I'm glad you want to be there. So I will pick you up in the morning and drive you to the service. I don't want you coming in alone like a . . ." Mose stopped.

"Like a what?" Miriam asked. "*Daett* and *Mamm* could bring me."

Mose ignored the suggestion. "I will pick you up. It will look more appropriate and decent."

"I'm sorry," Miriam said weakly. "I didn't mean to cause problems for you."

"It's not your fault exactly." Mose settled

243

further into the buggy seat. "But there were plenty of questions asked the other Sunday by the ministry. Thankfully, I had answers for all of them because you are a virtuous woman, Miriam. Let's keep things that way. I can't have your parents bringing you to the services like you're in pursuit of a bishop."

"Thank you for your kind words." Miriam shivered.

Mose pulled up to a stop sign and turned north on State Road 39. The steady clip of his horse's hooves filled the buggy again. Miriam took a deep breath and tried to relax. Her conscience stung, even with *Mamm*'s words of comfort at home, so she had to say something about Tyler.

"I do need to confess something," Miriam whispered into the silence of the buggy.

Mose jerked his head up. "Confess?"

Miriam faltered. "I mean, I do have a past, you know. I was promised to a man before."

"I already know that." Mose had turned to stare at her.

Miriam tried to still the beat of her heart. "I have memories of Wayne, and they still haven't gone away."

Mose shrugged and relaxed. "I see," he said. "So that's what's bothering you. I had not planned to speak so plainly, Miriam. I

244

know your mind is pure and filled with a desire for the Lord's will, but I too have memories of my marriage with Rachel, and I'm sure I will always have them. You shouldn't be ashamed of your engagement with Wayne. I'm sure you loved the man, but that's in the past now, and we can build a new life together in the will of the Lord."

Miriam let out a long sigh of relief. "You are so kind, Mose. I can never thank you enough."

His glance was tender. "Your desire for the Lord's will is so pleasing to me, Miriam. I'm honored that the Lord has brought your steps to walk with mine. There's no reason to doubt your intentions. In all this time I've known you and asked questions about your character, not one shadow has risen to cloud the sky. And you have acted most appropriately around me, so I have no complaints."

A slight smile had spread across Mose's face. "I do wish to say, Miriam, that I had not expected to find another *frau* who so pleased me, but the Lord has been *gut*. I know you never knew Rachel, but she was beautiful like you are, and filled with a humble and a broken spirit."

Miriam had looked away and clutched the buggy blanket with both hands, but no words would come.

Mose regarded her with a kind look. "You have little to say, as Rachel also said little. Those are the best women — the ones graced with a meek and quiet spirit. They comfort a man's heart first of all and fill his house with the grace of the Lord."

Miriam tried to breathe evenly as her conscience stirred. She could not think about Tyler right now. She had already tried to confess, and the words wouldn't come. Perhaps she needed a little more time. Ahead of them the first signs of the auction appeared with the long line of cars parked in the field. Mose's gaze was already fixed on the auction site in front of them, and in the distance the excited auctioneer's chant rose and fell.

Mose turned toward Miriam again and said, "Looks like they've already started, but that pile of farm parts over there is still safe. That's what I've come for."

The buggy bounced into the field, and Miriam hung on. Mose had a big grin on his face. His hand reached over to squeeze Miriam's for a moment. "May the Lord bless this evening and our time together. I know I've already enjoyed being with you tonight. You are a woman of great favor with God, Miriam."

Miriam managed a weak smile as she followed Mose out of the buggy. She waited until he had tied his horse and stayed close beside him as they worked their way through the crowd. Few people paid any attention to them. They already looked like a married Amish couple, Miriam was sure. Thankfully, the thought wasn't unpleasant. Maybe Mose's words of praise had reached her heart and begun its *gut* work.

CHAPTER TWENTY-TWO

Sunday afternoon found Miriam sitting on the backless wooden bench with her hands clasped. The line of the young, unmarried women around her stilled when Bishop Miller stood to his feet. Since the deacon of the district was a candidate, Bishop Miller had brought along a visiting minister from his district to help him officiate. The two had emerged from upstairs only moments ago with three songbooks in the visiting minister's hand. The long drama of the day was almost over.

This was not the most important part of the service, Miriam reminded herself, even if it felt so. Communion Sunday was a day spent in memory of the death and resurrection of Jesus Christ. That topped the list of the day's activities, but the fact that the next few minutes could change Mose's life and hers forever somehow overshadowed even communion.

Miriam stiffened as Bishop Miller walked toward the two local ministers and the deacon who sat on a bench by themselves. With only three votes needed to become a candidate, all three were included in the lot. This had been the expected result. Each now had an equal chance at the bishop slot. Miriam's gaze rested on Mose's face. It appeared fixed and drawn, and the other two were equally burdened.

Mose had been silent for the most part on the drive over to the service this morning. Miriam had wanted to wrap her arms around him in the buggy and pull him close. Not that she felt like his *frau* yet, or even the woman he loved, but the emotion of the moment had gotten to her. Great uncertainty must be swirling in Mose's heart over the question of whether the Lord would choose him today for the heavy duties of a bishop's office.

Maybe she would hug him on the way home if she wasn't too nervous. Mose had agreed to stay for supper at *Mamm* and *Daett*'s place tonight. He would need that extra attention, especially if he didn't have the slip of paper in the book he drew. Mose hadn't said so, but he would take the rejection hard. He had more of his hopes set on the Lord's choosing him than he would admit.

Miriam shifted on the bench as Bishop Miller faced the three candidates. The bishop still didn't speak for a long time as the congregation waited. Clearly this was a time for reverence and godly fear.

"As you can see," Bishop Miller began, "the congregation of the Lord has chosen all three of you as worthy candidates for the lot of bishop. In this office you are to lead the flock of God, nurture the injured, and reprove and rebuke all sin. This choice speaks well for each of your lives and also for the congregation, which is led by three such worthy men. So now is the time for us to see whom the Lord has chosen. Will each of you choose books beginning with the oldest candidate, Minister Kemp?"

The visiting minister set the three songbooks on the bench in front of the three and straightened them out before he removed his hands. Each appeared identical. With a bowed head Minister Kemp reached forward and chose the middle book. No order was required, Miriam knew. Each man could follow the Spirit's leading in his choice, except the deacon, who came last and took what was left. But that in itself was a choice, and if the deacon was chosen he would he highly honored to have been anointed by the Lord without the touch of a man's hand.

Mose went next and took the outer left songbook. He took his seat again, the book held limply in his hand. The deacon took the remaining songbook.

Bishop Miller cleared his throat but said nothing as he stepped forward. He took the songbook from Minister Kemp's hand and flipped through the pages. No one moved. Even the smaller children didn't make a sound in the crowded house.

No paper was found, and Bishop Miller handed the songbook back. Miriam couldn't make out the expression on Minister Kemp's face. Was the man relieved or disappointed? She shouldn't even ask the question at such a holy moment, but never before had the selection of bishop mattered as much to her.

Bishop Miller took Mose's book next and opened it. The paper fluttered to the floor, and Bishop Miller bent over to retrieve it. Miriam's gaze was fixed on Mose's face. He appeared relieved. She was certain of it. The man had desired the office greatly, and now it had been given to him. But the Lord must know what He was about, Miriam told herself. This now also changed her life. She would become a bishop's *frau.*

"The lot has been found in your book," Bishop Miller said, stating the obvious as he stood back up again. "Would you please kneel, Brother Mose?"

Mose knelt, and Bishop Miller placed both hands on Mose's head. The bishop began his prayer: "Now unto the God of Abraham, Isaac, and Jacob be all the praise and the glory for this choice made in God's great wisdom. I charge you in the behalf of Christ, feed the flock of God, tend to their wounds, speak the words of life in season and out of season, teach, reprove, and exhort with all long-suffering and doctrine. And may the Lord always be with you." Bishop Miller paused for a moment before he offered Mose his hand. "Stand, brother, and take the office the Lord has given you in all humility and brokenness of spirit."

Mose stood, and Bishop Miller kissed him on the cheek. The visiting minister did the same, and Mose took his seat again. A song was given out, and Miriam found a comfortable spot on the bench until it was finished. The clock on the living room wall read ten minutes after four. The day had been a long one, but the community now had their new bishop.

A woman appeared in Miriam's side vision once the song ended and the service dismissed. Her voice was gentle. "Hello, Miriam. I'm Esther, Minister Kemp's *frau.*" Esther offered her hand. "I'm glad you could be here today."

"*Yah,* so am I," Miriam managed. "As you see, I don't know too many people. I didn't recognize you this morning."

"That's okay." Esther's smile was warm. "I didn't know who you were either when we shook hands in the washroom. But, Mary, the deacon's *frau,* told me."

Esther glanced over her shoulder as another woman approached and offered her hand. "I'm Mary. I know you don't know me, but it's *gut* to have you here."

"Esther just told me the same thing." Miriam tried to smile. "I'm sorry I don't know anyone."

"I'm sure that will change soon." Mary's smile filled her face. "Will you be moving into the community soon?"

"I . . . um . . . I don't quite know yet," Miriam said.

The two women laughed. The sound tinkled above the soft murmur of voices that filled the room.

"I suppose you can't be spilling your secrets just yet," Mary said. "But I can assure you that on our part you're very welcome to come anytime. We have heard only *gut* things about you and the little community out in Oklahoma."

"Thank you," Miriam whispered. Her knees grew weak as the realization washed over her. This was her welcome into the ministry team of this local congregation. And she was younger and would be the bishop's *frau.* No wonder she could hardly stay upright.

"You're very welcome," Mary was saying. "Now we'd best be going. I see Mose left a few seconds ago. You came with him, didn't you?"

"*Yah,* I did." Miriam forced herself to move. She almost reached for the bench to steady herself but managed to stay on her feet and avoid an embarrassment.

Mary led the way to the washroom where the women found their shawls and then slipped outside to the waiting line of buggies. The other women in the room gave Miriam shy looks. A few sent smiles her way, but no one spoke.

Everyone was tired, Miriam told herself. She'd have to beome better acquainted now that Mose was the bishop in the district. No doubt her ear would be the first one many of these women would spill their troubles into. Maybe she should reconsider the decision to complete the school year in Oklahoma and marry Mose soon after Christmas. If Mose brought up the subject of their wedding date again, she would tell him her change of perspective. A winter date would be right after the regular wedding season, but these were special circumstances. Betsy could prepare herself in that time and take over the schoolhouse. Miriam would miss the children and the prairie countryside, but this was now home, or soon would be. She had a responsibility the Lord was leading her into. Tyler was still back home, but she wouldn't have to face him much longer — if he was still around when she arrived back in Oklahoma. Miriam felt her face redden at the thought. Why had Tyler intruded upon this sacred moment when the call of God had been so clearly expressed in Mose's life?

"You have a *gut* evening now," Esther said in Miriam's ear as she smiled.

"And you too." Miriam smiled back. How quickly everything had changed. She felt almost like a new woman. No wonder the Lord had led her here early so she could experience this with Mose.

Miriam lowered her head and walked toward Mose's buggy. As she pulled herself up into the seat, she gave him a warm smile.

He didn't smile back.

"Mose," she touched his arm. "The Lord has chosen you. I'm so honored I could be here today. I've never been affected like this before."

Mose jiggled the lines, and his horse took off. He still didn't say anything, and Miriam waited. Maybe the shock of the ordination had rendered the man speechless.

"There is much that must now be done," Mose finally said. "Starting with our own lives, Miriam. I'm glad to see that you have also accepted the call of God. As you should know, this carries over into many things in our lives. We now have to adjust. We must together seek to walk worthy of this high calling of a bishop."

Miriam's mind whirled. What could Mose mean?

"Yah," she allowed. "I saw how the women looked at me after the service. I expect they will come to me for counsel — once we are wed, of course. Is this what you speak of?"

"Not exactly." Mose's voice was sharp. "I speak of the example you and I must be for the others. Nothing in our lives can bring reproach to the name of the Lord or the reputation of the community."

"Yah," Miriam agreed. "I expected noth-

ing less. That's how I have always lived my life."

Mose gave Miriam a stern look. "Okay. We will start then with your dresses. I know they are in line with the *Ordnung* now, but I want them a few inches longer. The world presses in on us all the time, and drift is easy. The people must see that my *frau* goes the other way, toward the Lord's ways and not out into the darkness."

"You . . . you think . . . that I . . ." Miriam couldn't find the words. Her dress was already a clear example of godly living. Moments ago neither Esther nor Mary had looked at her with any questions in their eyes. But Mose apparently wanted more.

"And your stockings." Mose glanced down at Miriam's feet. "You will wear only black ones from now on. Any off color is only more drift in my mind. We will run this district so there is no question where their bishop stands on holiness. We will do this even if there aren't enough votes to forbid dark brown stockings in the *Ordnung.*"

"But I have always worn these." Miriam tried to speak evenly. "And *Daett* is known for his strictness, and I have never rebelled."

Mose nodded. "That is *gut.* Your life has obviously prepared you well for your role as a bishop's *frau.* For that I'm thankful. And you will have plenty of time to make these changes before we say the vows during the next wedding season."

"Mose, please . . ." Miriam began.

His glance silenced her. "I hope you don't plan to protest. That wouldn't be fitting on this holy day when the Lord's will was shown so clearly before the whole congregation."

Mose's words stung. Why had he changed so? His selection as bishop was the obvious answer. But such a change for her — and now of her — was so unexpected. She had thought the ride home would be joyful with his selection, but that was clearly not to be the case. And all thoughts of giving him a hug had flown far away.

"You are still the woman I thought you were." Mose patted Miriam on the arm. His eyes gleamed for a moment as they rested on Miriam's face. "You are still beautiful, but I must not think of that now. Our wedding date will come soon enough."

Miriam kept her head down. Mose hadn't even asked her to marry him yet. Did he plan to skip that part, as if her acceptance didn't matter? Or was her presence here today all the answer Mose needed? Now that Mose was the bishop, his word was apparently sufficient to move things forward on their own.

You haven't asked me to marry you, Miriam wanted to say, but the words stuck in her throat. Mose expected her to say *yah* and had saved himself the bother of asking. And here she had wanted to suggest the idea of a wedding date after Christmas. Right now the thought of a wedding even next season sent a chill up her back. But surely Mose would soften by then. He was only caught up in the emotions of the moment, and she must try to understand.

Ten minutes later Mose approached the Yoders's lane and slowed down. "I won't be staying for supper as we planned," he said. "I need to spend time in prayer and fasting. Tell your *mamm* I'm sorry. Maybe I can come back some other time before you leave for Oklahoma."

"I'm sure everyone will understand." Miriam forced the words out. She tried to smile but her face was frozen.

Mose pulled his horse to a stop, and Miriam climbed down. "I'll see you at your sister's wedding then," Mose said, and he was gone.

Mamm met Miriam at the front door with a strange expression on her face. "Why is Mose leaving?"

Miriam took a deep breath. "He needs to

259

spend time with the Lord. It's been a shock to him, I think."

"Oh, dear." *Mamm* took Miriam in her arms, and her face glowed. "So Mose did make bishop today. Well, that is *gut* news. I know the two of you will be of great service to the community and the Lord's kingdom."

"He wants a wedding date in a year," Miriam whispered.

"A year?" *Mamm* held Miriam at arm's length.

"*Yah,* that's what he wants."

Mamm hugged Miriam again. "That time will be here, dear, before you know it, and what a holy man. But I never thought he'd wait that long to take my daughter as his *frau.*"

Miriam wasn't sure why, but none of this seemed wise. But she was just a woman, and what did she know?

CHAPTER TWENTY-THREE

On Thursday of the following week, Miriam's sister Shirley exchanged vows with Glen Weaver. The Yoders's neighbor, Mrs. Faulkner and her husband, Charles, had been given front row seats as special guests. Miriam looked over from her position and watched as they nudged each other with big grins on their faces. They had so far taken in the three-hour service with a great show of interest and now were watching intently as with a soft smile Bishop Wagler pronounced, "In the name of the God of Abraham, Isaac, and Jacob, I now join this man and this woman in holy matrimony. They are one before the eyes of God and man and are to walk together through life until death parts them. And let no man ever separate what God has joined together today before these many witnesses."

Shirley's face glowed as she held Glen's hand and gazed into his eyes. Bishop Wagler loudly cleared his throat, and Shirley let go of Glen's hand to lower her gaze to the floor. Glen reached out to give his new bride a quick squeeze on her arm before they both went back to their seats.

Miriam felt a rush of heat creep up her neck. Such a display of affection in public was unusual for an Amish wedding, but Shirley and Glen were an unusual couple. They had been through much and had grown to love each other deeply. Shirley adored Glen's soft and kind ways, and he was taken with Shirley's beauty and grace.

Mose gave Glen a tolerant smile after Glen sat down, but Mose's stern look didn't retreat too far. If Glen hadn't been Mose's *gut* friend, she wouldn't have been surprised if Mose would have begged off from his duty as best man today. Mose's ordination on Sunday had changed the man, but he had shown up this morning anyway. He had been a little grumpy, but he was there.

Earlier in the day, Glen's hearty "*Gut* morning. I'm so glad you have graced us with your presence, Bishop," had brought a momentary smile to Mose's face.

Now a song was given out, and Shirley's face glowed again as the congregation sang.

Miriam let her thoughts drift again. She hadn't been able to please Mose all morning, especially after Mose noticed her dress. The color was a complementary dark blue that matched Shirley's lighter blue wedding dress. But the color was not the problem. Shirley had made the dress and had missed the district's *Ordnung* dress length by an inch or more. *Mamm* had noticed first, and they had all agreed that Shirley had made a mistake. But Shirley was out of material, and *Mamm* had assured them that weddings were special days and no one would mind. If some people said something — which they wouldn't — *Mamm* would tell the truth. She'd say the family didn't have the extra money to spend on dress material over a question of an inch or two in length.

Mose hadn't said anything this morning about the dress, but she knew what his thoughts were by his frequent stern glances. She was the only one of her family who knew about Mose's view on the proper length of an Amish dress. No doubt Mose was disappointed that she was dressed today in a shorter dress than any Mose had ever seen her in.

But Mose should be happy on Shirley's wedding day, Miriam told herself. Or at least act so for Glen's sake, if not for Shirley's. Glen was Mose's *gut* friend. Mose shouldn't worry about an inch or so of dress length. And why had Mose been so quick to see the discrepancy? The other men in the congregation hadn't given her a second glance.

Even Bishop Wagler had greeted her with a smile. "Welcome back to Possum Valley, Miriam. I hope you can stay a little longer not so far in the future."

Bishop Wagler had turned to wink at Mose, and Mose had managed a grin. But the stern look had soon returned. Of course Mose had a right to examine her — she was, after all, his promised one. Not because Mose had asked to marry her, but because he had pronounced a wedding date on his own. Mose must think he had the right to such things now that he was ordained a bishop.

Miriam pulled her concentration back to the present as the song came to an end. Glen and Shirley stood first and were followed by the others. Miriam fell in beside Mose as the wedding party headed for Mrs. Faulkner's pole barn where the reception would be held. *Englisha* people weren't usually involved in an Amish wedding, but *Daett*'s buildings were all too small for the reception. Mrs. Faulkner had offered the solution herself, and *Daett* surprisingly had accepted.

Miriam kept pace with Mose's long strides. They walked a little behind Glen and Shirley, who gave each other constant loving glances and smiles. They also whispered in low tones, which elicited Shirley's occasional giggle.

Mose hadn't spoken to her since they left the ceremony, but she was to blame, Miriam told herself. What wicked thoughts she had entertained earlier about an ordained bishop. No wonder Mose was displeased with her, and he didn't even know the half. She ought to apologize for the dress. The lack of funds in the Yoder household was no excuse. If she had asked Mrs. Faulkner for help, the woman would have driven her to Sugarcreek for more material. Mrs. Faulkner might even have taken the trip at no charge, and she could have paid for the dress material. Weren't there matters in life more important than money? Things like your husband's opinion? She should have connected Mose's lecture to her on Sunday with this dress and done something about it. She still had much to learn about how to please the man and practice proper submission. An apology would be a start.

"I'm sorry about the dress," Miriam whispered.

Mose didn't look around. "So you knew

about it then."

There was no use to fudge. The truth was better. *"Yah,"* Miriam admitted. *"Mamm* saw it first, but Shirley was out of material, and we didn't . . ."

"You don't have to make excuses," Mose cut her off. "There are always ways to do the right thing if a person wants to. I would have paid for the material myself rather than see you in . . ." Mose dropped his gaze down toward Miriam's shoes for a moment ". . . that."

A deep blush spread over Miriam's face.

"I'm glad to see this thing shames you deeply," Mose said. He appeared pleased for the first time today.

Relief flooded Miriam. She could do the right thing after all. She could apologize. Silence fell between them as the cooks came out of Mrs. Faulkner's pole barn to see the wedding party arrive. Most of them wore aprons over their Sunday dresses and had huge smiles on their faces. Shirley gave everyone little waves of her hand as they walked past.

Glen went further and hollered out, "Thanks for all the hard work. I know we haven't eaten yet, so if I die from food poisoning I want to make sure you are properly thanked."

The cooks laughed heartily. One of them called back, "I've got a special mixture of hemlock stirred up for you."

Hilarity ensued, and even Mose joined in with a short laugh and said, "Spare me — that's all I ask."

That joke was a little self-centered, Miriam thought, but everyone chuckled.

"Thanks again," Glen concluded, and led the way toward the corner where the wedding party would be seated.

Shirley had decorated the *eck,* as the Amish called it, the corner laid out with fruit arrangements and a hand-drawn picture of a sunrise over the words, "Where you go, I will go. Your God shall be my God, and Your people shall be my people."

Mose read the words and grunted his approval. "That's a *gut* verse. That's the way the Lord has ordained things. *Yah!* We are meant to marry within the faith."

"I agree," Miriam said, but Mose didn't answer. Instead he stared at Shirley's fruit arrangements.

Noticing his gaze, Shirley asked, "Aren't they lovely?"

Mose hesitated. "They're okay, I guess. But worldliness often comes in through weddings first. So we cannot be too careful about the matter. Any display of the flesh is not pleasing to God."

Shirley appeared stunned by the rebuke, but Glen didn't seem bothered.

"Come on now, Mose," Glen said, "surely you have some *gut* thing to say for us."

Mose managed to smile. "I do give you both my blessing. You are my *gut* friend, Glen, and you have found a *frau* in the Lord. I pray you will bring up many *kinner* in the fear of God and teach them to walk in His ways. May your paths be always blessed. And you, Shirley, may you be clothed with the glory of the Lord, and may you always remember that you are first a woman of the most high God and seek to walk humbly in His ways."

Shirley turned all sorts of colors at the generous blessing, which neither she nor Glen had expected. Glen though, wasn't at a loss for words.

"Thank you, Mose," Glen said with a twinkle in his eye. "Or should say I 'Bishop'? Those were words I will always treasure. And thanks for being my best man."

"You're welcome," Mose responded. "I wouldn't have missed the opportunity unless I was home in bed deathly ill. And thanks to you for the high recommendation on this woman." Mose gave Miriam a quick glance. "Every word you uttered in her honor has been proved true and then some. She is blessed greatly by the Lord and will bring comfort and health to my old bones."

Now Miriam was blushing.

Glen laughed. "You're not that old, Mose. Come on. Today's my wedding day. Let us be merry."

"We must always walk in the fear of the Lord," Mose replied.

But he did smile, Miriam noticed. Glen had a *gut* effect on his friend, but then maybe Mose had a kind heart down inside all that gruffness. Wasn't that what she had told *Mamm* the other night? Now if she could only keep that truth in mind.

The wedding party quieted down as people began to pour into the barn. Most of them came past the corner table to congratulate Glen and Shirley and to give their marriage the traditional Amish blessing, "May you have a good beginning, a steadfast middle, and a blessed end."

Mose leaned toward Miriam to whisper. "I think our wedding date should be about this time next year. I like the weather for one thing, and the autumn breeze is still in the air."

"Whatever you want," Miriam whispered back. "I'll tell *Mamm* before I leave for Oklahoma, and she can begin to plan."

Mose appeared quite pleased. "Tell her not to make a large wedding. It wouldn't be appropriate for a . . ." Mose didn't finish. He meant to say bishop, Miriam was sure.

"We can plan the details once I'm back from schoolteaching," Miriam said.

Mose continued, as if Miriam hadn't said anything. "I don't want all of these decorations that your sister has placed up. We can't be too careful about the example we set for the community."

Miriam drew in a sharp breath and voiced her concern. "Mose, my family seems to miss your high standards by a wide margin. Are you sure I'm the *frau* for you?"

Mose didn't hesitate. "It's a settled matter, Miriam. The Lord wills our union, and you need to walk with me in the way of righteousness."

She might as well go for broke, Miriam figured, now that she had begun. "Shouldn't we be wed in the early summer? Once I'm back from Oklahoma?"

Surprisingly, Mose looked pleased. "I appreciate your eagerness, Miriam, but this must be done in the Lord, and *yah,* I do need a *frau* around the house, but I also never had any *kinner* with Rachel. So that gives me more flexibility. I have a chance to set an example for others. In our case we must not give way to the desires of the flesh. We must wait, and there will still be a whole life ahead of us . . . if the Lord wills it."

Miriam kept her head down, but still she protested. "I would feel better if I took up my duties as your *frau* once I returned from Oklahoma. People will wonder why we are waiting."

"They will understand." Mose didn't back down an inch. "And I won't be bringing you home every Sunday evening once you're back from Oklahoma. We've both dated before, and we're past that stage. Things will appear more appropriate if we don't hang around each other like love-struck teenagers."

Miriam didn't answer. What she thought apparently didn't matter. If Mose didn't want to act like a love-struck teenager, that was fine, but she didn't want to wait around all next year when there was a task in front of her just to impress people who wouldn't be impressed anyway. Widowers always married quickly. Did Mose expect to change that?

When Miriam didn't say anything, Mose added, "And I will not be visiting again in Oklahoma. Letter writing is the Lord's way of conducting a relationship under our circumstances. And it will be best if we are not around each other all the time." Mose gave Miriam a quick glance. "When are you going back to Oklahoma?"

"Tomorrow morning, early. Mrs. Faulkner is taking me to the bus station."

Mose nodded. "You'll be back then in time for schoolteaching on Monday."

"*Yah,* that's the plan." This was the first Mose had asked about her, but she wouldn't allow bitterness to fill her heart.

"Then we have today yet." Mose appeared pleased at that at least. "You are a woman of the Lord, Miriam," he said.

"Thank you," Miriam whispered. A cold chill tingled up her spine. She knew by now that Mose's kind words didn't lead anywhere. But she would have to learn patience. Maybe this was what the Lord wished to teach her by this experience. Her heart had much to learn — of that, she was certain.

CHAPTER TWENTY-FOUR

Miriam waved to Aunt Fannie and Mr. Whitehorse as she came down the steps of the Greyhound bus. The bus trip had been long and tiresome, but now that she was back in Oklahoma, it seemed as if no time had passed. Even Mose was a distant memory. The thought of her husband-to-be caused Miriam to wince, but she gathered her courage and put on a smile. Whatever was going on with Mose simply had to do with him adjusting to his new role as bishop. A change that sudden would be a shock for any man.

"Please move along, young lady," the bus driver urged, interrupting Miriam's thoughts. "I have your suitcase right here."

"I'm sorry," Miriam said, reaching for her suitcase. "And thank you."

The driver had already turned his attention to the next passenger awaiting her luggage.

Aunt Fannie hurried forward with open arms, and the two embraced for a long time. "You've come back to us," Aunt Fannie gushed. "It's so *gut* to see you again. It seems like forever."

Miriam laughed. "I've been gone for only two weeks."

"That's long enough," Aunt Fannie continued. "How was Shirley's wedding? I hope your *mamm* understood that we would have loved to be there, but . . ."

"Everyone understood," Miriam assured her. "Especially *Mamm.*"

"And what of you and Mose? When will he visit here again?" Aunt Fannie asked.

Miriam hesitated. "Mose won't be making the trip again to see me. It's so far . . ."

"Oh, no," Aunt Fannie said, patting Miriam's arm. "Well, look on the bright side, dear. Your qualifications are no doubt well settled in his mind."

Miriam tried to look grateful. The two women approached the car, and Miriam greeted Mr. Whitehorse. "It's nice of you to pick me up on a Sunday afternoon."

"You know I'd do it anytime," Mr. Whitehorse said with a grin. "You're the community's favorite teacher, but I also hear that wedding bells will be ringing for you."

Miriam blushed a little. "I see Aunt

274

Fannie has been keeping you up to date."

"It's about time I heard about your plans!" Mr. Whitehorse declared as he loaded Miriam's suitcase into the trunk. "I can remember when I first picked you and your sister up here several years ago. She's the one that just got married, right?"

"*Yah,* she's the one," Miriam said as she climbed into the car. Aunt Fannie waited until Mr. Whitehorse was in the driver's seat before she got in.

"I'm sure you heard that Mose was made bishop," Miriam whispered to Aunt Fannie as Mr. Whitehorse drove out of town. "And to think that I was able to be there and watch him choose the book with the lot in it."

Aunt Fannie's eyes grew large. "*Yah,* I heard. Miriam, that is so *wunderbah.*"

"Sorry to eavesdrop," Mr. Whitehorse interrupted. "But did you say bishop? Would this be the minister that was here a few weeks ago?"

"*Yah,* Mose Stoll. And he's a bishop now." Miriam said the words with care. Not for Mr. Whitehorse's sake, but for her own. She wanted the proper reverence to sink deep into her heart.

"Quite an honor, I suppose," Mr. Whitehorse muttered.

They drove on in silence until Aunt Fannie ventured, "Nothing much happened while you were gone — at least compared to what you must have experienced. A bishop's ordination, and for your promised one at that! And Shirley's wedding, of course. All we had to entertain ourselves with was Tyler Johnson's occasional visits. We had him over again last Friday night for supper. He's staying in Deacon Phillips's basement now and making himself quite at home in the community. It wouldn't surprise me if Tyler began to attend the Sunday morning meetings soon. Tyler told us how much he enjoyed that evening he drove you to the hymn singing."

Miriam jerked herself out of her reverie. That name. Tyler Johnson. She had almost allowed herself to forget.

Aunt Fannie hurried on. "Just think where this might be going, Miriam. We've not had a convert in some time, and Tyler's conversion would be quite an honor. Why, Mose might even be impressed. If I were you, I'd mention Tyler and all the latest developments in your next letter."

Tyler was the last thing she'd mention in her letters, Miriam decided. If she did mention Tyler, Mose would have more questions about the man than she wanted to explain.

Thankfully, Aunt Fannie finally seemed out of breath and settled back in her seat in silence.

In the distance, Clarita's water tower came into sight, and Mr. Whitehorse turned left on Highway 48. Moments later they pulled into the Bylers's driveway where Mr. Whitehorse popped the trunk, and Miriam dashed out to retrieve her suitcase. She paused at the car window to pay Mr. Whitehorse for the trip into Coalgate and added ten dollars for a tip.

"That's for the bother on a Sunday," she told him. "And tell your wife hello for me."

"I'll do that." He grinned. "She's with the grandbabies today, or she would have come along. And thanks." Mr. Whitehorse waved the cash in the air. "Always can use this stuff. Social Security isn't as secure as one would hope!"

Miriam waved him goodbye and set out for the house with Aunt Fannie a few steps in front of her. Jonathon met them on the front porch and flew into Miriam's arms for a long hug.

"Oh, what am I going to do when I don't see you anymore every day," Miriam cooed into his ear.

Jonathon giggled and retracted himself from her embrace to vanish around the corner of the house.

"Home again, home again, jiggity-jig," Uncle William sang out when Miriam walked in. "Just in time for popcorn making."

"Miriam will do nothing of the sort," Aunt Fannie scolded. "You get up and get Star ready for her so she can make a trip over to the schoolhouse. I know that's the first thing on her mind — not popcorn for you."

"I'll make him popcorn," Miriam offered.

Aunt Fannie stood her ground. "No sacrificing right now. I'll make the man popcorn, and mine's as good as yours. He only wants to be babied."

Uncle William laughed and disappeared out the front door.

"Now take your suitcase upstairs, and then you can go," Aunt Fannie said. "I'll have supper ready when you get back, and you can relax for the rest of the evening — because you're not going to the hymn singing after that long trip of yours."

"Thank you," Miriam whispered. "I do appreciate your understanding about the schoolhouse. I promise not to work — just think and plan for tomorrow."

Aunt Fannie pursed her lips. "*Yah,* but no guilt feelings now. Anyone would understand your wanting to visit the schoolhouse.

And you're a bishop's *frau*-to-be. Cheer up!"

Miriam felt her face color a little.

"Ah," Aunt Fannie cooed, giving Miriam a quick hug. "You're so modest about everything. Did the man kiss you?"

Miriam gasped. "Aunt Fannie!"

"*Yah,* I know." Aunt Fannie smiled sheepishly. "I'm a terrible one, but kissing a bishop . . . now that would be something!"

Miriam turned and fled upstairs, her suitcase bouncing behind her on the stairs. If Aunt Fannie knew the half! But how could it ever be told?

Miriam took a moment to look around. Aunt Fannie had obviously fluffed the quilt on the bed and dusted recently. Everything sparkled. In spite of Aunt Fannie's instructions, Miriam took the time to hang her dresses in the closet before she returned downstairs.

"All hitched up and ready to go," Uncle William sang out.

"Now remember, I'll have supper ready," Aunt Fannie promised.

"*Yah,* I'll be back soon." Miriam made a dash out the door before Aunt Fannie could make another remark about Mose's kisses.

Miriam drove Star out the Bylers's lane and toward the schoolhouse. Long before she arrived, Miriam searched for her first sight of the building. She loved her job and the community children she taught. Now that she planned to leave after this term was over, her heart was stirred even more deeply.

Miriam reached up to rub her eyes. Why was there an *Englisha* automobile parked in the schoolyard right where her buggy would go? She gasped. Tyler. There was no doubt about it — and on a Sunday afternoon at her schoolhouse! Miriam pulled back on Star's reins. She ought to turn the buggy around and flee back to Aunt Fannie's at once. But there was no suitable explanation she could offer to Aunt Fannie for her sudden reappearance. Instead Miriam set her chin and drove straight up to Tyler's car. This was her schoolhouse, after all. He had no right to intrude.

"Hi, Miriam," Tyler greeted, walking boldly over to greet her. He leaned against the buggy wheel as if he had every right to be there. "*Gut* to see you back."

"And you," she said, biting her lip. That was exactly the wrong thing to say. She pondered whether to even climb down or just turn the buggy around and leave.

Tyler turned his head sideways. "Your aunt told me you'd be back this afternoon, and she also mentioned you'd probably check in here, first thing. She knows you pretty well. And so do I." He looked quite pleased with himself.

"You have no business here," Miriam snapped. "I came over for a few minutes of peace and quiet. Aunt Fannie didn't tell you I'd be here so that you could disrupt my afternoon. And what if someone sees us?"

Tyler grinned. "We could go inside, I guess."

"We will do nothing of the sort," Miriam retorted. "You will leave right now."

"Fiery as ever," Tyler muttered. "Did the ogre get to see this side of you?"

"Mose is a bishop now." Miriam glared at him. "So watch your words."

"Oh, *my,* a bishop." Tyler raised his eyebrows. "Did the bishop get around to kissing you? Or is the bishop too holy?"

Miriam was speechless. The nerve of this man astonished her. He was as brash as Mose was bossy. Yet to her dismay, her heart was pounding so hard she could hardly breathe. Miriam tried to collect herself as Tyler's handsome face disappeared in front of her only to reappear on the other side of the buggy. Without permission Tyler climbed in beside Miriam and sat down. He gazed intently at her for a moment before he took Miriam's hands in both of his. Then he moved closer, slowly at first and then in a rush at the end. Miriam felt helpless, but also somehow strangely content to return his embrace. And then he gently placed his hands on her cheeks and kissed her softly. They clung to each other until Star twisted his head around to look at them.

Miriam gasped and pushed Tyler away. "Tyler! No! How could we? This isn't right!"

Tyler didn't bat an eye. "I think it's very right. Our flames burn well together."

"Oh!" Miriam moaned. "How could this happen? Tyler, you must leave and now!" She pushed on him with both hands until he leaped out of the buggy. "Go! Go!" she commanded. "Please, Lord, forgive me. I didn't mean what I just did."

"You do take this seriously," Tyler said regarding Miriam for a moment. "That was only a kiss. And, for your information, a very enjoyable kiss."

"If you don't leave right now, I will," Miriam ordered. She grabbed the reins, but Tyler held up both hands.

"Okay. I'm gone, but you've not seen the last of me. Remember that."

Miriam moaned again as Tyler drove out of the schoolhouse lane. He turned and waved, but she looked away at once. Oh, how had that happened? She had kissed another man. Mose would never understand this. She would have to tell him, and yet how could she? This would ruin everything. Everything! Oh, and the worst of it was that she had wanted to kiss Tyler. She had wanted to terribly!

Miriam sat in her buggy staring across the schoolyard. She had kissed Tyler. She, the community's faithful schoolteacher and a bishop's promised one, had kissed an *Englisha* man.

Miriam placed her head in both hands and sobbed as Star nibbled the grass near the hitching post.

CHAPTER TWENTY-FIVE

It was Thanksgiving Day, and Tyler had retired to his basement apartment at Deacon Phillips's house after a sumptuous feast. Now he opened the e-mail on his tablet and peered at the screen. Deacon Phillips's basement had no wireless connection, but Tyler had long ago signed up for Internet service for just such occasions.

A wry grin crossed Tyler's face. What would Deacon Phillips think if he knew that his tenant had all the trappings of the world right in his basement? Or that he had passionately kissed Miriam Yoder on Sunday afternoon at her schoolhouse. Either revelation might motivate Deacon Phillips to ask him to leave this comfortable basement den.

He had no doubt what his own motives had been on Sunday afternoon. He found Miriam fascinating and was drawn to her. He'd wanted to kiss her for a long time. That she had harbored equal feelings for him had only sweetened the temptation. And he had been correct. He'd expected all week that Deacon Phillips would accost him and demand an explanation. Though guilt had niggled at him, Tyler had pushed it away.

He doubted Miriam would confess her transgression, so he didn't fear a revelation from that angle. No, he was more concerned with the other buggy that had driven past the schoolhouse just after he'd climbed in next to Miriam. She hadn't noticed . . . but he had. She'd been too taken with his sudden action.

But so far no one had spoken up in accusation, so he simply took this as a warning to be more careful next time. Because there would be a next time. Of that he was sure. He should have gone to the Thursday evening youth gathering tonight, but Miriam wouldn't be there if he had judged her correctly. She'd expect him to show up and would stay away. But he'd see her eventually, and he'd hold her in his arms again. He'd always had a way with women, and apparently his charms extended even into this cloistered Amish community. After all, Amish women were human too. But that thought brought the guilt again. He had no right to exploit Miriam's innocence. He couldn't marry the girl unless she left the community. He knew that much. And Miriam wouldn't leave. Or would she? He'd have to find out.

Tyler focused on the e-mail in front of him. It was his pressing problem at present, and a whole lot less enjoyable than his pursuit of Miriam. This e-mail could prove even more explosive than flirting with an Amish bishop's engaged girlfriend. "Better think twice about what you're doing," Tyler read out loud. "You know what will happen to your softhearted pacifist friends if this keeps up. Maybe that's where the hurt should begin. Maybe a big kaboom would temper your stubbornness!"

Tyler stood to pace the basement floor. This wasn't the first threat. The warnings had increased though through the past week or so. His continued inquiries into corruption must have stirred up things. Who would have thought it? He might actually be onto something big out here in the middle of no-man's-land. Perhaps his ticket to fame as a journalist had indeed finally arrived.

Tyler laughed out loud. He had to keep his feet firmly planted on the ground. No more big dreams that ended only in disappointment. He might have stumbled onto nothing more than a local corruption scheme, which would barely make the local paper once uncovered. Put that way, the pursuit hardly seemed worth the effort. He probably would have dropped his search already, focused as he was on his attraction to the community's schoolteacher. But the two worked together. His search for corruption gave him a reason to stay in the community. Deacon Phillips and William Byler had spread the word among their brethren, but the cooperation came with limits. William had told him only yesterday, "Now you understand that the Amish won't testify in court under any circumstance, Tyler. I wish you'd drop this thing anyway. It's gone far enough. We don't want the police on our properties or the authorities asking our children questions."

But because his real focus had been on Miriam Yoder, Tyler had laughed off the suggestion and assured William. "They won't be asking you questions. I've done my research, and they'll come after me."

But he wasn't so sure now. He hadn't told William about the e-mails, and this one upped the ante. But he couldn't back down. No, not now.

"What exactly do you think is going on?" William had asked him.

Tyler had thought for a minute before he

answered. "At the risk of oversimplification . . ."

William stopped Tyler with a chuckle. "Try the full version on me. I might actually understand."

Tyler grinned. "Well, these smaller companies, such as the Olga Corporation, Westby Tabled, and Eastern Indian Market — of which there were a dozen or more, were used to supposedly funnel aid monies to people in need after the storm damage. So far I've only checked the Amish people. The companies listed the right names and addresses, but the monies or supplies never arrived. To cover their tracks, they had companies like Wymore Building & Supply and Howard Lumber supply the same people with the materials needed, so the work got done."

"Sort of like double billing," William muttered.

"That would be it," Tyler agreed. "The sums in each transaction are small when compared to the millions handled overall — amounts from ten to forty or fifty thousand dollars — but together they make a half a million dollars or so. And that could be the tip of the iceberg. What if this was done in other places, say the Chickasaw Reservation, which was also hard-hit? And then where did the money go? Because the smaller companies did dispense funds. Someone received thousands of hidden dollars. What if there is political corruption involved? There was a senatorial race on that year between Billet and Yentas. A battle close fought, and that money could have made a huge difference. And Yentas received a boost from some late fund-raising, if I remember right."

William laughed. "You have a wild imagination, Tyler. Thank the Lord we live a quiet and peaceful life away from all such things."

"You might have been more involved than you knew," Tyler said.

"Don't take us there," William warned. "Perhaps you should think yourself of a quiet and peaceful life — perhaps a life among us, Tyler."

Tyler joined William's laughter this time. "Now *you* have a big imagination."

William sobered. "The bishop thinks highly of you. Perhaps you should consider our way of life. The Lord might have His hand in this whole thing."

"I doubt if even the Lord could provide that sort of miracle," Tyler teased, but William had remained sober.

Well, that was that. He had no plans to back off his pursuit. Not even with threats like this. No good reporter retreated in the face of intimidation. Tyler tapped the "forward" e-mail icon and wrote, "Maybe this will persuade you that things are hot around here. We might be onto something big. Remember the Billet/Yentas contest that year? Dig deep. Will continue here as I can."

Tyler pressed "send." Now what? The logical next step was another meeting with Mr. Westree, the chairman of the Clarita Relief Fund.

Tyler tapped out a text message. "Need to meet again. New information found. Name the time and place."

Tyler sent the text seconds later and waited a few minutes. If Mr. Westree responded at once, that would give some indication of how concerned the man was. And that was exactly why Mr. Westree wouldn't respond tonight, and perhaps never.

Tyler gathered up his tablet and phone to slip out the back basement door to his car parked behind the barn. Deacon Phillips hadn't designated that spot, but Tyler's instincts told him the Amish would appreciate the consideration. Cars parked overnight in front of their barns didn't give the best appearance. Not for people who drove buggies, and especially not for deacons.

Tyler turned the car around, and as he drove by the farmhouse, he waved to one of Deacon Phillips's younger daughters, who was peeking out of the kitchen window. The oldest girl, Ruth, was at the youth gathering. She had offered him a ride earlier in her buggy, but he had declined. Ruth had a crush on him but hid it well at home. They both knew it would go nowhere. This was a young girl thing. Ruth would grow out of it in a few weeks . . . unlike Miriam. Miriam was another matter entirely.

Tyler turned left on Highway 48 and minutes later pulled into the Bylers' driveway. He hadn't planned to come here. A text from Mr. Westree would have sent him in another direction, but with no immediate response, he was being drawn to Miriam again. What he'd say if he saw her tonight, Tyler had no idea. Perhaps he could find some pretense to be alone with her.

Tyler parked beside the greenhouse and approached the Bylers's front door. Fannie opened it before he arrived and greeted him. "Howdy, stranger. You're a little late for supper."

Tyler forced a laugh. "I guess I do hang around here a lot. Is your husband home?"

"*Yah,* he's relaxing in the living room." Fannie held open the front door. "Come in and make yourself at home."

Tyler stepped inside and greeted William. "Sorry to bother you when you're not working."

William grinned. "I'm thinking you have mischief up your sleeve with that look on your face."

Tyler chuckled. "Maybe I do."

"So what can I do for you?" William asked.

Inspiration struck Tyler. "Is Miriam at the youth gathering? I've been working and haven't driven over there yet. I thought I might give her a ride if she hasn't left."

"Miriam is upstairs working on her school work," Fannie offered.

"She's still not caught up from her trip?" William didn't appear pleased. "The girl works too hard."

Fannie shrugged. "You know how dedicated Miriam is."

"She probably needs a break," Tyler offered. "Shall we ask her?"

Fannie's face lit up. "That's kind of you. Miriam does need to get her nose out of her work. She'll have plenty to do as the bishop's *frau* once they marry, but Miriam ought to enjoy her youth while she still has time."

"I agree!" William said. "Why don't you go insist she take a break?"

Tyler held his breath as Fannie hurried up the stairs. He half expected an outraged yell to tumble Fannie back down again, but the Amish didn't seem to have inappropriate outbursts.

Tyler stood to his feet as Fannie appeared with Miriam behind her, looking not at him but at the floor. Without saying a word, she headed straight for the front door.

"What's up with her?" Fannie whispered.

"Maybe a bad letter from the bishop?" William laughed.

"Well, see you all later," Tyler said as he hurried after Miriam, catching up with her on the front lawn.

She turned on him with anger written on her face. "Of all the sneaky, low-down tricks in the book. How dare you? Do you know the danger this puts me in?"

Tyler grinned. "I'm just driving you to the youth gathering, and I'll bring you right home again. What danger is there in that?"

Miriam sputtered something Tyler couldn't understand and climbed into the car. Guilt niggled at him, but Tyler pushed the emotion aside. He cared for this woman, but he would make no untoward advance on her tonight. He promised himself that.

Chapter Twenty-Six

Mose opened the mailbox as the cool evening breeze moved through his thick hair. His ruffled beard fell flat again when Mose turned his face into the wind. He took a moment to catch his breath before he examined the letters in his hand. Most of them were bills, and he ignored them. The Oklahoma return address caught his eye at once. The address was handwritten in a female style.

Miriam has written, Mose told himself, a grin spreading across his face. *If I had known this, I would have fetched the mail at lunchtime.* Then taking a second look at the envelope, Mose's face clouded. He looked closely at the handwriting again. Was he mistaken in thinking it didn't look like Miriam's handwriting? But he had seen it only seldomly, so likely it was indeed from Miriam.

Mose turned back to the house. Once

inside, he looked around with a shiver. The house looked lonely and unkempt. The place needed a *frau*'s touch. His supper sat on the kitchen table, warmed-over meat loaf he had brought home from his family's Thanksgiving gathering. He would eat the last of it tonight. Tomorrow he would have to make his own meals once more.

Mose glanced again at the female handwriting. "This has to be from Miriam," he said out loud. "Who else would write me from Oklahoma?"

The memories of Miriam's stay a week ago flooded his mind. He saw Miriam's gentle smile, her quick acquiescence to his every demand, and her soft touch on his arm, which he never fully accepted. He should have kissed the girl, Mose told himself. But his duty to the community and his high standards came first.

Mose sighed. Next fall seemed an awful long time to wait before Miriam's sweet presence came to live at his house. He should have taken Miriam up on her offer of an early wedding. The woman drew on his heart . . . but he knew if he didn't establish his authority before the wedding, it would only become harder afterward. Once they'd said their wedding vows, he could go soft and kind with Miriam. At least to some degree. A woman still had to learn obedience. This he had never forgotten with Rachel, and neither must he forget with his second *frau.*

Mose sat at the kitchen table under the gas lantern. He opened the envelope and slid out the single page. The handwriting was not Miriam's. He knew for sure now. He read the words.

Dear Mose Stoll,

I have something I should tell which concerns Miriam Yoder. I know that you were here awhile back and have fully researched Miriam's past. I don't wish to malign your efforts, but there is something you should know. Maybe this matter has only come up recently, but I doubt it. Such a grievous breach of character as I observed could only happen if the flaw has been there for a very long time. But let me tell you what I saw, and you can judge for yourself.

I was out with my husband last Sunday afternoon for a family visit that took us past the community's schoolhouse. As we approached my husband motioned with his head and said, "Isn't that Miriam's horse and buggy in the school-yard, along with that *Englisha* man's car, who's been hanging around the community?"

"That's impossible," I told him. "Miriam's at her sister's wedding and the bishop's ordination."

"But it *is* Miriam," my husband insisted. "As plain as day."

"Well, she must have come back early," I finally said.

I looked through our open buggy door as we passed, and what did I see but this Mr. Johnson kissing Miriam inside her parked buggy. I gasped so loud my husband jerked on our horse's reins and we nearly ran off the road.

"He's kissing her!" I told him.

My husband appeared irritated and laughed at me. "Now you're seeing things," he said. "Tyler has Bishop Mullet's and Deacon Phillips's approval, and you know what Miriam's character is like."

I was quiet and said no more. He is after all my husband, and yet I know what I saw. Please forgive my boldness, Mr. Stoll, but I had to let you know. I wish someone else would tell you, but I am the one who saw what I did. I could go to Deacon Phillips with this report, but it wouldn't be right to contradict my husband to his face in our home community. So I think this is best handled by your knowledge and judgment. For that reason I have written this letter and to clear my conscience of the matter.

Signed,
Your friend

Mose stood to pace the floor and glare at the white page. Could there be some mistake? But how? The woman was certain, and men didn't always notice such things even when they happened right under their noses, especially when the incident involved a woman with an excellent reputation like Miriam's. So what had gone wrong? How could he have missed this? But this was unthinkable! He ought to write Miriam at once and inquire into this matter. Perhaps there was some explanation. But what reason could be given for Miriam kissing an *Englisha* man? Apparently here was Miriam's weakness, and he had completely missed it. Thankfully the problem had surfaced now and not after they were married. He'd take steps to deal with this at once.

Mose groaned as the shame rushed over him. He'd never live this down. He simply couldn't have been this wrong in his judgment of Miriam. Nothing in her character pointed to this conclusion. She was too committed to the community, both in Oklahoma and in Possum Valley, and to the faith. That was part of what had drawn him to Miriam, and yet he had been wrong. At least he had held his ground and not given in to an early wedding. Now what must be done? Must he make another trip to Oklahoma? He had told Miriam he wouldn't, but this changed everything. He had no choice in the matter. He must go.

Thoughts raced through Mose's mind. Sunday was his first church service as the community's new bishop. He would be in charge. He had to be there. Only a funeral would serve as an excuse. If the community learned that their new bishop had raced out to Oklahoma to bring his promised *frau* under control, he'd be the laughingstock of Wayne County. Minister Kemp would nod his head and say that he had offered his sister Bethany as the proper choice but had been disregarded. Minister Kemp would further say that while the Lord's wisdom could always be trusted in the lot, this outcome required a great deal of submission on his part. And there were some who would agree.

His rule as bishop would be off to a rocky

start and might never recover. No, this must be kept under wraps. Still, someone had to be told. That was the first order of business. If the community here learned later that he had kept the matter secret on a subject that concerned him so intimately, his reputation would be damaged even further.

Mose grabbed up the letter, retrieved his hat and coat from the closet, and paused in the kitchen to turn off the gas lantern. He took a quick glance at the cold meat loaf, and his hunger stirred. He hadn't eaten since lunch, but he must not keep Deacon Yoder up late on this his first official call as the community's bishop. Who would have thought he would arrive with such news — a devastating accusation made against the woman he planned to marry.

Mose crossed the lawn in the falling dusk and rushed into the barn, where he harnessed his horse by the light that still crept in the barn window. He led the horse out by the bridle and had him on the road moments later. Tonight the steady beat of hooves on the pavement did nothing to steady his nerves. They sounded like the drumbeats of doom. Was his plan to take Miriam as his *frau* at risk? Deacon Yoder might advise that. Minister Kemp had already suggested that angle, and that was before this revelation. As a young bishop he would be expected to take advice easily. But could he stand the loss of Miriam? Could he abandon his hopes to see her in his house next year? Miriam's every act of submission had raised his opinion of her even higher. What more could he ask in a prospective *frau*? He simply couldn't lose her, even if he now knew Miriam had flaws.

Mose slowed the buggy as light from Deacon Yoder's house came into view. He pulled into the driveway and tied his horse at the hitching post. The front door opened in front of him, and Deacon Yoder's figure appeared on the porch.

"*Gut* evening," Deacon Yoder called across the lawn.

"*Gut* evening," Mose replied once he was closer. "I hope I'm not catching you at a bad time."

Deacon Yoder lowered his voice. "Church trouble already? I had hoped matters would stay calm for a while, but with a new bishop I suppose things will stir themselves up."

Mose swallowed hard. Surely Deacon Yoder didn't blame him for fomenting church problems? He wouldn't take offense anyway.

"This is a personal matter, I'm afraid," Mose responded. "Is it okay if we sit on the porch swing?"

"Personal?" Deacon Yoder appeared puzzled. "I'm afraid I don't understand."

"Read this," Mose told him. "I am shamed greatly, but I will not keep the matter hidden."

Deacon Yoder raised his eyebrows but took the letter. He read in silence.

"So?" Mose asked when the deacon finished. "What should I do?"

Deacon Yoder pondered the question for a while. "It must of course be dealt with, though I must say that unmarried women can kiss whom they wish, just not *Englisha* men. But it happens, you know, even to those who are promised, which I assume Miriam is?" Deacon Yoder gave Mose a quick glance.

"Yah." Mose settled back in the swing. "We have spoken of our wedding date."

"Which must now be put off, I would think, until this matter is resolved."

"The wedding is not until the next wedding season," Mose said. "I think there is plenty of time to work this out."

Deacon Yoder appeared puzzled. "But you do love the woman, and yet your wedding is not until the next season? You are a widower, after all, Mose, and a bishop now. You need a *frau* at your house."

"I thought we should set an example of

restraint." Mose bit off the words. He didn't like questions like this. Couldn't the deacon see the wisdom in his choice?

"Most men marry quickly after their first *frau* passes. You have already waited a decent amount of time."

"I am not most men," Mose snapped. "And I am not the problem here. Miriam is. Focus on that."

Deacon Yoder raised his eyebrows but soon spoke again, "You could cut off the relationship, I suppose. That's what most men would do, especially in your shoes as the new bishop. It's not going to look *gut.*"

"I want the woman!" Mose glared off into the darkness. "And I know Miriam's heart. She would not leave me for an *Englisha* man. Her character is too far above reproach."

"That's what you told us. And yet she is kissing an *Englisha* man." Deacon Yoder let the accusation hang in the air.

"Speak no more on that point." Mose raised his voice. "I know what the letter said. Tell me what we can do."

"Okay." Deacon Yoder paused. "Let's see. First, Miriam has not sinned exactly, but enough perhaps for a church confession. This should be given in Oklahoma, since that is where this happened and where Miriam lives. Second, I think you should be in attendance to receive the confession. It would look better that way. But I'd say you have some work in front of you. You could write ahead. Perhaps begin this conversation by asking Miriam for an explanation. You will wish to woo her back, I assume. She's not your *frau* yet. Remember that."

Mose got to his feet. "You speak words of wisdom, and I thank you. I'm sure you will support whatever action I take."

Deacon Yoder held out the letter. "She's your promised one, and you will have to live with her after you've said the vows. So do what you must."

Mose grabbed the letter and stuffed it back into the envelope. "Thank you again for your counsel."

A slight smile played on Deacon Yoder's face. "I'm sorry this had to happen to you, Mose, but we all have our trials given to us by the Lord. Looks like yours has arrived early in your second quest for a *frau*. May you find the grace to bear the burden."

"I'm sure I will," Mose said as he beat a hasty retreat. Already he was being laughed at, although he was sure the deacon meant no unkindness. The matter would remain a secret with Deacon Yoder for the time being. The man was known for his tight lips on church matters. But he knew how rumors could circulate. The unknown woman in Oklahoma who had seen Miriam kissing the *Englisha* man would soon let something slip, and then the news would be out. He would have to make the trip to Oklahoma soon. In the meantime he wouldn't write Miriam any more letters. Her guilt would grow with his silence, and she'd be even more ready to repent once he arrived with his strong rebuke. Mose untied his horse and climbed in his buggy to drive quickly out of the lane.

Chapter Twenty-Seven

Miriam awoke with a start and sat up in bed. What was that noise? It sounded like heavy shoes running through the hallway, followed by a shout from outside that she couldn't understand. The voice was clearly Uncle William's. Some emergency must have occurred, but why would her uncle race outside in the middle of the night?

Miriam reached for the ticking alarm clock but stopped when her glance passed to the bedroom window. A soft flicker of red blinked on the drapes. Something outside was burning. But what? With a cry Miriam threw the covers aside and pulled on her heavy housecoat. The red light from the window was clearly increasing in its intensity. From below, the stair door opened with a bang, as if it had been thrown against the wall with great force.

Aunt Fannie's urgent call filled the stairwell. "Miriam! Fire!"

Miriam opened her bedroom door and stuck her head out to answer, "I'm coming!"

Miriam grabbed a scarf from the top dresser drawer and tied it around her loose hair. This was an emergency, and the scarf would have to do for a *kapp.* She didn't have time to put up her hair. Outside in the hallway Miriam took the stairs with care. Whatever the need was outside, she wouldn't gain anything if she broke her leg on the way down. On second thought she should have taken the time to light the kerosene lamp. But it was too late now. Miriam felt her way with her hands and moved faster when the flicker of red light from the fire reached through the living room window. With a rush Miriam entered the living room where Aunt Fannie stood by the window with a quilt draped over her shoulders, her head bare. Wild light rose and fell on the house walls. Miriam hurried to her aunt's side, and Aunt Fannie reached for Miriam with one arm. One look outside was all Miriam needed. The barn was on fire, and not just one corner. The whole length of the building was engulfed in flames that reached ever higher skyward.

"Has someone called the fire department?" Miriam asked. Of course they had, but what else was there to say?

"I'm sure William ran down to the phone shack," Aunt Fannie answered. "Not that it will do much good. The whole barn is gone, but at least the horses are out to pasture this time of the year. Oh, Miriam, what have we done to provoke the Lord's wrath?"

"You haven't done anything," Miriam said at once. "These things happen."

But deep down guilt filled her heart. If anyone was at fault, it was her. Had her unconfessed sin with Tyler brought the judgment of God upon her innocent relatives? But surely a stolen kiss in a moment of weakness didn't deserve this. Miriam pulled her silent aunt close to whisper, "You should get dressed. There will be plenty of people here soon. And there's nothing we can do outside."

Aunt Fannie shook her head and moved toward the front door. "Come. We will stand with William if nothing else. The people will understand."

Miriam followed her aunt outside. The faint form of her uncle came down the lane from Highway 48 with slow steps. Uncle William shielded his face with his hands and stayed on the far side near the wire fence. Aunt Fannie met him near the house. With a loud cry she wrapped her arms around him. The quilt slipped to the ground and Aunt Fannie's nightgown fluttered in the light breeze. Her long waist-length hair was colored with strange light from the flames that leaped into the sky.

"It'll be okay," Miriam heard Uncle William say. He bent sideways and picked the quilt up to place it back over his *frau*'s shoulders. The two stood together, their faces turned toward the burning building.

Miriam gave a silent cry of her own and dashed back to the front porch. She couldn't stand her aunt and uncle's pain, and they needed this moment alone to grieve. Maybe she could comfort Jonathon if he awakened, but she hoped he wouldn't. This was a horror a young child should be spared. She wanted comforting arms around her own shoulders right now. She wanted to bury her head in a man's chest and weep, but there was no one. Aloneness crept over her. Then a dizzying awareness struck her. It was Tyler she wanted beside her right now. Mose seemed like the fire itself — fierce, intense, and destructive. But that was the kind of sinful thinking that perhaps caused God to send this tragedy on them. *Yah,* it had to be. What was her future to be with a man like Mose? Yet she knew she could never choose Tyler's wildness, his mystery, his handsome face over all that was decent, upright, and just among her people. She couldn't jump the fence into the *Englisha* world.

"Nay, I cannot," Miriam silently screamed toward the heavens.

The crackle of the flames answered her, as if to mock the will of her heart to overcome. How could this weakness be in her? She had kissed Tyler. There was no sense in denying the truth. And worse, she had enjoyed the moment. Only the intensity of her own emotions had brought a shock of reality, and she had come to her senses with an explosion of anger. But Tyler saw through all that. She was sure he did. Why else would he have dared show up and finagle a trip to the youth gathering in his car? Her anger when Tyler picked her up had served only to raise Aunt Fannie's eyebrows. Thankfully her aunt had written off the indiscretion to her tiredness as she had stomped out of the house right in front of them all.

Little good that had done. On the way home Tyler had stopped his car short of her uncle and aunt's driveway, and they had kissed again. Tyler had been the one who stopped their kiss and had started the car to drive on again. And now the world was on fire. She was too weary to wonder anymore. She wanted only to sleep and sleep until somehow this all went away. How could it be that she, Miriam Yoder, *baptized* Miriam Yoder, faithful-to-a-fault Miriam Yoder, was in love with an *Englisha* man, and she could do nothing about it? No wonder Uncle William's barn was in flames. She was somehow to blame for this. The tears trickled down Miriam's cheeks as she gazed into the fiery light.

The wail of sirens and bright lights in the distance interrupted Miriam's thoughts. She wiped her eyes and glanced into the house. Jonathon would awaken now, if he hadn't already. With all the noise there was no way to hide this tragedy from his eyes. Perhaps it was better if Jonathon got to see his *daett*'s barn burn rather than rise from bed in the morning to see only black, ugly ashes on the ground.

Miriam slipped into the house and pushed open Jonathon's bedroom door to approach his bed.

"Jonathon," she called, gently shaking him. "Wake up."

He groaned and opened his eyes, but alarm soon filled them.

She should have thought of a less dramatic way of waking him, but it was too late now.

"You need to come with me," she ordered.

The wail of sirens was louder now, and Jonathon ran to his bedroom window to look outside. Miriam followed to drape her arms over his thin, bare shoulders.

"It's a fire," he said. "The barn."

"*Yah,* come."

"Is it the middle of the night?" Jonathon asked, looking up at her.

"*Yah,* but you must come."

"Why is the barn burning?" Jonathon asked as he returned to his bedside to pull on his small pants.

Miriam helped him with his shirt but didn't answer. Words seemed too heavy to utter right now, and what was the answer?

"Why?" Jonathon insisted. "Why would the barn burn?"

"Just come." Miriam took his hand. "I wish you didn't have to see this, but perhaps it is for the best."

He asked no more questions but followed Miriam. In the living room, Jonathon went to stare out of the window with wide eyes. After a moment, Miriam took him by the hand to lead him outside. Aunt Fannie noticed them and came at a fast run. She scooped up Jonathon with both hands, and sat with him on the porch step. With slow strokes she ran her hand through his hair and whispered murmuring sounds. Aunt Fannie needed her own comfort, Miriam decided, so she sat on the other side of the pair and draped her arm around Aunt Fannie's shoulders.

"Oh, dear Lord," Aunt Fannie prayed out loud, "have mercy upon us. Forgive us our sins. Remember not our trespasses that we have done . . ."

Miriam covered her face with her free hand and tried to join in her aunt's prayer, but the words froze on her lips. Hot waves from the fire blew their way, and Jonathon snuggled deeper into his *mamm*'s arms. None of them moved as the firemen set up their trucks and the first blast of water lifted skyward.

It was all too little, too late, Miriam told herself. The firemen seemed to know this and concentrated their efforts on the side toward the house. The greenhouse roof received a share of the attention. The men sprayed a sheet of water on the wall and roof facing the barn. The metal steamed in the fire's light and added to the surreal feeling that hung over the place.

Aunt Fannie had ceased her prayer, her gaze fixed on the activities around them. Miriam saw numerous headlights appear on the highway, and then slow down as people parked along the road. Aunt Fannie still had the quilt wrapped over her shoulders with Jonathon under it now. Tyler should be here, Miriam told herself. It was a horrible thing to think, but she couldn't help herself.

"We should fix something to eat," Aunt Fannie muttered as she rose to her feet. "And we should both get dressed properly. Jonathon, don't get off the porch," Aunt Fannie ordered before she turned to go.

Miriam followed her aunt inside.

"We'll fix something after we've changed." Aunt Fannie motioned toward the bedroom. "I'll be right back."

Miriam took a kerosene lamp and hurried upstairs. When she had changed, Miriam returned to the kitchen. By the feeble light of the lamp, she searched the cupboard and placed what she found on the table. There were several pies, a plate of brownies, and cookies — that should be enough.

"We should make coffee," Aunt Fannie said as she reappeared fully dressed. "There are a lot of firemen out there. They should have something."

"I can make both pots in here," Miriam offered, running the logistics through her mind. "We can serve off the front porch unless you want to bring up the small table from the basement."

"The front porch is fine." Aunt Fannie seemed distracted and returned to the living room window for a moment.

"Just go back outside," Miriam told her aunt when she returned. "Take what you can carry, and I'll bring the rest."

Aunt Fannie gave Miriam a quick hug and exclaimed, "What would I do without you tonight? William's heart will be broken to pieces. We have no extra money laid up to rebuild that I know of, and how can people give again when . . ." Aunt Fannie didn't finish her sentence. "Sorry, Miriam. I shouldn't have such a breakdown. I know that somehow the Lord will provide."

Miriam wanted to say something, but the words wouldn't come. Her guilt was like a cold stone that froze her emotions. Aunt Fannie picked up what she could carry and left. Miriam waited until the water was boiling and then strained the coffee. She left more water to heat while she took the first two pots outside. A few firemen had already gathered near the porch steps and took the cups of coffee eagerly from her hands as she poured them.

"Thank you," the first one told her.

Another also thanked her and then said something to the other fireman that caused Miriam's heart to jump.

"I wonder if they're getting this kind of service at the other fire?"

"That's an Amish homestead too, isn't it?" the second fireman replied.

"Yep, that's what I heard."

"Isn't that strange? Two Amish barn fires the same night."

"Arson, I would say, but the big boys will have to confirm that."

Miriam clutched Aunt Fannie's arm. "What is it they're saying?" Miriam whispered.

Aunt Fannie turned her face, and Miriam saw her aunt's tear-streaked cheeks. "*Yah,* William told me," her aunt choked. "It's Deacon Phillips's barn. The Lord must have stirred His wrath greatly toward us as a community."

A sob escaped Miriam's lips, and the cup of coffee she was holding crashed to the concrete porch floor. Tyler was staying with Deacon Phillips. And here was where she lived. Two fires. *Yah,* this was surely the Lord's judgment. Like with Elijah of old, the fire had fallen from heaven.

CHAPTER TWENTY-EIGHT

The middle of the following week Miriam pulled the buggy into the Bylers' lane, and Star lifted his head to whinny as they approached the remnants of the burned-out barn.

"Take it easy," Miriam called calmly to him. "It's okay."

Crews of local Amish men had gathered last Saturday to help with the cleanup, but the police had stretched crime-scene tape between the trees encircling the ashes. No one had been allowed in or out. Police cars had been parked in the Bylers' driveway until late Saturday night. Only after Uncle William had begged them to leave until Monday morning had they left so that the family could spend Sunday in peace. The officer in charge hadn't appeared happy about the decision.

"We have our duty to perform, Mr. Byler. Surely you understand that," the officer had snapped. "And our job is to protect all our citizens — including you Amish."

"The Lord gives us protection," Uncle William had said. "We will trust Him."

"Doesn't look like you made out too well here," the officer said, waving his arm toward the burned building.

Uncle William hung his head. "We believe we should submit to the Lord's will, whatever it is."

The officer had grunted but said no more. Great shame had fallen over the community with the intrusion of the police. Deacon Phillips had fared no better when clear signs of arson were found behind his barn. Someone had set both fires on purpose.

Tyler hadn't shown his face on Sunday at the service or the hymn singing. Miriam's heart ached. What was the cause of this tragedy? Were Tyler and she to blame? Was Tyler asking the same questions as she was? But how could he? Tyler wasn't from the community and never would be. Her heart was the one that had clearly betrayed her. And to make matters worse, she learned on Monday morning from one of the schoolchildren that Tyler had moved out of Deacon Phillips's basement the day after the fires. Had Tyler left for his own reasons after he had taken such liberties with her, or had

Deacon Phillips asked Tyler to leave and kept the matter a secret from everyone for a few days? Either option sent stabs of pain through her.

Perhaps tonight those questions would be answered as this morning Uncle William had announced, "Tyler wants a meeting with Deacon Phillips and me here at our place tonight."

Aunt Fannie had brightened a little and responded, "So we will be seeing him again. I have the women's sewing this afternoon, but I'll be home in plenty of time to get ready."

Miriam was as anxious for answers as everyone else. But was Tyler about to expose their relationship tonight? Why would he? Did Tyler hope to get her to leave with him now that he planned to leave the community? Surely not. She would just have to wait and see. With the meeting held at her aunt and uncle's house, she would at least learn something. Aunt Fannie would tell her both the *gut* and the bad.

"Mostly bad," Miriam told herself as she parked by the greenhouse and climbed out of the buggy. Her mind spun as she wondered why it seemed the Lord's face had turned from her. She had trusted Him to heal her heart of its wrong desires, but it had seemed only to fall even lower. She had kissed Tyler, not once but twice. Hot streaks of shame ran along Miriam's face.

Miriam forced herself to unhitch Star and lead him into the temporary shelter the men had erected behind the greenhouse. She left him there in the makeshift stall where he began to munch happily on the strands of hay still left in the manger. Miriam retreated again. A wisp of a breeze stirred the ash pile in the barn foundation and made the fallen timbers creak against each other. The sound was soft and muted, unlike the noise healthy wood made when moved by the wind. But everything was troubled right now. The burned-out barn was really the least of her worries.

Even Aunt Fannie, whose faith rarely wavered, was disturbed. Her aunt made little exclamations to herself while she worked in the house. "Why, Lord? What have we done? Protect us, please." Or the oft repeated, "Let not our will be done, but Yours, Lord."

Miriam pulled her gaze away from the burned hull of the barn to enter the house. Jonathon came at a run and flew into her arms. She held him for a long time. He had rebounded well from his trauma last week and would have played in the soot if his *mamm* had let him. No red tape stopped Jonathon like his *mamm*'s commands. Miriam had yet to see him venture anywhere near the ashes.

Miriam set Jonathon on the floor when Aunt Fannie bustled out of the bedroom in a clean dress and apron, announcing, "The meeting with Tyler is right after supper. I figured I wouldn't have time to change later."

Miriam nodded. "I'll stay out of sight. It's not like I'm involved."

"*Yah,* but you can listen in from the kitchen while you wash dishes," Aunt Fannie said. "It's got to be something serious after what we've been through the past few days."

"Did you learn any news at the sewing today?" Miriam asked, changing the subject.

"No, but I think maybe I've come to accept the Lord's will better. The women spoke words of encouragement I needed to hear. They also said that Tyler had left Deacon Phillips's place because he feels that he's to blame somehow. Did you know that?"

Miriam hid her face before she answered. "I learned that Tyler had left from the schoolchildren on Monday morning."

"And you didn't tell me," Aunt Fannie scolded. "You know how much Tyler means

321

to me. He's such a comforting presence in the community. I always felt he was a sign of the Lord's good pleasure on us, but now he's moved out of Deacon Phillips's basement. Maybe that's what Tyler wishes to speak of tonight. How he can come back."

Miriam looked away. What if her aunt found out all that had gone on? The thought was almost too terrible to contemplate. Her aunt's faith would be shattered in both Tyler and herself.

The two women entered the kitchen to work in silence on the supper preparation. Aunt Fannie had kept the menu simple — broccoli soup and toasted cheese sandwiches. Jonathon stuck his head in at regular intervals to peer about hungrily.

"It'll be ready before long," Aunt Fannie finally assured him. "Just run and play, but stay away from you know what."

Jonathon vanished again and didn't return until Uncle William's footsteps came in with his. The two seated themselves at their regular places.

Uncle William looked up with a smile on his face. "At least we still have the greenhouse and a temporary shelter so our animals have a place to live."

"*Yah,* we have much to be thankful for," Aunt Fannie answered his smile. "And we have each other. How are things going over at Deacon Phillips's place? I assume that's where you came from this afternoon."

"About the same," Uncle William said. "He can't clean up yet either. But I was talking to him about the meeting tonight. Tyler's acting awful strange — that's all I can say. We both wonder if this had anything to do with all those questions Tyler kept asking of us." Uncle William hung his head for a moment. "If it does, I'm ashamed I helped Tyler answer them."

"But how could that be?" Disbelief showed in Aunt Fannie's face.

Uncle William didn't look up. "I had best keep silent until I know what I speak of, but I may have sinned greatly in what has come upon us."

"You? Sinned?" Aunt Fannie couldn't have appeared more surprised.

"Our faith has strong guidance on these matters." Uncle William fell silent for a moment. "But let us pray so we can eat."

They bowed their heads in silent prayer. When he had finished, Uncle William dished soup into Jonathon's bowl and then filled his own. After the first bite, he continued, "From how the law enforcement people are acting, both of us think there is a connection."

Miriam's head spun. Uncle William thought this was about something else entirely. But what? Now she would have to listen by the kitchen doorway for sure.

"There's also other news in the midst of our troubles," Uncle William said with a smile. "Deacon Phillips said Mose is coming this weekend again. On Saturday."

Cold chills ran up and down Miriam's back.

"Bishop Mose!" Aunt Fannie exclaimed.

Uncle William had a twinkle in his eye. "That's what I've heard. So I guess he'll come preach for us. Did you know anything about this, Miriam?"

She had to say something. But what?

"Did you know this, Miriam?" Aunt Fannie asked.

"No." Miriam kept her head bowed over her empty bowl. "Mose hasn't written since I've been back from Shirley's wedding."

Aunt Fannie stared at the wall. "That's true, now that I think about it, and that's been a while. There has been plenty of time for a letter to arrive. Didn't you send him one?"

"I was waiting for him to write," Miriam replied. This was partially true, but guilt over her kiss with Tyler on her first Sunday back completed the story. "Wise woman,"

Uncle William chuckled. "The strategy must have worked. The man's on his way out here."

Aunt Fannie was worried, though. Miriam could tell.

"There's no use writing him now," Miriam tried to tease, but from the look on Aunt Fannie's face, she had only made things worse.

"There may be much repentance necessary before this is over," Uncle William muttered.

Miriam glanced up sharply. Was Uncle William speaking of her?

"Aren't you going to eat anything?" Aunt Fannie asked with a glance at Miriam's still-empty bowl.

"I'm not that hungry," Miriam managed, but she ladled out a small dipper of broccoli soup and added a few crackers. Jonathon grinned at her as she ate, and Miriam tried to smile back. The effort hurt, but Jonathon didn't seem to notice. Thankfully, Aunt Fannie seemed taken up with Uncle William at the moment.

Once the silent prayer of thanksgiving was offered to end the meal, Jonathon was up like a shot.

"Poor boy," Aunt Fannie muttered as he disappeared out the washroom door. "I imagine the barn animals are more cheerful than this house right now."

Uncle William gave his *frau* an awkward pat on the arm. "The Lord will see us through this dark valley. That's His promise."

Miriam caught a glimpse of a car pulling into the driveway, followed by Deacon Phillips's buggy.

Aunt Fannie also noticed. She stood up and walked to the kitchen doorway. "Looks like everyone timed it just right."

Uncle William had a weary look on his face. "May the Lord help us — that's all I can say."

"Amen," Aunt Fannie echoed.

Miriam ducked out of sight as an officer climbed out of the car with Tyler. Aunt Fannie noticed the same thing and gasped.

"Maybe he's here to investigate some more," Miriam suggested.

"Well, he's coming in, so we'll know pretty soon," Aunt Fannie said.

What a valley of sorrows, Miriam thought. And to top it off, Mose would come this weekend. She would have to confess her sin to him, and it would not be easy. Mose might call off the engagement. Not that he had asked her to marry him to begin with, but all the same, their plans could come to an early end — and just as well. Miriam deserved all of this and more. Likely the shame of this transgression would follow her for the rest of her days, and she'd never live the report down once Mose spilled her secret.

"We'll make it through this," Aunt Fannie said in Miriam's ear. "Even with an *Englisha* officer in the house. Take courage, Miriam. You're white as a sheet."

"What do you think he wants?" Miriam whispered. Tyler had obviously brought him. The same Tyler she had kissed. The Tyler that was from another world so foreign it boggled her mind. How could she have opened her heart to this man? Miriam grasped the back of a chair with both hands and sat down. The whole kitchen spun in circles around her, but she managed somehow not to faint.

Chapter Twenty-Nine

The late Saturday sunlight filtered in through the drapes on Miriam's bedroom window. She shouldn't hide out here, Miriam told herself, but she had to catch her breath for a moment. Mose had been due to arrive this morning at Deacon Phillips's place, and she had waited all day for his buggy wheels to roll into the driveway. But he hadn't come. Maybe the Greyhound bus had been late into Coalgate, but that was doubtful. Miriam still didn't know why Mose was making the trip, but she was sure he wasn't coming for a friendly visit. Mose must have found out about Tyler. What else could explain this trip? Mose hadn't bothered to notify her of his arrival. And it wasn't like him to leave that to others. Mose was here to bring correction to her life — if he settled for that after she confessed the whole story. Nothing would surprise her at the moment.

A crew of community men had shown up early in the morning to clean up Uncle William's barn, now that the police had removed their yellow tape. The crew was almost finished and would leave soon. Likely Mose knew of this and would time his visit so he could speak with her alone.

She had helped Aunt Fannie serve the men lunch. That's when her aunt had finally noticed her nervousness, but there hadn't been time for a private discussion with the other women around. Several of them had arrived to help fix dinner and clean up afterward. A few of the women were still in the yard waiting for their husbands to complete the barn cleanup.

In the stillness of the house, she had fled upstairs to escape Aunt Fannie's questions, but her attempt was in vain. She could hear Aunt Fannie's footsteps coming up the stairs at this very moment. At least they would have their conversation in her bedroom without fear of interruption. She might as well tell Aunt Fannie everything. Her transgressions would eventually be made public once Mose arrived.

"Please help me, dear Lord," Miriam prayed as Aunt Fannie entered the bedroom without a knock.

"Miriam, what's going on?" Aunt Fannie

stood before her with both hands on her hips. "You are all *fahuddled.* I know Mose is coming, but you don't seem the least bit happy about it. And now that I think twice about the matter, why haven't you received any letters from him since you've been back? And why didn't you write any? Start talking, Miriam."

Miriam tried to steady her voice. "I told you why I didn't write. Why Mose didn't . . ."

Aunt Fannie stopped Miriam. "There's more to this, Miriam. I want you to tell me what's been bothering you."

"Oh, Aunt Fannie, it's just so awful!" Miriam started to cry. "I don't know why I did what I did. I tried not to, but I couldn't help myself. I've searched my heart, and I can't believe what I find there. Oh, Aunt Fannie, it's the most horrible, terrible thing to ever happen to me. And I think Mose knows about it!"

Aunt Fannie sat down on the bed and didn't say anything for several long moments. "I have no idea what you're talking about, so let's back up and start at the beginning. What did you do that's so wrong?"

"Tyler and I kissed! Twice!" Miriam blurted out. "I mean two different times.

Oh, I don't know what's wrong with me. I couldn't help myself."

"You did *what*?" Aunt Fannie was on her feet again.

"Oh, Aunt Fannie," Miriam wailed. "What am I going to do?"

"When did all this happen?" Aunt Fannie sat down again, ashen-faced.

"The first day I was back from Possum Valley, on that Sunday afternoon when I went back to the schoolhouse with my buggy. And then when Tyler brought me home in his car from the youth gathering."

"And Mose knows this?"

"I don't know how he could . . . but I know I have to confess to him . . . then he'll know for sure." Mirian burst into a fresh set of tears.

"He must already know," Aunt Fannie muttered. She walked over to the window and looked out. "Why else would he not write? Why else would he come all this way and not even tell you, of all people, he's coming?"

Miriam choked out, "But who . . . and how?"

"Someone must have seen you at the schoolhouse," Aunt Fannie said. "Oh, Miriam, how could you! This is beyond you. You've never acted like this before. Now

331

your sister Shirley — *yah,* that I can understand. Shirley used to pull these stunts, but
not you."

Miriam buried her face in her pillow and
moaned.

"Well, you're right about confessing to
Mose." Aunt Fannie's face was set. "That
might help. It's your only chance. And there
must still be hope. Why else would Mose
make the trip out here? He must still love
you."

"Love me?" Miriam muffled her voice.

"You don't have to act surprised." Aunt
Fannie gave Miriam a glare. "You're an attractive catch. Why else would Tyler have
kissed you? Oh, how could I have been so
wrong about the man? Here he was seduc-
ing you and bringing the police into our
house, to say nothing of what still lies
ahead."

For a moment only Miriam's muffled cries
could be heard. Then Aunt Fannie spoke
up again. "I know what, Miriam. Let me
talk with Mose first. I'll tell him I just
learned of this thing myself and that Tyler
pulled the wool over all of our eyes. I'm not
the deacon's *frau* or the bishop's, but I am
a woman. He'll listen to me."

Miriam shook her head. "I think it's best
that I go first. I have done this, and I must

redeem this. There is no other choice."

"But he . . ." Aunt Fannie stopped. "Well, okay. Perhaps you know best. But I'll make it easier for you if I have a chance."

Miriam tried to smile but in vain.

"Come." Aunt Fannie took her hand. She led Miriam down the stairs like a child. Aunt Fannie let go only moments before they stepped into the living room. Through the window they could see the small group of women still in the yard. One of the men had a buggy ready to go, so it wouldn't be long before the yard was empty. Miriam pulled in a sharp breath. Mose was there, standing with his back turned to the house and in deep conversation with Uncle William.

"Help us, dear Lord," Aunt Fannie whispered.

Terror gripped Miriam. The man could ruin her, and she could no longer put a *gut* face on this. Mose might even plan to excommunicate her — if she repented or not.

"Do you think he'll put me in the *bann*?" Miriam whispered.

"How could he?" Aunt Fannie retorted. "You did a mighty stupid thing, but the *bann* isn't for kissing another man. Not unless you're married."

"I remember when you told me about your . . . transgression," Miriam said. "Uncle William was going to force a church confession out of you. You weren't married when you kissed your former *Englisha* boyfriend at that chance meeting."

Aunt Fannie paled a little. "*Yah,* but that's not the *bann.* And if you have to make a church confession, you'll still have Mose."

She could handle that, Miriam told herself. The shame would cut deep, but others had had to confess their faults in front of the whole church. However, she had never done so before and didn't want to now. From her reaction, pride must have crept deep into her soul. And did not pride always come before great destruction? *Yah,* it did. No wonder she had fallen.

"I can do that much." Miriam looked up at her aunt's face. Horror was written there. "What?" Miriam managed.

"Tyler might have changed everything in the past few days!" Aunt Fannie said. "Perhaps this is no longer an ordinary situation."

Miriam saw what Aunt Fannie meant — the fires, the police, the yellow crime tape, the long conversation in the living room on Friday night about arrests and courtrooms and testimonies. Uncle William had been

334

white-faced under his dark beard when Tyler and the police officer had finally left.

"Oh, Miriam." Aunt Fannie clutched her arm. "I can't believe this."

They might as well believe, Miriam told herself. Outside Uncle William was shaking hands with the last of the soot-covered men, obviously thanking them for their help. Mose's straight form broke away from the group and strode toward the house, his head bowed low. He raised it only to nod to the three women still in the yard. He appeared tired, like a weary man after a long day's work. Mose paused by the water hydrant where the men had cleaned up for lunch and splashed water on his face and beard. He rubbed on the soap for a long time before he rinsed and dried himself with the towel hanging on a nearby bush.

"I'd better leave you alone," Aunt Fannie whispered, vanishing in the direction of the kitchen.

Miriam watched, transfixed. Mose was still a young man, but his beard was lengthy for his age and untrimmed. Straggly hairs floated sideways as he dried them with the towel. His eyes blazed even from this distance, and Miriam stepped further out of sight.

This man was to be her husband. Her

335

whole body trembled at the thought. Would his kisses be tender? There was no way she would find out now before they said the vows together. But what right did she have to know? How could a kiss be trusted to tell the truth of a man's character? If it could, Tyler was the man she should marry instead of Mose. Yet Tyler had nothing to offer her. He had waltzed into the community and taken advantage of them all. Tyler had been after nothing but a corruption investigation, which had nothing to do with the community's best interest. And Tyler didn't take no for an answer when it came to matters of the heart, even when he left nothing behind but broken pieces. Her mind went back to the Wednesday night meeting she had overheard from the kitchen.

"Drop the whole investigation," Uncle William begged Tyler. "We're sorry we ever got involved."

"*Yah,* please, Tyler," Deacon Phillips seconded.

"It's out of my hands now," Tyler insisted.

"He's right," the officer agreed. "The state is involved now, and we're sorry for the trouble you've all had. But we'll see what help can be provided."

"We want no help from the state," Deacon Phillips said in no uncertain terms. "That is not our way."

Tears sprang to Miriam's eyes at the memory of that night. Her reverie ended when Mose pushed open the door. Miriam jumped. She whirled about, but he had already seen that she had been watching him from the window. No emotion showed on his face.

"Miriam," he said.

She wanted to race to him and fly into his arms the way Jonathon did when she came home from the schoolhouse, but her body wouldn't move.

"You know then?" Miriam forced the words out.

"That you have been cavorting with that *Englisha* man who has brought all this trouble on your community?" Mose spat the words out.

"Mose, please," Miriam begged. "I know there's no excuse, but —"

Mose cut her off. "So it is true? I had hoped in the depths of my heart that you might at least deny the matter."

"And lie to you?" Miriam couldn't keep the surprise from her face.

Mose's laugh was harsh. "How is that worse than kissing an . . ." Mose stopped, as if unable to say more. He recovered himself quickly. "You are my promised one,

Miriam. And I am a bishop, and this *Englisha* man is a troublemaker, a rabble-rouser of the worst sort. And he brings the law into the community, officers who ask questions of us. The whole community is in an uproar when I arrive, and with *gut* reason. Now two of our people have had their barns burned down because of this *Englisha* man. He has come among us like a wolf in sheep's clothing. And now he has seduced you. How could you, Miriam?"

Miriam covered her face with both hands and slowly lowered herself to her knees. She crept forward until she could see his ash-covered shoes.

"What is this, Miriam?" His voice was harsh above her.

"I have fallen, Mose." She forced herself to speak loudly enough for him to hear. "I know I have. I'm unworthy to ask your forgiveness. I simply say that I am guilty. You may do with me as you wish."

"Get on your feet, Miriam," he said. "I am not the Lord that you must humble yourself before me."

She longed for his hand to reach down and lift her up. His slightest touch would have helped heal the jagged pain throbbing in her heart. Miriam waited, but in vain. There was only the sound of his sharp intake of breath above her. Slowly, Miriam placed her hands on the floor and stood. She trembled in front of him, her head bowed.

"Look at me," Mose ordered.

Miriam brought her head up and tried to keep back the tears.

"Will you take your punishment for this?" His tone was brisk. "Willingly? Whatever it is?"

"*Yah,*" she whispered.

"Even the *bann*?"

Miriam choked and clutched her chest.

"Even the *bann*?" His voice rose higher.

"*Yah.*" Miriam stifled her sob.

"Then that is *gut.*" Mose stepped back. "I will not speak to you again until a time of seclusion for you is completed. I will speak with your bishop and tell him you have agreed to a voluntary time of excommunication to seek and find the proper repentance. So consider yourself blessed, Miriam. After the shame you've brought upon all of us, but especially me, this is a light punishment. The length of the *bann* will be announced tomorrow after the service, and the school will be closed for that time. Do you understand?"

Miriam dropped her head again and wept silently.

"I'll take that as a *yah,*" Mose said, and closed the door behind him.

Miriam didn't move until Aunt Fannie's hands slipped around her shoulders and helped her to the couch. The two clung together until Miriam's sobs had quieted down.

"It's only for a little while, dear," Aunt Fannie whispered. "You can make it."

"I wish I were dead," Miriam said. "I wish the day I was born had never been."

"Come now." Aunt Fannie clucked her tongue and tucked Miriam's wet hair under her *kapp.* "You're not quite Job yet, I don't think."

CHAPTER THIRTY

Miriam clasped her hands and kept her head down. The three-hour church service would end soon, and the worst thing to ever happen in her life would happen. She would be placed in the *bann.* This story would be part of the tale she would have to tell her children and her grandchildren — how Grandma had fallen for an *Englisha* man and . . .

The tears stung, but Miriam resisted the temptation to wipe them away. She doubted if any of the unmarried girls sitting on either side of her knew what lay ahead. The chatter all morning before the service had been about the fires and the questions the police still asked of the community men.

The women were horrified as they whispered their questions to each other.

"Can you believe what they're asking? Did any of us notice any illegal billing or activity when we rebuilt after the tornado?"

"Did we receive more goods than we needed for our building?"

"Or who was our main supplier for the materials? Don't they know?"

"*Yah,* and did not Tyler Johnson supply all this information?"

The last question stung the most. Never had anyone imagined the welcome they had given Tyler would turn into such a nightmare. The police officers wanted the Amish to give testimony in court, but such a notion violated the convictions of even the most liberal-minded member in the community. Bishop Mullet had forbidden any further cooperation with Tyler. So why had Tyler shown up this morning for the service? The reception given Tyler by the men had been frosty from the looks on their faces. She had tried to stay out of sight once Tyler came into the house. Thankfully, he had taken a seat toward the back, but he would still see her humiliation or hear it. Bishop Mullet would make an announcement after Mose finished his sermon. Maybe no one would pay a lot of attention with all the excitement that already happened in the community. But that was a vain hope. The excommunication of the community's schoolteacher could not be missed, or the fact that school would be closed afterward.

Still, the memory of all this would eventually be dulled. People would forget. Aunt Fannie had said so this morning. But Miriam knew she would never forget.

Miriam tried to focus on the last of Mose's sermon, but the words blurred together into a solid sound she couldn't understand. At least his face wasn't as grim this morning. But the fierceness from yesterday afternoon hadn't left her memory. Mose figured he was letting her off easy. But how was the *bann* easy? Even for what she had done? It was Tyler who was to blame for the fuss in the community. Maybe Mose wouldn't have been so extreme if he hadn't arrived right after the two barns had burned and the police officers had been asking questions and wanting court testimony.

Miriam forced her thoughts to stop. She couldn't give in to bitterness. The pain was already enough without an added burden. If she wanted to live as Mose's *frau* sometime in the future, she had to accept this punishment. But what would *Mamm* and *Daett* say in Possum Valley when they found out? That question had reduced her to fresh sobs in Aunt Fannie's embrace last night.

Miriam tried again to listen to the sermon. Mose was in the middle of a point with both arms raised. His voice thundered in Miriam's ears. "Repent, said the prophet John. Repent, and prepare the way for the Lord to come. Repent, and make straight the path. Repent, and bring every mountain low. Repent, and fill in the low places of every valley. The Lord God has the same message for His people today. Those who lift themselves up must be brought down, and those who humble themselves before the almighty hand of God will be lifted up. This is what repentance brings. The Lord will walk among us again if we repent. The world tells us, do your own thing, seek your own pleasure, think your own thoughts. But God tells us, 'My ways are not your ways, My thoughts are not your thoughts.'"

Miriam hung her head again and let the tears flow. Mose was preaching at her, she was sure. Apparently Mose didn't think she had fully repented; otherwise, why would she have to suffer the *bann*? Or maybe Mose believed in punishment to bring about a full repentance, one that her heart couldn't reach on its own. She had to believe that, or insanity would knock on the door.

Miriam lifted her head for a moment to wipe her eyes. She stopped, transfixed. Tyler was leaning far around one of the men's backs to look at her. A big question was written on his face. But it was the kindness in his eyes that sent a fresh stab of pain through Miriam. She thought this day couldn't hurt more than it already had, but Tyler's look brought a rush of emotion to the surface. A wail almost slipped out of her mouth. Miriam dropped her head and slipped one hand in front of her mouth. Had she cried out or not? Apparently not. None of the girls on either side of her turned from their focus on Mose's sermon. A few moments passed before Miriam breathed evenly again. But she kept her eyes turned away from Tyler's section of the room.

One of the girls seated beside Miriam squirmed and finally looked her way. If Mose's sermon hadn't drawn his audience in, she would have attracted attention long ago with her tears. Miriam set her chin. Enough of this! She would think on the sermon until the awful moment arrived in a few minutes. Fresh tears threatened at the thought, but Miriam kept her resolve and her gaze away from Tyler.

Mose wrapped up his sermon with a final, "Let us prepare our hearts for battle against the world, the devil, and our own flesh. Every day the temptations come. None of us are above giving in to weakness, for it lies near to every human heart. But in repentance, in humility, in brokenness of heart, and in a willingness to make restitution for our sins . . ." Mose held that part out for a second and looked right at Miriam. She dropped her head and bit the inside of her lip until she tasted blood. But surely that was better than tears. Mose had said he wouldn't speak to her again until the *bann* was over, but that must have excluded his sermon. Surely she wouldn't be used like this once they said the marriage vows. She couldn't stand having her husband preach at her in church. Mose wouldn't, Miriam assured herself, and she wouldn't be tempted to kiss *Englisha* men after she was Mose's *frau.* Nor would Mose excommunicate her again. She had to believe that too.

"And now," Mose continued, "I have come to the end of my time of speaking today. I confess to a frailty of the flesh from my travels last week and from sharing in the trials this community is experiencing right now. I pray the Lord would grant all of you great mercy, but I remind you to take up this cross with joy in your hearts. I know on my part I will share with the brethren and sisters at the home community of your sweet spirit and of the hospitality you have shown me. We will pray for you and wish you God's greatest blessings. So if I have preached anything in error today, I leave that to the brethren to correct in their testimony. Perhaps Bishop Mullet can go first, followed by Deacon Phillips. I don't know many of the men here, so if the bishop wishes to choose another man, that's fine with me."

Mose sat down, and Bishop Mullet spoke first. He named Ezra Kauffman to also give testimony, but Deacon Phillips went next. When Ezra finished, Bishop Mullet got to his feet to say, "Will the members please stay in after the final song? Thank you."

Miriam tried to breathe in the long moments it took for the nonmembers, including Tyler, to file out. The young boys made their way quickly, but it took longer for the younger girls to gather the smaller children and take them into the kitchen. When all became quiet, the members turned in expectation toward the ministers's bench.

Bishop Mullet stood slowly to his feet and cleared his throat. "I have asked all of the members to stay behind due to a very serious matter that has come to our attention. This is on top of everything else that has happened in the past few days. I regret to say that our beloved sister Miriam Yoder has found herself in a moral failing which requires our attention." Bishop Mullet paused to clear his throat again. "I don't wish to give too many details. The rest of the ministry and I have spoken about this with Bishop Mose. He is the one who has brought the matter to us and has spoken with Miriam. We didn't know for sure what steps to take at first, but we have come to an agreement." Bishop Mullet glanced around the room before he continued. "Miriam has agreed to a voluntary time spent in the *bann*. We as a ministry have decided on an excommunication of one week that we think is appropriate. Because this is voluntary, we don't have to vote or bring further shame to a member who has sought repentance. I have spoken with William Byler this morning because Miriam's *daett* isn't here, and he agrees that Miriam has shown all the signs of deep sorrow. Mose on his part will not be cutting off his relationship with Miriam. Rather, Mose will stay around until the week is over so that he can meet with Miriam again and restore what has been damaged between them. I trust that is okay with everyone. Remember that we are in an unusual time right now, and we are doing the best we can with what we have to work with." Bishop Mullet glanced at the other ministers. "Do any of you have anything to say?"

Deacon Phillips whispered something, and Bishop Mullet leaned closer to hear.

"Yah," Bishop Mullet said once he stepped back. "I had forgotten to mention that school is out for the week of Miriam's *bann.* Let us use the time for prayer and fasting, not just for Miriam but for ourselves. If anyone has time on their hands, they can bring their children along to the work sites this week. We hope we can have both Deacon Phillips's and William Byler's barns rebuilt in that time, if the Lord has mercy on us. You may now be dismissed."

The girls seated on both sides of Miriam turned to stare. *What have you done?* was the question written on their faces.

Telling them wouldn't help. How could she explain why she had kissed Tyler Johnson while she was promised to Bishop Mose? Bishop Mullet had left the specifics of the transgression unspoken, and she would leave it there. The news would leak out soon enough.

Miriam fled through the kitchen and out into the washroom. More than one woman stared at her, but she didn't pause. She wouldn't stay for lunch and bear the further shame of having to eat at a separate table.

By the next Sunday service, this would be over. At home with her uncle and aunt, she could handle the shame, but not in public. The Lord didn't ask people to take up a cross bigger than they could carry. Uncle William had agreed to have Star ready for her when the service was dismissed. She would go home and cry alone.

Miriam found her shawl and tried to take slow steps across the lawn. The young boys at play didn't give her more than a passing glance. But they didn't know about her shame. Uncle William had Star ready when she arrived at the buggy. He held Star's bridle and stroked his neck until Miriam could climb in.

Uncle William gave Miriam a kind look before he let go. "Bishop Mullet tried to make things easy for you."

"*Yah,* I have much to be thankful for." Miriam bit her lip again. "And thanks for your kindness. You didn't have to do this."

"It's the right thing to do," Uncle William said, handing Miriam the reins.

Uncle William gave Star's neck a final stroke before Miriam drove off. Miriam kept her head down until she was past the house on the road. Then her tears came as great sobs racking her body. Star seemed to sense her distress and turned his head more than once to look back.

The drive finally came to an end when Miriam stopped in front of the greenhouse, but she couldn't climb out of the buggy. She couldn't stop sobbing. Only the sound of a car's tires behind her brought a quick gasp and instant soberness. She dared not guess who it was. Her only hope was that it was a customer who didn't realize the nursery was closed on Sunday. But no, she knew who it was . . . who it had to be.

"Miriam," Tyler called out. The sound went through her like a jolt.

She froze.

"Miriam," he repeated. "What's wrong?"

What is wrong? she wanted to scream, but she kept her voice even and said, "I guess you should know that answer."

"I don't know a thing." He gestured wildly back toward the road. "What was that all about? You know I don't understand Amish ways or customs. One of the men gave me a few details after the service was out. Then you went tearing out of the driveway like a wild woman. Did I understand that you've been excommunicated because of me?"

Miriam gave him a hard stare, but her heart pounded so hard she could hardly breathe. Mose's discipline must not have done its work because Tyler appeared as handsome and attractive as ever.

"It was because of me, not you," Miriam said, suddenly very tired of it all.

Tyler waved his hands about again. "No, I think it's because of that old ogre back there. The one who jawed for over an hour. The one that plans to marry you."

"That would be Bishop Mose Stoll." Her voice trembled, and Miriam bit the inside of her lip again.

"He's an ogre." Tyler was unrepentant. "He made you cry."

"Oh, Tyler, you simply don't understand," Miriam managed. "You never will. Please leave. If you care for me at all, just leave!"

"Really?" He studied her closely. "You know you could run away with me, Miriam. We could marry tomorrow if you wish, down at the courthouse. I think we'd be happy together, Miriam."

"Please, just go," she ordered as she managed to climb down. With knees that trembled, she unhitched Star from the buggy.

Tyler stood there and didn't offer to help, but he was gone when she returned from the temporary shelter set up to house Star and the few other animals. Miriam looked up the road in each direction. There was no sign of Tyler's car. Miriam pulled her wet handkerchief out of her pocket again, but

her eyes were dry. There were no tears left
to cry.

Chapter Thirty-One

Tyler typed the last paragraph of the article in his hotel room before he reread the title, "Amish Aid Exposes Political Corruption."

That should grab readers' attention, Tyler told himself. He scanned the rest of the story:

The Amish reject political affiliation and rarely vote, yet in the small community of Clarita, Oklahoma, Amish people have found themselves in the center of a political firestorm. Though initially reluctant to answer questions on how funds were distributed to them more than two years ago through the Clarita Relief Fund set up to aid in tornado reconstruction, the Amish still agreed to cooperate. The information they gave was crucial in the subsequent investigation and helped untangle a web of financial deceit where still unknown amounts of monies were only partially channeled by the Clarita Relief Fund to Amish homes and businesses destroyed or damaged by the storms. In a scheme involving double-billing, Amish building projects received barely sufficient funds to finish their projects while all of the overrun was diverted to political causes.

This scam was ingenious in that no one thought the integrity of such godly people would be questioned. Nor was it apparently thought that anyone would ever dig deeply into how funds allocated to the Amish were distributed. But as the Amish themselves would say, "The Lord makes sure that sins do not remain hidden."

I will write later about my involvement in the initial discovery work, but suffice it to say for now the trail of corruption leads to the highest levels of Oklahoma state politics. After threat letters were repeatedly sent to me and two Amish properties were burned to the ground in clear intimidation attempts, federal investigators are now involved. Sitting US Senator Yentas denies that his political campaign was involved in any way or received any of the diverted monies. He has referred all questions to his lawyers. However this ends, the Amish are due our gratitude and respect. They wish to remain out of the courtroom as befits their convictions and religious beliefs. It is my hope that the investigators in charge will respect these wishes. There must be some way in a modern political corruption investigation to leave room for privacy in the lives of such exemplar men and women. The least we can do is cause them no harm.

I have nothing but good to say about the time I stayed in the community. I was taken in as a friend, even though I was clearly an outsider. I was given the hospitality and trust these people display so freely. May God bless them. I will always remember my brief stay with such a godly people with great tenderness and a thankful heart.

Tyler attached the document to an e-mail and pressed "send." His editor might have a few changes, but this should do. He really didn't need to explain his own role further. The media had the information they needed about a freelance journalist who had exposed what others had failed to see. He planned to say nothing about Miriam Yoder or his feelings about a certain bishop she was engaged to. He hoped the reporters weren't hounding William Byler's place right now or Deacon Phillips's. His departure from the community had already left enough of a bitter taste. The truth was he had exploited the Amish in their acceptance of him. His conscience had informed him of that a long time ago, and no rationalization had persuaded it otherwise. He considered writing an apology to Deacon Phillips, but that wouldn't change much. The Amish didn't harbor grudges, and they valued a changed life more than spoken words.

After this had all settled, he had in mind a book project about his few weeks spent in the Clarita community. With the level of interest the public had in Amish affairs, he ought to make the *New York Times* Bestseller List for sure. His experience had the sizzle of all the hot buttons: corruption, politics, and love. He'd have to tell it all if he wrote the book — how he had felt when taken into the community's embrace and how his attraction to an Amish girl who was promised to a young bishop came about. He'd have to reveal Miriam's passionate kisses and include her voluntary excommunication as punishment for her transgressions. And lastly it would have to include Miriam's brave refusal to leave the community with him.

The rejection still stung. His pride was badly battered. He wasn't used to such treatment from women. Hilda had complained a little when he called her yesterday, but they had a date scheduled tonight. All would be forgiven and forgotten.

"Oh, well," Tyler sighed. "It's back to where I left off. For better or for worse."

He would have to accept reality. Miriam had given him the boot. And what would he do with her in his world anyway? He had offered Miriam marriage, but perhaps her refusal was for the best. How could he deal with an ex-Amish woman living with him in Oklahoma City? Even if Miriam had tried, she couldn't have changed overnight, and in some things her heart might never change. Miriam was who she was. Probably the charm of the community had affected his judgment. He had played games with their young people and attended their meetings, but that didn't mean he was one of them. They knew that, even if he didn't.

Maybe an early lunch with Hilda would help clear his mind. Or Mimi Coons? He hadn't called her in months. Mimi worked for an online newspaper, so at least they had journalism in common. That was how they had met in the first place. Mimi might have a regular boyfriend by now, but maybe she'd want to meet him for an interview. He was hot news and had refused to answer more than the basic questions from any other reporter. An intimate look at his time among the Amish would be the first step in his book project — if he could persuade himself to write it. He wanted to keep that private for now. And he had to get over Miriam first. Her tears were not his business now. And Miriam had the bishop to comfort her. They'd be married soon and have a dozen children before that many years rolled by. So why should he be so sentimental?

Mimi would be just the ticket to restore both his edge and his injured ego. There would be admiring glances and hints from Mimi. They made a pretty good couple, he had to admit. Mimi would get what she wanted out of lunch, and he would get what he needed: a female who pretended to adore him.

Tyler punched "contacts" on his phone and found Mimi's number. Thankfully, he hadn't deleted it. Quickly he typed in the text. "Tyler here, from way back. Sweet memories! Remember? Want to do lunch? The Amish are hot stuff right now, you know."

He pressed "send" and waited. The bait might not be enough. Perhaps he should have made the message stronger and offered an interview outright. She'd be skeptical of him — and with good reason.

Tyler grinned when the tone sounded seconds later on his phone. With glee he read the message. "Name the place and time."

He still had his charm.

Tyler typed in his answer: "Perino's, off the turnpike, N. May Ave. @ 11:30."

That should be downscale enough. Not fast food and not a formal restaurant. Just a quiet place to have a good meal. When no response came, Tyler glanced at his watch. He'd have time to change and make it down to North May Avenue with minutes to spare.

Tyler headed toward the bedroom where he pulled on a clean pair of jeans and shirt. His glance into the closet took in the black, collarless Amish suit he had asked Deacon Phillips's wife, Katie, to sew for him. She had begun the work a week after he first made contact with the Amish community. He had acted on impulse and had planned to wear it to a Sunday church service, but Katie hadn't finished before his schedule had been interrupted. She had handed the suit to him, all wrapped up in plastic, on the evening before the fire. On his last Sunday in the community, he was no longer welcome. To wear the suit would have been like pouring salt in an open wound.

"Oh, well," Tyler said aloud. He shrugged. He should wear it for his lunch with Mimi. She'd get a kick out of the outfit, and it would play his part well.

No, he wouldn't do that, Tyler decided. The Amish had gotten to him more than he realized. The least he could do was refrain from subjecting their way of life to ridicule.

Tyler gathered up his tablet and phone. Moments later he was driving across town. He encountered no delays and arrived on time. His life in the outside world ran with ruthless efficiency. His edge had been blunted in his weeks among the community people, but he had recovered it. Their slower pace and flexibility had drawn him in, but that was all behind him now.

Tyler parked and locked the car. Mimi was waiting inside, dressed in a sharp, dark blue dress. Tyler saw visions of young Amish girls clad in the same color, only the dresses had been longer and fuller.

"Howdy, stranger!" Mimi waved her hand.

"It has been a long time," Tyler agreed.

"So come sit down and tell me how I get

an exclusive with you."

"The blood is in the water, I see," Tyler teased. "Why should I give it to you?"

She gave him an adoring look. "Because I'm so special."

Now Tyler laughed. "That's true, but . . ."

"Come on." Mimi leaned forward on the table. "Let's order and you can give me the scoop. We'll even split the check."

"Okay, but you have to worship at my feet the whole time," Tyler said with a laugh.

When the waiter had taken their orders, Mimi started in. "So what was it like in Amish Land? Totally boring, I'm sure."

He gave her a glare. "Not so much. They are much more interesting than you might imagine."

"Really?" Mimi wasn't convinced.

Tyler saw Bishop Mose's face as he preached that last Sunday and remembered Miriam's tears.

Mimi noticed. "Your face betrays you. There must have been a girl."

"Um, let's not go there," Tyler said. "I haven't figured out that part of the story yet." There were places in the last few weeks he had no intentions to revisit with anyone. Having Miriam's face inches from his as he embraced her in her buggy was one of them. That would have to wait for the book if he had the courage to write it.

"All right, then. What *can* you tell me?"

Tyler managed a smile. "Well, I must say I was surprised by what I found. The original idea was to write a nice public interest piece on how the Amish businesses as well as their private homes were faring some two years after a tornado had been through the area. To begin, I was welcomed into an Amish home the first evening of my arrival and was served a great Amish supper. I got to meet the family, a small one by Amish standards, and the community's schoolteacher who boards there, a Miriam Yoder."

Mimi scribbled notes and looked up expectantly.

"You may not need that," Tyler said.

"Why not let me decide? Continue," Mimi said.

"Okay, but scratch the reference to the schoolteacher."

Mimi smirked. "Aha. So your famed charm with women reaches all the way into the exclusive community of the Amish. I guess I'm not surprised."

"Don't go there," he snapped.

Mimi's smirk widened. "That's usually exactly where one should go. You know that, Tyler."

"It's not a big deal." Tyler gathered his

emotions together. "Anyway, I was served supper and got to talk with the man of the house, William Byler. He was friendly and answered a lot of questions. Mr. Byler introduced me the following week to the community's deacon, in whose basement apartment I ended up staying before all was said and done. I also had a meeting with Mr. Westree, the chairman of the Clarita Relief Fund, who wouldn't answer my questions to any degree of satisfaction. Working on a whim at first, I pursued my suspicions and soon was sure I had hit pay dirt."

"Don't brag," Mimi interrupted. "It never sounds good."

"Then scratch it, or write the piece so it doesn't brag. You owe me one anyway." Tyler gave her a fake glare.

Mimi chuckled. "I'm a fearless person to be in your debt. So tell me about this schoolteacher, Miriam Yoder."

"No, I said we're not going there." Tyler's glare wasn't fake this time.

"Hey," Mimi shrugged, "there are other ways of finding out these things. For that matter, I can go interview her myself."

"Okay," Tyler retorted. "Miriam Yoder is a woman of great character, whose sterling reputation in the community was on everyone's lips. Wherever she went praises fell before her like rose petals before a queen."

"You expect me to write *that*?" Now Mimi glared. "Cut the corn, Tyler. So perhaps I was wrong. Maybe for once you met a girl who didn't succumb to your charms. That's the real problem, isn't it?"

Tyler grinned. "I'm going to ignore that and continue with the real story here. After I got closer with my questions, I soon began to receive threats. They started mildly but soon increased in severity. I kept my editor in the loop, but neither of us felt we should back off. Then the two fires happened to some of the principals in my story. Of course, the Amish wouldn't cooperate, being big on forgiveness and all, and so the rest was up to me and the law enforcement folks, with no more help from the Amish victims."

Mimi leaned across the table and whispered, "Yada, yada, yada. That's the story you already told. I want to hear about the schoolteacher. That's the untold story. Tell me, and I'll worship at your feet for days."

Tyler got to his feet. "I think we'll call things even. Thanks for the adoration. My shattered psyche is on the mend."

"Hey, our meal hasn't even arrived yet.

That Miriam Yoder must have been something."

"That she was," Tyler said as he left.

CHAPTER THIRTY-TWO

Mose was on the road early on Friday morning in Deacon Phillips's borrowed buggy. He was headed over to help with the day's construction project at William Byler's place. All week he had worked where needed. By Thursday most of the barn on Deacon Phillips's property had been rebuilt. The few odds and ends would be completed today by Deacon Phillips and two other men who had agreed to return for the day. The rest of the community's men and large crews from the Amish communities scattered around the state planned to erect William Byler's barn by nightfall.

The visiting carpenters had stayed over from yesterday and been put up in the area's homes and barns. Mose had given up the basement apartment at Deacon Phillips's place so that the women who had accompanied the vans as cooks had a place to sleep. He had joined several men on sleeping bags in Deacon Phillips's newly built barn loft.

They had awakened before dawn to a delicious breakfast cooked in Katie's kitchen and served outdoors until sunup. Mose looked behind him and pulled partly off the road as two vans passed him full of the men in straw hats and a few women in dark shawls. Everyone waved heartily, and Mose stuck his hand out of the buggy to respond. They were all in *gut* spirits this morning. He was too. The reconstruction had gone well this week, and the weekend was finally close when the *bann* would be lifted and he would speak with Miriam again.

All week he had chafed under the restrictions he had placed on their relationship. He should have allowed for a time when he could rebuke and chasten Miriam further. That way he would have cleared the air between them. They would have been ready to move on to other things on Sunday afternoon. He had limited time to spend with Miriam now as he planned to leave for home Monday on the Greyhound.

Oh, well, it was done. Mose stuck his head out of the buggy again for a long breath of the prairie's morning air. He had come to like the land out here. No wonder Miriam was so attached. He was surprised she hadn't made more of a fuss about the need to move with him to Wayne County once they had wed. But that was Miriam's character. She was self-sacrificing and wished to please her husband-to-be. Where her transgression with Tyler Johnson had come from, he still couldn't understand. He wanted to get to the bottom of all this, and he should have done so on Saturday evening when he first met with Miriam, but his furor had been too great. No *gut* thing came out of the wrath of man, Mose reminded himself. Of this he was sure. But Miriam's acceptance of her discipline had settled his temper. Not all women would have taken a time spent under the *bann* with so little protest.

Mose settled in the buggy seat again. Deacon Phillips had opened up to him earlier in the week with details about Tyler Johnson. Nothing he had heard surprised him. The man had sneaked into the community under a false pretense, and Deacon Phillips had fallen for the man's story. Deacon Phillips had gone so far as to give Tyler a place to stay in his basement apartment. The man's charms must have been immense. No wonder Miriam had fallen. The thought made him feel better, and yet it still shouldn't have happened. Women were supposed to be more sensitive about deception and notice it sooner. Why hadn't Miriam known the truth about Tyler? The question burned through his mind. He had done things in his *rumspringa* time that he now regretted, but he had never kissed an *Englisha* girl. He had gone on a date with an *Englisha* neighbor girl a few times, but that was all the further things had gone. How could Miriam have fallen so low? Miriam had such a *gut* reputation throughout the community, and her character was above reproach until . . .

"Well," Mose muttered. "We all have our weak points."

He would comfort himself with that thought, but it would not do to let Miriam know that he held any understanding for what she had done. There was no danger the *Englisha* man Tyler would return, but still . . .

"Tyler's left us for *gut,* I'm afraid," Deacon Phillips had told him. There had been a twinge of sorrow in the deacon's voice. Did Miriam feel the same? Would Miriam remember the man's kisses? Likely! But so he remembered Rachel's kisses and always would. Miriam couldn't replace the life Rachel and he had lived together. There had been no *kinner,* but Rachel had spent many an evening close to him on the couch as they read *The Budget* together. No, he would never forget Rachel. He would have to move past his anger. Miriam would be his married *frau* soon enough, and they could build their own memories with *kinner* this time — if the Lord didn't object. Surely he wouldn't be left childless by two women?

Mose pulled back the reins as he approached the Bylers' place and saw vehicles parked along the road. Who would that be? There were huge vans everywhere with people all along the road. This must be the news media, Mose told himself. The men from the community had spoken together yesterday about what they would do if such a thing happened. They had decided that in no case would there be any cooperation offered or photography equipment allowed on the Amish properties.

So today their fears had come to pass. The Amish were already in the news in all the local papers in connection with the political corruption case Tyler had uncovered. It was only natural that the media would seek to cover the rebuilding project of the burned out barn. Well, William had kept them out on the road from the looks of things. That was the best any of them could do. The Lord would have to take care of the rest.

Mose drove with care as he approached.

The Byler driveway had large vans parked on either side of it. His buggy would barely fit through.

"Whoa there," Mose called to his horse as they came closer. "Take it easy, old boy."

Two men ran toward the buggy with fancy equipment held above their heads and long trails of wires strung out behind them. "Whoa there." Mose spoke louder this time, but his horse threw its head in the air and whinnied loudly.

Mose gripped the lines as one of the men shouted, "Do you know Miriam Yoder, the Amish schoolteacher?"

Mose gulped for air and leaned out of the buggy. Had he heard correctly? How did these men know his *frau*-to-be?

The men moved closer at once. A long pole was stuck almost into his face. "Do you have any comment, sir, about her affair with Tyler Johnson?"

Mose jerked his head back inside the buggy. *"Das ist ein leig,"* he exploded, but surely the men didn't understand Pennsylvania Dutch. Even if they did, he had best say this in English. Mose leaned out again. "This is a lie," he said, his voice raised high.

The long pole ended up inside his buggy as the men plunged forward. "Do you have personal knowledge of this affair, sir?"

Mose's ears rang with the question. His horse reared high into the air and took off. It was all Mose could do to hang on to the lines as they dashed between the two vans. The long pole caught on the buggy door and bent sideways. There was a loud twang, as the buggy dashed into the Bylers' driveway. Mose came to a bucking stop beside the greenhouse with his head in a daze and his hands clamped on the lines.

As Mose caught his breath, William stuck his head into the buggy with a grin. "It's not every day we see a bishop come in like a rowdy youngster. Did your horse get away from you?"

"There're asking questions about Miriam," Mose said.

William sobered. "They are? How can that be?"

"I don't know," Mose replied. "Unless Tyler is talking. Would he do such a thing?"

"I don't think so," William muttered.

"They say Miriam had an affair with Tyler," Mose told him.

"You don't say!" Horror filled William's face. "But that's not true."

"I suppose not," Mose allowed. "But we'd best tell them, don't you think?"

"Miriam would do no such thing." William still wasn't finished.

Mose's head spun. The shouted questions had deeply disturbed him. They were the sound of a world he knew little of, and yet they were here. He had spoken the truth. To ignore the reporters further would do no one any *gut*.

"You don't doubt Miriam, do you?" William stepped closer to ask.

"It doesn't matter," Mose finally allowed. "The question is what must be done. This will be in the local papers tomorrow if I don't miss my guess. How will the community live this thing down, or *my* community, since I'm involved? We must answer this charge more fully."

"But how? They are *Englisha* men . . ." William stared toward the parked vehicles by the road with their bright lights turned toward them. "All they can do is ask questions."

"Go tell Miriam she must go out with me and answer this matter," Mose ordered. He climbed down from the buggy. "She must tell them there is nothing to this."

William appeared doubtful but turned to hurry toward the house. Mose unhitched his horse and waited for twenty minutes until three people appeared. Fannie was with William and Miriam. The two walked on either side of the white-faced girl.

"Have you told Miriam?" Mose addressed William.

"Yah," William replied. "She will say what needs saying."

Miriam kept her eyes on the ground and said nothing.

"I will also go with her," Fannie said. "It will seem more appropriate."

He couldn't argue with that, Mose thought. The woman was wise. He hadn't thought of how it would appear if he stood beside Miriam alone.

"You had best come too," Mose told William.

Together they approached the vans again. The workers on the barn stopped to watch as the *Englisha* men ran from their vehicles toward them. Mose came to a stop at the end of the driveway and held up his hand.

"I am Bishop Mose Stoll," he said, his voice steady. "And these are William and Fannie Byler, whose barn we are rebuilding today."

"Do you know Miriam Yoder?" a loud voice interrupted him.

Mose stepped closer to Miriam and placed his hand on her arm. "This is Miriam Yoder, who is promised to me in holy marriage. We do not know where these rumors have come from about how Tyler Johnson

375

spent his time in the community, but none of them are true."

The long poles ended up in Miriam's face. "Are you Miriam Yoder?"

"Yah," Miriam managed.

"Do you know Tyler Johnson?"

Miriam nodded. The questions came thick and fast.

"What was your relationship with Mr. Johnson?"

"Does this affect your engagement to Mr. Stoll?"

"Does the community's vaunted forgiveness extend to fallen women?"

"Will you be seeing Mr. Johnson in the future?"

Mose stepped forward and pushed back the long poles. "Enough," he shouted. "These questions are all unfair. Tyler came among the community as a sheep in . . ."

Mose was drowned out by the chorus of shouts. "Let the woman speak for herself."

He had better, Mose decided, and he stepped back. Miriam would handle this properly. His future with Miriam hung on it.

Miriam spoke softly. "I knew Tyler Johnson, *yah*. He's a nice young man, and we saw each other at the youth gatherings. But that's what all the young people from the community do. We talked and enjoyed each other's company. I don't know what Tyler . . . Mr. Johnson . . . told you, but any comments about an . . . affair . . ." Miriam choked on the word, ". . . are completely untrue."

"You did not date Mr. Johnson then?"

"I did not." Miriam kept her gaze steady.

"What was your opinion of Mr. Johnson?"

Miriam looked away. "He appeared to be a nice young man. He succeeded in uncovering a political corruption scandal, so his time in the community was not wasted."

"Can we see your classroom, Miss Yoder? Will you be teaching today?"

Mose took over again. "This is enough. We have now answered your questions."

William turned to lead the way back, and Fannie had her arm around Miriam's waist.

"Is she really your fiancée, Bishop?" The last question was delivered with a laugh.

Mose turned and walked away without answering. He had totally misjudged the situation. These people could not be trusted. Once again he had made a wrong decision and embarrassed himself.

"What have we now?" the watching Amish workmen greeted him when he got back to the worksite. "An Amish television evangelist?"

Mose forced himself to join in their laughter but said no more about the matter. They were all hard at work ten minutes later while the camera crews hugged the road and flashed their bright lights at them.

CHAPTER THIRTY-THREE

After the hymn singing, Miriam slipped out of the washroom door with her shawl pulled tight over her shoulders. The brisk December air had a bite to it, not unlike the evening that lay ahead of her. She would speak with Mose tonight as the *bann* was lifted and he would drive her home. The horrible episode with the *Englisha* newspeople didn't count as part of the *bann*. Mose had barely looked at her other than when the cameras had been in their faces. She had tried to play her part after Uncle William had explained why the media people were there. That Tyler would spread such an awful rumor caused more hurt than how Mose had acted.

Her face had burned with shame at the accusation of what the world called an "affair," but Uncle William was right. If she had refused to respond and had stayed in the house, Mose would have thought she was guilty of more than a kiss with Tyler. Now her only hope was to get a fresh start with Mose . . . if he would still have her.

Miriam searched the darkness for the buggy Mose was driving while he was in Oklahoma. For once he had acted like a real suitor by coming to the hymn singing and now driving her home. Perhaps he was trying to make amends for the hard time she had gone through this past week.

"Please help me, dear Lord," Miriam whispered, offering a quick prayer as she caught sight of Mose's buggy parked at the end of the line. She tried to slip past the other buggies unnoticed, but she knew all eyes must be on her. The *bann* wouldn't affect her reputation greatly, but people were still curious. Mose still hadn't revealed to the community what had been her moral failure. Nor would he, which was as much to shield himself from shame as anything.

But those weren't decent thoughts, either. Miriam pushed them away. Behind her, Miriam heard the soft footsteps of other girls as they hurried to their families's buggies. Miriam kept her head down. The community currently had two other dating couples, and both of them had left earlier. Mose had waited longer. He must not want to appear eager to leave with her. He was big on his dignity, which was appropriate for a bishop. She might as well get used to it.

Miriam pulled herself up the buggy step and slid into the seat beside Mose. His figure cut a stark outline against the prairie starlight that twinkled outside the open buggy door.

"*Gut* evening," Mose said, his voice gruff.

"*Gut* evening," Miriam responded.

Mose didn't offer a buggy blanket, and he kept his door open. Perhaps Deacon Phillips had borrowed the blanket for some other purpose, Miriam thought. The notion did little, though, to warm the chill that cut through her shawl.

Mose didn't seem to notice as he said, "The Lord's blessing has returned to us as we humbled ourselves and sought His grace this past week."

Miriam hung her head. "I'm so sorry for what happened. I hope you can forgive me."

"I suppose we all have our weaknesses." Mose's tone had lightened a little. "I was stirred in my heart today as I thought of your gracious spirit this past week, Miriam. You are a true woman of the Lord who has humbled herself in the sight of the congregation. I'm glad we decided to work through this problem."

"You are kind to forgive me," Miriam whispered.

"Things will go better for us this way," Mose said with confidence. "Whatever happened between you and Tyler has now been properly repented of. A woman who humbles herself is a truly beautiful woman, Miriam."

Miriam kept her head down and said nothing.

Mose continued, "Our wedding day will be a day of great gladness, not only on this earth but in heaven. The cause of God and His church will be glorified. Together we will stand and serve the congregation and each other in holiness and godly fear. I believe the Lord will give me *kinner* this time, Miriam. I feel a great hope rising in my heart."

Heat streaks ran up her face at Mose's words, but thankfully the darkness hid them. She would marry the man, but he didn't have to speak so openly about *kinner.* Not yet, at least. The wedding wasn't until next fall, unless . . . perhaps she should bring up the subject again. They might as well get this over with and begin their lives together.

Mose ignored her for a moment to gaze out into the star-filled skies. "The world cannot harm the people of God, Miriam," he said. "That *Englisha* man tried to spread those awful rumors about you. But the Lord knows you have repented, and He protected us on Friday morning. Let the world say what they will, but we will find hope in the Lord. God has given us a fresh start now."

The horrible thought rose again, and Miriam spoke this time. "Mose, you don't think I really . . . Mose, please. Tyler and I did nothing more than kiss, and I have confessed that."

Mose regarded Miriam for a long moment. "I know how the *Englisha* people are. This Tyler must have many girlfriends. Why wouldn't he think of you as another one of those?"

"But Mose," Miriam protested.

He silenced her with a stern glance. "We will say no more about this. The *bann* has cleansed whatever you have done. Tyler's actions with the fires and bringing the police into the community are enough to explain why such a harsh method was necessary. Any righteous man or woman would see what needed to be done, and you agreed quite readily to the punishment, so surely you felt the guilt of your actions."

Miriam clutched her hands together. Her whole body felt so weak it couldn't move.

"But I told you, we only kissed. We did no such evil thing as was rumored." Miriam struggled to keep her voice steady.

"Okay." Mose smiled. "If that's the way you want it, I will say no more about the matter." Mose settled back in the buggy seat. "I hope there will be no more indiscretions in the future. Not that I can imagine how there could be, since Tyler's gone, but I still say this as a godly warning."

"I don't suppose there can be," Miriam told him. "But if you feel any doubts, maybe you had best assign someone to watch me each day until the wedding."

Her sarcasm seemed to escape him.

"I have spoken with your Uncle William," Mose said. "He will make sure that things are watched more closely from now on. He now sees where he made grave mistakes in trusting this Tyler fellow and welcoming him into his home. If that hadn't happened, perhaps you would not have been tempted like you were."

The tears stung, but Miriam tried to hold them back.

Mose slowed for the Bylers' driveway and parked by the hitching post. Miriam climbed down from the buggy to wait while Mose tied his horse. She expected flashbacks from the times when Wayne used to bring her home. Wayne would tie his horse at this exact spot, and her heart would sing with joy as she waited for him. Only she wouldn't have been on her side of the buggy but right by Wayne's side, perhaps even with her hand on his as Wayne secured his horse.

But none of those visions returned. Rather, she saw Tyler parked down the road on that evening he had taken her to the youth gathering. Tyler had known enough to stop well short of Uncle William's driveway before he had taken her in his arms. Miriam stifled a whimper and pushed the memory away.

"Did you say something?" Mose asked as he appeared in front of her.

"No, I was just waiting." Miriam fixed her gaze on the ground. Soon this would end, she comforted herself. Courage gripped her, and she reached out to grab Mose's arm. "Can't we move up the wedding date, please? Don't you think this has gone on long enough?"

Mose hesitated before he pulled his arm away. "That is not the Lord's way, Miriam. We must not give in to a solution that seems easy." Mose paused, and a fierce look filled his eyes. "Is this why you pushed for an early wedding date before? Because of this temptation with the *Englisha* man? You had to have known of Tyler when you were in Wayne County, and you did not tell me? Is this not so?"

Miriam's head spun. Now she had only made things worse. Mose had obviously not thought of this angle yet. "Is that any worse than what you already suspect me of?" Miriam tried to breathe evenly as she waited for Mose's answer.

Mose was silent for a moment and then said, "We had best leave that alone. The *bann* has taken care of your past. There isn't much else we can do beyond what we have done." Mose studied Miriam's face as the tears trickled down her cheeks. He seemed touched, finally, and took her hand. "Come, there has been enough sorrow now. The great apostle told us that we must take up the erring member after a proper repentance." Mose led the way toward the house. "We must leave this behind us now and move on."

Miriam didn't pull her fingers out of his hand when she opened the front door, and Mose didn't either. Together they entered the house and seated themselves on the couch. Mose faced Miriam, and a smile crept over his face as he placed his free hand over the one he held. "You wouldn't have something to eat, would you? I'm starved."

Miriam forced herself to stand but had to grab the back of the couch for support. "Whoa there," Mose teased. "Looks like you need some food yourself."

She needed something else worse, Miriam told herself, but Mose wouldn't understand. She wanted to be held close and comforted after what she had been through. Mose could at least give her a hug, couldn't he? They were promised to each other. Would a hug be such an unholy thing?

Mose regarded her for a moment. "Do you need help in the kitchen perhaps? Maybe with finding the pies? I'm sure my nose will lead me right to them," he joked.

Miriam forced a smile, though the effort cost her more than Mose would ever know. But she might as well get used to forced smiles. Mose wouldn't change much — if at all — after they said the marriage vows. The *bann* he had prescribed for her this past week shattered that illusion.

"Come," Miriam forced the words out. "You can sit at the kitchen table while I find something."

"That would be *gut,*" he said. "I would love to watch you. I haven't had that much chance to be with you this week, and I do have to leave tomorrow. I won't be seeing you again for a long time. I won't make the trip again. You know that, don't you?"

"*Yah,* I know that," Miriam answered.

Mose smiled his thanks as he followed Miriam to the kitchen. He had once again misunderstood her, and she wouldn't correct him. She would need all the months until school was out to prepare her heart to see Mose again. Much prayer and submission would be needed. That was something Mose obviously wouldn't understand either.

CHAPTER THIRTY-FOUR

It was Christmas Eve, and Miriam was driving home from school with the lines held loose in her hand. Star seemed to sense her mood and responded with a slower pace as they approached Highway 48. School hadn't let out for the Christmas holidays until noon today because a week had been lost as a result of her *bann.* The pain of that memory lingered, and her work seemed to take twice as long to finish. Miriam hadn't completed correcting all the student papers until a few moments ago. But it was better to work late now so she wouldn't have to return to the schoolhouse until the Monday after New Year's Day.

Miriam's gaze lingered on the open prairie, and a sigh escaped her lips. More than a week had passed since Mose left on the bus for his return trip to Wayne County. She had written him last Friday evening and mailed the letter on Saturday, even though

Mose hadn't written yet. There would be no repeat of her mistakes from before. She would do her part to make her engagement with Mose work. Her marriage to Mose would be the end of the road for her. All choice would end once the vows were said, but joy would surely come afterward. It would have to. Didn't love grow in the hearts of all married couples who lived in the fear of the Lord?

Maybe Mose would change once they were wed. Mose would take her in his arms, and her heart would be comforted — if she could make it through the months ahead. That was the trial, and obviously Mose knew this and planned to test her to the fullest. This was Mose's right, Miriam reminded herself. She had revealed her flaws to him when she kissed Tyler Johnson. Thankfully, Mose still planned to marry her. For that she ought to get down on her knees each night and give thanks to the Lord.

Miriam glanced up toward the heavens and whispered, "Thank You," but her heart felt like lead. Well, there was nothing she could do about that except wait until the vows were said and love for Mose came into her heart.

Star jerked his head skyward as they approached the Byler driveway. He whinnied as if he wished to add his own prayer. A slight smile crossed Miriam's face but vanished at once. She pulled the buggy to a stop beside the new barn and climbed down. Her heavy heart would lift by the time school began after the New Year, Miriam promised herself. She couldn't appear in front of her students with this sadness on her face. She hoped they hadn't noticed the depth of her sorrow so far. She had tried to show a happy face each day, but ever since the *bann* she had struggled to maintain a cheerful attitude in school.

A startled look crossed Miriam's face when the front door opened and Aunt Fannie hurried out to meet her.

"What is it?" Miriam called out. Had she been wrapped up in her own troubles while something terrible had happened at home again?

"This just came." Aunt Fannie caught her breath to wave an envelope. "A letter from Mose. I thought you needed to see it at once."

"Is there news?" Miriam clutched Star's bridle with both hands.

"Silly," Aunt Fannie said. "I wouldn't read your mail, but it's the first one from your promised one to arrive after he's been here. I thought it might cheer you up."

Nothing will cheer me up, Miriam almost said. Instead, she forced a smile. "I suppose I should read it right now — after I put Star in the barn."

Aunt Fannie helped Miriam unhitch the buggy and followed her to Star's stall where she said, "I know you remember the time several years ago when William found out that I kissed my *Englisha* boyfriend after I began dating him. I feel bad when I remember how supportive you were back then and how little comfort I've been to you as you went through a much worse situation." Aunt Fannie hung her head.

"You mustn't blame yourself," Miriam protested. "No two situations are alike."

"Still, I feel so helpless," Aunt Fannie continued, taking Miriam's hand. "You seem to always make the right choices, even when they're hard. I trembled when I was faced with a little church confession, and here you went through the *bann.*"

Miriam forced a laugh. "Only for a week, and Mose made it easy."

"You know that's not true. The *bann* is never easy." Aunt Fannie gave Miriam a tight hug again. "Come, let's eat a quiet supper, and tomorrow we have nothing to do but celebrate the Lord's birthday."

"Are we staying home?"

"Is there somewhere you'd like to go?" Aunt Fannie gave Miriam a kind look. "Because I can arrange something."

"Nay, I'd much rather stay home." Miriam tried to appear cheerful.

Aunt Fannie didn't appear convinced. "Maybe William's family has something going we can attend."

Miriam shook her head. "No, thanks. I'm fine staying home."

"Well, okay," Aunt Fannie gave in. "I guess most of the community is taking a quiet day off since school didn't let out until Christmas Eve."

Miriam hung her head. "That's my fault. My sins seem to follow me everywhere I go."

"Oh, you poor dear!" Aunt Fannie exclaimed as she took Miriam's hand and rubbed it in affection.

"My letter." Miriam held up the envelope. "I should go read it. And then I'll be right down to help with supper."

"You take your time." Aunt Fannie held the front door open for them as Jonathon raced out of the kitchen to leap into Miriam's arms.

Miriam held him tight and kissed the top of his head.

"There's ice cream tonight!" Jonathon

yelped when Miriam let him go.

Miriam turned to her aunt. "You made ice cream?"

"A little something special to cheer you up," Aunt Fannie said, wiping away a tear.

Jonathon looked like he didn't know what the tears were about, and so with a shout of joy he ran off to play outside.

"I'll read Mose's letter and be right down," Miriam declared.

Miriam hurried upstairs. She opened the envelope and took out the single page. But she shouldn't be disappointed at its shortness, Miriam told herself. Even short letters could supply some measure of comfort.

Miriam read quickly . . .

Dear Miriam,

Greetings in the name of the Lord. I had a blessed trip back to Wayne County this past week, though bus travel always makes for weariness of body and soul. The Lord's grace was with me. I arrived home to find the farm work suffering, but I hope to catch up after Christmas. My mother has Christmas breakfast planned at her place, and I can't miss that. One shouldn't work on the Lord's birthday anyway, even if the date is a little questionable, coming from the *En-*

glisha as it does.

My sisters brought in plenty of food for over the holidays, but that can't go on forever. I couldn't impose to such an extent even if they had the time. I think you met them when you visited here, but I know everything was a little strange that Sunday. That will change once we are wed and you have moved into the house here in Wayne County.

All three of my sisters have large families of their own. One has three *kinner,* and the other two have five each. My six brothers are likewise blessed with *kinner.* The oldest brother, Michael, has eight. I pray that the Lord will likewise grant grace to us. This matter has been heavy on my mind since I have been back from Oklahoma. The shame of the past will lie far behind us if the Lord will make our marriage fruitful. I pray the Lord will see fit to grant this desire of my heart. In my new calling as bishop, I long for a ministry that is successful both in the church and at home. I know this cannot happen unless *kinner* are granted to us. I trust that you will join me in prayer on this matter.

I will preach the Sunday after Christmas for the second time since my bishop ordination. And my first communion service will be in the spring. There will be plenty to keep my mind and soul occupied. And of course there is the farm work, which will be heavy this spring.

I pray that you are well and continue to walk in the Lord's will.

Sincerely,
Mose Stoll

Miriam bit her lip as the tears stung. Not one kind word. Had that been too much to expect after all that she had done for Mose while he visited? Couldn't he at least have expressed his love for her? Aunt Fannie's kindness had soothed her spirit, but she wanted the love of the man she planned to marry. Surely that wasn't too high an expectation?

A twinge of bitterness stirred, and Miriam suppressed the emotion at once. She must not go there! Ever! That road led nowhere. Obedience to *Daett* and now to Mose was the life she knew. That road might be rough, but she should be honored to become the wife of a bishop. And her *kinner* would be blessed to have such a *daett.*

Miriam folded the page quickly. She would not think of *kinner* right now, or of Mose. Aunt Fannie had ice cream downstairs, and the family would eat, and laugh, and enjoy each other's company tonight. Tomorrow she would rest. With her body renewed, perhaps she would feel better about all of this.

Miriam took a deep breath and hurried downstairs.

"You do look more cheerful," Aunt Fannie pronounced as she walked in the kitchen.

Miriam didn't say anything. Aunt Fannie didn't need to know how little the letter had comforted her.

"Shall I bring the ice cream up?" Miriam asked, heading toward the basement door before Aunt Fannie could answer. Jonathon, who had already come back inside for supper, was in the basement, parked in front of the hand-cranked freezer. Little dribbles of ice water ran down the side of the wood and past his toes.

"It's delicious," Jonathon said happily.

"Did you eat some?" Miriam scolded.

The guilt on Jonathon's face was answer enough. "Only a fingertip, that's all."

"You shouldn't," Miriam explained. "If the container is still inside the salty ice water and you lift the lid off, salt can get into the ice cream."

"It didn't," Jonathon assured her. "But please don't tell *Mamm.*"

"The salt will tell the story." Miriam gave him a stern look. "Remember that. Sins are always found out."

He nodded soberly. Miriam considered that was a lesson she learned herself the hard way. The salt had definitely betrayed her.

"Can I help?" Jonathon held out both hands when Miriam lifted the stainless steel container from the ice water.

"Grab the bottom," she ordered. "And hold on until I get a better grip."

He clung to the container as if his life depended on the effort. Miriam looked at his innocent face and tears formed as she wondered, *Will I one day have wonderful* kinner *like Jonathon*? She couldn't imagine it when she remembered Mose's stern face. Would he allow joy and happiness in their home and ice cream on Christmas Eve, or would life be all work, and duty, and seeking the church's blessing?

"Does the salt make you cry?" Jonathon appeared puzzled. He adjusted his grip, and Miriam did likewise.

"Let me take it now," Miriam said lightheartedly.

Jonathon seemed to forget his question as he followed Miriam upstairs. His eyes glowed as she set the container in the kitchen sink and dipped the ice cream out with a spoon. His finger crept forward again, and Miriam touched his leg with her foot. Jonathon jumped, and a look of guilt rushed over his face.

But he still protested. "I can't get any salt in it now."

"Depend on a child to figure out a way around everything," Aunt Fannie said.

"It's still better not to," Miriam told Jonathon.

Jonathon took his place at the table and stared expectantly at the ice cream heaped high in its new home.

Footsteps were heard coming through the washroom door, followed by Uncle William's cheerful face. He hollered, "What have we here? Ice cream!" He seemed even happier than Jonathon. Warm circles rushed around Miriam's heart. At least tonight some joy had crept back into her life.

"Now, go wash up and come for supper," Aunt Fannie ordered.

Uncle William's face darkened for a moment as he turned to Miriam. "Thought you ought to know that Tyler fellow is back in the community. He stopped in at Deacon Phillips's today. He's come back to say how sorry he is for how things have gone with the fires and the police and all."

"Oh, William! Did you have to say that!" Aunt Fannie snapped. "We're having a quiet evening at home. Miriam doesn't need more stress in her life."

"Sorry," Uncle William muttered. "But Miriam doesn't have to worry. We all understand the danger now."

Miriam dropped the ice cream spoon and fled into the living room to compose herself. What would her aunt and uncle say if they knew the unwanted thrill that had shot through her at the mention of Tyler's name? The thrill quickly turned to shame, though, and Miriam knew she must try to somehow save this evening and not drag the rest of the family down with her. They deserved to enjoy their ice cream with joy in their hearts. She would fake joy; there was no other option. And later she would cry out to the Lord once she was alone upstairs. She would have to beg once more that somehow the Lord would change her heart. She could not go down this path with Tyler again.

With a set face Miriam reentered the kitchen. Thankfully, Aunt Fannie didn't say anything, but joined in with her effort at laughter and light conversation as the meal began.

CHAPTER THIRTY-FIVE

Miriam closed the schoolhouse door and stepped out into the light dusting of snow swirling around the corner of the building. The wind pulled on her scarf. Winter had decided to make an appearance just in time for the first day of school after the Christmas recess. The chill cut through her dress, and Miriam pulled the thin coat she had grabbed this morning tighter around her shoulder. Tomorrow she would have to wear warmer clothing.

A few of the *Englisha* houses in the distance still twinkled with their Christmas lights in the front windows, but none of the cheer reached Miriam. Inside, an even deeper winter cold lay heavy on her soul. It had been there since Christmas Eve and showed no signs of abatement. If there were snowdrifts of the heart, hers were ten feet high and still piling up.

Halfway to the small shelter where Star

waited, Miriam lifted her face into the wind and squinted. Was that Tyler's rental car? She was sure a vehicle was creeping up the school's driveway. Miriam pulled in a sharp breath and rubbed her eyes. The image went away. The wind burned her eyes as it whipped in off the prairie. Was this what happened when people lost their minds? Didn't they see things that weren't there?

With a small cry, Miriam rushed toward her buggy. Her hand trembled as she placed her book bag inside and entered the shelter. The cold had crept in unhindered, and Star's nostrils sprouted blasts of steam.

Miriam stroked the horse's beautiful face with both hands and asked, "Have I lost my mind?"

Star blinked and chewed slowly.

A wild laugh threatened to burst out of Miriam. She *had* gone mad. She was talking to her horse as if he understood. The Christmas respite had done her no *gut.* She wasn't as refreshed as she had been after previous Christmas breaks, when she had come back filled with a yearning to begin the second half of the school term. Now her heart felt like ice.

Four more months of school remained before she would leave this place forever to wed Mose in Wayne County. A cry escaped her this time, and Miriam clung to Star's halter. Somehow she had to gain control of herself. There was no reason for this exhaustion. She had done little but putter around Aunt Fannie's place ever since Christmas Day. Aunt Fannie had seen to that.

"You need rest after what you've been through," Aunt Fannie had instructed Miriam.

Miriam slipped on Star's bridle as he whinnied loudly.

"We can drive fast," Miriam said in comfort. "Home to your warm barn."

Miriam hitched him to the buggy and climbed in. Star dashed out of the school driveway, and she hung on to the reins. Usually joy would ripple through her at this fast run home, but now there was only the wind in her face and the heavy feeling in her heart. She would have to speak with Aunt Fannie. She couldn't face her students like this tomorrow morning, but hiring another substitute or delaying school again was unthinkable. She had already cost the school enough with her troubles. The schoolboard had been nothing but patient and understanding so far, but they had limits too.

Star made good time and didn't slow down until Uncle William's new barn came into view. The snow had blown from the roof and piled in small drifts along the east side. Little swirls lifted skyward with each gust. Star whinnied loudly again, and Miriam hung on to the reins as they took the turn into the lane with a clatter of buggy wheels. Uncle William's face peered out of the barn door as Miriam pulled to a halt. Star's breath blasted white into the sky. He tossed his head, and Miriam waited to catch her breath before she climbed down.

"Are you okay?" Uncle William asked as his head appeared beside the buggy door.

"That was some ride!" Miriam replied, trying to sound cheerful.

Uncle William wasn't deceived. "Maybe you'd better let me unhitch, and you can get into the house."

"I'll be fine," she said halfheartedly.

"Now, do as I say," Uncle William commanded, sounding fatherly. "I don't want you to overdo yourself."

Miriam wouldn't argue. He was probably right, so she climbed down and retrieved her book bag, attempted a quick smile, and turned toward the house.

When she opened the door, Jonathon flew into Miriam's arms as usual, giggling as Miriam hugged him. Then he ran off to resume his play.

Aunt Fannie peered out of the kitchen doorway. "How did your day go?"

"Okay, I guess." Miriam sat on a kitchen bench with a sigh. Usually she came back from the schoolhouse refreshed in her spirit. Not today, and there was no use trying to fool Aunt Fannie.

"There's a letter from Mose," Aunt Fannie offered hopefully. "Maybe that will cheer you up."

Miriam said nothing. Didn't Aunt Fannie know by now that a letter from Mose would only make her worse? *Yah,* she knew. She had seen her niece mope around the house all Christmas week.

"I wish there was something I could do," Aunt Fannie said, her hand resting gently on Miriam's arm.

Miriam didn't answer and looked away.

"Tell me, Miriam," Aunt Fannie insisted, "what is it that's happened since the *bann* was lifted that has you so down? I had hoped you'd be back to your normal happy self by now."

Miriam finally whispered the words. "It was on Christmas Eve when Uncle William said that Tyler had stopped in at Deacon Phillips's place. That set my heart spinning, even though I didn't want it to."

Aunt Fannie's hand tightened on Miriam's arm, her voice gentle. "Miriam, are you in love with Tyler?"

Miriam gasped. "How can you say such a thing?"

"Because you show all the signs." Aunt Fannie pulled Miriam close. "Of course, you know such a thing cannot be. Such a match will not bring you happiness — only more misery."

"*Yah,* I know," Miriam said. "I will marry Mose, and that will be the end of it. It must be the end of it."

"In this condition?" Aunt Fannie frowned. "You aren't fit to be anyone's bride right now."

"Mose won't care." The words slipped out, their sound harsh. "He just sees all the benefits I'll bring to him. I'll be a *gut frau,* and keep his house, and support him in his bishop work, and bear his *kinner.*"

"Miriam!" Aunt Fannie gasped. "Why are you so bitter?"

"I don't know." Miriam struggled to control her anger. "Something has happened to me. I don't feel like the same Miriam anymore. I feel so different inside. I think I've gone mad."

"You're not considering refusing Mose?" Aunt Fannie appeared dazed.

"Nay. I will marry him."

Aunt Fannie appeared relieved. "We all go through times like this. You will survive."

"I hope so," Miriam said, standing to her feet. "I really hope so."

Aunt Fanny hesitated and then said, "Miriam, I want to be honest with you. You need to know that Tyler has been back in the community more than just the once William mentioned. We don't know much about what he's up to, but we've heard that he's trying to make things right with Bishop Mullet and Deacon Phillips."

"Tyler is around again?" Miriam didn't know whether she was happy or troubled at the words.

"Remember, any feelings you have for him can only end in misery." Aunt Fannie's voice was firm. "He's from another world, and he will never be part of us. You know that."

"*Yah*. What is so hard for me to bear is that I thought Tyler had feelings for me. But now I just feel he was using me. It was all about his news story, wasn't it?"

When Aunt Fannie didn't respond, Miriam glanced over at her aunt. A look of guilt fell on Aunt Fannie's face . . . and Miriam noticed.

"Don't you agree?" Miriam asked. "It was never really about me. It was about the scandal. I was used. And then he even apparently started that rumor about . . ." Tears formed, and she choked on sobs.

Finally, Aunt Fannie spoke. "Miriam, perhaps there's something else you need to know. We weren't going to tell you, hoping this would all pass and you'd find happiness without bringing up something that would only stir your emotions more."

Miriam looked puzzled. "What could you possibly tell me that would help?"

"Wait here a moment," Aunt Fanny said, as she turned and went into her bedroom. She quickly returned with a newspaper. "I guess you should read this editorial. It came out in the paper shortly after all those reporters were questioning you and Mose out by the driveway."

Miriam took the paper from her aunt.

In a column on the opened editorial page, Miriam read . . .

TYLER JOHNSON'S DEFENSE
OF THE AMISH

Tyler Johnson, the freelance journalist who has uncovered a political corruption case involving a sitting US Senator, is now using his influence not to further his own interests but those of a little-known Amish community near Clarita. The community figured heavily in the original corruption allegations, but Mr. Johnson is attempting to change that perception. He has pled with federal law enforcement investigators to minimize the community's involvement and to focus instead on the real perpetrators of the corruption who carried out their nefarious scheme under the guise of helping the Amish community recover from the damage of the tornadoes that ripped through the community two years ago.

According to Mr. Johnson, the peaceful lifestyle and nonresistant beliefs of the Amish could be threatened or severely strained by the court testimony necessary in the federal prosecution of the political corruption case. Mr. Johnson has made a vigorous defense for the community's beliefs, which are traceable to the sixteenth century and a little-known group of dissenters during the Protestant Reformation.

As if the drama were not interesting enough, Mr. Johnson was originally quoted by a locally based online magazine as having had a romantic dalliance with Miriam Yoder, an Amish schoolteacher from the Clarita community. Mr. Johnson now insists he was misquoted. He claims no such relationship existed. "All of the Amish women," Mr. Johnson says, "are models of decorum and have outstanding reputations, especially the community's schoolteacher. Miss Yoder is engaged to an Amish bishop, and I wish her all the happiness in the world." Mr. Johnson's account was apparently verified by Miss Yoder's fiancé, Bishop Mose Stoll, who in an unusual move, spoke recently with reporters outside of an Amish reconstruction project at the home of Mr. William Byler, a Clarita Amish man whose barn had been burned to the ground in an unsuccessful attempt to end Mr. Johnson's investigation.

It is the recommendation of this paper that authorities honor Mr. Johnson's request to respect the local Amish community's admittedly quaint traditions and also to refrain from casting aspersions on individual members of the community without evidence of wrongdoing.

The remaining two paragraphs of the editorial trailed off into meaningless clatter as far as Miriam was concerned. Miriam let the paper fall from her fingers to the floor.

Tyler had defended her? To the whole world? Tyler hadn't even revealed their kisses. Surely the story of how he had kissed an engaged Amish woman would have sold plenty of copies. But Tyler hadn't told.

Miriam picked up the paper again and stared at the words. Tyler's tenderness reached off the pages and passed through her whole being. *Yah,* it turned out he was a wonderful man, and he hadn't been using her . . . but the fact remained that Tyler was not for her. Miriam brought herself up sharply.

"Thank you, Aunt Fannie. Thank you so very much," Miriam said, setting the paper on a nearby table.

CHAPTER THIRTY-SIX

The February sun peeked through the heavy clouds scurrying across the prairie sky. Miriam bent her head against the wind and hitched Star to the buggy. Another school week was at a close and every bone in her body ached. Even the children had noticed her crushed spirit this past month. Miriam was sure of it, hard as she tried to act her usual cheerful self.

"What is to become of me?" Miriam asked Star.

He turned to stare at her and blinked his eyes. Miriam patted Star's neck before she climbed into the buggy and drove out of the schoolhouse lane. She had hoped the turning of a new calendar page this month would make a difference. She had even sent a prayer heavenward while she stood staring at the twenty-eight numbered days on the calendar. But the days until March still seemed far away and heavy.

At home in her dresser, more of Mose's letters lay still and empty. They were filled with his plans and all about the happenings on his farm. He was doing well, and his preaching as the community's new bishop pleased the people. Miriam knew she should be with him. Maybe then Mose would show her a little affection. But why couldn't Mose say something kind and affectionate in his letters? Mose knew she supported him. She had shown that plainly enough. Why couldn't he at least sound like he cared for her? Even the smallest form of endearment would have brought tears to her eyes.

Maybe Mose was just different. She had been used to men like Wayne who had kissed her often during their engagement. The memory brought a sting of pain. She had no right to think of Wayne's kisses — or, more importantly, Tyler's.

She was spoiled, that was all. Mose was a bishop, a leader among the people. And he wanted her as his *frau.* That was the Lord's way. Eventually she would come out of this depression. Didn't all things come to an end, both *gut* and bad?

Miriam turned onto Highway 48 and lowered her head against the wind. Star did the same. He picked up speed, apparently in a hurry to arrive at Uncle William's warm barn. Miriam let him pick the pace, and they soon whirled into the Byler driveway.

Uncle William came out of the greenhouse to help unhitch with his hat pulled low over his ears.

"Kind of brisk yet," he greeted her.

Miriam attempted a smile. "*Yah,* but winter has to end sometime. Thanks for helping," she said to him as he led Star to the barn.

"Miriam, are you okay?" He paused with his hand on the bridle.

"*Yah,* school went well." Miriam forced another smile. "I'm fine."

"Okay," he said, and went on. She was not about to tell her troubles to Uncle William. He could do nothing to help her. No one could . . . except Mose.

Miriam retrieved her book bag from under the buggy seat, and with a final glance over her shoulder headed for the house. Aunt Fannie met her at the door, but there was no sign of Jonathon.

"He's playing upstairs," Aunt Fannie explained.

But there was more to this, Miriam was sure. For some reason Jonathon had been told to stay upstairs when she came home.

"Come." Aunt Fannie took Miriam's arm. "We need to talk."

Her heart pounding, Miriam joined her aunt on the couch. Had she done something wrong?

Aunt Fannie stroked her arm. "William I are really worried about you, Miriam. And I'm sure Mose would be too if he knew. You're not the happy, cheerful schoolteacher we used to have."

Miriam sat up straight. "I'm sorry about that. I've tried to put on a *gut* face at school. Maybe I can do better next week."

"No, Miriam." Aunt Fannie's voice was low. "This has gone on long enough. I need to intervene in some way. Ever since Christmas you've been moping around as though you've lost your dearest friend. I think it has to do with Mose."

Miriam looked down at the floor. She would say nothing against her future husband.

"Miriam, I want you to show me Mose's letters. All of them since you were put under the *bann.*"

Miriam gasped. "But I shouldn't."

Aunt Fannie was gentle. "Something is wrong, Miriam, and we need to know what."

"But, his letters?" Miriam hesitated.

"Go get them," Aunt Fannie ordered.

Miriam waited. Was she really in bad enough shape that Aunt Fannie had to intervene? And Uncle William? He was involved too?

Miriam rose and took the stairs in slow motion and retrieved the letters from her dresser drawer. She had planned to keep them to show her children and grand-children someday — hers and Mose's.

Surely Mose wouldn't approve of her showing the letters to her aunt, so Miriam was torn. But Aunt Fannie wouldn't take no for an answer. With a groan Miriam descended the stairs and handed the letters to Aunt Fannie. Aunt Fannie began at once to read, taking her time on the first two, but scanning from there until she reached the last page of the most recent letter.

In his letter from this week he had written the details of his sermon. It was all there in black and white, and Aunt Fannie read each word. Mose had written as if he liked the words, without any concern over how they affected her. Then the final line in the letter was Mose's attempt at humor: "Minister Kemp must also be impressed with how things are going. He told me once more that his widowed sister Bethany is still looking for a husband. I laughed and told him that this area in my life is already taken care of."

Aunt Fannie set down the letter. "This is awful, Miriam. I'm so sorry."

"I suppose I deserve it," Miriam muttered.

Aunt Fannie ignored her answer and asked, "Miriam, has Mose ever said anything kind to you? Has he ever . . . touched you?"

Miriam knew her face showed the answer.

"Not even since you've been engaged?" Aunt Fannie asked, her voice rising.

"Mose never asked me to marry him." The words slipped out. "He just planned the wedding. I guess Mose knew I wouldn't object."

Aunt Fannie stood to pace the floor. "I've heard of a lot of hurtful things in my life, but this . . . I'm at a loss for words."

"He's going to marry me." Miriam came to his defense. "He's overlooked my sins and is still willing to have me. That's enough . . . isn't it? And besides, I thought you liked the man."

"I do!" Aunt Fannie exclaimed. "But I also like you, Miriam. You're dear to my heart, and this is wrong. This man is like ice." Aunt Fannie searched for more words. "Well, anyway, I know how a woman about to become a *frau* acts when she's about to be blessed with a husband . . . and this is not it, Miriam."

"But he's . . ." Miriam began before the tears choked her voice. Then great sobs wracked her body, and Aunt Fannie pulled her close.

When the tears slowed, Aunt Fannie held Miriam at arm's length. "I have to tell you this, Miriam. It's not fair if I don't. Tyler has been asking to speak with you."

Miriam wiped her eyes with her handkerchief. "At this point, what difference does that make?"

"None, really, I guess. Except he's not sneaking around. That much is to his credit. And he's been staying away in obedience to Uncle William's forbidding him to contact you."

"Tyler's not from our world." Miriam met Aunt Fannie's gaze. "What can he possibly say to me that won't be just more hurt?"

"I don't know," Aunt Fannie said. "I just had to tell you in light of these letters. Why, there's not a single line of endearment toward you in any of them!"

"Maybe that's just his way," Miriam defended.

"No, this kind of courtship is not normal, especially from a man who's been married before. Why isn't the wedding date this spring after school is out, or even next month? Most men would demand such a thing. Were you not willing to be married sooner?"

Miriam glanced away before she answered. "I suggested it twice, but Mose said no. Especially since I fell so low with Tyler. And maybe my motives weren't too pure for wanting to marry soon. I wanted to wed so I could get away from my weakness." The tears began again, stinging her eyes.

Aunt Fannie gave Miriam another long hug. "I have to speak with William about this. He will want to know."

"But what if Mose finds out that I told you of our private conversations and showed you his letters?"

"We'll take care of that," Aunt Fannie promised.

How that was possible, Miriam had no idea, but the weight on her shoulders had lifted a little.

Miriam squeezed her aunt's hand. "Thank you for listening. I've had only Star lately to tell my troubles to."

"Oh, you poor thing." Aunt Fannie was in tears herself. "I'm going out to see William right now."

Miriam fled upstairs and grabbed Jonathon for a long hug when he peeked out of the front room.

"Does that mean I can come out now?" he asked.

"Yah." Miriam played with his hair. "I'm

sorry you had to stay in the room at all."

"*Mamm* said it was important." Jonathon's face was sober. "Really important!"

"Oh, you're such a dear." Miriam gave him another hug.

Jonathon wiggled out of Miriam's arms and ran downstairs. Moments later Miriam heard the washroom door slam. With numbness running through her whole body, Miriam entered her bedroom to stare at the corner of the dresser drawer where the stack of letters had been. Aunt Fannie had taken them with her to the greenhouse. Mose's letters! A chill ran up the back of her neck. Mose would learn of this, and he would not understand. She had allowed other people to read his love letters. Only there was no love in them. Miriam trembled and closed the drawer. The image of the missing letters didn't fade away, though. They became larger in her mind until that was all she could see. Mose had wanted this time of their life blessed by the Lord, but she had failed him once again.

She had no tears left to cry. Surely her shame would follow her forever. What had happened to the determined young woman of only a few months ago who had been so happy living in the Lord's will as a single girl? Now she had the promise of marriage in front of her, and to a bishop at that, and all she could do was mope.

Straighten up, Miriam ordered herself. Somehow there would be a way out of this mess. She would write Mose tonight and tell him how truly sorry she was that Aunt Fannie saw the letters.

The front door slammed, and Miriam brought herself out of her thoughts to hurry downstairs.

"Everything's going to be okay, Miriam," Aunt Fannie told her, stepping close enough to squeeze Miriam's hand.

"Why? What did Uncle William say?" Miriam couldn't keep the fear out of her voice.

Aunt Fannie hesitated. "William agrees with me. Something must be done about this, and it's more than we can handle."

Miriam stared out the living room window as Uncle William's buggy drove out of the driveway. "Where's he going?"

"To see Deacon Phillips." Aunt Fannie led Miriam to the couch again. "We need some advice from the ministry on how to handle this."

"You would punish me again?" Miriam felt the coldness creep through her.

"No, Miriam," Aunt Fannie said. "You've been punished enough. It's time now to look at the other side of this picture. Maybe we haven't been seeing everything."

"Like what?" Miriam kept her gaze on the floor.

"We want you back," Aunt Fannie assured her. "The old Miriam who was so full of joy. The person the whole community so loved and appreciated. Everyone knows you've done your part. It might be . . ." Aunt Fannie stopped.

Miriam waited, and when Aunt Fannie didn't continue, she looked up. "Might be what?"

Aunt Fannie struggled for a moment. "Let's just leave it at that for now. You're not wed yet, and this dating period is to find out whether you are suited for each other."

Now the tears sprang up again. "And so you think I'm not suited for Mose."

Aunt Fannie's eyes brimmed with tears. "No, Miriam. It's what we never looked at before. Is Mose suited for you? Is he worthy of you?"

CHAPTER THIRTY-SEVEN

Under the bright television lights Tyler pasted on the expected smile. The anchor of the local Oklahoma show leaned forward. "So you're at the height of your fame right now, Tyler. A little unprecedented for a freelance journalist. How did you accomplish this feat?"

"I hope to rise much higher," Tyler quipped. "Perhaps I'll take over your chair before long, Dennis."

The anchor chuckled. "Good answer. But tell me, how did this happen?"

Tyler kept his smile bright. "I pursued an assignment from an editor I often work for. He wanted a public interest piece on the Amish, a report on how they had recovered from the tornado that ripped through southeastern Oklahoma a couple of years ago. That story line got me a hearing with the Amish, who opened their homes to me, invited me for supper, and showed me how their rebuilt properties were faring. Sensing more to the story, I dug deeper, followed my instincts, and soon there was a trail to follow."

"You make that sound so easy," said the anchor, grinning. "But that's unusual access for a journalist among the usually media-shy Amish. How did you accomplish that?"

Tyler glanced up at the ceiling. "Maybe I had some aid from above. Who knows? That makes the most sense to me, but the Amish and I did learn to trust each other rather quickly."

"Any truth to the report that you had a romance with one of the young Amish maidens, in particular a young school-teacher?" The anchor gave Tyler a sharp look.

"Why does everyone always come back to that?" Tyler forced a laugh. "I've answered the question in detail. A romance would have closed the door for me with the Amish, not opened it."

The anchor leaned forward again. "Your fellow journalist, Mimi Coons, insists that she reported accurately. Miss Coons also claims as your former girlfriend that your charms are well documented."

Tyler made a wry face. "Is that supposed to help or hinder the reporting?"

The anchor ignored the remark. "Miss Coons has a new article up this morning. Have you seen it?"

Tyler sat up straighter. "No."

A look of glee filled the anchor's face. "This is what Miss Coons has to say." He motioned toward a large TV screen now filled with script. The anchor read aloud, "Following my conversation with Tyler Johnson about his time spent among the small Amish community in Clarita, Oklahoma, I have been challenged by Mr. Johnson on my version of what transpired at our interview."

"I never said what she claims I said," Tyler interrupted.

"Let's see then," the anchor continued, and the screen scrolled down. "In an attempt to buttress my claims, I have made my own inquiries into the small Amish community at Clarita. The local sources couldn't supply me any further information, but I was assured that the kind of access Mr. Johnson speaks of is unprecedented for the Amish. So I stand by my original claim. Mr. Johnson had the inside track somewhere, but only he can give us the details."

"See," Tyler laughed. "It's a dead-end street. The Amish are a godly people. They have their strange ways, but those are to further their chosen way of life. In no way did I or anyone in the community compromise their faith. I have gone out of my way to ask for respect from the investigators. The Amish's desire to avoid testifying in court is deeply ingrained in their belief system, and the investigators have agreed. With ulterior motives perhaps, because they have plenty of other witnesses now to interrogate. I suppose a scene in which the Amish refuse to testify in open court and are held in contempt is the last thing any decent investigation needs. That could reflect badly in the public's opinion, to say the least. And any appeals court would likely uphold the Amish religious objections to testifying anyway."

"You seem well versed in the Amish faith." The anchor smiled. "Ever think about going back?"

Tyler hesitated. "I still have contact."

"Will you elaborate?"

"Not really." Tyler grinned.

"Now you're leading me around," the anchor scolded.

"Just don't misquote me, as Mimi . . . Miss Coons did," Tyler warned.

"So there was no romance, even an Amish version of it?" The anchor gave Tyler a steady look.

"I'm afraid that's a story for another day," Tyler shot back. "I think you're out of time."

The anchor chuckled. "And that's it for us today, folks. Thank you for watching. And the best of luck to Mr. Johnson and his romance with the Amish maidens. Maybe we'll have him on for his Amish wedding announcement someday."

The music rose and the TV lights dimmed.

"Very funny, I'm sure," Tyler said, glaring at the anchor.

"I believe you're hiding something," the anchor responded. "Maybe I should take a trip into Amish country myself and meet this schoolteacher of yours."

"Happy hunting," Tyler quipped. He stood up and was escorted back to the makeup room, where he cleaned his face. The makeup didn't come off easily, and Tyler grumbled, "This is the last time I'm going on one of those things."

"I heard that." His escort stuck her head around the corner. "You'll come back if you get the chance. This is television. Good PR for you."

Tyler finished and was shown out. He wondered if the statement was true. Would he continue this kind of life? Would the success he was experiencing give him what he wanted? Next week this hoopla would be over, and certainly by the time the corruption trials began in the spring, he'd be old news. In fact, he felt old now. Not rejuvenated as he'd always imagined. Fame was supposed to lead one to the fountain of youth, but that hadn't happened.

Tyler's cell phone beeped, and he glanced at the text. "Can't make tomorrow but will reschedule. Gladly!" He had taken Lisa Burke out for dinner last week after they had met at a party. Tomorrow night he was to meet her again.

A smile played on Tyler's face, but it soon faded. He returned the phone to its holder without a response. He was bored with everything — the fame, the fortune, the charm, the whole thing. The date with Lisa might rejuvenate him, but the relationship wouldn't last. It never had before. Hilda had finally stopped texting after he wouldn't respond. And it wasn't Lisa's fault, either. Tyler was sure of that.

The truth was, the girl he wanted to see was Miriam. He wanted to be back with her people. What an odd thought. Tyler sobered at the notion. Was the community something he should seriously look into? Not in an investigative way. He'd already done that. But as his possible future? The thought wasn't new. He'd seen it float by a few times before but hadn't wanted to take a serious look.

Of course, Miriam was at the center of the question. He couldn't get his mind off her. Hilda hadn't done the trick. Nor had Lisa. No, it was Miriam he wanted to be with, which was why he'd kept tentative feelers in the Amish community. He'd gone so far as to ask Deacon Phillips two weeks ago whether he could speak with Miriam.

"I want to do things right this time," Tyler had offered.

A patient look had crossed Deacon Phillips's face. "You're not one of us, Tyler. It's for the best that you not speak with Miriam again."

He had felt a scolded schoolboy, but the truth was he also felt taken care of, as if he belonged somewhere, perhaps was even loved. That was the strangest feeling of all. Correction and love had never connected for him, and yet there was that component to the deacon's words. He wouldn't violate Deacon Phillips's wishes. The deacon's words were like a path he had to follow. And he knew it was best for Miriam. She was going to marry that bishop. He had stared at the man's face on TV and hadn't liked it. There wasn't a kind look in his eye when his glance shifted toward Miriam. Yet Miriam had stood bravely by his side, her face set. He couldn't imagine Miriam kissing the man.

"Skunks!" Tyler exclaimed. It was all a mess, and he could do nothing about it. Well, there was one thing he could do, but it seemed utterly impossible. He could join the Amish. Then he could marry Miriam. Miriam would never leave the Amish . . . nor did he want her to. Her Amish life was an asset for her, not a liability. Why did the English always see being Amish as a sort of prison, when the Amish were some of the freest people he'd ever met. He was no longer impressed with his life out here "in the world," as the Amish would say.

He could see his future where he was. Mostly he would spend average days and nights with girlfriends that all ultimately bored him. He couldn't imagine marriage with a girl from "the world."

Tyler sighed. He would consider joining the Amish. Who would care if he disappeared into a reclusive community? Tyler grinned at the thought. His charm and money might be missed by his girlfriends. On the other hand, his money didn't carry weight with the Amish. But maybe his charm could still be put to good use. If he didn't miss his guess, the deacon's wife,

Katie, certainly had hopes he'd join the community. Their daughter Ruth had turned up her nose at him the last time he stopped by. And afterward Ruth had peeked out of the kitchen window and made sure he saw her look of disinterest before she retreated again.

Tyler chuckled. Crushed puppy love — that's all Ruth had. Miriam, on the other hand, had never turned up her nose. She had rejected him in a deeper way, like a woman whose heart had reached his. Tyler groaned. Who would have thought his life would take this turn? The least he could do was to be honest with Deacon Phillips.

But Tyler could hear the deacon's first question already: "And why would you wish to join the community?" And the one that would follow: "Why would we want to have you after what has happened so far?"

Deacon Phillips might not ask the second question that way, but he would think it. And the answer was the truth: "Because I'm in love with your schoolteacher."

There! He had said the words, and he felt better already — more wholesome. Tyler laughed. He would wax eloquent with the deacon. Not that the man would be easily persuaded by his charm — and there was still the problem of Miriam's engagement.

She wouldn't break it. He was sure of that. So why should he waste his time?

He didn't know, but he had to try. If he didn't, he'd always wonder what could have been. He'd think and dream of what life could have been like with broadfall pants and suspenders and Miriam by his side. There would be drawbacks, but with Miriam's love, they could be overcome.

Deacon Phillips would be sure to point out the conflict of interest involved in his proposal. His professed interest in the community came with the love of a woman. Well, he'd just have to be honest and see where things led. This time he would cut no corners, take no shortcuts, steal no kisses from engaged women. He would go in openhanded and open-faced, and the sticks would fall where they would.

"May the best man win!" Tyler declared aloud. "The outsider against the bishop. The heart against the head."

CHAPTER THIRTY-EIGHT

Mose settled into his rocker at the end of a hard day's work and tore open the envelope in his hand. Why would Deacon Phillips from Oklahoma write him a letter? Surely Miriam hadn't transgressed again? He couldn't face the shame the second time. Minister Kemp would laugh heartily at his continued trouble with the young schoolteacher and do more than drop hints about his widowed sister Bethany with two children. Mose didn't doubt the need for a man in Bethany's house — just that he was the proper candidate. The next time the subject came up, he'd tell Minister Kemp that he was in prayer for his sister. Mose chuckled at the thought.

Mose returned his focus to the page in front of him and began to read.

Dear Bishop Mose,

Greetings in the name of the Lord. Praises be to the Most High God and our precious Redeemer and Lord. I hope this finds you in good health and prosperous in soul and body. We are looking forward to spring weather soon out here on the prairie. I don't remember Ohio having this cold a winter, but we've had quite the time of it. Seems like my bones feel the weather more each year.

But anyway, it has fallen to me to write this letter as the deacon and also because of my close contact with you while you visited our community. I assure you of my continued friendship and affection, and also of my respect for your new office. I pray the Lord may prosper you greatly. But I wish to raise an issue with you. Our concern as a community has been great these past weeks concerning our schoolteacher, Miriam, who is your promised one. We in no way wish to interfere in what the Lord has done or wills, but as you know, our people believe in community, and in speaking to what we see. We know that such efforts are feeble at best and greatly subject to error. In this we ask your forgiveness if we speak out of turn or stray into things that are not the truth.

It seems to us that Miriam has been greatly troubled since you left before Christmas. We thought at first this was the effect of the discipline placed upon her while you were here. But now we are well into March and our happy, cheerful schoolteacher is not back with us. I'm sure you can see how this would be a cause for concern with all of our parents as well as the ministry. I do hasten to say that Miriam has not complained or spoken unworthily of her position as your promised *frau* or against you. Miriam has not complained at all. I know these details only through her uncle and aunt and what I and others have observed. William has been over to visit me, and his concerns as well as Fannie's bear sufficient weight that I promised to write you. I assure you that they are both on your side and wish only what is best for your proposed marriage and for your calling in the church. Please do not think otherwise.

So I ask with great trembling of soul and some question as to the wisdom of this whether you could find it in your heart to visit again. Could you spend some time with your promised one and show her the proper tenderness and affection she needs from the man who will be her husband? I know you were once a married man, and so you must fear your passions, but you should be able to do much with the limited freedom the Lord gives a dating couple.

I have spoken last Sunday with Bishop Mullet on this matter, and he also expressed his grave concerns about Miriam's mental, physical, and spiritual health. I told him I planned to write you, although we did not discuss details. I'm sure Bishop Mullet will wish to have conversations with you if you should decide to visit. But in observing Miriam's present state of mind and emotions, something must be done.

Again, may the Lord's greatest blessings be upon you,

Deacon Phillips

Mose snorted and laid the pages down. "Now what kind of letter is that?" he asked the empty house. "Here I am all alone without a *frau,* suffering with my own cooking, the load of the church on my shoulders, and now they think I'm not taking care of Miriam." His voice had risen higher until it echoed up the open stairwell. "Tenderness and affection!" Mose declared. "That comes after the vows are said and the woman lives in the house of her husband. Whoever heard of such newfangled ideas among the people of our faith?"

Mose paused to listen to the echo of his words. He ought to preach more at home, he thought with a smile. His voice sounded *gut.*

But Mose soon sobered. From the sound of it, it was entirely possible William and his *frau,* Fannie, had read his letters, along with Deacon Phillips. Mose grimaced and got up from his chair to pace the floor. The pages of the deacon's letter fluttered down, but Mose ignored them.

The nerve — reading his letters! Exactly what did they think was wrong with his letters anyway? He had written nothing inappropriate. Well, maybe he shouldn't have made a joke about Minister Kemp's sister Bethany, but that was meant as a compliment to Miriam. What was this nonsense about tenderness and affection and another trip out there? And what of the whole community being concerned for Miriam's welfare? The Oklahoma community must be more liberal than he had noticed when he visited. This explained why Bishop Mullet had watered down the necessary discipline on Miriam to one week instead of the two weeks he had asked for. That's what happened when the hand of the church was too light. No wonder Miriam was struggling with her recovery. She had not been properly cleansed of wrongdoing.

He would remember that in the future and not give in next time. Now Miriam was being influenced by these liberal ideas. What if Miriam brought these ideas with her when she moved back to Possum Valley and to Wayne County after the wedding? He'd end up with a *frau* with these fancy ideas in her mind, and he'd never get them out. Nay, he certainly wouldn't go out to Oklahoma for another visit. That was out of the question. The arson fires in the Clarita community had given him cover the last time, but he'd be the laughingstock of Wayne County this time. Minister Kemp would call him Eager Beaver Bishop or some such thing.

No, there was but one way out of this. The deciding factor was the liberal church drift that had been exposed in this letter. He'd have to lose Miriam, and that was a shame. He truly didn't want to give her up, but the situation was what it was. He shouldn't think about this too long, or he'd give in to Miriam's charms again. His relationship with Miriam was no longer a position he could justify, and his office in the church came first.

Mose grabbed up a pen and paper from his desk but paused. No, he would do this his way. No one need know he wrote the letter to Miriam. He couldn't mail the envelope until the morning anyway.

Mose hurried to the washroom and took his hat and coat off the hook. If he hurried he could be back before his regular bedtime. Bethany lived in a little tenant house behind her brother's larger home, and he'd sneak in the back way. Dusk would fall soon, and Minister Kemp wouldn't have to know until Bethany told him in the morning.

Mose hitched his horse to the buggy as his thoughts raced. Surely Bethany wouldn't turn him down, and so it was best this way. Miriam hadn't been *gut* for him all along anyway. She had tried his patience to the limit, and a bishop shouldn't have such a *frau.* With the problems he had with Miriam so far, what would she do to him if he lived with her and they had *kinner* together? That could be nothing but a road filled with more pitfalls than he wished to envision.

Mose urged his horse on and didn't slow until he turned into the bouncy gravel lane near Minister Kemp's home and parked behind the small barn. Mose tied his horse quickly and took rapid steps toward the tenant house.

Bethany's surprised face appeared at the front door before he arrived, her ample frame filling most of the opening.

"Bishop!" she exclaimed.

"Can I come in?" Mose nearly bowled her over as he brushed past. He felt better now that he was out of plain sight.

Bethany still looked puzzled. She bounced down on the couch and motioned for him to do the same. "What a surprise. I'm trying to collect myself. What on earth?"

Mose laughed. "Well, it's not hard to figure. I've come to see you."

"Me!" The puzzlement still hadn't left.

"Yah," Mose acknowledged. He wasn't sure how to proceed exactly, but he felt perfectly at home here. That much comforted him. This might actually work, he told himself.

Bethany still stared at him. "Are you hungry perhaps?"

Mose laughed again. "I've had supper, thanks."

For the first time, Mose noticed the faces of Bethany's two small girls peering out from the kitchen.

Bethany followed his gaze and stood up to shoo them into the bedroom, where she closed the door. With a smile Bethany lowered herself back onto the couch. "This is quite unexpected, Bishop, but a great honor."

Bethany had begun to comprehend, Mose told himself. He allowed a smile to creep over his face. "Your brother has spoken highly of you. I thought I would speak with you myself on the matter. Time is slipping away, you know. I'm not getting any younger, and neither are you." He gave her an appraising look. Bethany would definitely need to lose some weight, but he would deal with that later.

She had colored slightly. "I thought you were writing to Miriam Yoder. Didn't you make a trip out there not so long ago?"

Bethany knew good and well that he had, but Mose nodded as if this were a serious question. "My duties did call me out there, but I'm back now to stay. And my relationship with Miriam . . . well, you don't have to worry about that. It may be at an end."

That didn't make a whole lot of sense, but Bethany didn't seem bothered.

"My girls and I have greatly appreciated your sermons, Bishop." Bethany's smile was nervous. "I'm glad you've come tonight. I had never dared hope this day would come." She laid her hand on his arm, and he didn't pull back. There was no need to, and he did appreciate her admiration.

"I'm glad you do," he said.

"Our souls have been fed greatly, Bishop. More than I can ever say. The Lord has clearly been at work in our community of late, even if I must say so when my brother was also in the lot for bishop."

"Then the Kemp family didn't take things too hard?" Mose gave her a sideways glance. He hadn't planned to speak on this matter, but she had brought it up.

"There are no hard feelings." Her hand stroked his arm. "We saw clearly what the Lord's will was, and everything since has pointed in that direction."

Mose cleared his throat. "Then I might as well say why I'm here. I need a *frau,* Bethany. Would you consent to say the vows with me before too long?"

Bethany got on her knees with tears in her eyes. She clung to his hand with both of hers. "Words fail me, Bishop. You know what my answer is. What else could I say, but *yah*? I never dared dream of this day."

"Then come up!" he ordered. "We are to kneel only before the Lord."

Bethany trembled and struggled to stand. She lowered herself back on the couch.

"When can this happen?" Mose was all

business now.

"The wedding?" she whispered.

"*Yah,* of course." He was brisk. "I need a *frau,* and you need a husband. Look at you!" He gave her another sharp glance that took in her ample girth.

"Oh, Mose." She sighed but seemed to miss the point. "Happiness fills my heart so I can hardly speak, but I will talk with my brother in the morning, and *yah* this can happen soon. Very soon. Oh, the Lord is blessing me and my daughters more than I can ever say! Can I kiss you before you leave? So I can think of your kind words and tender heart in the days ahead?"

Mose smiled. "I suppose so." He leaned toward her and Bethany took her time. Her face glowed when she finished. "Oh, Bishop, thank you. You don't know . . ."

Mose silenced her with a wave of his hand. "Speak no more of it. We have a lifetime in front of us, and you will have your duties as a bishop's *frau.* I suggest you begin by showing some restraint with your eating. You must be an example to the other women in all godliness and holiness."

Bethany's smile faded. "I will fast until the wedding!" she declared. "I will not disappoint you, Bishop."

She might or she might not, Mose figured.

At the moment her willingness was all he asked for. "I'll be back soon," he said over his shoulder.

Bethany didn't ask when but stood on the porch to wave goodbye. When Mose turned for one last glance, the faces of Bethany's two girls peered out from her skirts. The road had been long and rough in his travels to his second marriage, Mose told himself, but he had finally found the right woman.

Now there was only Miriam's letter to write, and the thing would be done.

CHAPTER THIRTY-NINE

Dusk had fallen and Miriam was sitting on the couch in the living room with Uncle William and Aunt Fannie seated in their rockers. Jonathon was nestled against her, smiling up into her face. Miriam tried to return the smile, but the effort was feeble. She wrapped her arms around his shoulders instead and pulled him tightly against her. Uncle William glanced at them as he reached for the family Bible and opened it. Without comment he began to read, "Blessed are the undefiled in the way, who walk in the law of the Lord. Blessed are they that keep his testimonies, and that seek him with the whole heart."

Miriam let her thoughts drift as Uncle William read on. The words didn't provide as much comfort tonight as they often did. For one, the Scripture talked of a person who had things right in her life. Miriam didn't. Not anymore. And for another, an unopened letter from Mose was tucked in her dress pocket. Aunt Fannie had handed it to her with a concerned look when she arrived home from school. Miriam hadn't found the strength to open it yet. No doubt the letter would say more of the same about Mose's farm life and how successful he was in his ministry. In the meantime she could barely get out of bed in the mornings. The only comfort she had was the kind words so many of the community people had said to her these past Sundays. Had Aunt Fannie shared her problem with the other women? Or perhaps Deacon Phillips's *frau,* Katie, had done so.

Katie had been the first to touch her elbow after the church services yesterday and whisper in Miriam's ear, "Dark clouds always have their silver linings, dear. We all love you, Miriam. Remember that."

Miriam had been unable to respond properly, other than to squeeze Katie's hand.

Katie had moved on, but the encouragement didn't stop. Others had approached her, and the touches and soft whispers were delivered with sincere smiles.

"I know life's hard sometimes, but we're praying for you."

"Just cry out to the Lord, Miriam, and He'll see you through."

"Our children so appreciate you. Don't forget that."

"We pray for you every night at devotion time, Miriam."

In spite of their comforts, Miriam felt she was to blame for her situation and needed to straighten out her life. In any event, tomorrow she'd have to answer Mose's letter. That would take a great effort, but it must be done. What could she say to a man whose life seemed so perfect when your own was such a mess? Had God perhaps forsaken her? This wasn't the first time the question crossed her mind, and she certainly wouldn't have blamed the Lord if He had.

Miriam focused again on Uncle William's words. "Make me to understand the way of thy precepts: so shall I talk of thy wondrous works. My soul melteth for heaviness: strengthen thou me according to thy word."

Yah, Miriam told herself. That was more like what she felt. Miriam pulled Jonathon even closer until Uncle William finished a few moments later. They all knelt, and Uncle William read the usual evening prayer. His voice rose and fell with the familiar German words. Miriam let her mind lift heavenward as she prayed her own prayer. "I want to do Your will, Lord. It's strength that I lack. I know that I have failed both You and Mose, so please forgive me and help me."

A measure of peace settled over her. Uncle William soon said amen, and they all sat up again, but no one moved to go except Jonathon, who dashed off the couch to play upstairs.

Aunt Fannie finally looked her way to say, "Maybe you should read your letter from Mose now, Miriam. You've been under a cloud ever since I gave it to you."

Miriam took a deep breath. "*Yah.* I'll go into the kitchen, but I think I'm okay. The devotions tonight helped a lot."

Aunt Fannie's compassionate gaze followed her. Miriam didn't dare look at her aunt too long lest the tears come. She opened the envelope. The letter wasn't long, but Miriam still sat down to read.

Dear Miriam,
Greetings in the name of the Lord. I hope this finds you well.

Miriam stopped and stared at the wall. Was Mose changing? He had never begun a letter like this. Miriam blinked the tears away and continued to read.

I have been doing the usual things

around the farm. Spring will break soon, I hope. This has been a hard winter for us in Wayne County, and as always one must not complain but be thankful for what the Lord sends.

But to the point of my letter. I received correspondence from Deacon Phillips today, in which he reported that you have not been well in mind or spirit for some time. This, of course, troubles me greatly. Deacon Phillips did not say what the reason was for your ailment, but he did imply that our relationship might not be the best. I'm not sure what that means, but I do have my opinions on what the problem could be.

I wish you had written me yourself about this, but perhaps the shame of your ill health was too much for you to disclose. Deacon Phillips's letter has brought me many troubled thoughts as you can imagine. We have already been through so much, Miriam. As you know my journey toward you began when I first visited Oklahoma on the advice of your now brother-in-law Glen Weaver. I don't want to scold Glen because he did what he thought was best. I also know that your *daett* praised you highly, as did the community in Oklahoma. I wish to leave all that as it is and pray that the Lord will bless them and that you will be granted *gut* health in the future.

But I think it is best if we break off the engagement, Miriam. With your fragile condition, it might also be better if I offer no explanations. Believe me, I regret this deeply. I had looked forward to having you here in Wayne County as my *frau,* but sometimes it's time to admit that a wrong road was taken and to make amends. I will not hold any hard feelings toward you, as I have already moved in the direction the Lord has revealed to me, and I might say, to others of the ministry in our district, and this is how things should be.

So may God bless you, Miriam, as He has blessed me.

Sincerely,
Mose Stoll

Miriam's hand shook. She stood to her feet and clutched the chair for support. The warmth from the evening's devotions disappeared into thin air. She was clearly unworthy of a place by Mose's side as his *frau.* Mose had finally done what he should have done when she kissed Tyler that first time. Her moral failure had been great, and

Mose was right to come to his senses.

Miriam entered the living room with the letter in one hand. Her voice sounded distant, and her ears rang. "I guess I should have let you read it first." Miriam handed the letter to Aunt Fannie. "I have failed completely."

Uncle William stood up to read over his *frau*'s shoulder. Miriam waited with her hand on the couch to steady herself.

A soft smile filled Aunt Fannie's face when she looked up. "Maybe it's for the best, Miriam. Things weren't going well anyway."

"You're just being kind," Miriam whispered.

"Fannie speaks the truth," Uncle William echoed. "The whole community has been very concerned about this, Miriam. Perhaps this is the Lord's way. Mose wished you nothing but the best, and I'm sure you feel the same about him."

Miriam nodded, unable to speak.

"Many of us in the community have been much in prayer about this." Aunt Fannie reached over to touch Miriam's arm. "I wrote your *mamm* about the matter, and she wrote back to say they support whatever happens, and now Mose has made his decision. We must accept this as the Lord's way."

"But I've . . ." Miriam stopped. That she was a failure was obvious, and yet no rebuke was written on either Aunt Fannie's or Uncle William's faces. They appeared concerned, but there was no scorn. The tenderness from Aunt Fannie's touch still lingered on her arm. Miriam slid down on the couch, and her aunt came to sit beside her. They clung to each other while Uncle William stood vigil by the rocker.

"Do you feel better now?" Aunt Fannie studied Miriam's face once she let go.

Miriam didn't answer. She didn't know how she felt. Maybe she was a little relieved that she would not see Mose again — at least not anytime soon. No longer would she have to wonder if she met the standard as Mose's promised *frau*.

"Come." Aunt Fannie took Miriam by the arm and led her back into the kitchen. "Sit," Aunt Fannie said. "I'm going to make you hot chocolate, and we're going to talk."

Miriam's legs wobbled as she sat down at the kitchen table. Aunt Fannie busied herself with the kettle and brought over the bowl of hot chocolate and a bag of marshmallows from the pantry. While the water heated, Aunt Fannie sat down beside Miriam. In a kind voice she began, "This is hard for me to say, Miriam, but I have to confess that I was wrong about Mose. I told you so awhile back, but I want to make myself clear now. I misjudged the man completely. I know he's a bishop, and some unmarried woman will likely make him the perfect *frau,* but that's not you. William and I have spoken at length on the matter, and we have consulted often with Deacon Phillips and Katie about your condition. We are all of the same mind. We knew that at the very least some changes would have to be made in your relationship with Mose. This is what Deacon Phillips said in his letter to Mose, but none of us tried to end the relationship. That was up to Mose and you, and Mose has obviously decided you were too much trouble for him. That was his loss. You're in no way to blame for any of this."

Tears stung Miriam's eyes again, and Aunt Fannie gave her a quick hug. "Don't cry, dear. I know you looked at this as some sort of endurance test, but marriage is not supposed to be like that. A man and a woman must walk in love with each other and the Lord. Mose wasn't treating you right, Miriam. And if he doesn't want to change, it's best if he ends the relationship as he's done. Can you believe that, Miriam? Can you hope a little again? All of us want that cheerful, happy Miriam back who used to bless our community so greatly."

"But what is to become of me?" Miriam whispered. "When I get old, I will always remember this failure. Think of what you're saying, Aunt Fannie. I could have been a bishop's *frau,* but now I'll be just a withered-up old maid."

Aunt Fannie laughed. "I don't think that will happen. For one thing, you can always remember that a bishop once courted you, but he wasn't *gut* enough. That's a much better way to look at this."

Miriam attempted a smile, but the tears crept down her cheeks instead. "I have to get well somehow, for the sake of my school-children if for no other reason. Will they scorn me when they find this out?"

"No one will scorn you," Aunt Fannie assured her. "We will feel only joy in our hearts when we see smiles fill your face again."

"I'll try," Miriam muttered.

"Nay," Aunt Fannie chided. "You don't have to try anymore. We will help you. All of us will with our prayers and with our thankful hearts. We're glad, Miriam, that you live among us."

Miriam hid her face in her hands. "You shouldn't speak like that."

Aunt Fannie ignored the protest. "And I

want to say this also. Bishop Mullet and the rest of the ministry deeply regret the decision to place you in the *bann*. They feel it was done in the heat of the moment when things appeared badly for Tyler's reputation. But Tyler has come back often since then, and he's tried to make right what he could. The man's character has impressed both Bishop Mullet and Deacon Phillips."

Miriam looked away. "Tyler has nothing to do with this."

Aunt Fannie ignored the comment to continue. "Did you know that Mose wanted you to be in the *bann* for another week, but our ministry refused? Of course they all have to work together, so what happened, happened, but I wanted you to know that. You are greatly loved here, Miriam."

Miriam lifted her face and wept silently.

Aunt Fannie waited a few moments before she spoke again. "Another thing. I'm now free to say that Tyler has asked to court you, Miriam. He has spoken at length with Deacon Phillips, but he was told it was a forbidden subject while you were engaged to Mose. He was also told that no one would interfere, other than to ask that Mose make some changes in his attitude toward you. Tyler seemed to think that would end your relationship with Mose, and apparently he was correct. Tyler has also asked to join the community, Miriam. I know you're in no condition to respond to that news, but I didn't want to dribble it out bit by bit in the days ahead or have someone else tell you."

Miriam choked back the sobs. "I have also failed Tyler, and I'm in no condition to see him again. You should know that."

Aunt Fannie nodded. "That's why we're going to help — William and I, and Deacon Phillips and Katie. You won't have to walk this road alone this time. I'm not expecting you to say anything tonight, or even anytime soon. You must get well first. Come, the chocolate is ready and we can relax better in the living room."

"Will you tell Tyler this — what Mose wrote?" Miriam pointed toward the letter now resting on the tabletop.

Aunt Fannie smiled. "I wouldn't show him the letter, but I think Tyler should be told that your relationship with Mose is over."

Miriam took a deep breath. She didn't want to think anymore, but the image of Tyler's face rose in her mind. She saw him as he drew close that Sunday afternoon in her buggy. Miriam stood with a shaky hand held tightly on the kitchen chair. "*Yah,* you should tell him," she whispered.

CHAPTER FORTY

The bright sunlight of an early spring Sunday afternoon filled Aunt Fannie's living room. Miriam unfolded the two letters that had arrived earlier from Possum Valley and placed them carefully in her lap.

"Going to read them again?" Aunt Fannie teased from her rocker.

"Must be really *gut* stuff in them letters," Uncle William joined in. "Almost as *gut* as this popcorn you made."

Miriam smiled at both of them but didn't say anything. The warmth of her uncle's and aunt's concern had enveloped her these past few weeks, and words weren't always necessary. They knew the letters from *Mamm* and Shirley had blessed her deeply, and *yah,* she would read them again.

Miriam opened the letter from *Mamm* and read:

Our dearest daughter Miriam,

My heart overflows with joy after your last letter and the one from your Aunt Fannie. We had been so concerned about how things were going, and I cannot tell you how relieved we are that you're feeling better. I understand that everything still isn't exactly right and may not be for a long time. Life on this earth is rarely perfect, but the grace of the Lord is with us through it all. As you know, this has always been a great comfort to me.

I feel bad about all the things that have happened to you. It's no excuse to say we didn't know about them at the time, but we honestly didn't — and I guess it was for the best. I don't think we could have done anything, and I would only have worried. I still can't believe you were in the *bann* for a week and no one told us. You must have suffered terribly. Why didn't you let us know? I thought the letter we received in December sounded a little down, but that's normal sometimes over the busy Christmas season. And you had just been home for Shirley's wedding, and of course we had such high hopes for Mose and you. Maybe that's what blinded us to what was happening right under our noses. I know you haven't said anything against Mose, and I wouldn't want you to, but I should have seen things more clearly. I know that now. A mother knows if she takes the time to look and listen. For this I am sorry, Miriam. I hope you can forgive me.

Daett says to tell you that he also is disappointed that the relationship with Mose didn't work out. He understands a little better now after he read Fannie's letter. Mose was the one who cut off the relationship, so don't blame yourself, Miriam. This will all work out for the best. The Lord has something better in mind for you. We will continue to pray and keep you in our thoughts. For my part, I can't wait until you return in May and I can see your face again. I hope this hasn't aged you too much, because I still can't imagine how awful a week in the *bann* must have been. I don't think I could take it, myself.

With all our love and affection,
Your *mamm*

Miriam turned to Aunt Fannie. "What did you tell *Mamm* anyway?"

"I only said what needed saying." Aunt

Fannie sent Miriam a kind look. "And how sorry I was that we didn't understand what was going on sooner."

"Mose . . ." Miriam stopped. She wasn't going to defend the man any longer. He was gone from her life, and there was no doubt she felt better about that — guilty at times for the relief, but definitely better.

"Tyler will be at the hymn singing again tonight," Aunt Fannie said with a smile. "You shouldn't be afraid to speak with him if you want to."

Miriam was silent for a moment, and then said, "I don't understand any of this . . . but one thing I do know is that I'm not going to marry an *Englisha* man."

"That's a *gut* point," Uncle William spoke up. "And if Tyler doesn't plan to join the community, you shouldn't have anything to do with him."

"He's not going to join," Miriam said dropping her gaze. "I don't know what's gotten into both of you that you actually think that could happen."

"I agree that Tyler has to prove himself," Uncle William said. "But Deacon Phillips thinks he's genuine, so we'll have to see."

"Just trust the Lord," Aunt Fannie said, smiling weakly.

In the silence that followed, Miriam

picked up Shirley's letter and tried to focus, but the words blurred. The recent events had worked out so strangely, so unexpectedly. She knew for sure that her chance to marry Mose was over. If there was any doubt, there had been whispers at church this morning that Mose was already promised to someone else.

"It wouldn't surprise me if their wedding was planned for late this spring," Katie had said.

There had been no admiration in Katie's voice for Mose's quick change of affection. Why there wasn't a wholesale condemnation of her by the community, Miriam still couldn't understand. She had transgressed by kissing Tyler. They all knew that marriage to a bishop was an esteemed accomplishment. A woman who failed to keep such a relationship was usually pitied. Yet she felt nothing but support and kindness from all of the community's women.

Even Bishop Mullet's *frau,* Ellen, had given her a hug this morning and whispered in Miriam's ear, "We're all praying for you."

That everyone in the community seemed to care moved her deeply, but their acceptance of Tyler was another matter. That was the surprise. Was Aunt Fannie now trying to push her into Tyler's arms? Even

Deacon Phillips and Katie seemed in on the effort. But how was such a thing to happen? She couldn't open her heart again, not after yet another disappointment with Mose. Ivan, Wayne, and now Mose. It was too much!

Miriam sighed, and Aunt Fannie reached over to put her arm around her. "It'll be okay. Just talk with Tyler tonight if he wants to talk with you."

Miriam didn't answer. She would have to see about that, if and when the time came.

Miriam focused again on Shirley's letter, and this time the words stayed in place.

My dear, dear sister,

What horrors have you been through! When I heard the news, I was so angry that Glen had to work for an hour to calm me down. I was ready to make a trip up to Wayne County and have it out with Mose myself. But Glen prevailed and talked some *gut* sense into me. He's much more understanding of Mose, and of Mose's despicable actions, than I am. I don't care if you did kiss that *Englisha* man. Mose had no right to throw you into the *bann* for a week. Or even for a day. The nerve! Friends are often so unlike each other. With how kind and thoughtful Glen is, I assumed Mose would be that way too. Was I wrong! What a nasty man, Miriam. I don't care if Mose is a bishop. He had no right to use you like that.

Miriam smiled in spite of herself. As usual, Shirley didn't hold back her feelings. Glen was *gut* for Shirley, though. He could handle her. What a sight that would have been if one of the Yoder girls had driven her buggy up to Wayne County and chewed Bishop Stoll's ears off. They would never have lived down that scandal. Thankfully, Shirley had listened to her husband. That was the decent attitude for any *frau* to have, and look how much embarrassment Shirley had saved herself and the rest of the family.

Miriam folded the pages and rose to her feet. "I guess I'd better get going to the hymn singing. Deacon Phillips is serving supper tonight for the young folks."

"William's gone to get Star ready for you," Aunt Fannie said.

"Oh." Miriam stopped to stare at the empty rocker. "I didn't even see him leave. I'm so distractible these days."

"*Yah,* but you're doing so much better," Aunt Fannie assured her. "And you're happy again. You're just not ready to admit it."

Miriam pressed back the tears. Her aunt did understand her. There was no question about that. "I guess I should be going," she whispered.

Aunt Fannie's kind look followed Miriam out the front door. Uncle William had hitched Star to the buggy and held his bridle at the end of the walk.

"You didn't have to do this," Miriam said. "But thank you."

Uncle William grinned. "You have a *gut* evening now. And behave yourself."

Miriam clutched the reins as Star took off down the lane. She let go with one hand for a quick wave. Uncle William teased her more these days. He seemed to pay more attention to her, and she appreciated his effort. Still, she needed to get fully well so all these *wunderbah* people could go on with their lives. She couldn't depend on others to carry her as they had of late.

Star set a brisk pace down Highway 48, and Miriam let her thoughts drift. Things would never be quite the same again. She could feel that. The ideal would be if she could return to being the satisfied girl she had been early last fall. Her schoolteaching job had fulfilled her. She really felt as though she needed nothing more to complete her life. Now she couldn't imagine a return to the girl she had once been.

She was no longer the old Miriam, but was it possible the woman she was now might share a life with someone like Tyler? The thought left Miriam weak. Unless he did join the community . . . which she still couldn't believe . . . that would mean she would have to leave the community. Had she changed that much? Nay, she knew she had not.

Miriam slowed Star for the turn onto the side road leading toward the hymn singing. Darkness threatened to creep into her soul again, but Miriam rallied herself. Aunt Fannie prayed for her each day, and the Lord answered such selfless prayers. She would have to believe this.

With a lighter heart Miriam approached Deacon Phillips's place. She was a little early, and only a few buggies were parked beside the barn.

"Whoa," Miriam called out as she brought Star to a stop.

Just then Tyler came toward her, apparently planning to help her unhitch Star. Miriam shuddered. She doubted her legs would hold her if she tried to climb down the buggy steps. Tyler looked so handsome in his Amish suit and black hat, she couldn't breathe.

"Hi," Tyler chirped. "If it isn't Miriam Yoder herself."

"I heard you might be here."

"Yes, I am. Or rather, *yah,* I am," Tyler teased. "Don't I look handsome tonight?" He gestured toward his outfit. "Only wore them today for the second time."

"Well, you at least look decent," Miriam allowed. Her legs seemed to work now, so she climbed down from the buggy.

Tyler patted Star on the neck and then bent forward to loosen one of the tugs. Miriam was impressed that he seemed to have learned how to unhitch a horse, but he would not charm her again regardless of what happened. She glanced around at the empty barn lot before she spoke. "Tyler, you know it's true that my engagement to Mose is off, but that doesn't change anything between you and me. I can't come out to your world, and my world involves more than just wearing a set of Amish clothing."

Tyler's face was sober as he answered. "I understand that, Miriam. And I wouldn't dream of luring you into my world. I'm sorry I ever suggested that — and I'm sorry for my flippant attitude and for the things I said about this Mose fellow. I hope you can forgive me."

Miriam swallowed hard before the words would come out. *"Yah,"* she said. "Of course I forgive you, but that doesn't change anything. For my own sanity, I can't let my heart stray into something that's not possible."

"So it did stray?" he teased. She realized he had stepped much too close. "Or maybe it was beginning to stray?"

Miriam felt streaks of fire flame into her face. "You know it did, Tyler. I'm not going to lie. But . . ."

He silenced her with an upraised finger. "Don't say anything, okay? Just let me find my way through this, Miriam. I'm working with your deacon on this matter, and he's providing me guidance. I want to do this right."

"Tyler, I can't be hurt again." Miriam forced the words out. "I *can't.*"

Tyler studied Miriam for a moment, and his face softened. He reached out for her hand. "I won't lead you on, I promise. If I can't do this right, I'll leave and you'll never see me again."

Miriam tried to breathe as her fingers lingered in Tyler's hand. Before either of them could speak again, another buggy turned in the lane, followed by two more behind that. Tyler let go of her hand, and they unhitched Star from the buggy.

"I love you, Miriam," Tyler whispered before he led Star toward the barn. "You would be worth going to the ends of the world."

Miriam turned around and pretended to look for something on the floor of the buggy until she could collect herself. Feelings of sorrow and joy rushed through her together. Never in all the weeks Mose had courted her or written letters from Wayne County had he said such words. But the fact remained, Tyler was still an *Englisha* man.

CHAPTER FORTY-ONE

Several Sunday evenings later, Miriam opened the front door to Aunt Fannie's living room and motioned for Tyler to enter. A kerosene lamp flickered on the desk. Tyler turned to Miriam and grinned. "Very romantic!"

"Don't say that," Miriam whispered. "Aunt Fannie left it burning for us before she went to bed."

She was jittery, and had been ever since Tyler had asked whether he could drive her home. He'd made the request at the youth gathering last week, apparently intending to court her according to the community's *Ordnung.* With that in mind she had consented, and now she was in Aunt Fannie's house on an official date with an *Englisha* man. Well, a former *Englisha* man who planned to join the Amish community.

Tyler peered around the living room. He had been here before, so the place should

470

have been familiar to him, but Uncle William and Aunt Fannie had always been present. Miriam closed the front door behind her. She knew she was acting worse than a schoolgirl with her first crush. Yet in many ways, this was all new. At least the idea of Tyler as a suitor without her feeling guilty was new. Aunt Fannie and Uncle William had already signaled their approval of the date, and so had Deacon Phillips and half of the community, it seemed.

Miriam made her way to the couch and sat down, her stomach all aflutter. She would have to catch her breath before she could serve Tyler any food.

"Yep, right romantic," Tyler repeated as he came over to sit beside Miriam, giving her a kind glance. "My, you're lovely tonight."

The words made Miriam wonder if she might actually pass out. She hadn't heard words like that since before Wayne had died.

"Did I say something wrong?" Tyler peered at Miriam.

"Nay," Miriam gasped. "I just wish you wouldn't say things like that."

"So what am I supposed to say?" Tyler put on a puzzled look.

"I don't know . . . just not that."

Tyler laughed. "I can't help myself. You're

just so lovely, you know."

"Tyler . . . I'm going to scream if you don't stop," Miriam threatened.

Tyler glanced at her again and said, "I admit I have much to learn, but I'm enjoying every minute of it, especially when you're the teacher."

Miriam ignored the comment. "Let me get you something to eat."

"Is that what comes next?" Tyler regarded Miriam with a tilt of his head.

"When it comes to food, there's little difference between an *Englisha* man and an Amish man," Miriam said over her shoulder.

Tyler chuckled at her feeble attempt at humor. Miriam entered the kitchen thinking how odd it was that she had just said something she would never have dared breathe in Mose's presence.

Miriam's hand shook as she lit another lamp in the kitchen. Even only a room apart, she could feel Tyler's presence close to her. The pleasantness of it flooded her senses. This was too *wunderbah* to possibly continue — yet she hoped that it would. She so wanted this to work. This was a dream from which she hoped never to awaken.

With the lamp lit, Miriam found a plate of brownies and filled glasses with milk. She carried both back to the couch where Tyler had seated himself again. A look of expectation filled his face. "So what is this fancy food you serve?"

Miriam had to smile. "Nothing fancy at all. Just plain old brownies and milk. Can't get simpler than that."

Tyler grunted. "I like simple. That's what you are. Uncomplicated, yet deep and mysterious."

"Oh, stop it," Miriam warned. Tyler grinned.

He took a brownie and sat back to sip his milk. "Ummm. Delicious. Did you make these?"

"*Yah,* of course."

"How do you have time with your schoolteaching?" Tyler asked, regarding Miriam with skepticism.

"I don't usually," Miriam admitted. "Aunt Fannie does most of the cooking. But I knew you were coming, so I baked these myself yesterday."

"Especially for me?"

"Well, the others ate some," Miriam allowed. "Jonathon had to be told twice he could have only one, and I had to test them to make sure I wasn't poisoning you."

"But you put the rest of the family at risk first?" Tyler kept a straight face.

Miriam laughed. "You know what I mean."

Tyler helped himself to another brownie. "I'm going to put on weight — that's all I can say. You and Deacon Phillips's wife make food to kill for."

"So you're back in the basement apartment?"

"No, I just stop in for meals sometimes. They invite me to talk about things. Deacon Phillips is quite helpful. I don't think it's for my sake, though. More like for yours. You're quite respected and loved, Miriam — you know that."

"Please." Miriam looked away. "I said no more of that."

"And you think I'm going to listen?" he teased. "I'm practicing how to be an Amish man and boss my wife around."

"Tyler." Miriam caught her breath. "I did try my best with Mose to obey. You know that."

"Sorry." He touched her arm. "I didn't mean it that way. I know those are sacred things to you. I'm just not used to it — that's all. I'll learn in time."

"Then you are serious about joining?"

"I plan to, if you continue to let me bring you home on Sunday nights."

"Is that the only reason?"

He thought for a moment. "I'll be honest. I don't think I would join if it weren't for you, Miriam. But I do also want to change my life. I don't like the way I've been living. I was drawn to the life of the community from the first time I visited. I don't say I'm a natural, but I was tired of where I was roaming. I wanted to settle down, but out there in the world it didn't seem possible. Then I met you and the rest of the community. It made a difference. But it started with you. But I'm not going to lie about it. If you chased me off, I wouldn't continue to live in the community."

Miriam's mind spun. "Does Deacon Phillips know this?"

"Yes, I have told him so from the start." Tyler was matter-of-fact. "He said there are many reasons for joining the community, and if a willing heart was involved, a woman like you could be one of those reasons."

"He did not!" Miriam stifled her gasp.

"Yes, he did," Tyler assured her. "And he said I should tell you when you asked — and he did not say *if* you asked but *when* you asked. It seems the deacon has you figured out. He said he wasn't going to make things easy on me, and there would be no shortcuts. They would have to feel certain that I was serious and wouldn't leave you afterward or lead you astray."

Miriam took a deep breath. This she had not expected, but her heart certainly felt no disagreement.

"Let me put it to you this way," Tyler continued. "You've told me some of your past experiences with Amish men, and I've learned more details from Deacon Phillips and your uncle. We don't have to rehash all that, but am I a greater risk than any of the other men?"

"You make it sound like I'm a woman who lives on the edge." She forced herself to look at him.

"Perhaps," he said. "Now I have a question for you."

"Yah?"

Tyler suddenly appeared nervous. "Miriam . . . do you . . . love me?"

Miriam didn't look away. "You know the answer to that."

"Even knowing I could lead you away from your faith?"

"You could never do that." Miriam's voice was hushed. "My faith is too strong. But I suppose you could someday leave me . . . and leave the faith."

"Leave you?" His finger stroked her arm. "I don't think I'm capable of that."

"I don't think so either," Miriam allowed.

"Of course, I love you. I loved you even when I wasn't supposed to. How then could I not love you more now that our love is permissible?"

He slowly reached over and planted a gentle kiss on her lips. Miriam dropped her gaze to the living room floor. Tyler kept his eyes on her. Then, after several silent moments, he said, "I think I'd better go now. I'm not used to driving horses after dark, and I won't have you along to help."

Alarm filled Miriam's face. "That's true. You have to be careful. You don't know how the *Englisha* are with their cars."

They both laughed at the irony, and Miriam followed him to the front door.

"Can we do this again next Sunday evening?" he asked.

Miriam hung on to the door edge and nodded. Her smile was answer enough. Never had she opened her heart to a man as she had with Tyler, an *Englisha* man — or rather a former *Englisha* man.

Tyler grinned and leaned in for another kiss. Miriam let go of the doorframe to lift her face toward his, and they clung to each other for a long time.

He turned to leave, and Miriam stepped outside on the porch to watch him climb into the borrowed buggy and drive off. As he rode into the dark, Tyler turned to wave. She watched until his buggy lights had vanished, and even then she remained still. She didn't want this moment to end. She wanted the memory of his kisses to linger in her heart forever. When she stepped back into the house, Aunt Fannie was standing there in her nightdress, her voice atwitter. "I couldn't wait until morning to find out how it went. I do declare, I'm as dizzy with excitement as if I had been on a date myself!"

"Did you see us . . ." Miriam stopped as streaks of heat rushed into her face.

Aunt Fannie giggled. "No! I wouldn't stoop so low as to spy on your moments together. But does that mean . . ." Aunt Fannie's face glowed.

Miriam tried to collect herself. "He's coming back again next Sunday," she finally said.

"You are a match made in heaven," Aunt Fannie said.

"I know," Miriam whispered. "Tyler brings all the pieces of my heart together."

CHAPTER FORTY-TWO

Miriam ran out of Aunt's Fannie front door with one hand on her *kapp* as the wind whipped past her face. The early morning squall had cleared, but the wind was still blustery. An hour ago she had stood by the living room window wringing her hands in frustration. What if the rain didn't quit in time for the Saturday outing Tyler had planned? Tyler hadn't said where they were going, but she had gotten the impression *gut* weather was needed.

"You'll still enjoy the ride," Aunt Fannie had called cheerfully from the kitchen.

Miriam had forced a smile, but now the wait was over and the clouds had cleared. Out of breath, Miriam arrived at Tyler's buggy just after he managed to turn it around in the driveway. Tyler had a new horse and buggy of his own, but he was still a little unsure of himself.

Tyler leaned out of the buggy door to

exclaim, "That's what I like to see — a woman eager to see her man!"

"What woman wouldn't want to see her man . . . if that man was you?" Miriam teased back as a deep blush spread over her face. Tyler laughed. "Hop in, and we'll be off. I like a woman who is all rosy-cheeked on a windy Saturday morning."

Miriam ignored the comment as she climbed up. "You're doing right *gut* with the horse and buggy, and you look like a real Amish man in your new suspenders and pants. Did Katie make those for you?"

Tyler chuckled. "I've tried not to impose more on Deacon Phillips's household than necessary. I ordered my pants from an Amish seamstress who advertises in *The Budget.*"

I could make them for you, Miriam almost said, but she held back the words. She was already forward enough with her expressions of love for Tyler. The time to sew his clothes hadn't yet arrived. An Amish woman should be hesitant to sew a man's clothes until after their wedding day. Miriam looked away as her blush deepened.

"So how are plans coming for the last day of school?" Tyler asked once he was safely out on Highway 48.

"I'm working on it — the program that is.

The eighth graders are having some problems with their long memory work and are begging me for something . . . well . . . less lengthy, but I haven't found anything suitable yet."

Tyler grinned from ear to ear. "I'll have to come over and watch you practice someday."

"You'll do nothing of the sort," Miriam shot back. "You'll have me a blubbering mess, and I'll lose all the respect the children have for me. I'll be unable to control the program from then on. Now, would you like that?"

Tyler laughed. "I doubt I'd have quite that effect, but that does sound interesting."

"You won't come," Miriam told him, nestling against his shoulder, more to hide her face than anything. The steady beat of his horse's hooves on the pavement filled the air as Tyler drove north on Highway 48.

"Don't you want to know where we're going?" Tyler finally asked.

"You're not going to tell me, so I'm going to act very disinterested."

Tyler's laughter filled the buggy.

"You're enjoying yourself way too much this morning," Miriam said, looking up at his face.

He reached with his free hand to touch

her face and whisper, "You've brought me great joy, Miriam. I'm not ashamed of that."

Miriam didn't answer and leaned tighter against Tyler's shoulder.

"I think I had better tell you where we're going," Tyler finally said. "Because we're almost there."

Miriam sat up straight in the buggy seat.

"See that farm over there?" Tyler pulled back on the reins to point as a car passed them. "I want to buy it. That's my real estate agent now. We have an appointment."

Miriam stared as vague memories filled her mind. Wayne had brought her north of the community several times during their engagement to look at . . . could it have been this very place? It looked familiar . . . but how could it be? She must be mistaken. Their plans had never gotten far before Wayne passed.

"Is something wrong?" Tyler looked over at Miriam.

"Nay." Miriam took a long breath. "It's a cattle ranch, isn't it?"

"Yes, it is. Do you know the place?"

"I think I've driven past it before, but I've never been inside," Miriam dodged.

Tyler persisted. "Tell me, Miriam." He had pulled the buggy to a stop beside the road.

Miriam squeezed her eyes shut. "Tyler, do you remember my telling you about Wayne? And how I had inherited the two million dollars I eventually donated to the relief fund?"

"Yes, I remember," Tyler said.

"Tyler, this is the very place Wayne wanted me to use some of my money to buy. For us. For Wayne and me."

Relief spread over Tyler's face, and he smiled. "You had me scared there for a moment. I thought with your high standards about money you would object to living on such a nice farm. You have no objections then?"

"To what?" Miriam managed. "If anything, I thought *you* might, because it's the place I was going to buy for Wayne and me to live on. But you know I have no money now, Tyler. This beautiful place can't be cheap. Surely you don't plan to take on that amount of debt?"

Tyler grinned. "Well, that certainly sounds more like the Miriam I know."

"But what about Wayne? Do you mind that I was going to build a life with him here?"

"No, of course not. I'm sorry you lost Wayne, but the Lord has arranged for us to meet and fall in love. The life we build here will be our life together . . . not yours and Wayne's."

"But the debt! With this acreage, it must cost at least a million dollars! How can you buy it with your income? Surely what you've made as a freelance journalist couldn't be much."

"You're right there, Miriam. But hasn't it occurred to you that I could only survive as a freelance writer if I wasn't dependent on the income from it?"

Miriam met his gaze. "You have a million dollars?"

Tyler looked away. "A bit more than that, I'm afraid. And I have a woman I love who doesn't love my money. Now isn't that something?"

Miriam was sure those were tears in Tyler's eyes. Miriam took his free hand in both of hers to say, "I had no idea, Tyler, but I do love you. More than I should, I think. You make so much right in my life. I'm the one who should be crying now."

He laughed and came closer and began to trace her face with his free hand. "You're a wonderful woman, Miriam, and I love you," he whispered. "Marry me this fall. Once I've been baptized. Move with me to this house, and we'll raise a family together."

"Tyler!" Miriam reached for him with

both hands and pulled him close. The moments seemed golden as the wind gusts moved the buggy from side to side. Tyler's horse peered over his shoulder as if to ask them why they had stopped for so long.

"What will it be?" Tyler finally asked. "Will you marry me? We can't sit here all day. The Realtor is waiting."

"You know I will," Miriam managed.

His soft chuckle filled her ear. "We have a lot of plans to make, and I suppose the wedding has to be in your hometown of Possum Valley. But we have all summer to plan . . ." His voice drifted off and he took the reins and they drove in silence up the long driveway.

"I hope you like it," Tyler said as he came to a stop. "They've lowered the price because it's been on the market awhile, but the money isn't a consideration. This place is for you, and . . ."

"Hush." Miriam reached up to touch Tyler's lips. "Let's just look at it, and if you like it, I'll be happy."

"Thank God for Amish brides," Tyler muttered as he climbed out of the buggy.

Miriam followed him down to the ground. The Realtor was out of her car and waiting for them at the front door.

"Hello, there, Mr. Johnson," the Realtor

greeted them. "This must be Miriam, the young lady you were telling me about."

"Yes, it is," Tyler replied, taking Miriam's hand.

"I'm Ann Cavendish," the woman said, introducing herself. "I certainly hope you like this property. It's been sitting vacant, just waiting for the right people who will love it as their home."

Ann unlocked the front door and led the way inside. "The entryway opens to this large and beautiful living room. And it's adjacent to the ranch-style kitchen, just perfect for someone who loves to cook."

When the tour was over, Tyler whispered, "Do you like it, Miriam?"

"We could have church in the living room and have room to spare," Miriam whispered back.

Tyler turned to Ann. "What is the asking price again?"

Ann glanced at her papers. "Eight hundred and fifty thousand."

Tyler smiled. "Let's offer seven hundred and fifty."

Ann's eyes grew large, and she sat down on the couch. "What bank will you use for the loan application? Because if you haven't spoken to a banker yet . . ."

Tyler silenced her with a wave of his head.

"No bank will be involved. This will be a cash offer. Maybe that will help things along. We can close in thirty days, I think."

Ann gulped. "Okay." She scribbled on the papers in front of her.

Miriam hid her smile. Tyler had enjoyed that moment way too much. Miriam reached over to squeeze his arm, and he winked at her.

This man she loved was to be her husband, Miriam told herself, and this was to be her new home as soon as this fall. It was all too much to comprehend.

"Will there be earnest money to accompany the offer?" Ann looked up to ask.

Tyler didn't hesitate. "Yes, ten thousand should suffice."

Ann's look had changed from astonishment to giddiness. She was likely thinking of her commission, Miriam thought. Pulling Tyler aside as Ann wrote the offer, Miriam asked in a low voice, "Where did you get your money, anyway?"

Tyler's eyes twinkled. "Now you ask. You've already given your word to marry me, and you can't back out just because I robbed a bank."

Miriam playfully slapped Tyler's arm. "You mean thing. Don't tease me like that."

They clung to each other in silent gales of

laughter.

"Ahem." Ann cleared her throat behind them. "I'll need your signature on the offer and the check, of course."

Tyler gave Miriam another wink before he joined Ann to sign the offer. Miriam drifted off for a solo tour of the house. She could already envision where the couch would go and how the bedroom furniture would fit in. She stood still and drank in the surroundings. In the distance she could imagine Tyler's laughter and her aunt's and uncle's voices as they visited on Sunday afternoons. Bishop Mullet would preach in the living room at the Sunday services, and here her *kinner* would be born. She would . . ."

"Miriam," Tyler called.

Miriam collected her thoughts and hurried back to say, "Just looking around."

"Look around all you want." Ann beamed, clutching Tyler's check as if it might disappear.

Minutes later, Tyler helped Miriam into the buggy and untied the horse. He climbed in, and on the way out of the lane, Miriam asked, "So tell me. How did you come into so much money?"

"The same way you did," Tyler said. "My father was a wise investor for many years.

When he passed away five years ago, his money came to me. I've also been a wise investor, learning from Dad. The money has allowed me to pursue my own interests, which has included some travel, the ability to be a freelance writer, and now, best of all, the means to buy a home for the woman I love."

Miriam squeezed his arm. "Where to now?"

"Well, we'd best head back to your aunt's place for the rest of the day and start scribbling out some plans."

"Aunt Fannie will be so excited," Miriam sighed.

Tyler pulled Miriam close with his free arm. "But first we have to stop along some shady spot for something we missed, don't you think? It'll only take a few minutes."

Miriam smiled with great contentment but said nothing, her heart overflowing.

Chapter Forty-Three

It was a beautiful fall evening. Dusk had fallen, and Miriam and Tyler were sitting in the corner of Mrs. Faulkner's pole barn. In this exact spot a little less than a year earlier, Shirley had celebrated her wedding with Glen. Miriam had been with Mose that day and on pins and needles over his constant criticism. But Mose Stoll was only a memory now, while Tyler was more real than he had ever been to Miriam. She was now his *frau,* as Bishop Wagler had heard them say their vows to each other earlier in the morning.

"Whatever happened to that bishop of yours you once dated?" Tyler leaned closer to tease, as if he'd read Miriam's thoughts.

"He's married now," Miriam whispered back.

"The poor woman," Tyler said with a grin. "Married to an ogre."

"Stop it," Miriam ordered. "Someone will

hear us."

"Who cares?" Tyler said, louder this time.

Miriam's cousin Lois, who was the witness for her side of the family, smiled at them. "You two have been whispering together all day."

"That's because we have much to whisper about," Tyler said, appearing quite satisfied with himself.

James, Lois's partner, leaned closer. "My special blessing on your marriage, and thanks for making us a part of your special day."

"You're welcome," Tyler said. James continued, "I live up in Wayne County, so maybe you can give me details of how you two came together. I don't think I ever heard the story."

Miriam blushed. She hoped James didn't know too much about her engagement with Mose. She wasn't going to jog his memory.

Tyler got a dreamy look on his face. "It's a long story, really. I don't think we can do it justice here."

"I suppose not," James chuckled.

"I've heard some of it from Shirley," Lois said. "It sounds most interesting. But I doubt if she told me everything."

"I hope not," Tyler said, and they all laughed.

"I heard you came to the community in Oklahoma as a reporter," Lois said.

"That I did, and I decided to stay after Miriam charmed my socks off." Everyone laughed except Miriam.

"You know that's not true," she protested. "I'm not that much to get impressed over."

"See. Isn't she something?" Tyler said. "Modest and righteous the woman is."

Miriam's color deepened, producing more laughter.

"There's got to be more to the story than that," James probed.

"Well," Tyler allowed, "I did finally get around to making up my mind about Miriam, and the community. I was baptized some two months ago, just before we traveled out here to prepare for the wedding. I insisted that Miriam come sooner, but she said baptisms were milestones in Amish life and she wouldn't miss mine. So here we are, after Miriam's parents okayed me. That took a little doing."

"Oh, it did not," Miriam spoke up. "*Mamm* and *Daett* loved you the first time they laid eyes on you."

"You *are* quite charming," Lois said. "In a *gut* way, of course."

"Hey," James protested. "What about me?"

Lois had colored a little and quickly leaned over to squeeze James's hand. "You have plenty of charm of your own."

"To charm!" Tyler declared. "And to love, and to Miriam Yoder . . . er, Johnson, who is now my *frau.*"

James nodded and turned his attention to Lois. Miriam took Tyler's hand under the table as they conversed in whispers.

Finally, as the crowd continued to thin in front of them, James got to his feet.

"Well!" he declared. "It's been a long day, and we had best be going. I see only old people left around here."

"Now don't be calling us old," Tyler warned.

James laughed and shook their hands. "You two make it good now."

"Thanks so much for helping out," Miriam said. "And you too, Lois."

The other witnessing couple also stood and said much the same thing. Matthew and Rosy Lapp were friends of Deacon Phillips and Katie. Tyler had asked the deacon to pick a witness for him because he had no family among the Amish.

"Thanks to you too." Miriam gave them both a big smile. "Tyler and I are very grateful."

"I would have been up the creek without

a paddle if you hadn't helped out," Tyler quipped.

They both smiled and excused themselves. In the stillness Tyler took Miriam's hand again. "Now it's just you and me, sweetheart."

Tyler's face swam through Miriam's teary eyes, and his hand tightened on hers. She couldn't speak, and Tyler seemed to understand. They sat in silence until the last person had found his way out of the pole barn. Miriam's *daett* came back in to turn off all the gas lanterns except one. He turned to give them a quick smile and then retreated. Miriam pulled on Tyler's hand and led him outside into the soft fall moonlight.

Tyler knew enough to grab the gas lantern and take it with him. Hand in hand they walked up the road to the main farmhouse as the soft glow of light fell on the road in front of them. The whole Yoder family had temporarily moved over to Mr. Bland's old farmhouse for the rest of the week. Tyler and Miriam would have the place to themselves for a few days. After that they'd stay in Possum Valley for another month to visit relatives. Miriam's room upstairs had been used by her younger sisters in the years she had been away from home, but Miriam had restored it close to what the décor had been in her growing-up years. It was important that Tyler see that part of her life. She wanted nothing in her life hidden from him, as he had hidden nothing from her in their often-long conversations since their engagement.

Stars twinkled overhead as the two walked toward the dark farmhouse. An especially bright one seemed to reach all the way from the heavens to cast its ray on the farmhouse lawn.

"A star," Tyler said, astonishment in his voice. His free arm tightened around Miriam.

"Yah," Miriam agreed. "It is the Lord's sign that He will always be with us."

Tyler was silent until they approached the front porch. "Is an Amish man allowed to carry his bride across the threshold?" he asked.

"You may do whatever you wish," Miriam whispered back.

"I do believe I have myself a *frau,*" Tyler said.

DISCUSSION QUESTIONS

1. As the story opens, Miriam thinks she has fully accepted her single life. Do you agree? What does this say of one's ability to cope with uncontrolled events in life?

2. Why did Miriam accept the less than attractive advances of Mose Stoll? Can you imagine yourself in a similar situation? What would your reaction be?

3. What are your feelings on Mose Stoll as he sets out to make sure his next frau is suitable marriage material? Do you sympathies for him? Do you know anyone who is like Mose?

4. Should Tyler have pursued Miriam once he was aware that she was both attracted to him, and rejected him? What do you think of his obvious attempts to interfere

with what he considers an intolerable situation?

5. Do you think the kiss was something Miriam wished to have uncovered? Does how Miriam once handled a similar situation between her beloved Wayne and Esther Kuntz play any part in the scenario.

6. Was Mose's attempt to recover Miriam's affections after the kiss, a wise decision? Should he have used another method that might have succeeded?

7. As the Amish barns burn, what are your feelings about Tyler? Should he have pursued his corruption investigation to this extent? When is it time to back down or to stand tough?

8. What advice would you have given Miriam during her dark time of excommunication?

9. Why is Tyler drawn to join the community? Could he have reformed his life without such a dramatic choice? Could Miriam have fit in such a life?

10. What causes Miriam to accept Tyler as

potential husband material? Would Miriam have done so for any other reason?

ABOUT THE AUTHOR

Jerry Eicher's Amish fiction has sold more than 700,000 books. After a traditional Amish childhood, Jerry taught for two terms in Amish and Mennonite schools in Ohio and Illinois. Since then he's been involved in church renewal, preaching, and teaching Bible studies. Jerry lives with his wife, Tina, and their four children in Virginia.

The employees of Thorndike Press hope you have enjoyed this Large Print book. All our Thorndike, Wheeler, and Kennebec Large Print titles are designed for easy reading, and all our books are made to last. Other Thorndike Press Large Print books are available at your library, through selected bookstores, or directly from us.

For information about titles, please call:
 (800) 223-1244

or visit our Web site at:
 http://gale.cengage.com/thorndike

To share your comments, please write:
 Publisher
 Thorndike Press
 10 Water St., Suite 310
 Waterville, ME 04901